CW00530691

PRAISE FOR DIANE A

'*Mosaic* flows like a novel, which once started is hard to put down. It is a compelling family history of extraordinary people against some of the most frightening events of our century. The depth of emotions evoked is stunning. I was thrilled and deeply moved.'

—Joseph Heller, author of *Catch 22*, on *Mosaic*

'Diane Armstrong's book is a source of delight to the reader. Written with fervour and talent, it will capture your attention and retain it to the last page.'

—Nobel Prize-winner Elie Wiesel on *Mosaic*

'A most remarkable book about one family's experience ... a rich and compelling history ... Just as AB Facey's *A Fortunate Life* and Sally Morgan's *My Place* have become part of the national literary heritage, so too has *Mosaic* earned its place in our social dialogue as part of our cultural tapestry.'

—*Daily Telegraph* on *Mosaic*

'Diane Armstrong's novel is a nuanced rendition of the moral conundrums individuals face in extremis. She concludes that "perhaps no sin is unforgivable, if you can understand the sinner". Among survivors, forgiveness and understanding are highly charged and hotly contested notions. Armstrong's novel is a sincere contribution to that fraught discussion.'

—Louise Adler, *The Australian*, on *The Collaborator*

'Sometimes, if you are a writer, you read a book and experience a form of envy when you wish that you had been fortunate enough to uncover the story yourself. I had a little shard of that feeling in my heart when I read Diane Armstrong's new novel ... the reader is in for a story that hinges on moral ambiguity—a satisfyingly rich and complex zone of shades of grey prompting questions about courage and personal responsibility.'

—Caroline Baum, Plus 61J Media, on *The Collaborator*

'Guaranteed to hook you with its powerful and emotive journey back into a turbulent history, *The Collaborator* is a superb and compelling novel that comes highly recommended.'

—*Canberra Weekly*

'Armstrong takes two apparently totally disconnected lives and weaves them together in an intricate historical design that enables her to tell touching human stories and also to explore serious philosophical issues such as the nature of goodness, evil, crime, guilt, forgiveness, and gratitude.'

—*Historical Novels Review* on *The Collaborator*

'Author Diane Armstrong re-knits savage history into a successful weave of heroism, betrayal, vengeance, and hope ... a well-researched, compassionate story.'

—*Washington Independent Review of Books* on *The Collaborator*

'Armstrong expertly weaves each of these threads together to create a cohesive and engrossing page-turner that pays homage to the courage and resilience of Jersey islanders during World War II. Readers of historical fiction will devour this.'

—*Weekend Australian* on *Dancing With the Enemy*

'A fascinating story of betrayal, collusion, revenge and redemption.'

—*Who* on *Dancing With the Enemy*

'I found myself replaying the scenes in the book like a film reel in my mind ... *Nocturne* is one of those novels that will leave you

reading into the night and will stay with you, like the notes of an unforgettable melody, long after you've read the last line.'
—*Australian Jewish News* on *Nocturne*

'A moving and poignant celebration of survival ...'
—*Booklist* on *Mosaic*

'A consummate writer at the top of her form ... remarkable for her narrative dexterity and emotional resonance. A bold adventure of a novel ... a fine fictional debut from a writer who's already made her mark.'
—Sara Dowse, *The Canberra Times*, on *Winter Journey*

'A cleverly crafted mystery ... a good story, well told. Armstrong's skill in weaving an elaborate fabric out of her characters and subject matter stand her in good stead.'
—Andrew Riemer, *The Sydney Morning Herald*, on *Winter Journey*

'A complex and often heart-and-gut-wrenching novel. The book intelligently explores the need to confront and acknowledge evil before it can be exorcised. Armstrong's supremely confronting basic material is crucial to our understanding of ourselves as "warped timber" humanity.'
—Katharine England, *Adelaide Advertiser*, on *Winter Journey*

'The best and worst of the human spirit are dredged up in this profoundly moving, compelling and superbly written story.'
—Carol George, *Australian Women's Weekly*, on *Winter Journey*

'Like Geraldine Brooks, Diane Armstrong's historical research is expertly woven into the fabric of a fictional tale, providing an engrossing "action" of heroism and resilience which will appeal to both fans of fictional dramatic/romantic sagas, as well as lovers of insightful history.'

—*Australian Bookseller & Publisher* on *Nocturne*

'Easy reading, racy ... Diane Armstrong's *Nocturne* is in the category of blockbuster with extra heart. The stories of the role played by young women in the Warsaw revolt arc extraordinary ... Armstrong keeps us turning the pages and may well introduce a new readership to a story that must keep on being told.'

—*The Age* on *Nocturne*

'A gallant and gut-wrenching story. The accounts of the two uprisings ... are dramatic and heart-breaking ... superb reading.'

—*Australian Book Review* on *Nocturne*

'*Nocturne* had me captured from its opening chapters ... it is an inspirational account of how ordinary people are forced to find strength and courage within themselves when the world around them falls apart.'

—*Vibewire* on *Nocturne*

'A stirring and powerful tapestry into which she has masterfully interwoven the story of her family with the enormity of the Holocaust, commuting fluently between the individual and the historical, the particular and the universal.'

—*Australian Jewish News* on *Mosaic*

'Her rich account of lives good and bad, love, joy, bravery, greed, and bitterness is a testament to the human spirit. Armstrong's stories will bring smiles and tears.'

—*Marie-Claire* on *Mosaic*

'It is no small achievement and it bristles with life ... *Mosaic* is a work of many levels. But ultimately it succeeds because most of its characters demonstrate how the human spirit can soar way, way above adversity.'

—*The Sydney Morning Herald* on *Mosaic*

'A haunting Holocaust history that deserves shelf space alongside Primo Levi and Elie Wiesel. Diane Armstrong's work is a monumental accomplishment—both accessible enough and powerful enough to linger in our consciousness long after we have turned the last page.'

—Barnes & Noble on *Mosaic*

'*Mosaic* has the epic sweep and emotional depth of a nineteenth-century novel. Her skilful blending of vibrant individual voices across the generations makes this memoir a touching tribute to the healing powers of storytelling as well as to the unquenchable human spirit.'

—Amazon.com on *Mosaic* (one of Amazon's Top Ten memoirs 2001)

'A vivid, heartwarming family memoir. The plot and her characters move along in a fast-paced, tightly woven narrative.'

—*Publishers Weekly* on *Mosaic*

'Armstrong weaves in these individual tales with great skill. They flow in and out of the narrative in rhythm with the ship's slow movement from the old world to the new.'

—*The Age* on *The Voyage of Their Life*

'Armstrong's triumph in this history is to avoid judgment or argument ... she allows readers to enter into the mindset of the refugees, to empathise with them.'

—*Weekend Australian* on *The Voyage of Their Life*

'The characters become familiar and absorbing ... almost unbearably moving.'

—*Australian Book Review* on *The Voyage of Their Life*

'She is a natural sleuth … her writing is clear, incisive, yet imaginative.'
—*The Sydney Morning Herald* on
The Voyage of Their Life

'While it is a good read, *The Voyage of Their Life* is also an important historical document in that it gives humanity and dignity to the stories of dispossessed people arriving in post-war Australia.'
—*Wentworth Courier* on
The Voyage of Their Life

'Diane Armstrong's study of the *Derna* is an important contribution to post-war Australian history. Her careful research combined with her excellent writing skills make this book essential reading for anyone interested in the development of Australian society.'
—Dr Suzanne Rutland, *Australian Historical Society Journal*, on *The Voyage of Their Life*

© Jonathan Armstrong

Diane Armstrong is a child Holocaust survivor who arrived in Australia from Poland in 1948. An award-winning journalist and bestselling author, she has written seven previous books.

Her family memoir, *Mosaic: A chronicle of five generations*, was published in 1998 and was shortlisted for the Victorian Premier's Literary Award for Non-Fiction as well as the National Biography Award. It was published in the United States and Canada, and was selected as one of the year's best memoirs by Amazon.com. In 2001, *The Voyage of Their Life: The story of the SS* Derna *and its passengers* was shortlisted in the New South Wales Premier's Literary Award for Non-Fiction.

Her first novel, *Winter Journey*, was published in 2004 and shortlisted for the 2006 Commonwealth Writers' Prize. It has been published in the United States and the United Kingdom Poland and Israel. Her second novel, *Nocturne*, was published in 2008 and won the Society of Women Writers Fiction Award. It was nominated for a major literary award in Poland. *Empire Day*, a novel set in post-war Sydney, was published in 2011, and *The Collaborator*, set in Hungary and Israel, was published in Australia, the US and the UK in 2019. Her fifth novel, *Dancing with the Enemy*, set on the island of Jersey, was published in 2022.

Diane has a son and daughter and three granddaughters. She lives in Sydney.

Also by Diane Armstrong

Fiction
Winter Journey
Nocturne
Empire Day
The Collaborator
Dancing with the Enemy

Non-fiction
Mosaic: A chronicle of five generations
The Voyage of Their Life: The story of
the SS Derna *and its passengers*

THE
WILD
DATE
PALM

DIANE
ARMSTRONG

THE WILD DATE PALM
© 2024 by Diane Armstrong
ISBN 9781867245162

First published on Gadigal Country in Australia in 2024
by HQ Fiction
an imprint of HQBooks (ABN 47 001 180 918),
a subsidiary of HarperCollins Publishers Australia Pty Limited (ABN 36 009 913 517)

The right of Diane Armstrong to be identified as the author of this work has been asserted by her in accordance with the *Copyright Amendment (Moral Rights) Act 2000*.

This work is copyright. Apart from any use as permitted under the *Copyright Act 1968*, no part may be reproduced, copied, scanned, stored in a retrieval system, recorded, or transmitted, in any form or by any means, without the prior written permission of the publisher. Without limiting the author's and publisher's exclusive rights, any unauthorised use of this publication to train generative artificial intelligence (AI) technologies is expressly prohibited.

This is a work of fiction. Names, characters, places, and incidents are either the product of the author's imagination or are used fictitiously, and any resemblance to actual persons, living or dead, business establishments, events, or locales is entirely coincidental.

A catalogue record for this book is available from the National Library of Australia
www.librariesaustralia.nla.gov.au

Printed and bound in Australia by McPherson's Printing Group

MIX
Paper | Supporting
responsible forestry
FSC
www.fsc.org   FSC® C001695

For Justine, Jonathan and Adrianne,
with love and admiration.

PROLOGUE

Leah, 1967

If you had to choose a single image to represent your entire life, just one that you would be remembered by forever, what would you choose? I can see you're frowning, you're rummaging through the messy drawers of your life, examining this and discarding that as you try to select something significant that will do you justice.

But I don't even have to think about it. I want to be remembered by a lone date palm growing wild and untended in the desert wastes of the Sinai. As you'll soon discover, that image doesn't do me justice, but it's typical of my entire existence because it's really my sister's story. All my life I loved and hated her, admired and envied her in equal measure; all my life I lived in her shadow, and even now, so many years later, I still can't separate from her. Of course it's his story too. I worshipped him, but he's not part of my story either: it was Shoshana he loved.

Like a fairytale, our story began in the shadow of the Crusader castle that looms above our orchards and vineyards. The castle was built long before we arrived, by the Knights Templar to protect the pilgrims who journeyed to the Holy Land eight or nine hundred years ago. Eventually Arabs conquered the castle, murdered the Crusaders, and then fought among themselves. Later the Mongols came and in turn were conquered by the Mamelukes, and eventually they all abandoned their prize, leaving it to the implacable effects of sun, wind and time. Once it had towers, moats and drawbridges; rampant lions carved into its walls. Today it's just a crumbling ruin, a reminder that in the end desperate deeds and misplaced loyalties all turn to dust.

In our personal domain, my handsome, brilliant brother was the king, my beautiful, heroic sister was the queen, and, like all powerful monarchs, they affected the fate of individuals and nations for generations to come. As for me, I was a minor moon eclipsed by two dazzling suns. If I had disappeared one day, I don't think anyone would have noticed, and the world wouldn't have been a poorer place.

I've compared our story to a fairytale, but when I think about it, it more closely resembled a Biblical parable: a group of Jews following their patriarch from a country where they had been persecuted to the land that Moses promised them. Sound familiar? Only it wasn't a land of milk and honey when they arrived. Far from it. It was a desolate area of sand dunes and arid wastes where thorns and thistles grew, and swamps bred mosquitoes and malaria. My father cleared this land of rocks with his bare hands and lived under the thumb of a benevolent but despotic overlord. There was even a plague of locusts. Much later, people compared Shoshana to Joan of Arc, but I think of her as Deborah, the warrior princess. And to complete the Biblical allusions, I was named Leah. Remember the girl who stole her sister's lover?

You might think it strange that I'm the one speaking to you, a minor actor unexpectedly thrust centre-stage. But the ways of the world are unfathomable, and destiny is a mystery that is concealed from us until the day we collide with it and our eyes are finally opened to the significance of our lives.

CHAPTER ONE

Zichron Yaakov, 1910

The black-edged notice on page two of *Hapoel Hatzair* caught Shoshana's attention. She took her foot off the treadle, put aside the muslin blouse she was sewing for her sister, picked up the newspaper, paused, and began to read aloud.

'Last Thursday morning at dawn, Miss Malka Reichman left her lodgings. When she did not return, the landlady knocked on her door but no one answered. Worried about her young tenant, she let herself in, and found this note on the bed:

"From a distance, life looks beautiful but that's a cruel illusion. Reality bears no resemblance to what I imagined I'd find in Palestine and I can't stop asking myself why I left my village and those I loved to come here. If only someone loved me, if anyone had touched my soul and understood it, I could bear my loneliness but I feel so alone in a blackness that surrounds me. I could

never kill myself on a bright sunny day, but this is a cold and grey morning, and the sea is rough. I am not afraid to die. I read somewhere that we come from eternity and return to eternity, that our individual life is only a moment of consciousness in eternal life, something we can only understand when we are dying. Perhaps that's when it will all become clear to me. Please tell my parents I died of malaria."

'It is assumed that Miss Reichman met her death in the sea. Her body has not been found. Her parents in Russia have been notified.'

Shoshana stopped reading, and the silence in the room was broken by her mother's sobs. Shoshana and Leah exchanged glances.

'What a dreadful story,' Leah said. 'I could never kill myself.' She turned to her sister. 'Could you?'

Shoshana looked pensive, but before she could reply, their mother broke in. 'You can never tell what desperation might drive you to do.' She wiped her eyes. 'I can understand how that poor girl felt.'

The sisters looked at each other again. Batya was a strong, decisive woman who had an opinion about everything but kept her feelings tightly knotted. Shoshana rose from the well-scrubbed wooden table and poured them tea from the silver samovar, one of the few belongings their mother had brought from Romania.

Batya put down her glass and sighed. 'That's exactly how I felt when I arrived here,' she said with a faraway look. 'You can't imagine how it feels to leave your familiar world behind and come to a desolate place in a foreign country. I cursed the moment I'd left my village. Imagine if you were suddenly transported to a wasteland where you had to start a new life.'

'But you didn't want to kill yourself, did you?' Leah sounded alarmed.

Batya hesitated for a moment. 'I had a husband and a small child to look after, so I had to keep going. But for years I felt a stone crushing my heart.'

Shoshana glanced out of the window at the stone gates of their home, and the olive groves, orchards and vineyards on the slopes below. 'It's hard to believe that less than thirty years ago this was a wasteland.'

Batya sighed again. 'If I spent a whole week describing what we went through, you still couldn't picture it. Sometimes I can hardly believe it myself. I don't even know how we survived.'

'You've never told us about it,' Leah said, then added, 'You never told me, anyway.'

Shoshana glanced at her younger sister and recognised the implied complaint. Perhaps because Leah was the youngest, she always felt excluded from family discussions. Or perhaps it was because Shoshana and their older brother Nathan had such a close bond.

'I've been too busy to dwell on the past,' Batya said.

'Maybe you didn't want to relive a time when you were so unhappy,' Shoshana suggested.

Leah's envious eyes lingered on her older sister. As usual, Shoshi had a way of cutting through to the heart of things.

'For forty days and forty nights, like Moses in search of the promised land, our small group wandered from port to port. The Turks tried to stop us from landing in Palestine because we were Jews,' Batya began. 'And when we finally found a harbour where we could dock, all we could see were swamps, rocks, weeds, spindly grasses and thorny plants. I couldn't help thinking how lucky Moses was, because he never got to set foot here.'

Once started, Batya's reminiscences gathered momentum. The sisters drew closer, hardly breathing for fear of interrupting the long-suppressed memories pouring out. Their mother described stepping off the boat, her legs unsteady after the long voyage, her head dizzy from the rolling of the ship on a journey she thought would never end. As she and the other refugees trudged up the steep hill past abandoned shacks of oak branches packed with mud and topped by straw matting, she kept her eyes on the rock-strewn path to avoid tripping. The mules pulling the carts that carried all their possessions stumbled, and the men had to shout and flail their whips to keep them moving.

'I thought your father was crazy,' she said, as if suddenly remembering her daughters' presence. 'All I saw was sandy soil and stony ground, but he saw vines and fruit trees. He talked about reclaiming the land that God had promised Moses, and making the desert bloom.'

'So Abba was the one who pushed you to come,' Shoshana said as she refilled her mother's glass.

Batya nodded. 'He didn't let up. If not for him I never would have come here.'

'Women are always at the mercy of men's dreams and desires,' Shoshana said.

Leah stared at her sister. The things Shoshi came out with. Her thoughts turned to Eli, to the meaningful look in his dark eyes when he had danced with her at the Purim party and the thrilling things he had whispered. She wouldn't mind being at the mercy of his desires.

'The way grew steeper and rockier,' Batya was saying, 'and no amount of yelling at the mules and prodding them did any good. The poor animals just stared back with desperate eyes, whinnied, and refused to move, so the men had to unload the carts and carry everything on their backs. At that point I sank onto the ground and burst into tears. Your father took the baby from my arms, sat down beside me, and reminded me why we had come. He wasn't an educated man, but he had a way of explaining things that made sense. "I think you've forgotten what our life was like in that village. Like the Israelites, we were also living in bondage, in a land where we were despised and oppressed. Remember how the Cossacks rampaged through our village like wild beasts, grabbing young girls and leaving them bloodied and broken on the ground? Have you forgotten how they nailed men to the oak trees and set them on fire? And the locals who accused us of blood libel and came after us with scythes? Is that how you want to live, is that the life you want for our child, God forbid? No matter how hard it is, at least here we'll live in our own land, and no one will oppress or persecute us. It's better to be a poor man on your own scrap of land than a prosperous one at the mercy of others."

'"That's all very well," I told him, "but there's nothing here."'

'He reminded me, "We didn't have any choice. This was the only land the Arab owner offered to sell."'

'I couldn't help myself and said, "Well in that case, the seller was a lot smarter than the purchasers."'

Shoshana smiled. She could imagine her mother making such a tart comment.

Batya's mood suddenly lightened and she sat forward. 'I'll tell you something interesting. While the men were trudging up the hill, bent under the weight of tables, beds, trunks and boxes, pausing every few minutes to catch their breath, straighten their backs and mop their foreheads, we women sat on the ground with our children. We weren't used to the heat and sweat trickled from under our kerchiefs while babies fretted and toddlers grizzled. We were all exhausted, but your brother Nathan, who was nine months old, didn't utter a sound. He was looking around him with such an alert expression, as if he was fascinated by his surroundings and already assessing future possibilities. Fruma, one of the women in our group who had been suckling her baby, was adjusting her blouse when she looked across at Nathan and said, "You can see that one is a *halutz*, a real little pioneer. He looks as if he's already figuring out where he's going to build his house!"

'We all laughed, but from the moment we landed, he looked as if he recognised this land and knew he'd come home.'

Batya paused and looked at her eldest daughter. 'When you were born six years later, I wondered if you'd be like him.'

Shoshana and Leah exchanged knowing smiles at their mother's pride in her firstborn. They didn't resent it. Nathan had always been the star of the family, and from the time they could walk, they had been his enthusiastic apprentices, grateful to be part of the discoveries he made during his rides across the hills and wadis. His love for the flowers, bushes and even rocks of this land was infectious, and they were always eager to run behind him as he gathered plants and taught them their strange botanical names.

What Nathan had started as a hobby became an obsession that earned him international fame – in the hills of Upper Galilee he had found the botanists' holy grail, the origin of wild wheat.

'I don't think there's much chance of me ever matching Nathan's achievements,' Shoshana said as she returned to her sewing machine. 'Unless I become famous for reproducing French fashions in Zichron Yaakov.'

Leah sprang from her chair, and a moment later the front door banged behind her.

'What's wrong with your sister?' Batya asked. 'Is she in one of her moods?'

With a shrug, Shoshana left her sewing machine and followed Leah outside.

'Come and try the blouse on again to make sure it fits.'

Leah was staring straight ahead. 'Of course it will fit. You've made all my clothes and they're always perfect. You're the smart one. You can do everything.'

Shoshana was about to make a conciliatory comment when Leah turned towards her with a conspiratorial smile. 'I've got something to tell you, but don't you dare tell anyone. Promise?'

Shoshana nodded, relieved that her sister wanted to share a secret with her. She admired Leah's dainty figure and pretty face framed by soft fair curls, such a contrast to her own height and strong features, and she couldn't understand why her sister often sounded disgruntled and resentful.

'You remember that Purim party we went to in Hadera last month?' Leah was saying. Her cheeks were flushed and she spoke faster than usual, twisting the hem of her skirt as she always did when she was nervous. 'Nathan's friend Eli was there, just back from France. When we danced the *hora* he held my hand so tight.'

She paused and Shoshana waited, uneasy at what might follow.

'He said I reminded him of the rosebuds he saw in the Luxembourg Gardens in Paris,' Leah whispered, blushing at the memory of his dark eyes burning into hers. 'Shoshi, he's so handsome. I can't stop thinking about him. I think I'm in love.'

Shoshana stared at her sister. Oh no, she thought. Oh no.

CHAPTER TWO

Zichron Yaakov, 1910

The sun had finally gone down, and in the blessed coolness of the evening Shoshana and her sister set out for an after-dinner stroll along Ha-Meyasdim Street. Zichron Yaakov's main road was lined with small houses and shaded by oaks and pine trees. Mouth-watering smells of roasting meat and yeasty bread wafted into the street from neighbouring kitchens.

As they passed, neighbours appraised the sisters' outfits and commented on Shoshana's white organza blouse with its large sailor collar and her blue skirt that flared towards her ankles, but Shoshana knew the smiles were as false as the compliments. 'Everyone thinks you're stuck up. You think you're better than us,' the girl next door had once told her. Shoshana had been shocked. Was it their large pink stucco house with its interior courtyard they envied? It stood out in a town whose plain, squat houses and unpaved side streets resembled the villages they had left behind in Eastern Europe.

Perhaps they resented that the Adelsteins were such a close family and kept apart from the rest of the townsfolk. Was it because Nathan, who knew more about the plants of Palestine than anyone else, had recently become world-famous? Or because she and Leah were always dressed to the nines in the French fashions she copied from the illustrated magazines?

Either way, Shoshana didn't care what small-minded people thought, and she smiled back despite the grudging nature of their admiration. She looked fondly at her sister. In her rose-coloured dress with its flounced hem that almost touched her buttoned shoes and a wide sash that accentuated her small waist, Leah resembled one of the porcelain figurines her mother displayed on the sideboard. Tall and full-bosomed herself, Shoshana preferred a simpler, more streamlined design in blue, a colour she favoured ever since Eli had told her that she should be charged with stealing a scrap of sky and inserting it into her eyes. She could still see the provocative way his eyes burned into her as he said it. Then she stopped smiling as she recalled what Leah had confided earlier that day. She hoped their evening stroll would give her an opportunity to find out exactly what had transpired between Eli and her sister. But before she could broach the subject, their friend Miriam caught up with them, out of breath, her lips parted and beads of sweat on her forehead. It didn't take long to discover why she was in such a rush to talk to them.

'Nathan has been away for such a long time. When is he coming home?' she asked, her eyes wandering from their broad-brimmed hats to their new clothes. Shoshana knew that Miriam's mother and Batya had long entertained the hope that one day their son and daughter would get together, but although Miriam's hungry eyes never left Nathan whenever they met, Shoshana knew he didn't return her feelings.

'We haven't had a letter from him for quite a while,' Leah said. 'We thought he'd be back by now but he must still be meeting scientists in Berlin.'

Shoshana said nothing. She suspected that Nathan's trip, ostensibly to discuss the implications of his discovery of the original wild wheat with German botanists, had been motivated by an urge that was sexual rather than botanical. She knew he was in love with a married woman who had left Palestine for Berlin, but from what he had told her, she sensed that the object of his passion was stringing him along, flattered by his attention and enjoying the power it conferred.

'You're wasting your time,' Shoshana had told him, 'she'll never leave her husband.' But he was too besotted to listen.

Now, looking at Miriam's crestfallen expression, she thought of all the local girls who had their eyes on her brother while he insisted on pursuing a woman who was married and lived in Europe. For as long as she could remember, women of all ages were attracted to Nathan. More than his rugged features, it was probably his self-confidence, bordering on arrogance, that challenged them.

For some reason that Shoshana couldn't understand, Nathan only wanted women who weren't available. Perhaps the chase appealed to him more than the conquest. Or he hadn't yet met the woman who was right for him. The woman in Berlin certainly was not.

Miriam walked on with slumped shoulders, and Shoshana was about to ask Leah about Eli when a couple they knew stopped them. From their eager expressions, it was clear they were bursting with news.

'Did you know that Russian firebrand Olga Mankiewicz is coming here on Sunday to give a speech?' The speaker was an elderly woman with a black scarf over her grey hair. 'I can't imagine who invited her here. She's going to get everyone worked up. Probably start a riot with her new-fangled ideas.'

Her husband chuckled. 'That would be interesting.'

Shoshana had read about Olga in an article in *Hapoel Hatzair*. It described her as a fervent socialist with revolutionary ideas that created a sensation among audiences whenever she spoke. Apparently she had run away from home at fifteen, moved to Minsk, and several years later organised a strike in a factory owned by her brother, who, she claimed, was exploiting his workers.

Shoshana, who had already seen notices about Olga's forthcoming lecture, couldn't wait to hear her, but she was astonished when Leah turned to her and said, 'Yes, let's go and hear what Olga Mankiewicz has to say.'

Leah had never shown any interest in politics or social issues. In fact, she became so visibly bored during discussions about Arab labourers or Turkish corruption that she often left the room. But Shoshana didn't have to wait long to discover the reason for her sister's unexpected enthusiasm for the Russian socialist.

'Eli was talking about Olga at the Purim party,' Leah said as her cheeks crimsoned. 'He said she was a remarkable woman with a charismatic personality.' Then she added casually, 'He'll probably be there as well.'

So that was it.

'Speaking of Eli,' Shoshana began, but before she could finish her sentence, Leah stopped to chat with a friend, and the opportunity was lost.

*

All Sunday, Leah was in a fever of activity, trying on one dress after another and discarding each in turn. One made her look too young, another was too old-fashioned, one was too fussy, another too plain. As she ran in and out of Shoshana's room, increasingly agitated at her inability to achieve the effect she wanted, Shoshana was dismayed by her sister's determination to attract Eli's attention.

On the way to the Town Hall where the lecture would take place, they passed the synagogue that Baron de Rothschild had erected in honour of his father, and as usual Shoshana was struck by the grandeur of Ohel Yaakov with its marble Holy Ark, rosette window, and wraparound upstairs gallery for the women. Unlike her parents, Shoshana only went to synagogue on the main holy days, but she always felt awed by the beauty of the interior, and amused by the men whose eyes frequently strayed from their prayer books to the girls sitting upstairs who nudged each other as they pointed and whispered. She noticed several glances in her direction but there was only one man whose attention she craved, and he never came to synagogue at all.

The sisters joined the crowd milling outside the Town Hall that had once housed the offices of the baron's managers. All around them, people were repeating stories they'd heard about the speaker. Each was more shocking than the last. Apparently Olga had been interrogated by Russia's dreaded secret police but had been released after one of the interrogators fell in love with her, one woman said, raising her eyebrows in a meaningful way.

'That's nothing,' her companion responded. 'The Russians called her a terrorist because she carried a loaded pistol.'

'She used it too,' someone chimed in. 'Killed a man who was about to denounce her, stuffed his body into a trunk, and sent it to a fictitious address!'

Another rumour said she was planning a revolution. Each new story evoked a frisson of anticipation to hear this scandalous woman.

But Leah didn't seem interested in the gossip. From the moment they entered and sat on the hard wooden chairs, she kept leaning forward to see who was sitting in front, then turning to check who was coming in. Irritated by her sister's restlessness, Shoshana nudged her.

'For goodness' sake, Leah, settle down. You're making a spectacle of yourself with all this wriggling and jiggling. If he's here, we'll see him after the lecture.'

But a moment later, her sister dug her nails into her arm. 'He's over there, on our right, two rows behind us,' she whispered.

Shoshana's heart was also beating faster, and she forced herself not to look, but after a few minutes she couldn't resist sneaking a glance in his direction. Their eyes met, as if he'd been waiting for this moment. A lock of dark hair fell over his forehead, and under his thick arched eyebrows, his coal-black eyes held hers with a tantalising expression of passionate intensity.

A moment later a young woman with round spectacles and dark hair gathered into an untidy bun stepped onto the podium. Olga Mankiewicz was short and plain, and wore a loose shapeless dress that Shoshana imagined Russian peasant women might wear, but as soon as she began to speak, she was transformed.

As she described a world where women were treated equally and had the same opportunities as men, she seemed lit by an inner fire. Olga's warmth radiated throughout the hall and touched every-one. It was as if she was speaking directly to each person there as she described a utopian existence they could all enjoy if only they opened their minds to new ideas.

'When I arrived in Palestine a few years ago, I was shocked to see that farmers employ Arab labour to tend their land and that women are confined to traditional household duties instead of working alongside men, that they are prohibited from using their skills and fulfilling their potential.'

Men in the audience began to mutter and interject, but Olga's charm and good-natured manner soon silenced them.

'Don't worry. I'm not criticising men and I'm not suggesting that every woman should put on long pants and till the soil,' she smiled. 'But I'd like you to consider that when 50 per cent of the popula-tion are deprived of their rights, then the entire community suffers, economically and socially.'

Shoshana was rapt. Finally she was hearing ideas that had already occurred to her, though in a tentative, half-formed way.

'Life here shouldn't merely be transplanted from Europe with its outmoded traditions. I would like to see it transformed into some-thing better. That's why your parents came here, isn't it? Not to recreate the past but to create a better future. I'd like to see Jewish farmers working alongside Arab workers, and Jewish women work-ing with their men on equal terms. I've come here today to tell you about a collective I've set up in Lower Galilee which I hope will revolutionise the way people live and work.'

The hall was quiet and every eye was on Olga. Although the ideas she expressed were foreign and challenging, they listened.

'The workers on my collective farm share their expenses and make joint decisions about how to work. They do the work themselves and don't hire others to work for them. Their pooled wages provide shelter, clothes and food for new workers. Those not capable of physical work are allocated other tasks, such as accounting. Apart from farm work, we have cultural activities. For instance, one of our members, David Ben-Gurion, is teaching Hebrew. Women are equal and some plough the land behind the oxen.'

There was renewed muttering as some women shook their heads, and men scoffed at the idea of their wives ploughing. 'Women build a nation and men protect it,' the man next to Shoshana said loudly until he was shushed by those around him.

'I understand how strange my ideas sound to you,' Olga said. 'Almost as strange as the idea of leaving Romania and Russia behind, as strange as coming to Palestine must have seemed to those your parents left behind.'

Some nodded, others shook their heads, but even those who disagreed with her vision were intrigued by the world she described.

'Most of you here are farmers, and I believe that a collective agricultural economy is a viable proposition for Palestine. My collective has already repaid its debts and made a profit. It has also demonstrated that women are capable and willing to work alongside men. In conclusion, I'd like to tell you that this has been the happiest year of my life, because I've created something that could become a blueprint for the future development of this land.'

Shoshana was enthralled. Not so much by the agricultural or economic aspects of the collective, but by the achievement of this young woman who had a dream and the courage to realise it. She admired Olga but she envied her too. Would she ever find a cause to believe in and the strength to fight for it?

In a daze, she followed the crowd streaming out of the hall. Outside, people gathered in groups, talking over each other, arguing and interrupting. Leah had already caught up with Eli, and they were engaged in conversation. Leah's eyes were shining, and the way she was looking at Eli made Shoshana uneasy. Just then Eli saw her, stopped talking, and his eyes lingered on her. The blood rushed through her body and the air palpitated around her.

Unsettled and confused, she walked home. Had she read too much into his gaze and imagined the desire in his eyes?

Preoccupied with the turmoil in her head, she didn't notice her mother standing in the doorway of their home, holding an envelope.

'Someone slipped this under the door for you while you were out,' Batya said, handing it to her.

She read it and almost forgot to breathe.

I see your soul in moonbeams, and in the flames of the setting sun
I see your passionate heart.

She sank into an armchair and pressed it against her lips. So she hadn't misread his glance.

CHAPTER THREE

Atlit, 1910

Astride her grey mare, Shoshana cantered along the ridge of Mount Carmel, her thick brown hair unpinned and streaming behind her. Riding always cleared her head, and after receiving Eli's poetic note, her feelings had see-sawed between delirious joy and nagging guilt. How ironic that she and Leah were both in love with the same man; that her happiness would cause her sister disappointment.

Leaning forward in the saddle, she urged Zahra on until clods of earth flew under her hooves as they galloped towards Atlit, past vineyards where fellahin in loose robes snipped clusters of purple grapes, and wadis whose rocky outcrops formed a dramatic contrast with the rural landscape.

Out of breath, she pulled on the reins and brought the mare to a stop under the shade of a date palm near the ruins of the Crusader castle. As soon as she stopped riding, her troubling thoughts returned.

When she looked down at the cobalt water of the Mediterranean sparkling in the sun, she saw a small boat moored in the bay. A short, thin man in a pith helmet and creased khaki shorts jumped ashore, notebook in hand. A moment later, he started up the hill at a surprising pace considering the steep slope and the searing heat. Alone in the boat, the skipper lay back and fanned his sweating face with a large palm frond.

The man with the notebook stopped at the foot of the castle, mopped his forehead, took out a metal pannikin and held it to his lips, which were caked with dust. He flopped onto a slab of sandstone, mopped his brow again, took out a notebook and proceeded to sketch. Who was he and what was he doing?

She trotted towards him.

Engrossed in his work, he didn't notice her until she was so close that when Zahra flicked her tail, she knocked the pencil from his hand.

He looked up and glared.

'I say, you should be more careful instead of galloping around as if you own the place.'

'I do own the place,' she retorted. 'At least my parents do.'

'Are you trying to tell me you own Atlit castle?' he demanded.

She laughed. 'Not the castle.' She waved her hand in the direction of the vineyards and the township beyond them. 'Just a house in that village and the vineyard beyond it.'

She dismounted, smoothed down her long riding skirt and sat on the sun-warmed rock beside him. She put out her hand. 'I'm Shoshana Adelstein,' she said.

'I'm Lawrence. Friends call me Ned,' he said. 'How come you speak such good English?'

Was he being condescending? She decided to put him in his place. 'As a matter of fact I speak five languages.'

'That's impressive.'

She noticed he spoke with a lisp. Mollified by the compliment, she thrust her hand into the pocket of her long riding skirt and offered him some large dates. 'From our date palms,' she said.

As he chewed the luscious sweetness of the date, she looked down at his notepad. 'Why did you come here? Don't tell me you've come all this way just to draw ruins.'

'I'm stationed in Cairo. At the moment I'm sketching Crusader castles on this coast and this is the most impressive one I've seen.'

She gave him a shrewd look. He didn't strike her as a tourist wandering around Ottoman Palestine sketching Crusader castles. Did he work for British intelligence? But before she could frame the question, he asked, 'How long have you lived here?'

He listened attentively as she told him the story of Zichron Yaakov, starting with her parents' arrival in a wilderness of sandy wastes and malarial swamps nearly thirty years ago.

'Within one year, most of their group had returned to Romania, but my father refused to give up,' she said.

Lawrence nodded. 'I admire his tenacity. What's the name of your town again?'

'Baron de Rothschild named it Zichron Yaakov after his father. It means "the blessing of Jacob" in Hebrew.'

He smiled. 'Ah, Hebrew. The everlasting miracle of Jewry.'

'Are you being sarcastic?'

'Not at all. Just stating a fact.'

'The settlement would have failed if it hadn't been for Baron de Rothschild,' she continued, and told him how the philanthropist from Paris had come to their rescue and financed the venture. 'He planted vines and fruit trees, but he was autocratic and treated the newcomers like serfs, so my father decided to become independent of his financial support.'

'A wise decision,' Lawrence commented.

Shoshana looked at him, surprised how easily she conversed with this stranger whose lisp had now become less pronounced.

'Your father was right,' he said. 'People can't breathe under the yoke of a despot. In the end they have to break free.' He was surveying her with interest. 'But why are you here on Arab land?'

Shoshana took a deep breath. 'Have you read the Old Testament?'

'Of course.'

'Then you know that God promised this land to the Israelites.'

He chuckled. 'And you're keeping Him to a promise He made over three thousand years ago?'

'I wasn't aware that there was a time limit on land ownership conferred by God.'

He paused and stared into the distance. 'Like your father, I also have a dream.'

Impressed, she listened as he told her that from childhood he had fantasised about Arabia's exotic deserts and its Bedouins, a world that was such a contrast with his dreary, colourless country where he felt he didn't belong.

'I believe that the Bedouin tribes that roam the desert fighting against each other should unite, overthrow the Turks and create their own independent nation. And I intend to lead them into battle.'

She grappled with this baffling idea. 'But how will you convince those warring tribes to unite? Anyway, why would they let you lead them?'

'Because I'm the only one who can. You'll see, one day I will write my will among the stars.'

She looked at him and marvelled at his belief in his own destiny. The white-hot rays of the sun formed an aura of bright light around him, and instead of a small man with a long face who spoke with a slight lisp, she glimpsed a messianic figure with a burning ambition who could inspire men to follow him.

Lawrence picked a yellow wildflower from the ground and twirled it around, studying its petals. 'Unusual plant,' he said.

Shoshana nodded. 'My brother Nathan has identified and catalogued hundreds of plants that are unique to this place,' she said proudly.

'Your brother?'

'Nathan is a botanist. There's nothing he doesn't know about the plants and rocks in this area. Ever since he was about six, he has brought specimens home, sketched them, and catalogued them.' She smiled. 'The only time he ever shouted at me was when I put a plant in the wrong envelope. A few years ago, he discovered the elusive wild wheat that is the mother of all wheat.'

'Why is that significant?'

'It indicates that civilisation began in this part of the world, with wheat cultivation. Nathan writes scientific papers and lectures all over the world.'

'He sounds like a man with a destiny,' Lawrence said.

Like you, she thought. She rose, picked up the horse's reins, placed her laced-up leather boot in the stirrup and swung herself onto the saddle.

'Goodbye, Shoshana Adelstein,' he said. 'One day I too will write a paper, maybe even a book.' He gave a lopsided grin. 'You never know, I might even mention meeting you.'

She was still smiling as she galloped away, marvelling at the rapport she had formed with this unusual man. She wondered if his dreams would be realised, but she would never know. It wasn't likely she'd ever see him again.

As she cantered home, her heart felt lighter. There was no need to worry about Leah's infatuation. After all, she was only eighteen. She was bound to get over it in no time.

CHAPTER FOUR

Zichron Yaakov, 1910

Observing her daughter at the sewing machine several days later, Batya sensed an impatience, almost a desperate energy, in Shoshana's usually languid movements.

She stopped kneading the dough for the Shabbat *challah*, wiped her floury hands on her large white apron, and placed them gently on her daughter's shoulders. 'You seem troubled. Is something bothering you?'

Without looking up, Shoshana sighed. 'My life doesn't amount to anything. I haven't achieved a single thing.'

Batya burst out laughing. 'But you're still young. What can you possibly achieve? You're not even married yet. Although it's time you started thinking about it. You're almost twenty-two.'

'What does marriage ever achieve for women?'

Batya, who knew her daughter well, could read the unspoken criticism her remark implied.

'I have two wonderful daughters and a brilliant son,' she said, and added, 'You've been unsettled ever since you heard that Russian revolutionary. You shouldn't envy her – women like that don't have easy lives or steady relationships.'

'Women like that!' Shoshana repeated. 'Why shouldn't women try and make the world a better place? At least their lives mean something.' She stopped the treadle. 'And don't tell me I'm good at dressmaking.'

With a sudden movement she pushed back her wooden stool and stood up. 'I need some fresh air. I think I'll go for a ride.'

*

Shoshana knew that Olga's lecture was only part of the reason for her restlessness. Ever since receiving Eli's note, she had been in a fever of excitement to see him again, impatient to assure him that she returned his feelings, but almost a week had passed without a letter, a visit, or even a chance encounter. Meanwhile Leah gave her meaningful looks and secret smiles, clearly still infatuated.

'Be careful,' Batya called out. 'I keep telling you it's not safe for a young woman to ride alone all over the place like you do.'

'Don't worry, I'll take my pistol,' Shoshana replied, and took the small firearm inlaid with ivory from her drawer. Nathan had bought it for her in America during one of his lecture tours. On her way to the stable, she could hear her mother calling out that she should take Leah, but she quickened her step and pretended not to hear. Leah was the last person she wanted to accompany her.

Eli Ginsberg lived in Hadera, several kilometres away. Like Zichron Yaakov, it had prospered thanks to Baron de Rothschild, who had introduced vines to this region and planted Australian eucalyptus trees in the swampy terrain to ward off the mosquitoes that caused the disease that was the curse of all these settlements.

The Ginsbergs were intellectuals from Russia. Like most of the settlers in this region, they had fled because of pogroms, but unlike the others, they had absorbed the revolutionary ideas that were permeating Russian society and threatening its stability. There was a rumour that they had even known Tolstoy.

Everything about Eli was exotic, Shoshana thought as she spurred Zahra to gallop over the scrubby hills and rugged wadis until she felt she was flying. She had recently read *Wuthering Heights* and in Eli's poetic intensity she recognised her Heathcliff. He could quote Karl Marx and the French authors he had met during the four years he'd spent in a Paris academy. He spoke Arabic like a Bedouin as he had been taught by one, and, although she hated to admit it, he could shoot more accurately and ride faster than she did. And unlike all the single men and women who continued to live under their parents' roof, he had built a tiny house for himself on an unpaved side street of his village.

Past the mudbrick hut where the Druze chief lived with his veiled wife and daughters, she continued to climb the gentle slopes of Mount Carmel, and then made her way down towards the sea coast. As she rode, she recalled the eccentric Englishman she had met at Atlit and marvelled at the depth and intensity of their conversation. It was as if they had known each other for years. His words reverberated in her mind and convinced her that one day he would achieve his dream.

Close to Eli's village, she slowed Zahra to a trot past a stand of grey-green eucalyptus trees and breathed in the astringent scent of their foliage. In her impulse to see Eli, it hadn't occurred to her that he might not be there, or that he might be engaged in some activity that precluded the tete-a-tete she yearned for. She passed his family home, which had hosted the Purim party where she and Leah had met him just over a month ago, and turned into the lane behind it.

As she dismounted and tied the mare to a knobbly cypress trunk, her confidence deserted her. What excuse could she possibly give for turning up like this, without sending a message or having a reason for her visit? She despised false modesty but would he be shocked by her unconventional behaviour?

But as soon as he opened the door and their eyes met, she knew she needn't have worried. As she stepped inside, it was clear from his expression that he knew why she had come.

They stood without speaking, and when he touched her arm through the fine cotton of her long-sleeved blouse, she felt the thrilling warmth of his hand spreading throughout her body.

'I couldn't wait to see you,' she blurted.

He increased the pressure on her arm and his eyes didn't leave her face. He was standing dangerously close now, and his lips brushed her cheeks as he bent down and, in a voice thick with passion, he whispered, 'You know I live alone. How brave are you?'

'Braver than you can imagine,' she whispered back in a voice she didn't recognise.

Taking her hand, he led her from the spartan living room furnished with just a wooden table and two chairs, into his bedroom and closed the door. She looked into his face and knew she didn't care about flouting conventions. This was what she wanted, and she knew that after this there would be no turning back. Standing behind her, he took out the pin that secured her thick hair, which spilled down her back. Pushing it aside, he pressed his lips to the nape of her neck. The unexpected sensation of his warm mouth on her neck made her quiver. She turned, flung her arms around him, and pressed her partly open mouth against his with an ardour that surprised her. With impatient fingers he unbuttoned her blouse and bent down to kiss her breasts. They undressed quickly and lay on his bed, caressing each other's bodies until they clung to each other and he entered her gently with melting tenderness.

Later, as she lay against him in a daze of erotic intoxication, he stroked her hair. 'I've never met a woman like you. So natural and sensual. I compared you to a moonbeam but I was wrong. You're a bolt of lightning.'

Then he added, 'Your sister is more like a moonbeam.'

She felt as if he had thrown a bucket of icy water over her. By mentioning Leah at such an intimate moment he was practically bringing her into their bed. She sprang up and started buttoning her blouse with trembling fingers.

'Leah told me you compared her to a rosebud,' she said coldly.

He nodded, apparently unconcerned by the comment or her tone. 'She is. Pink, pale and pretty.'

Then with a laugh, he encircled her waist and pulled her down onto the bed. 'But you're not pretty. You're magnificent. Like the sun, you draw everyone towards you. Just be careful not to scorch us all with your heat!'

*

All the way home, Shoshana tingled with excitement, astonished by her audacity and thrilled by their mutual passion. He was hers and she was his. If she fell pregnant it wouldn't matter. Theirs was a perfect physical and spiritual communion. They were destined to be together. While Zahra's hooves flew over the hills and valleys, she relived every moment, every sensation and every word. Her future lay before her, bathed in sunlight.

She paused on the summit of a weathered sandstone mesa and gazed down at the canyon below. Would her family be able to tell by her elated mood and flushed face that she was no longer the girl they knew, that she had just had an experience that had changed her forever? Surely they would see the change in her. She took a long breath as she surveyed the windswept rock formations of the wadi and the hardy plants and thorny bushes that flourished in this unique landscape. In an effort to compose herself, she paused beside a rampart of rock where the wind-borne seeds of a palm tree had lodged inside a crevice. Against all odds, without any soil, the tree had taken root in this inhospitable place and its roots were clinging to the rough surface.

*

When Shoshana arrived home, Leah was standing at the door holding up a letter. She followed Shoshana into the stable and watched while she removed the saddle and watered the mare. Could Leah detect something different about her? But her sister was preoccupied, glancing down at the letter in her hand.

'Guess what,' she said, waving it around. 'It's from Nathan, and he's been invited to lecture at some major American university. In California, I think.'

Shoshana was crestfallen. Nathan had already been away for several months. She missed him and the close connection they shared.

'So I suppose he'll be staying over there?' she asked.

Leah's curls bounced as she shook her head. 'I don't think so. Here, you read it.' And she thrust the letter into Shoshana's hands.

Nathan's letter filled two pages with his small, neat handwriting, and as Shoshana scanned it, her face lit up.

'That's fantastic,' she gasped when she'd finished reading. Turning to Leah, she said, 'He's definitely coming home!'

From Nathan's letter, it appeared that he hadn't stayed long in Berlin because he'd been invited by prominent botanists to lecture in California.

After I described our soil, water problems, and the plants I had collected, I explained that this land had once supported entire civilisations and could be fruitful again. In support of my theory, I quoted extracts from the Bible and the accounts of ancient historians, and they were enormously impressed. One of them told me that he could count on the fingers of one hand scientists who knew as much about botany, geology and ecology as I did.

Shoshana looked up from the letter with a smile. One quality Nathan lacked was modesty, but she could imagine how impressed those scientists would have been to hear a botanist from a tiny settlement on the other side of the world quoting from scriptures and ancient texts as he discussed plants, rocks and agronomy in support of his belief that arid land could become fertile again. She had never doubted that Nathan was exceptional, but it was exciting to have that conviction confirmed by top scientists in America.

They were so excited about the similarity between our condi-tions and those in California that they have agreed to fund an experimental agricultural research station here in Atlit, which will benefit us and them. This unique collaboration holds infinite possibilities for our future, it's beyond my wildest dreams. It's exactly what we need to develop our agriculture, but until now, nothing like this has existed here. They want me to be the director of this project, so I'll have to appoint staff. I'm assuming you will work with me, Shoshana. I heard that Eli Ginsberg has recently returned from France, and I plan to ask him to work with us. What do you think?

This suggestion couldn't have come at a more fortuitous time, and Shoshana could hardly keep still at the thought of Nathan's tri-umph and the prospect of being able to see Eli every day as they worked together on Nathan's new project.

'What about me?' Leah said. 'How come he hasn't asked if I'd like to work there too, only you and Eli?' Then she brightened up. 'Oh well. At least I'll be able to come over and see Eli every day.'

Shoshana felt a stab of guilt about the unresolved situation between them, which she had tried to ignore. She wasn't as articu-late as Nathan and dreaded confrontations. Perhaps without any encouragement from Eli, Leah would soon get over her infatuation.

Just then, hearing their voices, their mother came outside and saved Shoshana from having to comment. 'Perhaps Nathan thinks you're too young,' she said. Then she turned to Shoshana. 'I sup-pose this research station is good news, but I can't help wonder-ing if we can trust those Americans. They always have their own agenda.'

In her bedroom, Shoshana stood by the window, but she wasn't looking at the courtyard or the street beyond it. She felt sorry for

Leah. How would her sister react when she found out how intimate she and Eli had become?

She reread Nathan's letter, more slowly now, to absorb every word. As he hadn't mentioned the woman in Berlin, she assumed he had finally realised that she had been leading him on. On the other hand, he devoted a paragraph to describing the alluring wife of one of the American scientists, and, knowing him, she could read between the lines. Typical, she thought. Another unavailable woman.

It was Friday and Shoshana went into the kitchen to help her mother skim the fat off their chicken soup. Leah was setting the Sabbath table when their father came in from the vineyard. Moshe Adelstein had broad shoulders and strong hands the size of dinner plates. He exuded inexhaustible energy, and Shoshana could visualise him carrying furniture and farming implements up the slope to their new settlement back in 1882.

The sisters rushed to tell him Nathan's news and thrust the letter into his large hands. A man of few words and measured praise, he read the letter several times before making a comment.

'We know how remarkable our Nathan is, but unfortunately so does he. I just hope he doesn't put them all off with his arrogance.'

Looking fondly at his eldest daughter, he said, 'I heard something interesting from one of the men in the vineyard today. He just got back from Haifa, and everyone there was talking about the latest developments in Constantinople. Apparently a new group calling themselves the Young Turks have taken over the government, and they've reinstated the constitution.'

'That's good news, isn't it?'

Moshe shrugged. 'They haven't bothered us too much so far but you can never tell which way a fresh wind might blow.'

Just then, Batya called her daughters to the table to light the Sabbath candles, but as they intoned the blessings, Shoshana only heard Eli's passionate voice murmuring words of love.

CHAPTER FIVE

Caesarea, 1911

At the sound of pounding hooves, Shoshana dropped the brush with which she was scrubbing the pine table, ran to the window and almost stopped breathing. Eli was dismounting from his mare and she ran outside to greet him, her heart about to burst through her chest. Squeezing his hand, she led him into the house and noticed Batya's knowing glance.

The past few months had been the happiest in Shoshana's life. Winter had ended, the days were longer, warmer and brighter, and taking advantage of the weather, she and Eli had hiked in the mountains, swum in the sea, and raced each other on horseback along the slopes and valleys. Sometimes they rode to their cave, a secluded eerie high on the ridge of Mount Carmel, making love and lying on the sun-warmed rocks, watching butterflies flitting around as they listened to the haunting sound of jackals at dusk on distant hills. After these trips, she came home flushed and glowing, and hurried to her room to avoid her mother's disapproving comments.

Just the other day Batya had said, 'You're too wild, Shoshana, and he's too volatile. Excitement is all very well, but take it from me, a woman needs a stable, dependable man in her life. Like Abraham Khadry.'

Shoshana had burst out laughing. As if she'd be interested in this businessman from Constantinople! Apparently he was looking for a young wife; her mother had mentioned him several times in recent weeks.

'Don't waste your time, Ima,' she'd said. 'He'll just have to keep looking.'

'It's time you thought about your reputation,' Batya continued. 'Our neighbours are already making comments about your friendship with Eliezer.'

Shoshana shrugged. 'Why should I care what they think? They've always envied us, and they're always looking for something to gossip about.'

'You should take Leah with you just the same, and some friends as well,' Batya persisted. 'It will look better if there are more of you. You should look after your sister. She's miserable when you're out.'

Shoshana knew why Leah was unhappy, and from time to time, she invited her to join them on their jaunts, but she only felt gloriously alive when she was alone with Eli. As their intimacy grew, so did her passion for him. Each time they made love, his sensitive fingers unlocked the thrilling secrets of her body.

And now, as if conjured up by her daydream of their last encounter, here he was, tying up his horse outside their door, and she rushed to greet him.

'I thought we might ride to Caesarea this morning,' he said.

She could already envisage them riding side by side along the coastal plain that led south towards the ancient Roman town, perhaps stopping in a secluded cave along the way to make love.

Then he added, 'The three of us.'

She hadn't noticed Leah standing beside her, her face already lit up in anticipation.

'Oh yes, let's,' her sister said.

Shoshana opened her mouth to say something and stopped. Surely he had just meant her? Or was he fanning Leah's romantic infatuation, leading her on? She glanced at her sister's face and softened. Leah was gazing at him like a puppy anticipating a longed-for treat. Shoshana reasoned with herself. Perhaps he didn't have the heart to disappoint Leah. After all, they would have other opportunities to be alone.

'We'll have a picnic,' Leah exulted, almost skipping towards the kitchen. A moment later, she was bustling about inside, packing olives, bread, dates and grape juice while Shoshana frowned at Eli, who shrugged with an expression that implied it couldn't be helped.

Half an hour later, mounted on their horses, they started trotting towards the coast. Leah, who wasn't as confident on horseback as they were, trailed behind, and Shoshana welcomed the opportunity to talk to Eli whenever they paused to enable her sister to catch up.

It was spring, her favourite season, when everything palpitated with promise but also, she sensed, with a hint of danger.

Past orchards whose orange trees blossomed with an intoxicating perfume, they rode over carpets of yellow and white crocus, daisies, rock rose and thorny broom. As they waited for Leah, Shoshana pointed to a clump of red-tipped flowerets.

'Squill. The Druze and Bedouins regard it as a medicinal plant. Fatima, the sheik's wife, told me she uses it for her heart condition. Some of our neighbours are also using it – they think it's better than the tablets the doctor prescribes. I think my mother uses it too.'

He was looking at her with admiration. 'How come you know so much about plants?'

'Nathan, of course. I can't wait for him to return and set up that experimental agriculture station in Atlit so I can help. You'll work there with us, won't you?'

'How could I turn down an offer to spend my days close to you?' He raised one thick black eyebrow in that seductive way of his.

As they rode on together towards a stand of tamarisk trees, a flash of yellow feathers caught the sun, and Shoshana pointed to a ball of golden fluff hopping on the bough above them. 'Goldcrests. I love their soft buzzy chirping.'

'You love the music of nature,' he observed.

She smiled at him. How well he understood her.

Just then Leah caught up again, her cheeks bright pink from the ride. They sat down on a bluff overlooking the ancient harbour of Caesarea, and Leah spread out the food she had brought. Chewing on a date, Eli looked pensive. 'I dreamed about a palm tree last night.'

Leah sat forward, her eyes fixed on his face. 'What did it look like?'

'It was a lone tree that grew wild in the desert, but for some reason I was trying to water it.'

'Were you happy or sad?' she asked.

Eli surveyed her for a moment before replying. 'Sad. It felt as if I had died, and nobody knew.'

'What a strange dream,' Shoshana commented, tearing a piece of bread with an abrupt movement and reaching for a green olive.

Leah was still looking at Eli intently. 'Have you ever dreamed that before? I sometimes dream that I'm all alone in a strange place and can't find anyone I know. Do you believe that dreams are prophetic?'

Eli nodded. 'I've dreamed about death before.' Then in a lighter tone he added, 'Perhaps it means I should keep away from dates.'

Impatient with their shared stories about dreams, Shoshana pointed to the boats moored in the harbour below. 'It's hard to believe this port has been in use since Roman times.'

'Whenever I come here, I can feel thousands of years of history pressing down on me,' Eli mused. 'First the Phoenicians, then the Romans, and now the Turks, unfortunately.'

Tilting the pannikin to drink their vineyard's sweet grape juice, Shoshana asked, 'Why are you so interested in things that happened so long ago? They're irrelevant. Today we have our own problems to solve. Instead of looking back, we should look ahead.'

He could hardly wait for her to finish. 'Irrelevant? Whatever happens today has its roots in the past. Invasions, conquests, battles, persecutions, revolts, tyrants and liberators. History is an unending cycle of cause and effect and whatever happens today is the direct result of what happened before. Look at this land: pagans, Jews, Crusaders, Mohammedans and now Jews again.'

Gulls wheeled above them, screeching and swooping, and he paused until they flew away. He sat forward, and his black eyes glowed with an inner fire. 'When I lived in France, the people I met talked incessantly about the right of all people to be free from oppression and to live under their own governments. All over Europe, people are struggling to rid themselves of their oppressors, but we're living under the Ottoman yoke, at the mercy of the Turks who could easily confiscate everything we have and annihilate us on a whim.'

Shoshana was shocked. 'What makes you think they'd do that?'

He shook his head and a lock of hair fell over his forehead. 'The point is, they have the power to do it. Moses left Egypt to escape slavery, the Jews left Judea to escape persecution, and our forefathers escaped from Russia to free themselves from anti-Semitism. This has been our land for thousands of years and we shouldn't have to bow and scrape to our pasha like our ancestors did to the pharaoh and the tsar.'

They sat in silence, unnerved by the scenario he had conjured. But he hadn't finished yet. 'Already a new group has seized power in Constantinople. These so-called Young Turks are fanatical nationalists. We are just one of several ethnic minorities living within the Ottoman Empire. Who knows how they might decide to assert their new power? I wish Britain would overthrow the Turks. The British are cold people but they're solid and dependable, not corrupt like the Ottomans.'

This was too much for Shoshana to absorb. What a peculiar idea, that Britain should conquer Turkey. Her thoughts turned to the strange Englishman she had encountered at Atlit and his ideas about leading the Arabs to rise up against the Turks. But the scenario Eli had evoked was too far-fetched.

'I think you're exaggerating. The Ottoman Empire has always consisted of many different groups. Why should they suddenly turn against their own subjects?'

Leah had been listening intently. 'Surely you're not suggesting we're in danger and should rise up against them? How could we possibly do that?'

'I sense that times are changing and it will be impossible to continue as we are,' Eli replied. 'I'm not afraid of change, but what I can't stand is passivity. You have to stand for something, not stand aside. I've been convinced of that all my life.'

How clever he was, how passionately he expressed his ideas, Shoshana thought, enchanted by his hypnotic voice. But Leah! Shoshana had never heard her sister take such an active part in a political discussion before. She tried to dismiss her unease.

Eli was reminiscing about his school days to Leah, who watched him with the rapt expression of an acolyte listening to a prophet.

'Do you know what I did one day? We were taken to see a play set in a Russian *stetl*, and in one scene the anti-Semites were bashing Jews who were cowering and not fighting back. I couldn't stand watching that. I leapt onto the stage and shouted it was time they stopped portraying us as cowards who don't stand up for themselves.'

Leah's eyes widened. 'So what happened?'

He burst out laughing. 'I caused a riot! The actors tried to push me away, the audience applauded, whistled and catcalled, the director rushed on stage, dragged me away, and begged everyone to calm down and let the play go on, but by then it was too late and they had to stop the wretched performance.'

While Leah clapped and laughed delightedly at this triumph, Shoshana wished her sister had stayed home. Her mother regarded Eli as wild and reckless, likely to bring her nothing but trouble and heartache, but she admired his fearlessness and envied his strength.

If he ever decided to rebel, would she have the courage to join him? Or would she be one of the people he despised who just stood aside?

Her reverie was interrupted by the sound of children's voices floating up from the beach, where foam-tipped waves were breaking on the shore. Why was she wasting time worrying about something that would never happen?

They packed up their picnic and made their way down towards the steep tiers of the ruined amphitheatre where once thousands of bloodthirsty Romans had cheered at gladiatorial games. A light breeze ruffled her hair and she shivered.

The light was fading when they headed back to Zichron Yaakov and the wildflowers beneath the horses' hooves had already lost their brightness.

Eli turned to Shoshana. 'What do you think happens after we die?'

Startled, she shook her head. 'I don't think about it. Do you?'

'Very often. I think our lives are puffs of cloud that disperse into the air we came from, never to be seen again. We're snuffed out like a candle flame. No resurrection or afterlife. This is all there is, and we have to fight for whatever we believe in while we have the chance.'

Once again, she glimpsed the darkness that lurked beneath his exuberant nature, a darkness that excited and disturbed her. She decided to change the subject. 'What are you writing at the moment? A historical novel set during Roman times by any chance?'

He turned towards her. 'I'm writing a story about a man in love with two women.'

He was looking straight into her eyes and the intensity of his gaze made her look away. 'How is that possible?'

Now it was his turn to look surprised. 'Don't you think you can love more than one person?'

'At the same time?'

He nodded.

She shook her head, knowing that she would never love anyone as fiercely as she loved him, not now or ever. Speaking slowly, she said, 'I think you can love more than one person – in different ways of course – like your parents, your siblings, even your friends. But can you be in love with two people simultaneously? No, I don't believe that's possible. If you are truly in love with someone, you couldn't possibly feel that way about another person at the same time. If someone thinks they can, they are fooling themselves.'

She didn't realise she had raised her voice until Leah rode up beside her and asked, 'Shoshi, is something wrong? You sound upset.'

'I'm not upset. I'm just stating my opinion.'

'In your usual forthright way,' Eli commented with a disarming smile and a lift of his eyebrow. Leaning towards her, he whispered, 'But I love the way you challenge my ideas.'

She wasn't convinced and, still irritated, she gripped the reins and spurred Zahra to a canter, leaving Eli and Leah behind. Was he teasing her or did he mean what he said about her? What was this argument about? And why was she getting so worked up over it?

When she had calmed down, she looked back to see if they were following. They were nowhere in sight, and as she waited, it seemed that it was taking them longer to catch up than the distance warranted.

A few minutes later they appeared, chatting as they trotted side by side, and she heard the peal of Leah's girlish laugh.

'Were you trying to run away from me?' he murmured as he caught up with her. 'Don't waste your time, my darling. You will never succeed.'

The enchantment of the spring day had darkened, and as the neat houses of Zichron Yaakov came into view, a heaviness settled over her. For the rest of the day, she couldn't get his words, and the sound of Leah's laughter, out of her mind.

CHAPTER SIX

Zichron Yaakov, 1912

It was Shoshana who first noticed that clothes were hanging loosely on her mother's usually stout frame. At first, Batya rejoiced. 'Finally I look like those skinny women your father always admires,' she said.

But within a short time, her thinning face assumed a yellowish tinge, and she doubled over, complaining of sharp pains in her abdomen. Although she insisted that the squill tincture would cure her, her condition didn't improve, and despite her protestations, they sent their driver Nasser with their horse-drawn carriage to fetch Dr Hirsch from Haifa.

Shmuel Hirsch was a plump man with a bald head, jowly cheeks, and an authoritative manner that belied his kind nature. As Batya described her symptoms, he nodded thoughtfully without commenting except for a noncommittal 'Hmm' or 'I see.'

When he had finished examining her, he came into the living room where Shoshana, Leah and their father scanned his face anxiously.

Dr Hirsch spoke slowly, choosing his words with care. 'I've detected a mass in her abdomen,' he said.

'A mass?' Moshe Adelstein repeated. 'What kind of mass? What does that mean?'

Dr Hirsch glanced from him to Shoshana, as if assessing who was more likely to cope with bad news.

'A tumour,' he said.

Moshe grasped the doctor's arm. 'How serious is it? What can we do? Does she need an operation?'

Shoshana read the answer in the doctor's eyes.

'From her colour, I'd say she is jaundiced, which means the tumour is pressing on the bile duct. I'm afraid surgery won't help.'

'So what do you suggest? There must be something we can do.'

Her strong, confident father sounded panic-stricken, and Shoshana placed a comforting hand on his shoulder. Standing beside her, Leah tugged at her arm.

'I don't understand what the doctor is saying. What's wrong with Ima?'

'Your mother has a tumour, which I suspect is malignant,' Dr Hirsch said.

Leah looked questioningly at her sister, who squeezed her hand but didn't speak.

'If the pain worsens, I can prescribe something, but unfortunately there's nothing else I can do.'

As Shoshana escorted him back to the waiting carriage, he turned to her. 'I don't think your mother has very long. A few months at most. If the pain gets worse, let me know, and I'll give her an injection that will relieve it and let her drift away peacefully.'

Several days later, Shoshana was sitting on the edge of her mother's bed, racking her brain for something entertaining to say, when

Batya took her hand and whispered, 'I know I don't have very long, and there's something I want to ask you so I can die in peace.'

Her voice was so faint that Shoshana had to lean closer to hear what she was saying. She was about to demur but couldn't bring herself to utter empty words of false hope.

'Please take care of your father and Leah. They're not as strong as you are, and they'll need you, especially Leah,' Batya rasped. She rested a penetrating gaze on her daughter's face. 'I know I can count on you to look after her.'

Shoshana tried to blink away her tears and looked down, unwilling to meet her mother's eyes.

'If only Nathan were here,' Batya sighed. 'I hope I can hold on until he comes home but the pain is getting so bad that it would be a relief for it to end.'

Shoshana understood what her mother was saying and wondered if she should ask Dr Hirsch to administer the injection he had mentioned, but she hesitated. Nathan had written that he was on his way home. She decided to wait a few more days.

Batya died two days later.

*

For the next seven days they sat in slippers and ripped clothes on a low couch; all the mirrors in the house had been covered. After the prayers had been said, friends and neighbours came to commiserate and brought pots of soup, platters of chicken and slabs of cake. Moshe was dazed, and Leah sobbed. Only Shoshana looked composed and thanked each visitor for coming. She overheard two women talking as they glanced in her direction. 'Look how hard she is,' one of them whispered. 'Not even a tear.' Shoshana was shocked. Even during this mourning period, their neighbours couldn't refrain from carping.

Shoshana took charge of the household, burying her grief in a frenzy of cleaning, washing and preparing meals. Although she knew she could call on Leah to share the housework, hurrying from one activity to another dulled the pain. She couldn't give herself time to feel the loss that she feared might overwhelm her.

Eli understood that she needed time to grieve, but as weeks passed, he grew impatient. 'Whenever I come over to suggest a ride or a swim, you brush me off saying you have washing or ironing to do,' he complained. 'Is my company so boring that you find sweeping the floor more exciting?'

Another time, he took her hand. 'Shoshana, you're killing me. Can't you see I'm dying piece by piece? Life without you is death by a thousand cuts,' he said one afternoon and caressed her cheek. 'Why are you trying to push me away?'

'I'm not,' she replied, wriggling out of his embrace. 'It's just that I have so much to do.'

He wagged a finger at her. 'Just remember what I once told you – you might try to leave me but you'll never succeed.'

Her father still spent most of the day slumped in his armchair, staring into space, and she had to cajole him to get up and eat. As for Leah, she wandered around the house aimlessly, unable to settle to anything. The only thing that lifted her spirits was seeing Eli walk through the door, and Shoshana often saw them leaving together. At those times, she was overwhelmed with resentment and anger, which she tried to expunge by scrubbing the floor so vigorously her arms ached. She told herself she had no reason to feel jealous, as the notes Eli left for her were more passionate than ever.

Without you the sun has lost its warmth and the world has become cold and dark as it was at the beginning of time. It feels as if I've lost an arm, or half my heart. Come to me, my darling. I want to look into your beautiful eyes and hold you so that the world can come back to life and I can return to paradise.

She reread his letters until she knew them by heart and stored them in her bedroom drawer, but she didn't reply. She told herself she didn't have time.

Finally she wrote back.

Just because I can't express my feelings as well as you, doesn't mean they don't exist. My mind is less complex than yours but I feel things just as deeply. Do you always understand yourself? I can't explain why I'm keeping away, but this is what I need to do right now. I hope you understand.

As she reread her letter, the words sounded stiff, almost insincere, a lame excuse for neglecting something she was really trying to avoid. She supposed that succumbing to passion felt wrong, and depriving herself of his love was part of the grieving process.

His reply was immediate and fiery and he arrived in person to deliver it.

No, Shoshana, I don't understand. Grief doesn't cancel love. But I do understand one thing. Your words did reveal your feelings in spite of yourself. If you persist in refusing my embrace, I will kiss your little sister instead and I'll ask her to pass my kiss on to you.

Shaken, she reread his letter several times. What did he mean? Was he being flippant or was he trying to make her jealous? Was this an implied threat, that unless she changed her attitude, he would turn his attention to Leah? She dismissed that possibility. Eli was too honest and too direct. But she couldn't bring herself to question him about it or to resume the passionate relationship she craved.

Over the next few weeks, the change in Leah was noticeable, and each time she returned from a ride, swim or hike with Eli, she seemed to glow, as if illuminated by an internal lamp.

'He sent you this kiss and said to make sure I delivered it exactly the way he gave it,' she told Shoshana one afternoon as she pressed her lips hard against her sister's cheek. 'I know I shouldn't be saying this so soon after Mama died, but I've never been so happy.'

'Mama would be pleased you've stopped mourning.' Shoshana had trouble getting the words out and had to clear her throat several times before she could form them. She ached with longing for Eli, but she knew she was the one who had created the distance between them.

*

With Shoshana's encouragement, their father's depressed state lightened, and three months later he resumed work in the vineyard. While she served his midday meal one wintry afternoon, he looked up from the bean soup she had cooked, and there was concern in his eyes. 'Shoshana, don't you think it's time you settled down? A lovely and accomplished young woman like you should have a husband, a home of your own and children, God willing, instead of keeping house for an old man.'

Surprised, she sat down beside him. There was only one person in the whole world she would consider spending the rest of her life with, but she had pushed him away.

'I'm happy here, Abba. I don't want to get married.'

'But it's not right,' he persisted. 'Your mother, God rest her soul, would want to see you settled. Listen, I know a successful businessman who is looking for a wife. He moved from Haifa to Constantinople ...'

'Not Abraham Khadry? You've mentioned him before, and so did Ima and I told her I wasn't interested,' Shoshana interrupted.

'You see?' he said. 'Your mother also thought he was a good match for you.'

'So you want to get rid of me,' she teased. 'You're ready to marry me off to some old man who no one else wants and pack me off to Constantinople so you won't see me anymore.'

He waved his arm in protest. 'Stop your nonsense, Shoshi. I only want what's best for you. But it's your life, and if you don't want to get married, it's your business. I just hope you'll change your mind.'

She leaned over and kissed his furrowed cheek. 'So you can forget all about it because that will never happen. I love living in Zichron Yaakov and looking after you.'

But later, in her room, as she went over their conversation, the numbness of the past few months lifted, and for the first time since her mother's death, she felt a surge of excitement. Like a blind person whose vision has suddenly been restored, she recalled the pleasures she had cast aside. Eli above all. She longed to ride along the slopes of Mount Carmel with him, to lie down with him in their secret cave above the sea, to stroke every part of him and tell him how much she loved and desired him. She longed to feel his hands bringing her body to life, and to hear him whisper passionate words of love. As soon as she saw him again, she would tell him. For the first time in many months, she hummed as she cleared the table.

'It's good to see you in such a cheerful mood,' her father commented as he put on his hat and left for the vineyard.

Shoshana rushed to her bedroom to change her clothes. No more black dresses. She would wear the blue one Eli liked so much. She pinched her pale cheeks to bring colour into them and paced around the house. The light began to fade. Leah and Eli had gone riding on Mount Carmel and she wondered when they'd be back. Finally she heard the clip-clop of hooves, and the sound of voices. The waiting was over. She rushed to the front door, her eyes shining with anticipation.

Leah was laughing as she slid from the saddle into Eli's waiting arms, and together they walked into the house. Shoshana was about to ask if they'd had an enjoyable day when Leah glanced at Eli and went into her room.

Relieved to be alone with him, Shoshana sat beside him on the brocade-covered sofa and took his hand.

'There's something I want to tell you,' she whispered.

'There's something I want to tell you too,' he said.

She smiled and waited.

He cleared his throat. 'This has been tearing me apart for the past few months, but I've come to a decision.' He was looking deep into her eyes with a searching gaze. Squeezing her hand so hard that it hurt, he said, 'There's no easy way to say this. I love you, but I love Leah too. We're going to get married.'

The world tilted dangerously on its axis. Perhaps she hadn't heard correctly or had misunderstood.

'What are you saying?'

He was still squeezing her hand. 'You remember my story about the man who loved two women? You thought such a thing wasn't possible, but it is. I love you both and I wish I could cut myself in two.'

'But you've chosen my sister, so your love isn't equal, is it?' Her voice seemed to come from some empty far-off place.

He had tears in his eyes. 'My love for each of you is different because you are both so different. I adore your strength, my darling, but I don't think I could live with your intensity. I think I need a quieter, calmer love. But I will always love you.'

Fury gripped her. Fury with her sister who had stolen the man she loved, and fury with him. She sat cold and still as a stone, not trusting herself to speak. There was nothing to say. Maybe he loved her but he didn't love her enough.

Without another word, she rose, but before walking out of the room she turned to face him one more time. 'Don't delude yourself.' She spat the words. 'You've made your choice. You can't have us both.'

She was sitting on her bed when there was a soft knock on the door and Leah came in, radiant as summer sunlight.

Putting her arms around her sister, she whispered, 'Shoshi, I know you love him too but please be happy for me. I don't think I could live without him. I think Ima would approve, don't you?'

Shoshana's throat felt so swollen she couldn't speak. At that moment she loved her sister but hated her too. And she realised that, without being aware of it, she had kept her promise to her mother.

All night she lay awake in turmoil, and by morning her mind was made up. The pain of staying in Zichron Yaakov after Leah and Eli were married would be unbearable. Her disappointment turned to anger. Did Leah really think she would rejoice for her? And did Eli imagine she would hover in the background, ready to provide him with intellectual and perhaps physical stimulation? She had to get away from them both and there was only one way to do it.

CHAPTER SEVEN

Constantinople, 1914

From behind the latticed window, Shoshana watched raindrops bounce on the potted geraniums on the wrought-iron balcony. In front of her, craft of all sizes plied the Bosphorus: yachts, barges, steamers. Her favourites were the gulets, the traditional two-masted wooden boats that local fishermen used. She wondered if any of them were sailing to Palestine and how long it would take them to reach the coast she loved.

It had been two long years since she arrived in her new home, a palatial seaside mansion in Galata on the northern shore of the Golden Horn. She hadn't expected such a grand three-storey stone building with marble pillars leading to the front entrance and delicate fretwork decorating the long windows. Her astonishment delighted her husband. Abraham Khadry was also a surprise. Although her mother had described him as a merchant descended from a wealthy Baghdad family, one of whose antecedents had been banker to the Ottoman sultan, she had always imagined he was an old man. But when he arrived in Zichron Yaakov to meet her, she saw a likeable man of about thirty-five with a neatly trimmed black beard and an inclination for over-indulgence judging by the way his waistcoat buttons gaped over his stomach. Even though he was portly, he moved with a quick light tread, and she liked the softness of his voice and the admiration in his eyes whenever he looked at her.

'I'll make sure you never want for anything,' he'd promised. 'You'll have servants, a nice house, and whatever you desire.' But he didn't need to persuade her. She had already decided to marry him.

When she thought back to their wedding in Zichron Yaakov, she recalled how her legs trembled when she stood under the canopy in her long white satin wedding gown with its lace veil fanning out on the floor. While the rabbi intoned the wedding vows and the blessing, and Abraham smashed the symbolic glass with his Italian patent leather shoe, Leah had clutched her arm and her father had beamed, rejoicing in his daughter's excellent match.

The day she and Abraham left, Leah had clung to her. 'I'll miss you so much, Shoshi,' she sobbed. As for Eli, he had fixed his burning gaze on her and whispered, 'Don't forget, whatever happens, you'll always be part of me and I'll always be part of you.' She had averted her eyes and brushed past him without speaking.

At first, Constantinople bewitched her. She felt overwhelmed by its enormous size and the incessant noise and activity in its streets and marketplaces, by the pressure of its teeming population and the sound of horses and mules laden with huge panniers that transported goods all over town. She hadn't expected Constantinople to be so cosmopolitan, with Jews, Greeks and Armenians mingling with Turks in the bazaars.

But the novelty soon palled. She missed the vast skies and empty spaces of Palestine and the quality of the light that seemed to come straight from God. Most of all, she missed the freedom to gallop over the slopes of Mount Carmel and its rugged wadis, to breathe in the scent of its grasses, trees and wildflowers. Despite the opulence of the house, its narrow windowpanes didn't let in much light and she spent hours by her window, gazing longingly at the sea.

The house had become her cage and she chafed at the restrictions of her new life. She was shocked to learn that she couldn't go outside unchaperoned. 'It isn't safe,' her mother-in-law had said, listing the dangers and indignities that befell women who ventured out alone.

'The men regard them as loose women and grope, pinch and assault them. The government has recently passed a law to protect women but legislation is one thing and culture is another.' Fixing Shoshana with a meaningful look she added, 'The Turks regard lone women as prey. That's why you must never leave the house on your own.'

That first night in her new home, Abraham had taken her hand and led her to their bedroom; the tiled floor was covered by a magnificent silk carpet he had imported from Tabriz. Pointing at the intricate frieze around its edges, he explained that the Arabic letters spelled the name of the weaver who had created this masterpiece two hundred years before.

In their canopied bed, Abraham was a gentle but unimaginative lover, surprisingly inexperienced for a man of his age. Even now, two years later, she still didn't know that he had climaxed until he slid off her with a satisfied grunt. She supposed she wasn't sufficiently attentive. Although she wanted to make him happy and resolved every night to put Eli out of her mind, she yearned for his exuberant sexuality and the passionate, poetic words that aroused her desire. She was mourning the loss of a part of herself, as though her heart had fallen out of her body.

Abraham couldn't wait to show her around Constantinople in his horse-drawn carriage, and in his enthusiastic description of every medieval tower, mosque and sultan's palace, she sensed his love for the city. At first she was dazzled by the fairytale domes and colourful Byzantine mosaics that made her feel she was inside a kaleidoscope, but eventually she tired of Islamic art. She missed nature, but she enjoyed exploring the crooked streets lined with traditional timber buildings where Turkish men in tarbushes and black vests sat around small wooden tables drinking tiny cups of thick black coffee or smoking hookahs while leaning over a backgammon board.

Occasionally she lingered in the food markets, where sharp-eyed women in baggy trousers and head scarves sold glossy purple aubergines, vermillion tomatoes and pyramids of yellow, ochre and crimson spices. The mouth-watering aroma of yeasty flat bread baked in wood-fired ovens wafted over the stalls where men in floury aprons prepared spinach-filled pancakes called *gozleme*. They usually ended their stroll at Abraham's favourite pastry shop and brought home a selection of cakes smelling of rosewater and honey, which Shoshana found too sickly.

She became increasingly restless at the aimlessness of her life, a feeling that intensified whenever she received a letter from Nathan. He wrote that the recent yield of wheat and barley at the experimental agricultural research station at Atlit had exceeded all his expectations, vindicating his theory that, with skill, even arid land could become fertile. The Washingtonia palms he had planted on the road to Atlit were flourishing, and his American sponsors were delighted with his progress and planned to adopt his techniques in California.

His letter intensified her yearning for home and it took several days to recover her equilibrium. She was proud of Nathan's success, but envious, too. He was realising his dream. Sometimes she thought about the Englishman she had met at Atlit. Lawrence. He also had a dream, a more grandiose one than Nathan's, and she wondered if he would ever achieve it. But her own life had no goals and no triumphs. Only an unsettling longing to make her life count without any idea of what she could do.

To add to her discontent, Nathan often mentioned how lucky he was to have Eli working with him at the research station, and how happy their sister Leah looked. Leah's letters were brief. She missed Shoshana and wished she would come to visit. Apparently the wedding date hadn't yet been set. Her letters put Shoshana in a black mood for days.

Most disturbing were the letters from Eli with their intensity and intimacy. The most recent read:

> *Yesterday I stood in the doorway of your bedroom and gazed at your bed and felt like crying. It was excruciating to visualise your beautiful body stretched out upon it, like an erotic painting I once saw at the Louvre, and to know you were so far from me. You are my opium. I'm addicted to you, and I never want to be cured.*

His letters stirred her up. She knew she should ask him to stop writing and remind him that he'd made a choice and she had now made hers, but she couldn't bear to deprive herself of the guilty pleasure of his words.

That morning as she sat by her window and the early sunlight shone on the russet brickwork of the ancient Galata tower, the maid Fauza, in a white cap and apron over her black dress, brought her a letter from Zichron Yaakov on a silver tray. From the bold handwriting on the envelope, she knew it was from Nathan. His letter contained upsetting news. It appeared that Djemal Pasha, the governor of Palestine, had ordered the deportation of all foreign-born Jews from Haifa and Tel-Aviv. They had to leave all their belongings, which would be confiscated by Turkish officials. No one knew where they were to be taken, and all over Palestine, Jews were alarmed. The community leaders tried to intercede with the authorities but to no avail. They were expelled because they weren't Ottoman citizens. *Eli warned us that we couldn't trust the government now that the Young Turks have taken over. He says they don't trust minorities and want Turkey for the Turks*, he wrote.

Shoshana's heart ached for the victims. How terrible to be deprived of everything you owned and be expelled from your home, made destitute, and forced to rely on the charity of strangers. She recalled Eli's prediction about the Turkish government's attitude towards the Jews and wondered if this signified the beginning of a repressive policy. Eager to discuss this with Abraham, as soon as they had sat down to lunch and Fauza had withdrawn after serving their chicken broth, she told him about the deportations Nathan had described.

'I told you we couldn't trust this new government,' his mother said.

But Abraham shook his head. 'No need to panic. Our government must have a good reason for relocating these people.'

Shoshana felt her blood rising. How complacent he was. With his luxurious home in Constantinople and his lucrative business, he trusted the government and made excuses for it, ignoring the desperation of people who had been made destitute on account of their religion.

'Don't you even wonder why they only selected the Jewish residents for deportation? You can't tell me they had a valid reason for that.'

They stopped talking as Fauza returned with a platter of stuffed aubergines, grilled lamb skewers and rice pilaff, which she proceeded to serve.

After she left the dining room, Abraham turned to Shoshana. 'I don't think you should concern yourself with political issues you probably don't understand. But I'll tell you one thing to put your mind at rest. For centuries the Ottoman Empire has consisted of many minority groups, including the Jews, and it has never discriminated against us, so there's no reason to think they would turn on us now.'

'But they already have! There's a new government with a different agenda,' she retorted.

Abraham shrugged but his mother weighed into the discussion. 'Shoshana is quite right. They must have some ulterior motive for persecuting Jews. I know you're a loyal Turkish citizen, Abraham, but times are changing and you should open your eyes. Lately I've heard the cook and the driver blaming all their problems on the Armenians. They accuse them of all sorts of crimes. They refer to them as traitors. It makes me wonder, where has this hatred come from?'

With a sigh Abraham took out his monogrammed silver lighter and lit a cigarette. The air filled with sweetish smoke. Rising from the table, he said, 'I'll leave you two experts to sort out our political problems.'

Shoshana was keen to continue the discussion, but her mother-in-law changed the subject.

'I'm going to the bazaar tomorrow to buy silk for a new dress. Come with me and you can choose some for yourself. My dressmaker is good at copying the latest French fashions.' She gave Shoshana a meaningful look. 'I hope it won't be long before you have to buy looser clothes.'

Shoshana could hardly conceal her irritation. Her mother-in-law had made her desire for a grandchild increasingly obvious in the past year but Shoshana didn't reveal that a fortune-teller she had consulted in the bazaar had told her she would never have children. A prediction that didn't distress her. Having children with Abraham had never appealed to her.

*

The following day Shoshana received another letter and her hands shook as she tore open the envelope. It was from Eli. She stopped breathing.

> *I don't know how to tell you this so I'll just come out and say it. I know now that I've made the worst mistake of my life. I thought I wanted a calmer love but you were right and I was wrong. It's you I want, now and forever. Can you forgive me?*

She reread the letter several times and stared unseeing into space. It was wonderful but it was too late.

CHAPTER EIGHT

Constantinople, 1915

Watching the parade of soldiers in their helmet-like *kabalak* caps marching along the road that April day, Shoshana recalled the government's prediction of an imminent victory against the British. Although from a distance the determined military stride of the young conscripts gave the impression of strength, a closer look revealed boots in poor condition, khaki uniforms in a state of disrepair, and expressions that hinted at bravado rather than confidence.

'They're heading for Gallipoli,' Abraham said as the soldiers marched past. She supposed he'd heard that news from one of his acquaintances in the army.

It was the second year of a war whose causes were obfuscated in political alliances and secret treaties that made no sense to anyone Shoshana spoke to. That the murder of a minor royal in an unimportant nation by an insignificant assassin should have led to a conflict that now affected almost every country in Europe and ensnared even far-off Australia and New Zealand, was beyond the comprehension of normal people.

The war had ruined Shoshana's chance to visit Zichron Yaakov. Although she hadn't replied to Eli's letter, his confession had left her restless and unsettled as she paced around the house trying to convince herself that it was her home and family she longed to see again, not him. After all, it would be normal to want to see her family after such a long absence. Nathan had been away when she left, and she was eager to see the experimental research station.

Abraham had agreed to her visit and, palpitating with impatience, she had made all the arrangements. She had planned to leave the previous August, but as soon as war was declared, most of the trains were commandeered for the troops. Travelling was now out of the question, Abraham declared, and his tone forestalled any argument.

To complicate matters further, it appeared that the world was now carved into two opposing factions and for some reason, Turkey had entered the war on Germany's side. Abraham, who seemed to understand the arcane world of international politics, explained that they had allied with Germany because of Turkey's age-old fear of Russia.

That didn't make sense to her either and she hoped that the war would soon end so she could go home. Disappointed at being forced to delay her visit, she felt the separation more keenly and wept when she read letters from Zichron Yaakov. She spent hours sitting by the window but she didn't see the view.

The news from home was distressing. Nathan wrote that the Turkish authorities had begun conscripting young Jewish men into the army and she was horrified to learn from Leah that they had recently dragged Eli away. Having seen the thin, bedraggled soldiers in Constantinople, Shoshana hardly slept until Nathan's next letter brought good news.

Eli had been rescued. *As we know, baksheesh is the oil that lubricates every activity in the Ottoman Empire*, Nathan wrote. He had convinced Djemal Pasha that he needed Eli's help at the research station to continue producing large quantities of grain, which would become scarce during the war. *And as soon as I handed him a wad of Turkish lira, he suddenly agreed that Eli was far more valuable at Atlit than at the front.* Nathan's chutzpah always made her smile.

The front pages of the newspapers displayed bold headlines praising Turkey's military triumphs against the enemy. They had apparently thwarted a British attack by mining the Bosphorus and the British had retreated like a pack of marauding wolves abandoning their prey.

And now she read that the British had launched another attack, this time in the Dardanelles, and the war correspondents described how thousands of soldiers, many from Australia and New Zealand, had landed on the shores of Gallipoli to be shot down like fish in a barrel by the Turkish troops waiting for them on the hills above the beaches.

News of the fighting in the Dardanelles had reached Palestine. Nathan had got around the strict censorship that monitored comments about the war and written to Shoshana about what he described as the British debacle.

I can't understand their strategy. An English politician called Churchill had organised a landing on the Turkish coast that was doomed to fail. All those young lives thrown away.

His letter brought more distressing news. As the war had now entered its second year, food and other commodities had become scarce, and Turkish officials had swooped on Jewish farms and confiscated stores of wheat and barley, farming machinery, jewellery and any other valuables they could lay their hands on. As a result, many Jewish communities became impoverished, hungry and terrified.

The curious thing is that despite the expulsions, hardships and confiscations, many of our people still support our overlords and make excuses for them.

Shoshana sighed as she finished his letter, but she knew there was no point discussing it with Abraham. 'They are only targeting non-Ottoman Jews, not citizens,' he argued, ignoring their discriminatory policy. If only she could go home and see the situation for herself.

The more she thought about it, the more determined she was to make it happen. She had to get away from this stifling existence where she felt imprisoned. But how? Abraham would never agree. Besides, travelling alone by train through Turkey at any time was unthinkable, especially now in wartime when most of the trains swarmed with soldiers. The only possible solution was to find a male travelling companion without revealing her plan to Abraham.

The men who visited their home were either his friends or business associates, none of whom she could approach or confide in. Several months passed and she despaired of finding anyone. Then one cold November day, a visitor arrived from Zichron Yaakov. Miriam's father.

Joseph Steinman was a businessman who acted as an intermediary between the wine producers of their region and their distributor in Constantinople. He had always struck Shoshana as kindly and broad-minded, and, having known her all her life, she hoped he might be sympathetic. He was her only chance. As he was due to return soon to Zichron Yaakov, she watched for an opportunity to speak to him alone.

She had almost given up hope when one evening he arrived for dinner before Abraham came home. As soon as she heard the doorbell, she rushed downstairs just as Fauza had ushered him into the sitting room. As her mother-in-law was in bed with a migraine, Shoshana knew it was now or never.

Her mouth was dry and she clasped her hands tightly to conceal their trembling. 'Mr Steinman, there's something I need to talk to you about. I miss my family so much that if I don't get home and see them soon I don't know what I'll do,' she whispered. 'But I can't go unless someone accompanies me on the train. I know you're leaving in a few days and I was wondering if I could possibly come with you?'

He studied her for a few moments. 'And what does Mr Khadry think of your idea?'

She glanced anxiously at the door to make sure they were alone and spoke in an urgent whisper. 'He doesn't know and I can't tell him. He doesn't want me to travel because of the war but if you accompanied me, I'd be safe. Can you help me?'

He looked at her with a troubled expression. 'I'm sorry, I can't go behind your husband's back. I hope you understand. But don't worry. The war is bound to end soon and you'll be able to go home then.'

She leaned closer and spoke quickly. 'Abraham need never know you were involved. It would only be for a short time, just so I can see them. Then I'll come back.' But even as she spoke she despised herself for pleading a hopeless cause.

She heard a rustle, the door opened, and Fauza came in carrying tiny spinach and feta triangles on a Limoges platter. Shoshana wondered if she imagined the maid glancing at her with a look that implied sympathy. Several moments later Abraham entered, apologising profusely for keeping his guest waiting.

Shoshana hurriedly excused herself. 'I'm sure you have business matters to discuss, so I won't join you tonight,' she said and left the room.

Back in her bedroom, she held her head in her hands. How could she have been so stupid? Had she really imagined that he would agree to conspire with her behind Abraham's back? She hoped he wouldn't tell his family what she had suggested.

Too depressed to get up next morning, she was still in bed when Fauza knocked softly on the door.

'I've brought you fresh orange juice,' she said.

Instead of leaving immediately as she always did, the maid stayed in the room, straightening things on Shoshana's dressing table and glancing at her from time to time. Shoshana looked at this tiny self-effacing woman who had come to Constantinople from a small village as a girl and devoted herself to this household. It wasn't like her to hover around.

'Are you all right, Fauza? Is there something you want to tell me?'

Fauza hesitated for a moment before saying, 'Please forgive me, Mrs Shoshana, but I couldn't help overhearing what you said to Steinman *effendi*. What I wanted to tell you is that my nephew Mohammed is going to Izmit tomorrow. He's leaving in the morning on the Haifa train.'

CHAPTER NINE

Anatolia, 1915

The muezzin's dawn call to prayer was blaring from a distant minaret as Shoshana hurried along the crowded platform of Ahmed Pasha station towards the Haifa train, past black-clad women and men in traditional vests and black-tasselled tarbushes. Walking beside her, Fauza's nephew Mohammed carried her leather portmanteau. Every few moments, she glanced behind her to see if anyone from the house was following her, or whether the guard to whom she showed her ticket had noticed how her gloved hand shook and become suspicious.

After heaving her portmanteau into the compartment designated for women travellers, Mohammed wished her a good journey and walked alongside the train to find his own seat. Grateful that she was the only occupant of her compartment, Shoshana sank into the scuffed burgundy velvet seat, and drummed her fingers on her lap. Why didn't the train start? What if Abraham woke up, read the note she had left apologising for her sudden departure, explaining her longing to go home, and assuring him she'd soon return, and sent someone to the station to bring her back? She glanced anxiously out of the window, dreading to see someone searching for her. Finally the stationmaster's whistle shrilled, and in clouds of steam the train pulled away from the station, taking her from Constantinople.

Relieved, Shoshana breathed out and her thoughts turned to her homecoming. How amazed they would be when she appeared. No one in Zichron Yaakov had any idea she was on her way home. She would send Nathan a cable from a station close to home to let him know she was coming. The three-day journey ahead of her would be interminable.

But what would they say in Constantinople when they discovered she had fled? Her mother-in-law would wring her bejewelled hands and lament the ingratitude and deceit of a young woman who did such a scandalous thing behind her husband's back. Thinking about Abraham, Shoshana felt a pang of remorse. He wasn't accustomed to being thwarted, and would probably be furious, but she comforted herself with the hope that he'd forgive her when she returned.

Her thoughts turned to her marriage, which had been a terrible mistake. Did she really think she could live with a man she didn't love? But Abraham had deceived her by omission. He hadn't explained that she would become a virtual prisoner in a dark, suffocating house with barred windows. She reminded herself that she didn't get married to make herself happy. She had made an honourable decision and kept her promise to her mother by removing herself from Zichron Yaakov for Leah's sake. Of course she couldn't have foreseen Eli's change of heart. Or the ache of her own longing.

As the train gathered speed and the city buildings began to recede, she tried to figure out how she had arrived at this confusing point in her life. How did she convince herself that she could live in Constantinople, away from Zichron Yaakov? She hadn't anticipated that her yearning for home and for Eli would be almost visceral. She missed Zahra, her Arab mare, the scent of the dry grasses and wildflowers, and the shimmering silver leaves of the olive trees. Of course, she had given up her freedom and everything she loved for her sister. But she knew that her impulsive decision to leave Zichron Yaakov had been impelled by resentment and anger at Eli, just as the decision to return was prompted by the need to see him again, to breathe the same air he did.

For the first time, she considered the future. What if Abraham didn't forgive her when she returned to Constantinople? And even if he did, he would never trust her again, and he would never let her forget that she had deceived him. He would watch her every movement. Would her life become even more stifling?

But what if she never returned? Startled by that possibility, she sat up straight. Her father would say she had dishonoured him as well as herself by breaking a sacred vow. He had always maintained that a broken promise indicated a broken soul. He would be angry at the irrevocable damage to her reputation and her unforgivable insult to the husband who had offered her a comfortable life. He had never understood the longing of modern women for independence. But what would her mother have said? Perhaps she would have understood. Batya was rarely far from her thoughts. She continued to live in her mind, a constant silent companion and arbiter of her actions.

In turmoil now, her thoughts turned to Leah. What did Eli's change of heart mean for her? Had he admitted to Leah that it was her sister he couldn't live without? Leah's brief letters had never mentioned wedding plans. Did that mean she knew or suspected Eli's change of heart? Perhaps Leah was too busy looking after their father to write long letters. But now it occurred to her that their brevity was a weapon that concealed resentment she was reluctant to express openly. Leah never alluded to her relationship with Eli or explained why they still hadn't married. Had he confessed the truth? If so, could she and Leah ever be close again?

Or would the triangulated shadow of their situation eclipse their relationship?

She sighed. Too many imponderables. It was impossible to resolve these complex issues from a distance. Her thoughts turned to Nathan and her spirits rose. From his letters she knew how much he missed her:

> *Life without you is like a meal without salt. I'm doing such excit-*
> *ing work here but no one understands my dreams like you. I miss*
> *your wisdom and your strength.*

She brought her mind back to the present and glanced outside. There were fewer buildings now and more open fields as the train left the city behind. Lulled by the rhythmic motion of the train, she closed her eyes. She was back in the seclusion of their cave above the Mediterranean, and her body flickered at the memory of the pleasure they had shared.

One day merged into the next as the train began its ascent of the vast Anatolian plateau. She craned forward, expecting to see its steppes, picturesque villages and terraced valleys.

The conductor in a tight jacket and maroon fez knocked on the door. Giving her a brazen look that lingered on the curve of her breasts under her high-necked white blouse, he examined her ticket to Afula, the nearest railway station to Zichron Yaakov.

As soon as he slid the door shut behind him, she was lost in another daydream. She was galloping past olive groves and vine-yards, across the hills with Eli again. Then she looked outside and what she saw made her move closer to the window. Pressing her forehead against the grimy pane, she gasped.

Along the railway line, stretching far into the distance, all the way to the horizon, a ghostly column of men, women and children were staggering across the endless Anatolian plain. Many of the women, wrapped in threadbare shawls, cradled babies in their arms, or pulled exhausted toddlers by the hand, and in their gaunt faces she saw hunger, desperation and hopelessness. The children, thin and ragged, ran beside the train with pleading eyes and outstretched hands.

Striding beside their haggard prisoners, armed soldiers in khaki Turkish uniforms and *kabalak* caps wielded whips and batons with the brutality of those who know they won't have to account for their actions. In the distance, plumes of thick smoke rose from burnt-out villages.

Shoshana's heart hammered hard enough to burst from her chest. Who were these unfortunate people and where were they being taken? A little further on, she noticed something she wished she could unsee. It looked like a field that had been roughly ploughed, with clods of earth and rocks strewn all over it, but as the train drew closer, she realised that the lumps protruding from the ground were parts of human bodies.

Arms and legs were scattered all over the ground. And in among them were wild dogs, snarling and growling and tearing off hunks of flesh. Shoshana closed her eyes but it was too late to erase something she wished she had never seen: a dog chewing the remains of a child.

She wanted to scream, but her mouth was so dry she couldn't utter a sound. She was trapped inside a nightmare from which there was no awakening. It struck her that the people responsible for this massacre hadn't even felt the need to cover up their crime.

Unable to tear herself away from the scene unfolding before her horrified eyes, she watched the endless column of prisoners being herded along the dusty plain. At Izmit, the train shuddered to a halt, and she watched Mohammed jump down from his carriage and stride along the platform towards the exit. She wondered what he'd find when he returned home. Would his family be aware of what had happened to the unfortunate people she had seen? Would they assume these people had committed some crime? Or would they pretend not to know anything about it?

She tried to stand up but her legs trembled so violently she collapsed onto her seat. Several minutes later, she slid open the compartment door, and, gripping the rail, stepped onto the platform.

Most of the passengers stayed on board, and as she looked up at the train, she saw curious faces pressed against the windows. In another compartment, a man in traditional Turkish garb was pointing out something to the veiled woman beside him.

The conductor leaned against the train, smoking a thin Turkish cigarette whose scent wafted over the platform. He surveyed Shoshana with an impudent expression.

'Who are all these people?' she asked. 'Do you know where they are taking them?'

'Armenians. They're being relocated.' Taking one last drag of his cigarette, he tossed the butt on the ground, ground it with his shoe and spat. 'Good riddance.'

Shoshana stood in the shade of the station's awning, shaken by what she had seen and bewildered by his words. A shadowy figure wrapped in a dusty shawl sidled up to her. Without a word, the woman opened her shawl to reveal a baby with a skeletal body and a large bony head. Shoshana fumbled in her purse and held out a coin. The woman grabbed it so fast she scratched Shoshana's hand.

'Can you tell me what's happening here?' Shoshana asked.

Wild-eyed, the woman stared, and Shoshana wondered if she hadn't understood her Arabic. But when she began to talk, the words tumbled from her mouth with such feverish speed that Shoshana had trouble keeping up.

'Did you look out of the window? Can't you see what they're doing? The Turkish devils want to kill us all because we're Christians. In my village they hung stones around the necks of our priests, tied their hands and feet, and threw them into the river. Then they made a pyramid of thorny bushes, tied up all the village men and burnt them alive. We breathed in the ashes of their burnt flesh for days.'

She stared into the distance as she rocked the baby, caressing its lolling head with slow, loving strokes. Shoshana looked at the baby again and swallowed. Didn't the woman realise her baby was dead?

'They won't be happy until we're all dead,' the woman continued, still stroking the baby. 'They're torturing, murdering and raping in broad daylight, but no one cares. What about all the other Christians in the world? Why don't they help us?'

She grasped the lapel of Shoshana's jacket and Shoshana felt an urge to break free and put an end to this litany of horror, but she couldn't move.

The woman continued, 'How can this happen? Why doesn't someone stop it? Our priests tell us that if we sin we'll go to hell, but we're in hell now.'

As she went on listing the atrocities she had witnessed, Shoshana kept looking around, hoping the train would move on so she could escape from this woman's wild gaze, from the dead body of her starved child, and the harrowing stories that poured from her mouth. She wanted to block her ears and hurry back onto the train, but she forced herself to listen just as she had forced herself to keep looking through the window of the train.

When the woman fell silent at last, she stared at Shoshana with an expression of such searing intensity that she couldn't turn away. Her eyes were nails that impaled Shoshana.

'One day the Turkish devils will deny this ever happened, and people will believe them, because it's easier that way. But you're a witness, so you have to tell people what you saw. Don't forget us.'

Shoshana nodded, relieved to hear the whistle blow, but back on the train she couldn't get the woman's story out of her mind. Who should she tell? Would anyone care enough to challenge the might of the Turkish empire? And even if they had the courage, what could they possibly do about it?

Her brain was on fire. What she had seen would haunt her till her dying day, but she sensed its significance reached far beyond Turkey's borders.

As they continued their slow journey across the Anatolian plateau, Shoshana tried to grasp what she was witnessing. How could deportation and persecution of an entire ethnic group be perpetrated in broad daylight with impunity?

The scale of the expulsion was too huge and too well organised to be the result of a pasha's caprice. It must have been planned in cold blood in Constantinople.

Her thoughts turned to her own community. She knew that even before the war had begun, the Turks had been persecuting Jews in Palestine, expelling large numbers from Jaffa and Tel-Aviv, confiscating crops and equipment and imposing taxes that ruined many farmers.

She had been distressed by Nathan's description of the plight of the deportees who had arrived in Zichron Yaakov, distraught and destitute. All their lives they had been proud, hardworking people, but overnight they had been reduced to beggars.

Unable to look out of her window at the unfortunate souls being herded along the dusty track any longer, Shoshana pulled down the fraying tasselled blind to obscure the scene, but a moment later she rolled it up again, as the words of the woman at the station resounded in her head.

Because of the war, the journey took even longer than usual. Every few hours, the train jolted at an unscheduled stop, and would stand idle for several hours on the platform as hundreds of noisy young soldiers crowded into the other compartments. Occasionally she and the other passengers had to disembark and wait for another train to pull into the station.

Exhausted by the long journey and its horrific sights, she fell into a trance-like state. Suspended between wakefulness and sleep, she saw people being herded along the road and she recognised the residents of her village, trudging silently along the road, being driven to certain death.

Shocked by her vision, she gripped the armrests of her seat, her knuckles white. It was clear to her now. The persecution of the

Jewish communities and the expulsion of the Armenians were not isolated events. Both were part of the government's policy to eliminate minorities. The future had whispered its terrifying message to her sleeping mind: today it was the Christian Armenians of the Ottoman Empire; tomorrow it would be the Jews.

Charged with new energy, she sat up. In that moment she visualised her future unfurling before her and knew that it lay in Zichron Yaakov, not Constantinople. It wasn't chance that had led her to witness that atrocity on the Anatolian plateau. Freeing her people from the stranglehold of the Turks was her destiny, one she was determined to fulfil.

During the long delay at the next station, she hurried to the railway office and cabled her arrival details to Nathan, adding *I have left Constantinople for good.* She paused, and trembling at the audacity of her decision, she also sent a cable to Abraham.

CHAPTER TEN

Zichron Yaakov, 1915 to 1916

As soon as the train pulled up at Afula station, Nathan rushed along the platform until he saw Shoshana alight from her compartment, then flung his arms around her. In her powder-blue travelling suit and high-necked white blouse, she was an island of elegance in the sea of khaki-clad Turkish soldiers milling on the platform. But her face was white and strained, her eyes seemed fixed on something in the distance, and he thought she seemed dazed and disconnected. The hug she returned lacked warmth, and he supposed the long journey had taken its toll on her.

'You look exhausted,' he said. Picking up her portmanteau, he took her arm and led her towards the exit.

She stopped and turned to face him, and when she spoke, her voice seemed to come from some far-off place.

'I saw something along the way that will haunt me for the rest of my life. But it has also given me the purpose I have always longed for.'

Seeing his puzzled expression, she added, 'I'm still in a daze. I'll tell you all about it when we get home.'

'It's wonderful to have you back, Shoshi. We've all missed you so much.'

He placed his arm around her shoulders and they pushed their way past noisy groups of soldiers with bulging rucksacks, and as soon as they were outside, he paused and gave her a searching look.

'You cabled that you'd left Constantinople for good. What did you mean?'

'I meant what I said. I'm never going back.'

'But what about Abraham? Was it something he did?'

She shook her head. 'He didn't do anything. It was me. Initially I planned to spend a few months in Zichron Yaakov and then go back to Constantinople, but what I saw during the journey made me realise that my future is here.'

He stared at her. 'You've always been unconventional but leaving your husband ...' he trailed off, shaking his head.

'I think you'll understand when I explain what made me change my mind.'

They had reached the carriage. The horse was stamping in impatience, but the driver came towards her with a big smile.

'Welcome home, Miss Shoshana,' Nasser said as he helped her into the carriage. With a low whistle and a tug at the reins, he coaxed the horses to an easy trot.

As the carriage began to move, Nathan sat forward. 'Our experimental agricultural station at Atlit is succeeding beyond my wildest dreams. I can't wait to show you all the exciting things we're doing,' he said. 'Our wheat and barley yields have exceeded expectations and my American sponsors are delighted with their investment.'

He waited for her reaction, but she was silent, lost in thought, and after a pause he said, 'There's so much I want to talk to you about, and of course I want to know what happened during your journey, but I can see you're too tired to talk. It will probably take a few days before you're your old self again.'

She gave him that strange look again. 'I don't think I'll ever be the same. You know, I've always envied you because you've had a driving ambition and you've pursued it. Well, now I've discovered my mission.'

He leaned closer, waiting for her to reveal more, but too weary to talk, she closed her eyes as the carriage trundled along the road that wound above the coast.

*

When Shoshana opened her eyes an hour later, she sat forward eagerly, leaned out of the carriage and took a deep breath. The air was scented with the green freshness of the pines, grape vines and citrus orchards; silver olive groves shimmered in the sunlight.

Nathan followed her gaze. 'The enchanted castle of nature!' he murmured.

His face was lit up and she wondered if his love of nature and commitment to science would prevent him from participating in her mission to free Palestine from the Turks.

'Lately the Turks have been cutting down entire forests,' he was saying, and his eyes flashed with anger. 'They think they'll win the war by killing our trees. Not content with destroying the livelihood of our communities, they are denuding our environment.'

She nodded, hoping that he was angry enough to support her plan.

*

Her father was standing at the front door when their carriage pulled up and she was shocked at the change in him over the past two years. His hair had become greyer, his face was more lined and he looked frail. Moved by his appearance, she reached out to embrace him, but his arms stayed by his sides.

'You have disappointed me, Shoshana,' he said. 'I never imagined you'd behave in such a reckless, scandalous way. What you did to Abraham is unforgivable. I was mortified when I read the cable he sent me. He was outraged by your behaviour and I don't blame him.'

Then, without waiting for her to speak, he turned away and walked into the house.

She followed him inside. 'Abba, I understand how angry Abraham feels, and how upset you are, but let me explain.'

He turned towards her. 'How can you explain deserting a husband who has provided you with every comfort? And sneaking out of his house in secret. You've humiliated him and shamed yourself. What will become of you now, not married and not single? You'll be the talk of this town.'

It was the longest speech she could remember him making. 'Whether I'm married or not, I'm still the same person I was before,' she retorted. 'I have to do what's right for me, not for the gossips. You men think being married confers a higher status on women but ...'

'Being honourable confers a higher status on everybody,' he snapped. 'You made a marriage vow and you broke it. You will never convince me that you had the right to do that.'

Without another word, he went into his study and closed the door.

White-faced, she looked at Nathan, who squeezed her gloved hand. 'Don't worry. Abba never holds a grudge for long. He'll get over it. He missed you terribly. Sit down and I'll bring you a glass of tea. Then I'll have to get back to Atlit. I have two botanists assisting me at the moment as well as Eli.'

'Eli!' His name made her heart pound and blood rushed to her face.

Nathan came back from the kitchen with a glass of tea he'd poured from the samovar their mother had brought from her home in Romania, and they sat in silence while she sipped it, wondering how to broach the subject that had preoccupied her ever since reading Eli's letter.

She tried to sound casual. 'How's Leah?'

He shrugged. 'She keeps away, doesn't say much. I don't think things are going well with her and Eli. She'll probably tell you what's going on.'

It wasn't a conversation she was looking forward to.

'Anyway, now you're back, you can help at the research station,' he was saying.

She didn't have the energy to explain that there was no place for botany in the future she envisaged for herself or for him.

As soon as she finished the tea, he leaned towards her, kissed her cheek, and rose.

'I'd love to stay longer and talk but I can see you need to rest and I have to go. We'll talk more tomorrow.'

She was too exhausted to argue. A moment later she heard the front door close behind him.

After he left, she closed her eyes, and her trembling fingers traced the stitching of the petit-point upholstery of the settee. Although she had anticipated her father's disapproval, she was hurt by his coldness. He wasn't an effusive man, and she knew Nathan was his favourite, but she had always been comforted by his affection and quiet strength. It was another indication that nothing was the same anymore and never would be.

A moment later she opened her eyes and sat up. She wondered how long Leah had been standing watching her. With a cry of delight, Shoshana jumped up to hug her, but Leah's expression forestalled a display of affection.

Taken aback, Shoshana studied her sister. Leah looked older, thinner, and less radiant, as though the lamp that had lit up her impulsive, ingenuous spirit had faded and dimmed.

'Why did you come back, Shoshana?' Her resentful tone, and the way she addressed her by her full name and not its diminutive, felt like a slap in the face.

'I missed you all too much to stay away.'

'We both know who you really missed. Eli told me that you're the one he really loves, even though you're married. Anyway, you'll have to go on missing me because I'm going away.'

Leah sat down on the very edge of the settee, as far from her sister as possible, and twisted the hem of her long skirt around her fingers the way she always did whenever she was upset.

'What do you mean, you're going away? Where?'

'To the farm where Aunt Hannah lives. She moved there after Uncle Yosef died and she's been asking me to stay with her, so that's where I'm going.'

Hannah, their father's older sister, had moved to a small women's cooperative settlement, one of several inspired by Olga Mankiewicz. Shoshana recalled the evening when Leah had gone with her to hear the Russian revolutionary speak because it gave her an excuse to see Eli, and the memory of that evening added to her discomfort.

'As you can imagine, it would be unbearable for me to stay here now you're back,' Leah was saying. 'In any case, we've broken our engagement.'

Shoshana didn't know what to say. How ironic and how sad that Leah's decision to leave Zichron Yaakov replicated the one she herself had made two years earlier, for the same reason. She felt sorry for her sister and guilty for causing her unhappiness, yet at the same time she couldn't deny the relief she felt. And she was struck by the strength Leah showed by deciding to leave, a strength neither she nor Nathan had ever given her credit for.

Leah twisted her skirt again. 'I wish I was strong and passionate like you or clever like Nathan. I love Eli more than anything in the world, but I know I can never make him happy the way you can. I tried so hard to make it work, but deep down I always knew it was no use. I could never compete with you.'

Tears were spilling down her cheeks and Shoshana moved closer to give her a hug but Leah slipped out of her embrace and left the room, closing the door firmly behind her.

Shoshana sat still for a long time, trying to process what Leah had told her and what that would mean for her and Eli.

Her head was pounding. She went into her bedroom and was about to fling herself onto the bed, but when she pulled back the edge of the coverlet, she found a note tucked underneath and when she opened it, crimson rose petals fell out. Each one had been torn in two.

When you went away, you took my heart and left an empty, parched husk, but I knew you'd come back to me because you and I are two halves of a single soul. Did you know that when you and I were born, our souls were split in two and flung into the air? We were doomed to wander the world lonely and unfulfilled until our souls found each other again. I pressed my burning lips to these petals as I long to press them to yours. I'll be counting the seconds until I hold you in my arms so our bodies and our souls can be one again.

She reread his letter until she knew every thrilling word by heart and fell asleep clutching it.

*

When she opened her eyes, light was pouring in through the window, a dazzling white light that filled the whole world with brightness. It was already midday and the blood was singing in her veins. Only a few more hours, and Eli would have returned home from the station and they would be together again.

Those hours were the slowest she had ever lived through. She tried to eat something – she'd had no dinner the night before, and no breakfast – but couldn't manage more than a few mouthfuls of bread and honey. Each time she glanced at her wristwatch, only a few minutes had elapsed. She changed her clothes several times and finally settled on the white organza blouse with its large sailor collar and a long navy skirt fastened with a wide belt. Under her riding cap, she left her hair loose, the way he liked it.

Finally it was time to go. In the stable, she flung her arms around Zahra's neck and looked into the mare's liquid, expressive eyes.

'You thought I'd never come back, didn't you?' she murmured. Zahra nuzzled her as if she understood. After saddling up, she swung onto the horse's back, feeling like a prisoner released after a long captivity. Finally, she was free to ride again. Zahra didn't need much urging to quicken her pace, and they cantered past the Druze chief's hut, over the slopes of Mount Carmel and across the wadis, then trotted into Eli's village.

With feverish fingers and a pounding heart she tied up the mare and ran up to his front door. He had left it open, then there he was. For a moment they stood very still, gazing at each other as if spell-bound. She had forgotten how striking he was, how his face made the breath catch in her throat. She revelled again in the magnetism between them.

With a cry she rushed into his arms, and they clung to each other. He was kissing her eyelids, her cheeks, her lips and her neck, exploring her mouth while she caressed the honey-coloured skin she loved.

'That idea of yours about twin souls,' she began.

'Not only souls,' he murmured as he unbuttoned her blouse and pulled her down onto the bed. For a long time they caressed each other with a tenderness that ended in rapture.

She longed to stay with him but knew they had to be discreet to prevent more gossip. The mare tied outside would give away her presence to any passer-by. Abba was right. When their envious neighbours found out that she had left her husband, they would rejoice at the Adelstein family's disgrace, but if they discovered that she was carrying on an affair as well, their spite would have no limits.

The sun was setting when she rode back to Zichron Yaakov, and cool shadows dappled the road. As she relived every ecstatic moment of their reunion, she knew that their minds were connected as powerfully as their bodies, that he was part of her and always would be. She had wanted to breathe the same air he did, but he was the air she breathed.

CHAPTER ELEVEN

Atlit, 1916

On the following day Shoshana set out for Atlit. Dinner with her father the previous night had been strained. Nathan had gone out and Leah had already left for Aunt Hannah's farm. He continued to be cold towards her, but she hoped Nathan was right and he would thaw eventually.

Now she made her way along the avenue of lush Washingtonia palms Nathan had planted, impatient to share her plan. She smiled as she recalled how Nathan had once told her that stands of trees were connected just as humans were, that they shared the same roots and helped each other endure heat and drought, and that by soughing they communicated with each other.

But his phenomenal success and international fame as a scientist made her apprehensive. She didn't doubt Eli's support – not that they had had time to talk much about anything yesterday – but would she be able to convince Nathan to take part in her audacious plan? Or would he decide it was incompatible with his research? She knew that without his support she couldn't succeed.

Stopping to catch her breath, she shielded her eyes from the sun as she looked up at the massive ruin of the Crusader castle where she had met the charismatic Englishman. Nathan operated with the same self-assurance and conviction that he could achieve his goals, although his abrasive personality made enemies along the way. Lawrence, too, probably rubbed people up the wrong way, as extraordinary intellects usually did. She had never experienced that unshakeable confidence that Nathan and Lawrence shared, but now for the first time in her life her pulse quickened with the urgency of her mission.

The research station was a plain two-storey building with a tiled roof and a small wrought-iron balcony facing the sea. It sat on a patch of unpaved ground where a few low bushes straggled among the gravel. She dismounted and tied Zahra up in the shade of the building. As she approached the doorway she saw Nathan and Eli perched on stools at the long pine table, leaning forward to examine a plant. She had told herself to focus on her goal and not allow herself to become distracted, but seeing Eli again almost brought her undone.

As their eyes lingered on each other, Nathan looked up, caught the intimacy of their glance, and quickly looked away with an expression that told her he knew everything.

She waited to catch her breath, sank onto a stool, and cleared her throat. 'I want to tell you both what happened when I was on the train, and why it has affected me so deeply.'

Eli watched her with growing concern as she described the scenes along the Anatolian plateau. 'It was so horrible, I wish I could unsee it,' she said and closed her eyes for a moment as if to blot out the memory. 'But you know what was even more shocking? Those soldiers weren't even trying to conceal their crimes; they were in full view of the trains that passed by. They knew they wouldn't be held accountable for their actions. It's obvious that they were following government orders. An Armenian woman I met along the way told me that the Turks had been systematically burning their villages and torturing and killing the residents.'

Her mouth was too dry to continue and she swallowed, staring into the distance.

Eli moved closer and squeezed her hand. 'Nothing the Turks do surprises me.'

'Did the Armenian woman say why they were persecuting her people?' Nathan asked.

'Because they were Armenians. And Christians. In Constantinople people accused Armenians of being traitors, of helping the Russians.'

She paused and took a deep breath. 'The scenes I saw from the train, and the horrific stories she told me, reminded me of what the Turks were doing in some of our communities here, and I put two and two together. It couldn't be a coincidence that they've been targeting two non-Muslim groups. I think these Young Turks mistrust ethnic and religious minorities and want to get rid of them.'

She was speaking faster now. 'Don't you see? What happened to the Armenians could easily happen to us. I see it so clearly now: the only way for us to avoid their fate is for Turkey to lose the war. For Britain to defeat the Ottoman Empire.'

She looked from one to the other and waited for their reaction.

Eli was still squeezing her hand. 'You've had a terrible experience.'

'Yes, it was terrible, but if we make use of it, it might be our salvation.'

'Make use of it how?'

She looked quickly from one to the other, gauging their response. 'By helping the British.'

Nathan was frowning. 'You're moving too fast. Let's look at one thing at a time. I agree with you in principle that we'd be much better off under the British. Abba was only saying a few days ago that things have been much worse here since Djemal Pasha became governor of Palestine. The British are more law-abiding and less corrupt than the Turks, but you're forgetting one important fact. They're not remotely interested in Palestine. And as we've seen from their debacle in the Dardanelles earlier this year, they haven't got a clue about fighting Turkey or they would never have tried attacking from the coast when an overland assault from here would have taken the Turks by surprise and would probably have succeeded.'

He would have gone on, but Shoshana broke in. 'I've thought about that. They've made errors because they don't know how weak Turkey's defences are in Palestine, but that's where we come in. We can help them. We're living behind Turkish lines so we're in an ideal situation to provide them with the information they need. We can spy on the Turks.'

Eli was gazing at her with admiration. 'You've really figured it all out. It's a brilliant idea! I've always said we should break free of the Ottomans and be independent, and I'm all for spying on them to help the British. Some of my cousins agree. I'm sure they would join us.'

She was trembling with excitement. 'That's what I was thinking. We'll get together a group who think as we do, collect intelligence all over Palestine, and pass it on to the British in Cairo.'

'Your cousin Berish Leibovitz and Shoshana's friend Tova would probably join us,' Nathan said. 'They've all suffered from Turkish persecution. And I'm sure we'll be able to recruit others as well.'

'You know we're talking about espionage, don't you? We'll be risking our lives,' Eli said. Then he shrugged. 'So what? Better to die on your feet than live on your knees. If there's anything I learned from the philosophers I met in France, it's that life without freedom is meaningless, and freedom is worth fighting and dying for. I don't want to sit around and wait for the Turks to deport us and destroy our communities. I'd rather die in action than from inaction.'

'I agree,' Nathan said. 'But first we'll have to figure out a way to let the British know we want to help them, and that won't be easy. The British Military Headquarters is in Cairo.'

'So one of us will have to travel to Egypt to contact them.'

Nathan shook his head. 'That's impossible at the moment with the war on. The French are blockading the coast and the Turks are refusing to issue travel permits.'

'We'll have to find a way,' she said.

His gaze lingered on his sister, astonished by the determination in her voice.

'There's another problem,' he argued. 'Why would they take any notice of a small group of people in a little town they've never heard of, in a country they're not even interested in? And supposing we even manage to get to Egypt, we don't have any contacts there. You don't know the English. If we turn up unannounced, without an appointment, they won't agree to see us.'

'I'll figure it out somehow.' As she spoke, the image of the eccentric Englishman flashed across her mind. It was a long shot, but it was all she had.

*

Back home, Shoshana paced up and down, frustrated by her powerlessness. There had to be a solution. As the days went by, they heard more reports of the Turks' rapaciousness as they confiscated crops for their army, leaving impoverished farmers in ruin. It was increasingly obvious that intervention was urgent, but as Nathan had pointed out, obtaining a travel permit for Egypt was impossible. They might as well try to reach the moon.

Feeling desperate that her plan would prove impossible to realise, Shoshana tried to calm her nerves by riding across the slopes of Mount Carmel and along the coast towards Haifa to talk to people they knew and sound them out about the possibility of forming a spy ring.

'Be very careful,' Nathan warned. 'If word gets out to the wrong people, the Turks will find out what we're planning and I don't need to tell you what will happen to us. As you know, we have neighbours who would be happy to see us fall off our pedestal.'

With his warning still ringing in her ears, she rode towards a village outside Haifa to sound out Eli's childhood friend Aaron Sokolov. She had always considered him something of an enigma, a foppish fellow with pale blue eyes behind round metal-rimmed glasses. His love of stylish clothes gave him the look of a town dandy rather than a farmer.

But she knew that his appearance was deceptive. He was surprisingly strong and his fearlessness was legendary. He had once galloped into the desert on a camel during a sandstorm, risking his life to rescue a farm labourer who had become lost and would have died of thirst if Aaron hadn't turned up and saved him.

She found him in an orange grove, dressed in a shirt with a celluloid collar and a silk cravat, inspecting the fruit and giving instructions to the pickers. He beamed when he saw her and led her to the shade of a vine-covered pergola, where a servant brought them a jug of fresh orange juice.

'Shoshana! What a wonderful surprise,' he said, looking as if a longed-for dream had just materialised before his eyes. 'Are you visiting someone around here?'

Glancing around to make sure they weren't overheard, she explained why she had come, and while she talked, he kept nodding. 'Fantastic idea. Kick the damned Turks out. About time,' he said.

'Would you be willing to join us?'

'I can't wait. Just give the word.'

'I'm sure I don't need to tell you that we have to keep this secret. As soon as we've contacted the British, I'll send you a coded message by post, inviting you to a party at Atlit and we'll meet there to discuss gathering intelligence. But I should warn you that what we're about to do will be very dangerous.'

Behind their round glasses, his pale blue eyes never left her face. 'I'd follow you to the ends of the earth, Shoshana.'

Embarrassed, she changed the subject. 'I suppose your patrols with the security group are keeping you busy.'

Eli had told her that Aaron had joined a local militia dedicated to guarding the villages and keeping the peace between the Jews and their Arab neighbours.

He shrugged. 'They kicked me out last week. Said I disobeyed orders and accused me of provoking a fight with the neighbouring Arabs, one of whom got shot. They blamed me but it wasn't my fault. The Arabs were grazing their sheep on our land and destroying our crops.'

Riding back to Zichron Yaakov, Shoshana wondered about Aaron's team loyalty. His story about the militia gave her pause, and later that day she raised the issue with Eli.

'You don't have to worry about Aaron,' Eli said. 'He's inclined to be hot-headed but I would trust him with my life.'

She deferred to his judgement but her doubts lingered.

*

Since Leah's departure Shoshana had taken over the cooking, and she was in the kitchen, flouring, kneading and rolling the dough for their *challah* when her father came in from the vineyard, early as usual on the Sabbath.

He looked appreciatively at the stove where she was baking *cholent*, the traditional eastern European casserole of beans and brisket. Like most young women of her generation, she thought this dish was far too heavy for their climate, but it was her father's favourite, and ever since her return she had taken every opportunity to mollify him.

An hour later, the yeasty scent of freshly baked plaited *challah* filled their home. After she had lit the candles and said the Sabbath prayer, her father and Nathan said the blessings over the *challah* and the wine. Shoshana glanced at Leah's empty chair and looked away. It felt like a reproach.

'I don't understand you young women,' her father grumbled when they sat down at the table. 'First you left a good husband, and now Leah has left a good home without saying why she was going.

I know my sister is glad of her company, but I can't fathom why the girl wanted to live on a collective farm, especially one just for women, like a convent. When I asked her why she was going, she mumbled something about not being needed. I need her. Do you know what all that's about?'

Shoshana exchanged glances with her brother, who shrugged and spread his hands as if to say, who can understand women, and Shoshana rose from the table to bring in the pot of *cholent*. Moshe breathed in the rich, spicy aroma that always made him nostalgic for his childhood.

'Your *cholent* is good, Shoshi,' he said, 'and so was your mother's, but nothing can compare to the one my mother used to make.'

As usual this evoked a flood of reminiscences about life in the old country, and the struggle of their early years in Palestine, and his son and daughter smiled indulgently as they listened to the familiar stories. Shoshana noted that it was the first time since her return that he had addressed her by the affectionate diminutive of her name. She also noted that Nathan looked preoccupied.

After their father had gone to bed, they stayed up talking.

'Things must be a lot easier for you and Eli now that Leah is out of the way,' Nathan observed.

Was he being critical? She was about to make a sharp retort about his own non-existent relationships when he chuckled and pinched her cheek. 'Do you realise how alike we are? Here am I, desperately in love with a married woman who lives in Germany, and you, a married woman, in love with the man who was supposed to marry your sister.'

They sat in companionable silence, contemplating the complications of their love lives. 'I always sensed you were challenged by women you couldn't have,' she said.

'And what's your problem?'

She laughed. 'I'll let you know when I figure it out.'

After a pause, she said, 'Do you think we should let Abba in on our plan?'

He shook his head. 'Absolutely not. Why endanger him? Better if he knows nothing about it. Anyway, he wouldn't approve and he'd only try to talk us out of it.'

'I'm not so sure,' she said. 'He's always been a fighter. Let's wait and see.' She sensed their father would support their venture.

Nathan reached for the decanter of wine from their vineyard and poured it into their glasses.

'I've made some progress recruiting people for our spy ring,' she said. 'In the next few days I'm going to talk to Eli's cousin Berish, and to my friend Tova. From things they've said in the past, I'm sure they'll want to join us. If only you could get a travel permit for Egypt we could get started.'

'There's something I've been putting off telling you,' Nathan said as he drained his glass and refilled it. 'I have to leave tomorrow. Djemal Pasha has summoned me to Damascus. The dispatch said something about a locust plague.'

She was too shocked to reply. This meant the end of all her hopes. How could she possibly carry out her plan without Nathan?

He tilted her chin so that she looked straight into his eyes. 'Shoshi, I wish I could stay and help, but you don't need me. I know you can do it. You're strong enough and clever enough, and Eli will help you. Keep on recruiting people. I'm sure we'll get that travel permit eventually.'

She sighed. 'Perhaps Djemal Pasha won't need you for very long. Perhaps you'll be home soon.'

But from his expression, she could see that was a forlorn hope.

CHAPTER TWELVE

Cairo, 1916

As she stepped aboard the boat bound for Port Said several weeks later, Shoshana reflected on the improbable fact that her trip had been made possible by a plague of locusts.

She had been in despair. Nathan was in Damascus, and she was in limbo. The war was raging, everyone was a potential suspect, and the Turkish authorities refused to issue travel permits to the residents of Palestine.

And then swarms of locusts of Biblical proportions blackened the skies over Palestine and Syria, devouring every blade of wheat and barley in their path. Farmers were ruined and starvation loomed. Realising that the situation was dire, not only for the entire population but also for the Turkish war effort, Djemal Pasha had summoned Nathan to his headquarters in Damascus.

From the detailed descriptions in his letters, she could visualise her brother being ushered into a palatial chamber carpeted with patterned rugs and decorated with Izmir tiles, where a short man with an exuberant handlebar moustache glared down from his gilded armchair. 'You're supposed to be the famous agricultural expert, so solve this problem,' Djemal Pasha had sneered, adding, 'That's if you're as smart as they say you are and have any idea what to do.'

Nathan didn't miss a beat. 'I can do it if you provide me with thousands of soldiers and teams of labourers.'

Djemal Pasha almost leapt out of his throne-like seat. 'Are you making fun of me? Thousands of soldiers when we are at war?'

Nathan shrugged. 'If you can't feed your army, your excellency, you can't win a war. I'll need them to dig miles of trenches to drive the hatching locusts underground before they develop wings. It might take several months, but that's the only way to destroy them.'

After threatening to have Nathan hanged upside down if he failed, Djemal Pasha calmed down. 'You are now my commander-in-chief in the war against locusts,' he announced grandly. He installed Nathan in Damascus and bestowed extraordinary powers upon him, including access to the most prominent military and civil authorities in Palestine, Syria and Turkey, with priority over all government officials, and the power to recruit anyone he needed.

In another letter from Damascus, Nathan wrote, 'This appointment will be vital to our success.'

She understood what he meant. His access to Turkish dignitaries and the freedom to move freely behind Ottoman lines would enable him to gather information that would be invaluable to the British. That's if they ever succeeded in reaching the British in Cairo and arranging a way of transmitting intelligence. They had to find a way, she kept saying to herself. Every day the Turks tightened the yoke around their necks.

At home, the conversation invariably turned to the precarious situation of the Jewish communities in northern Palestine and the course of the war.

'God forbid that anyone should overhear this, but I think the best thing that could happen to us is for Britain to win the war, so we can get the Turks off our backs,' her father said one evening as they sat at the dining table, eating falafel and hummus in the flat bread Shoshana had baked.

This was the cue she had been waiting for.

'You're right, Abba,' she said. 'And that's why Nathan, Eli and I have decided to help them.'

Moshe put down his knife and fork and stared at his daughter. 'You're going to help the British? How?'

Slowly, step by step, she explained the plan, playing down the risks, and then braced herself for threats, warnings and predictions of calamities.

After considering what she had said, he steepled his fingers as he usually did when he was thinking. Then he said, 'I'm sure you know that what you are planning is very dangerous, so you don't need me to tell you that, though of course I'll be terrified if you're caught. This is an audacious plan but if it succeeds, the entire country will thank you. We couldn't do better than replace the Turks with the English. Of course it will be very risky, but nothing worthwhile is ever achieved without a struggle. But if you fail ...'

'We won't fail.'

She looked at her father and behind the grey hair and lined face she saw the steely determination of the pioneer who had overcome daunting odds to create a flourishing vineyard in a malarial swamp. She wondered why they had ever doubted him.

'Does Leah know about this?' he asked.

'We haven't told her anything. The less she knows the better.'

Moshe nodded. 'That's good. She's not as strong as the rest of us.'

She smiled. It sounded as if he had already included himself in the conspiracy.

'So the only thing holding us up is a travel permit for Egypt, and God only knows when and if we'll manage to get one,' she said.

'Never lose hope,' Moshe said. 'Just keep doing what you're doing, so when it happens, you'll be ready.'

With his advice in mind, Shoshana spent the next two weeks travelling around Galilee to recruit more members for their spy ring. Berish hadn't needed convincing to join the conspiracy. Nor had her friend Tova.

To each of them she said, 'As soon as we've contacted the British, we'll meet at Atlit. Till then, watch Turkish activities and collect any information that will be useful to the British.'

Days passed, and Shoshana's hopes were fading when, out of the blue, Nathan sent her a travel permit to Egypt. Because all letters were censored, he couldn't explain how he'd managed to obtain it, but she surmised that he had taken advantage of his position as director of the locust eradication program to ask for a personal favour on behalf of his sister.

A travel permit to Egypt! She read and reread it to make sure it was real. The minute her father walked into the house she rushed up to him and flung her arms around him. 'It's come!' she exulted. 'The travel permit! Now I can go to Cairo and contact the British!'

He studied her for a few moments without speaking. 'So you've crossed the first hurdle. That's good. Now you'll have to convince them that we're genuine. That won't be easy.'

His measured response was disappointing but failed to dampen her high spirits. She couldn't wait to tell Eli the news they had been waiting for, and next morning she met him at Atlit, where he was collating botanical specimens in Nathan's absence.

'I knew we'd do it!' he rejoiced, embracing her. 'Trust Nathan to come up with a solution. Now we're on our way and the Turks are on their way out! When will you leave?'

'Tomorrow.'

'Be very careful, my darling,' he said as he stroked her hair. 'You'll be alone in a strange country. I'll count the minutes until you return.'

'I won't be alone,' she said. 'Wherever I go, whatever happens, I will always have you with me because you're part of me, remember?'

Despite her light-hearted reply, she felt apprehensive. Getting a travel permit to Egypt had posed such a major hurdle that she hadn't considered what she would do once she got there.

*

'I know you'll succeed,' Eli assured her as they stood on the wharf the following day. 'The British authorities won't be able to resist you!' Then in a serious tone he added, 'Just remember, you are offering them a valuable gift.'

They clung to each other and then with a resolute tilt of her head, she stepped onto the gangplank. This was no time for doubts.

The voyage to Port Said was rough, and in between bouts of sea-sickness, Shoshana worried about her mission. Everything depended on her success and she felt unequal to the task.

Several hours later, she alighted at Port Said, dizzy from the rolling of the ship. On the pier, she was surrounded by thin horses harnessed to shabby carriages whose drivers jostled and shouted as they competed for the lucrative fare to Cairo. Although it would have been quicker, easier and less expensive to travel by rail, after her traumatic experience on the Constantinople train, she decided on a carriage instead.

She soon realised her mistake. The trip was long and exhausting, and she regretted her decision. After several hours of bumping and lurching over rough roads, they entered the capital. Past crooked foul-smelling side streets strewn with rank and rotting filth, they came to a surprisingly modern area of wide palm-lined boulevards. The driver told her that they had been designed by Baron Haussmann after the Suez Canal was built, but she was too absorbed in her thoughts to take much notice of the city's architecture.

She suddenly saw herself as the British might see her, a nobody from an insignificant part of an insignificant region of the Ottoman

Empire, attempting to convince them that her small group of conspirators could help them defeat the Turks. She had placed all her hopes on enlisting Lawrence's help, but now her confidence deserted her.

How was she to find him? What if he wasn't in Cairo anymore and had been posted elsewhere? But even if he was there, and she managed to locate him, four years had elapsed since their brief encounter at Atlit. He mightn't remember her and he might refuse to become involved. By the time her horse-drawn carriage deposited her in front of her hotel, her head ached from all the difficulties she anticipated.

The Grand Hotel Continental was a sprawling building situated in a large plaza where locals in loose white robes dodged horse-drawn carriages depositing Europeans outside the hotel's portico. As soon as the porter had placed her valise inside her cavernous room with its rattling ceiling fan, she changed from her rumpled travelling suit into a crisp white linen dress and went downstairs.

The large lobby smelled of cigars and perfumed cigarettes. Lounging in worn leather armchairs among potted palms, men in British army uniforms glanced up languidly as she passed before turning back to their conversations.

Some of the men entering the lounge wore strange wide-brimmed hats turned up on one side, and she heard one of the officers incline his head towards them saying, 'Colonials!' in a contemptuous tone. 'Did you hear about the riot they created in the brothel at Wazzir?' his companion said. 'Police had to be called. They were hurling furniture through the upstairs windows. An uncouth lot they are.'

She would have liked to hear more but she walked on. The hotel was obviously popular with British officers. Fate had led her to the right place. Stopping in front of two men reading newspapers under a standard lamp whose large shade consisted of small multi-coloured pieces of glass, she said, 'Excuse me, I'm looking for an officer called Lawrence. Thomas Lawrence. I think he works in the cartography section. Do you know where I might find him?'

The two put down their papers and exchanged glances. The younger one, whose fine sandy hair fell over his forehead, smirked. 'You're certain it's Lawrence you're looking for?' His gaze travelled down her body and up again until it rested on her face. 'Wonders will never cease.'

The man beside him, clearly embarrassed by his companion's rudeness, broke in. 'You'll find Lieutenant Lawrence at British Headquarters, in the Savoy Hotel on Midan Suleyman Pasha Avenue, madam. It's not far from here.'

Without giving herself time to register the unlikely coincidence that the officers she had encountered knew of Lawrence, she hurried outside where the doorman hailed a carriage for her. A short ride away, the Savoy was an oasis of elegant coolness after the heat and noise of the city, with high ceilings and chandeliers and a middle-aged receptionist who looked approachable. Shoshana introduced herself and asked for Lieutenant Lawrence.

'Please take a seat, Miss Adelstein. I'll let him know you're here.'

As she waited, she was heartened to know that the strange man she had met sketching the Crusader castle had obviously achieved some fame in Cairo, and she doubted it was for his draughtsmanship.

Several minutes later, the gilded metal doors of the elevator parted, and Lawrence emerged. He looked even more dishevelled and eccentric than she remembered, with a red sash tied around his waist instead of a belt, and trousers that stopped above his socks as if they'd been snipped off.

'Miss Shoshana Adelstein, I believe,' he said with an exaggerated bow. 'What brings you to Cairo?'

Before she could express delight that he remembered her, he said, 'I'm jolly pleased to see you again.'

After glancing around the lobby, he said, 'Before you tell me why you've come, let's go to Groppi's. We can talk there in peace. It's a Cairo institution with the best pastries and ice cream in town. And, unlike the other cafés in this male-dominated culture, it welcomes women.'

He walked so fast she had trouble keeping up with him, and was relieved when, several blocks away, they came to an entrance with an attractively tiled façade and entered a café sparkling with glass and silver. A waiter in a cropped white jacket and bow tie showed them to their table and handed them a menu with an exaggerated air of deference.

Shoshana scanned a long list of desserts, grateful to have a little time to compose herself. Putting the menu down, she asked, 'Are you still making maps?'

'That's one of my tedious activities I'm not at liberty to discuss. Let's just call them information gathering.'

She had sought him out because from their conversation at Atlit she had intuited that he worked for British Intelligence, and she sat forward, hoping he'd expand on this aspect of his work, but he said, 'One of my chores is editing a newspaper nobody reads, which is mostly filled with rumours and gossip. I've come to the conclusion that fiction is the best way of reconciling conflicting reports. The chaps here regard me as a charlatan anyway, and they might be right. Sometimes I do feel like a fraud.'

She demurred but recalling the supercilious attitude of the officers at the Continental Hotel at the mention of his name, she supposed that with his lisp and his attention-seeking attire, he probably was the butt of ridicule.

The waiter placed their desserts on the table with a flourish, and as she tackled a tower of chocolate ice cream surmounted by swirls of whipped cream, she wondered how to broach the subject on which so much depended.

Instead, she asked, 'What happened to your dream of leading desert tribesmen in Arabia?'

He looked at her appreciatively. 'So you remembered!' He gave a lopsided smile. 'I'm working on it. Never fear, one day it will happen.'

She believed him. In Atlit, she had envied his unshakeable self-confidence and his vision, but now she had also found her purpose in life, and reminded herself that she had come to Cairo hoping he would help her realise it.

He was watching her intently. 'I say, do tell me what on earth you're doing here.'

Now that the moment had come, her hands were shaking and her heart was beating very fast. So much depended on her ability to present their case and enlist his support. He had to take her seriously.

She toyed with the long-handled filigree spoon to give herself more time to think. 'We want to help Britain defeat the Turks,' she said slowly.

His lips twitched. 'I see. Who's we?'

'A group of us who live in and around Zichron Yaakov. I know it might sound improbable, but we're in a unique position to obtain information about Turkish troop movements and military defences that would be invaluable to the British.'

'Life is so improbable that I'm ready to believe anything,' he commented. 'So you're planning to spy on them. All I can say is, if the Turks catch you, pray for a quick death.'

'We don't intend to be caught,' she retorted.

'From what I remember, your area is populated by Jewish farming families. Not the kind of people who usually turn to espionage and expose themselves to such danger.'

'We believe it's essential for our survival. For the past year they've been persecuting Jewish communities in Palestine, dispossessing residents and deporting them. Now that I've seen with my own eyes what they've done to the Armenians, I'm convinced they intend to destroy us as well. We believe our only hope is for you British to defeat them.'

He looked up from his iced coffee. 'You're pitting yourselves against the Ottoman Empire to protect your communities and that's why you want us to win the war. So you and I share the same aim, the conquest of the Ottomans, although we're coming at it from different angles. We want victory for ourselves and you want to change overlords. Have you heard the story of the hens inviting the wolf into their yard? And supposing we do win, what happens after that?'

She frowned. 'What do you mean?'

'After the Turks have been defeated. What happens to the Arabs then? Do they get their own country? Don't some of your people want to set up a Jewish homeland there? I believe it's called Zionism.'

Unsettled by the detour their conversation was taking, she scraped up the last of the cream and said, more tartly than she intended, 'I know that Zionism is an idealistic notion that Jews should return to our ancient heartland because we've been persecuted in other countries. Regarding the Arabs, my brother and I have always believed that they should have equal rights with us. But coming back to your original question, we are prepared to take an enormous risk to help Britain win the war, and that's why I've come here, to offer our help.'

He studied her for what seemed a long time before saying, 'This is the most extraordinary thing I've ever heard. But it's just another improbable scenario that the world keeps throwing up, so why not?'

He paused again as if considering something. Then he said, 'You should go to Port Said to see my mentor Leonard Woolley. He works in Naval Intelligence and they're the people you should speak to. Where are you staying? The Continental?'

Shoshana nodded.

'I'll have a letter delivered there for you to give Woolley when you get there.' He paid the bill and rose. 'Time to go. There's a newspaper I have to edit. If you buy a copy, you'll boost the readership by a hundred per cent.' He shook her hand.

'Goodbye, Joan of Arc of Zichron Yaakov, and the best of British luck. You will need it.' And with that, he strode away.

*

Too restless to return to her hotel, Shoshana strolled among the exotic plants in the Ezbekiah Gardens and tried to calm her turbulent thoughts as she watched white swans gliding in an ornamental pond that reflected lush palms and tall bamboos. Had her conversation with Lawrence been productive? Did he see the potential of her proposal, or was he simply trying to fob her off by suggesting she travel to Port Said? What if he failed to write the letter? What if this Lieutenant Woolley refused to see her? She now saw the folly of placing all her hopes on Lawrence, a man no one took seriously. She straightened her shoulders. She couldn't fail. Somehow she would have to convince the British her offer was genuine. And why wouldn't they believe it? She was bringing them a unique gift.

She spent a restless night under a ceiling fan whose whirring kept her awake. Lawrence's comment about Joan of Arc, which she had taken as a compliment, bounced uncomfortably around her mind. It was a relief when spears of sunlight slanted through the wide wooden slats on the windows, warming her eyelids. As soon as she opened her eyes, she saw a letter that had been slipped under her door. It was addressed to Lt. C.L. Woolley in Port Said.

CHAPTER THIRTEEN

Port Said, 1916

Determined not to repeat the exhausting road trip back to Port Said, Shoshana bought a ticket at the railway station. It was early afternoon when the train reached Port Said, which bustled with merchants, sailors, hawkers and horse-drawn carriages. She hailed one and gave the driver the address on the envelope Lawrence had sent.

Glancing with interest at his young female passenger, the driver tried to engage her in conversation. When that failed, he resorted to pointing out local sights. 'Our famous Suez Canal, *madame*,' he said. Following her gaze, he pointed to the large grey warship in the canal. 'French ship, *madame*.' She noticed six women walking along the street wearing little caps and dark capes that reached halfway down their long skirts. 'Nurses,' he said. 'Working in Australian hospital.'

'An Australian hospital in Port Said?'

'Yes, *madame*. Many wounded Australian soldiers still here after battle in Turkey. Are called Anzacs. Funny name, no?'

His comment about the Australians reminded her of the sad vicissitudes of war that brought young men here from the other side of the world, and she wondered what had impelled these Anzacs to fight against the Turks.

Her reverie was interrupted several minutes later when the driver brought the carriage to a stop outside an imposing white building that housed British Naval Headquarters. Inside the sterile foyer, the young woman behind the counter told her that Lieutenant Woolley was busy and asked her to wait. 'It's cooler under the ceiling fan,' she suggested, indicating the rattan armchair in the corner, but Shoshana was too nervous to sit still, and paced around, listening to the sound of her footsteps on the tiled floor. Lieutenant Woolley was obviously an important man. What would he say to her proposal?

After a long wait, she was ushered into his office. Her heart was pounding. This was the man who held her fate in his hands. He was standing with his back to her, surveying the canal from the large window when she entered.

When he turned around, she saw a pleasant-looking man of about forty, with smoothly combed light brown hair cut very short and parted on the side, fashionably dressed in a slim-fitting grey double-breasted suit and a shirt with a stiff white collar. The jaunty red bow tie was a welcome hint of individuality, perhaps even rebellion against convention.

She cleared her throat. 'Lieutenant Lawrence gave me this letter for you,' she said, handing it to him. 'He said you were his mentor.'

He looked puzzled, then exclaimed, 'Oh, you mean Ned!'

Placing the letter on the embossed leather surface of his cluttered desk, he said, 'Did Lawrence tell you he worked for me on the archaeological dig at Carchemish? He's a remarkable young man, though very eccentric. He has a prodigious memory, and never forgets anything. He's what you call a maverick, doesn't really fit in anywhere because he's miles ahead of everyone.'

He stopped talking and noticed that she was still standing. 'Oh I do apologise. I've been rambling. Please sit down.'

She clasped her gloved hands tightly on her lap and tapped her buttoned shoe on the patterned rug while he unfolded the letter and proceeded to read it.

After placing it on top of a pile of papers on his desk, he looked at her intently. 'This really is most interesting. Most interesting. I've never come across anything like it, to be honest. What an extraordinary offer this is. Now if you don't mind, I'd like to ask my superior, Major Stewart, to come in and hear what you've got to say.'

With that, he left the office, and she stared at the grey waters of the canal as she tried to compose herself for a meeting that sounded crucial to her success.

Ten minutes later Lieutenant Woolley returned, accompanied by a tall man with iron-grey hair, a clipped moustache and stiff military gait who strode into the room and stared at her while Woolley explained why she had come to Naval Headquarters.

'Miss Adelstein, who lives in Palestine, has come to Egypt on behalf of her group who are offering to provide us with intelligence from behind Turkish lines. She's here at the suggestion of Lieutenant Lawrence from Military Headquarters.'

'Lawrence! Isn't that the little upstart who has made a laughing stock of himself prancing around trying to drum up support for an Arab uprising or something equally ridiculous? And as for Military Headquarters, that lot don't know their head from their arse.' As if suddenly aware of a woman's presence in the room, he added, 'Pardon my French.'

Shoshana's heart sank. The introduction she had placed her faith in had evoked a scathing reaction. Major Stewart's eyes were boring into her face. 'Anyway, who are you?' he barked. 'What group do you represent? You say you've come here offering to spy on the Turks for our benefit. We know nothing about you. How do we know we can trust you and this group of yours? For all we know, you might be peddling information to the Turks as well.'

Shoshana's face flamed and her fingernails dug into her palms as she tried to speak calmly. 'We are willing to risk our lives to help Britain by spying on the Turks, so obviously giving them information would be counter-productive, wouldn't you say?'

He gave her a disdainful look. 'How much are you going to charge us for your so-called intelligence? We have other sources. We're paying Arab agents for information, you know.'

This time she didn't hold back. 'Well in that case, you're wasting your money because those agents are useless. They haven't provided you with any worthwhile intelligence. They haven't even informed you about the inadequate state of Turkish defences. And that lack of information led to your catastrophic blunder in the Dardanelles.'

Leonard Woolley bit his lip as if suppressing a smile, but Major Stewart was not amused. His face reddened and swelled as he began to splutter. 'Now look here, young lady ...'

But she broke in, speaking quickly in her desperation to convince him. 'I understand that you don't know if you can trust us because you don't know us. We are not spies. Most of us come from farming families. Vineyards, citrus orchards and olive groves. My brother, Nathan Adelstein, is a world-famous scientist who has lectured in America. He runs an experimental agricultural station that the Americans have sponsored at Atlit, a place ideally located to gain information about Turkish troop movements. He has been appointed by Djemal Pasha to head a locust extermination project, and he has been given unique access to Turkish military installations. What we are offering you is priceless, and what's more, it's free. Our offer is idealistic, not materialistic. I realise this is unusual, so it's hard for you to understand, but we do not want any money from you.'

He snorted. 'This must be a first, Jews offering a service free of charge.'

Trembling, she rose and turned to Woolley. 'I appreciate that you took the time to see me and listen to me, but I can see that coming here has been a waste of time. We are prepared to risk our lives to help you, but instead of considering an offer that would benefit Britain at a time when it needs our help, Major Stewart has dismissed it and insulted us.'

Taken aback by her outburst, Major Stewart began to mumble, 'I say, Miss – Anderson, is it? – I meant no offence,' but Woolley, who had been silent until now, turned to his superior and said, 'If you will permit me, sir, I'd like a moment alone with Miss Adelstein.'

She was still shaking after the major left the room, and Woolley poured her a glass of iced water from a silver pitcher on the small mahogany table. 'Please overlook Major Stewart's unfortunate comment. I certainly don't share his attitude. I've studied the Bible and I know that Jewish history in Palestine goes back three thousand years. I admire the Jewish people and your courageous attempt to protect them, and I appreciate the generous offer you have made. Please sit down and tell me what kind of information you'll be able to provide.'

'But what's the use? Major Stewart has dismissed our offer. He seems determined not to accept our help.'

'Please trust me. I do see the value of your offer, and I believe I'll convince him to change his mind,' Woolley said.

She calmed down and reminded herself that she must not allow pride or personal feelings to stand in the way of her mission. 'Then please tell him that British knowledge of Turkish coastal defences is totally inadequate. For instance, your people don't realise how lightly manned their positions are. Between Gaza and Beirut there are thirty observation posts with only ten to fifteen soldiers in each one. The locust plague has depleted their numbers, and my brother has been given unprecedented powers to visit military depots and installations and talk to the top officials all over Palestine and Syria. Also, we live close to Afula, the biggest railway junction in northern Palestine, and we will be able to obtain information about troop movements and armament transports.'

He listened without interrupting, nodding from time to time to encourage her to continue.

'Right,' he said when she had finished. He sat down at his desk, picked up his fountain pen, wrote something on thick cream paper headed with the Naval Intelligence letterhead, and handed it to her.

'This is a list of the information we'd like you to provide. Among other things, we will need detailed information on Turkish heavy armaments and personnel, the condition of their troops, their weapons, patrols and military strategy, and the number and locations of their prisoners of war,' he said.

The turnaround was so sudden and dramatic that it took a few moments to sink in. Lieutenant Leonard Woolley of British Naval Intelligence not only believed her but had just given her instructions about the intelligence he wanted them to provide.

'After we've collected the information, how shall we deliver it to you?' she asked.

He considered her question for several minutes before replying. 'Obviously we'll have to settle on a reliable method of transmission. I'll arrange for one of our vessels to sail along the coast, but only on moonless nights so it won't be spotted by the enemy. We'll agree on a signal. When the captain approaches the station that afternoon, the ship will spew black smoke and sound three short horn blasts. The captain will then look for a white sheet hung out of the window in return, as a signal that you're ready to come down to the shore and deliver the intelligence. Once the captain knows the coast is clear, he'll return at midnight that night, anchor, and send a messenger ashore in a rowboat to collect your information and then return with it to the ship. On his return to Port Said, he will hand all the documents to me and I'll pass them on to Cairo.'

She started expressing her gratitude but he deflected her praise with a smile. 'We are the ones who should be grateful, Miss Adelstein.'

The following day, she sent a carefully worded cable to Nathan: *The pyramids in Cairo are even better than I expected.*

CHAPTER FOURTEEN

Zichron Yaakov, 1916

As soon as Shoshana walked into Eli's house, they wrapped their arms around each other so tightly she could hardly breathe. They stood for a long time without speaking. There was no need for words. It was enough to feel the beating of each other's hearts.

Finally they separated, and Eli listened with admiration as she described her meetings with Lawrence in Cairo, and then with Woolley in Port Said, and Woolley's commitment to provide a vessel to collect their intelligence.

'This is exactly what we wanted. Only you could have pulled off such a coup. Now there's nothing holding us up. Let's get started.'

'I'll send coded messages to the others tomorrow to say we'll convene at Atlit next Monday,' she said.

'While you were away I recruited two school friends, Reuven Berger and Eitan Grossberg,' he said. 'I think you met them at the Purim party we had here before you left for Constantinople. They have lots of ideas for gathering information.'

She nodded, but her expression told him her mind was elsewhere. 'Are you worried about something?' he asked.

'I know that all the people we've chosen are keen and loyal, and I know they're committed to spying on the Turks,' she said slowly, 'but I can't help wondering if they'll have the strength they'll need if they're caught.'

He looked into her eyes. 'Shoshi, none of us can possibly know that until we're tested.'

'I suppose so. We'll just have to make sure that never happens.'

Despite his entreaties, she didn't stay long. Although they had agreed after her return from Constantinople that it was safer to meet in their little cave in the overhang of Mount Carmel rather than at his house, Shoshana hadn't been able to resist rushing straight there. But the longer she stayed, the more likely his neighbours would notice her mare tied up outside.

Her father couldn't wait to hear her news. '*Nu?*' he asked as soon as he came home that evening. 'What happened?'

He slapped his palm on the table in delight as she gave him an account of her triumph. 'That English officer at Naval Headquarters sounds like a real *mensch*,' he commented after she had finished. The Yiddish word that denoted a decent person you could rely on was his highest compliment.

She smiled. 'Yes, I think he is. I trust him.'

For the next few days, she and Eli raced each other on horseback along the hills and valleys of Mount Carmel, swam in the warm waters of the Mediterranean and nestled inside their secret cave hidden from view. It was a joyous respite from responsibilities and worries, occasionally interspersed with excited plans for the future of their spy ring.

*

A week after her return from Egypt, Shoshana scanned the eager faces gathered around the table at the research station and reflected on the qualities they each brought to the dangerous task ahead. It struck her that every desirable trait contained within it the seeds of a potential problem.

Her eyes rested on Aaron, who was vigorously polishing his round glasses with a handkerchief. His courage and intellect were legendary, and Eli trusted him with his life, but she recalled that he had been expelled from his security group for insubordination. Could she rely on him to follow orders?

Sitting next to Aaron, Eli's cousin Berish Leibovitz was beaming as he told an anecdote at his own expense. Everyone liked Berish, whose affable nature lightened every gathering. After the Turks had dragooned his older brother into the army, imprisoned his father, and confiscated their crops, he couldn't wait to participate in their spy ring, but Shoshana wondered if he was smart enough for their clandestine work.

But she didn't doubt the commitment of his brother Joshua or her friend Tova, whose dark eyes blazed with fervour. Everything about Tova crackled with energy, from her curly black hair to her machine-gun manner of speaking. Shoshana suspected that she was ready to join any endeavour in which Nathan was involved, but she didn't think her brother was aware of Tova's infatuation. She had a major disadvantage, Shoshana thought – she was too available. Shoshana was relieved that Tova was the only one in the group who had asked her why she had returned from Constantinople, and listened sympathetically without judging her actions. The others seemed too excited at the prospect of espionage to question her about her personal life.

Across from Tova, Yankel Berlinger dominated the gathering with his confident manner and large stature, and listening to his booming voice, Shoshana realised that it would be difficult for him to blend into the background without being noticed.

On her left, Eli's friends Reuven and Eitan were discussing the best way to avoid Turkish patrols. But as she looked gratefully around the table, she reflected that they were all united by their unshakeable determination to do whatever they could to help Britain win the war. They were aware of the danger and willing to take the risk.

And now she was bringing the news they had all been hoping for, and their eyes were fixed on her as she described her meeting with Leonard Woolley.

'He promised to arrange for a British vessel to make regular visits here and pick up the information we've collected,' she concluded.

The excitement that had been building as she spoke now rose to fever pitch and they cheered, jumped up from their stools and hugged each other, rejoicing in her success. There were no more impediments. Their work could begin.

Tova drummed her fingers on the table. 'You said that your contact in Egypt, Lieutenant Whatshisname, would send a ship, but lots of ships pass Atlit all the time. How on earth will we know if it's the right one?'

'We've agreed on a signal,' she said, and described the process Woolley had outlined: the ship would give three blasts of the horn and blow black smoke in the afternoon, sail on, and return that night.

'But without definite dates, how will we know when to expect them?' Tova persisted. 'We can't be watching every afternoon in the hope that they'll appear.'

'The ship will only come on moonless nights so it won't be spotted.'

Yankel was shaking his head but before he could voice his doubts, she continued, 'When we know it will be a moonless night, we'll look for the ship's signal that afternoon, and as soon as we see it, we'll put out the sheet to signal that we're ready. That night two of us will go down to the water's edge with the documents and wait for the ship's return.'

'Do they know how wild and unpredictable this coast can be?' Reuven asked. 'Some days the sea is like a boiling cauldron. It would be impossible to come ashore.'

Shoshana nodded. 'Good point, but the captain will be familiar with the coast so I suppose he'll have to wait for a night when the sea is calm. After they've anchored, they'll row their messenger ashore in a small boat. After we've handed him our intelligence, he'll row back to the ship and give it to the captain, who'll deliver it to Lieutenant Woolley,' she said. 'The dangerous part for them will be rowing ashore and then back to the ship if the sea is rough. For us, it will be getting across the highway in the dark to avoid the Turkish patrols.'

With each question, she felt increasingly unsettled. The arrangement had seemed so foolproof, but now it occurred to her that so many things could go wrong. But there was no point dwelling on the precarious aspects of the arrangement, she told herself. She trusted Woolley. After all, it was in Britain's interests for his plan to succeed.

She felt Aaron's eyes on her. 'I'll go down to the shore and wait for the ship,' he said.

'I'll decide who goes down to the boat when the time comes,' she said, more crisply than she intended. As a woman, she was aware of the need to assert her leadership, but she hoped she had struck the right tone between authority and assertiveness.

If only Nathan was here to share this responsibility. But she had no idea when he'd be back from Damascus, or how the locust extermination project was progressing. Having heard locals complaining that the plague was ruining their crops, she feared the worst. Devout farmers called it a scourge from God, like the one described in Exodus. Except that this plague afflicted Jews, Christians and Muslims alike. She dreaded what might happen to Nathan if his strategy failed. Djemal Pasha wasn't known for his mercy towards those who disappointed him.

'Nathan will find a way,' her father had said when she voiced her fears. 'Have you ever known him not to succeed at anything he's set out to do?'

He wasn't equally flattering about Leah, whose letters were full of farming news and gossip. 'It's good you haven't said anything to her about our plan.'

She smiled when he referred to 'our plan'. Perhaps it infused some spice into his old age. Whatever the reason, espionage had brought them closer.

The arguments around the table had grown louder and she brought her attention back to the group.

'Let's talk about contacts who could be useful to us,' she said.

Aaron was the first to speak. 'Dr Shulman in Afula is a family friend. He looks after sick Turkish soldiers. As you know, Afula is the busiest railway junction in Palestine, so he's in an ideal position to find out about troop movements and weapons supplies. I've heard him talk about Turkish cruelty, and I think he'll be willing to help.'

'That's an excellent idea,' Shoshana said, recalling the soldiers milling on that platform the day she had returned home.

She felt Eli's gaze lingering on her, blushed, and looked away. If she was to earn respect as their leader, she had to appear strong and professional and avoid exchanging meaningful glances across the table like a lovelorn schoolgirl.

Yankel's booming voice cut across her reverie. 'Turkish officers often stop by our winery,' he said. 'They sound fed up with conditions in the army, and they're always complaining about their superiors. I reckon I'll be able to get them to talk about their weapons and their next posting.'

'I'll check out Turkish defences in the Sinai area and talk to the Bedouins,' Eli said. 'They always know what's going on and they have no love for the Turks.'

Suddenly he jumped onto the table and spread his arms wide as if to embrace them all. 'We'll help to defeat the Turks and show the world what we can do,' he cried. 'We're a brave new generation, afraid of no one, like the heroes of Masada.'

Shoshana gazed at him. How charismatic he was, and how his mercurial personality thrived on excitement and action. Everyone was laughing, but Aaron placed his hands over his face in mock horror. 'Let's not compare ourselves to them. Remember how they all ended up?'

When the laughter had died down, Tova sat forward. 'A woman I know is the housekeeper of the local pasha. From what she's told me, Turkish dignitaries often visit him and discuss the war. I'll ask her to pass on whatever she hears.'

After thanking them for their suggestions, Shoshana said, 'Over the next few days, I'll visit neighbouring villages and sound out people who might be willing to join us. We need as much support as possible.'

The sunlight pouring in through the window caught Aaron's glasses and momentarily blinded her. When she opened her eyes, he was standing beside her.

'You should come with me to Afula when I talk to Dr Shulman,' he said, looking straight into her eyes. 'He won't be able to resist you. No one can.'

Was he flirting with her? She dismissed that thought but conceded he had a point. Perhaps she should accompany him.

As they were saying their goodbyes, she felt she couldn't let them leave without saying something to inspire and impress them with the significance of the huge task they had undertaken.

Her voice was trembling with emotion as she began speaking. 'We don't need to swear an oath on the Torah, or seal our secrecy with blood, but we should never forget that we are engaged in a sacred mission to free our communities from oppression. What we do will never be forgotten. It will be remembered by generations to come.'

They filed out reverently like worshippers moved by an uplifting sermon.

Only she and Eli remained inside. 'Everything has moved so fast, I can't believe this is really going to happen,' she said. 'I only hope I'm equal to the task.'

He drew her so close that she could feel his heart beating under his shirt. 'Never doubt yourself. You're our Deborah.'

'Lieutenant Lawrence called me Joan of Arc.'

'While I was in France, I visited Rouen where she ...' Eli began but stopped abruptly. 'I prefer to compare you to our legendary Jewish warrior.'

They walked outside, and as she looked up at the ruins of the Crusader castle, the dunes that rolled around it, and the sea that sparkled below, she whispered, 'I love this land so much.' After a pause, she turned to him with a questioning look. 'Eli, do you think we choose our dreams, or do our dreams choose us?'

'Are you asking if I believe in destiny? I know that you and I were destined to be together, but sometimes I think our entire lives are dreams that we finally understand only when they are about to end. That we are only an instant of consciousness in eternity.' Then with a mischievous smile, he added, 'But I do know one thing in life that is solid and real.'

Clasping his arms tightly around her waist, he pressed his lips against hers, and she felt her body softening against him.

*

Two weeks later, Nathan returned from Damascus. His downcast face told the story. Despite all his efforts, the locusts had continued to hatch. 'I've resigned,' he said, and slumped onto the couch.

Shoshana poured him a glass of tea from the samovar, sat down beside him and waited.

'I couldn't get the workers to put in the effort we needed to contain the plague,' he sighed. 'They threw up their hands and said, "If Allah wants the locusts, who are we to fight them?" Some workers even roasted the insects and ate them.'

She put her arm around his shoulders. 'You did the best you could. But to think that after all those years of backbreaking work by our parents and the other pioneers to create these orchards and vineyards out of the malarial swamps, we might be defeated by a plague of locusts.' She paused. 'But tell me, how did Djemal Pasha react when you said you were resigning?'

'Better than I expected. At first he yelled and threatened me with all kinds of Turkish tortures, but fortunately he was distracted by an urgent summons to attend a war conference in Ankara, and left straightaway.'

He finished his tea and placed his empty glass on the table. 'Shoshi, you haven't told me what happened in Egypt. I gathered from your cable that it went well, but I want to hear everything.'

He insisted on hearing every detail, and when at last she finished, he patted her shoulder. 'I knew you could do it! So now we're really on our way.'

Finally it was time to ask the question she dreaded. 'But what about your scientific work?'

'I can put that on hold. I think it's far more important to fight for the survival of our people. But we do need to keep the research station operating, even if it's just ticking over. America is neutral and my American sponsors would never approve of using the research station as headquarters for espionage. If they found out they would withdraw their funding and we would lose the use of it, which is clearly essential for Woolley's signalling system to operate and the intelligence to be collected.'

She gazed at him with admiration. Her brilliant brother was willing to set aside the adulation of the international scientific world to devote himself to a dangerous political scheme that might not succeed.

'You're prepared to risk everything to fight for our people – many of whom mistrust and envy you,' she said, and added, 'Sometimes I think it's easier to love a land than its people.'

'I love my people even though sometimes I can't stand them,' he quipped, and they both burst out laughing. She knew exactly what he meant.

'Knowing you, you'll probably turn espionage into a science,' she said.

At that moment their father returned home from the vineyard, delighted to see his son again after his long absence and wanting to hear all about his assignment in Damascus.

After Moshe had gone to bed, Shoshana and her brother talked late into the night.

'So what information have you gathered so far?'

'Eli has been talking to the Bedouins in the Sinai and they've told him about the size of Turkish patrols in the area, and their routine. And Tova's friend has picked up news about the war from the pasha who entertains Turkish dignitaries. You know how good Yankel is at getting people to talk? Well, he plied the Turkish officers with wine and they've told him all sorts of things, including where they're about to be posted. All the things we've heard prove that the British need our help,' she mused. 'Tomorrow I'm going to Afula with Aaron to talk to the doctor there.'

'So we're amassing valuable intelligence for them and as soon as the ship arrives, we'll be able to deliver it,' he said. He took two glasses from the sideboard, filled them with wine, and handed one to her. 'Do you realise we have the future of the war in our hands? Let's drink a toast to Lieutenant Woolley.'

'And to his ship,' she said.

CHAPTER FIFTEEN

The Galilee, 1916

No one who saw the rider examining trees and rocks in northern Galilee would have suspected he was engaged in espionage. Despondent at the ravaged landscape where forests had been chopped down to make railway sleepers for the Turkish war effort, Nathan grieved for every tree as for a life cut short. Like the forests, farms had also suffered since the start of the war. The war against locusts had been lost and the creatures had devastated vineyards, barley fields and orchards. To make matters worse, the resulting food shortages were aggravated by the ever-increasing demands for crops by Turkish authorities unconcerned by the impoverishment of farmers. Weakened by hunger and depressed by their financial situation, people became more susceptible to disease, and typhus was rife in some communities.

Reflecting on the decline of his beloved homeland as he rode, Nathan mourned the loss of the lush, exuberant growth he had once seen in its orchards and fields. And in contrast with the deteriorating condition of the land and those who tilled and tended it, he saw the inexorable signs of Turkish progress. It was hard to believe the speed with which they had constructed the stretch of road between Afula and Nazareth. That had taken two weeks, while the long road between Jerusalem and Damascus had taken forty days, the time it had taken Moses and his people to walk from bondage in Egypt to freedom in the land of Canaan. Of course the Turks had accomplished this feat using whips on the backs of their enslaved labourers, who included old men and invalids. He knew this cruelty awaited them as long as the Turks were in power.

His back ached from long hours in the saddle and he dismounted, propped himself against the trunk of a palm tree and gulped water from his flask. With a sigh he rose, swung back into the saddle and continued his reconnaissance. The need for British victory was more urgent than ever.

Shoshana had predicted he would turn espionage into a science and she was right. Using his knowledge of botany, geology and agriculture, and his sharp powers of observation, he rode for three days from Haifa across the Galilee over to Rosh Pinna, filling entire notebooks with information. It seemed a lifetime ago that he had discovered the origin of wild wheat on these slopes, a discovery that had been hailed around the world as a botanical breakthrough. He could have led a comfortable life as a professor at a prestigious Californian university, basking in his fame, but he didn't regret taking a break from his career. Survival of their community was at stake.

During his ride, nothing escaped his notice. He paused to record details of crop conditions, the placement of Turkish artillery, the schedules of trains that carried troops and military equipment, the price of grain and the state of roads and railways. From time to time he stopped to examine new telegraph posts to figure out which trees the timber came from and to assess the condition of the roads along which it had been transported. Even the type of oxen the Turks used interested him. And while he filled his bulging notebooks with information that would be valuable to the British, he reminded himself that the spy ship would soon arrive. The sooner they could pass on their intelligence, the sooner the tide of war would turn in their favour.

*

While Nathan was gathering information in the north, Eli, who rode camels like a Bedouin, reconnoitred the southern desert region. He took every opportunity to stop and chat to local tribesmen, who invited him into their tents. Thanks to his father, who had sent him to study Arabic with the local chieftain, he could speak it fluently and even discuss the Koran. As a boy he had resented these sessions, preferring to spend the time riding, swimming and playing football, but now that his father was no longer alive, he was sorry he couldn't tell him he was grateful for his foresight.

During long, leisurely conversations interspersed with small cups of coffee and large platters of lamb pilaff, the Bedouins told him about new Turkish roads and telegraph construction, military bases and supply depots. They hated the Turks, who tried to repress their independent spirit, but Eli knew he had to be circumspect – although some of them were spying for the British, others were double agents.

*

By now the spy ring consisted of twenty-six members, mostly relatives, family connections and friends. Shoshana's discreet attempts to recruit local farmers often failed as they tended to be conservative and opted for the devil they knew. Why rock the boat when baksheesh usually succeeded in modifying Turkish demands? But what the group lacked in numbers, it made up for in determination. Worried that an excess of zeal might cause recklessness, Shoshana often warned them to be extremely cautious whenever pumping locals for information.

'Don't ask questions that are too direct, and if anyone questions your motives, explain you're gathering botanical, geological or agricultural information for some research,' she told them.

While the members of the group were fanning out in different directions, she decided to take Aaron's advice and accompany him to Afula to meet Dr Shulman, and then travel on to Jerusalem to meet another potential recruit – a very special one.

'If we're stopped along the way,' she instructed Aaron as they prepared to set out, 'we'll say we're travelling to Afula to consult a doctor there and you're escorting me because my brother is away.'

'You've thought of everything,' he said. 'You're a born leader.'

'I can't take credit for this trip. It was your idea.'

He started to say something but stopped and she was uncomfortably aware of his gaze lingering on her. It was a relief when it was time to leave. As she climbed into the carriage, the driver nodded in a way that denoted complicit understanding. The previous day she had taken him into her confidence. It would be impossible for him not to suspect something as he drove her around, but she knew she could trust him. Nasser, who was a Christian Arab, had been with the family for as long as she could remember. He hated the Turks and she knew he would approve of her mission.

As they settled inside the horse-drawn carriage, Shoshana noticed the look he gave Aaron. His stylish attire, so unusual in this rural area, was bound to turn heads, but perhaps that could be an advantage. He looked like a city-dweller setting out on a sightseeing tour rather than a spy.

Her friend Miriam had come out onto the street and stood beside the carriage with a puzzled expression.

'It's nothing serious, but I'm going to see a doctor in Afula,' Shoshana explained. Miriam was bound to repeat that to her mother, who no doubt would spread it around.

As soon as they set off, she began recording everything that might help the British understand the situation on the ground. On the road to Haifa, they came across military guards patrolling the highway, but to their surprise there weren't any on the coast. That confirmed what she had told Woolley, that Turkish coastal defences were far weaker than the British suspected. That turned her thoughts to the ship that would soon arrive to collect their intelligence.

In Haifa, they were stopped by a Turkish official who checked their papers. 'Your travel permit has expired!' he said, thrusting it back into her hands. 'You must leave your carriage and horses here or go back home, but you can't continue your journey.'

Aaron was bristling but Shoshana gave the official a smile. 'I'm sure there's some mistake. Perhaps we can sort it out,' she said smoothly and handed him a *mejidi*. With a quick glance to make sure no one was watching, he pocketed the coin and waved them on.

'It's amazing what half a crown can do in this country,' she remarked as they continued their journey.

When they stopped in Nazareth, a disgruntled Bedouin patrolman told them about a large Turkish arms dump in the courtyard of the Carmelite convent. That evening, during a spartan dinner of bread and olives inside the refectory, the nuns talked about the Turkish troops stationed in town. 'I feel sorry for those starving soldiers,' the mother superior said. 'They're just skin and bones. You should have seen how they threw themselves on our meagre fare. They told us that the officers steal their rations, so they have to steal the provisions meant for their pack animals.'

Before falling asleep on a hard bed in one of the convent's cells, Shoshana made a note of the army's shortage of food. How did they expect to win a war when they didn't feed their soldiers?

The following day they headed for Aaron's old farming community, which was nestled on a black basalt ridge above the Sea of Galilee. Despite his expulsion from the local militia that guarded the Jewish settlements in the Jordan Valley, Shoshana thought it was worth trying to recruit them. Being experienced and powerful, they would be a great asset.

Aaron had been against the idea. 'We're wasting our time. They won't support any organisation I'm involved in.'

He was right. The leader of the group shot him a disdainful look and then ignored him while Shoshana explained why they had come. He gave her short shrift. 'We don't want anything to do with your organisation. Espionage is against our policy.' And without another word, he walked away.

They continued on towards the River Jordan in silence. She was thinking that Aaron was more of a liability than she had suspected, and he was seething with resentment towards his former colleagues, who had not only disowned him but had become enemies.

Absorbed in her thoughts, Shoshana looked up in alarm. The long bridge ahead of them looked fragile and seemed too narrow to allow them to cross. The horse stopped, as if aware of the problem ahead. She looked questioningly at Nasser.

Pointing to a man sitting in a small rowboat on the riverbank below, he said, 'I'm sorry but you will have to get out while Mr Aaron and I pull the carriage across the bridge. I will ask the boatman to row you across to the other side.'

He took Shoshana's arm as they descended the slippery riverbank and spoke to the boatman, who nodded eagerly and helped her into the boat. It didn't take long to reach the other side but when she handed him the agreed amount, he shook his head, and insisted it wasn't enough. Rather than argue and cause a scene, she gave him another coin and quickly stepped ashore.

When she looked up at the bridge, she held her breath. Nasser was carefully guiding the horse, which was skittish, while Aaron tried to keep the carriage steady. Several times it looked as though horse and carriage would topple over and plunge into the water. Only Nasser's skill and patience succeeded in coaxing the horse to keep moving until they reached the other side.

Shoshana's legs were trembling when she climbed back into the carriage. 'I couldn't bear to look. I didn't think the carriage would make it,' she whispered to Aaron.

'I was worried too,' he said. He leaned forward and slapped Nasser's back. 'You did a fantastic job back there.'

Feeling calmer, they resumed their journey on the road to Afula. There they found a white-painted hospital building next to the railway station, and once inside they saw Dr Shulman's name on a door halfway down the corridor and knocked. When they entered, Dr Shulman was sitting at a small wooden desk reading a journal, but as soon as he saw them, he jumped up to greet them and pumped Aaron's hand. Beside the wooden examination couch stood a glass-fronted cabinet containing medical instruments laid out on a starched white cloth.

Gavriel Shulman was about forty, Shoshana supposed, a short man with wire-rimmed glasses, sloping shoulders and the beginning of a paunch. 'So long since I've seen you, my friend,' he said to Aaron. 'How's your family?'

Then he rested his bespectacled eyes on Shoshana with undisguised curiosity. 'I hope neither of you are ill.'

After introducing her, Aaron said, 'We've come for your help, but not as patients.'

'I'm intrigued. What can I possibly help you with?'

Instead of replying, Shoshana asked a question of her own. 'Can you tell us exactly what your job is?'

He seemed taken aback. 'My job? I'm a physician to the Turkish army. As you probably know, Afula is the most important railway junction in the country, and all the Turkish troops and officers come through here on their way to or from the battlefields in the south. My job, as you put it, is to check them all for infectious diseases like typhus.'

With a hint of pride, he added, 'Sometimes I treat the generals as well. Djemal Pasha has been in my surgery. So has von Falkenhayn, the inspector-general of German forces in Turkey.'

Shoshana and Aaron exchanged glances. 'So it must be easy for you to find out about troop movements, railway timetables, supply trains and their destinations,' she said.

He looked from her to Aaron, clearly at a loss. 'I don't understand. Why would I want to know these things?'

When she had finished explaining and asked if he would join them, he looked aghast. 'What you're asking me to do is treason. You're asking me to risk my head!'

She shrugged. 'As you see, my head is still firmly attached to my body, and yours will be too. We can set up a safe system for transmitting your information. No one will suspect you. And you'll make an important contribution to the defeat of the Turks and the survival of our communities.'

He was shaking his head. 'It's not that I don't want to help you,' he stammered. 'But you must realise, my position here ...'

Shoshana cut in. 'I do understand. It's a big decision. But you are in a unique situation here and the information you hear from your Turkish patients would be invaluable, while the risk to you would be minimal.'

She paused, sensing his hesitation, and added, 'If you join us, one day you'll be very proud that you were on the right side of history. Unless, of course, you're happy for the Turks to rule over us forever.'

The doctor sighed. 'Young lady, I admire your courage and your powers of persuasion, but I can't decide on the spot. I'll have to think it over.'

As they walked away from his surgery, Aaron wondered what Dr Shulman would decide but Shoshana was optimistic. 'I have a feeling he'll join us,' she said.

*

The sun was setting when they reached Jerusalem and Shoshana caught her breath when she saw the golden light on the city's ancient walls, towers, domes and mosques. They had come to Jerusalem to meet an engineer in the Turkish army, a contact that one of Aaron's friends had recommended, and planned to see him the following morning.

Overnight they stayed in an elegant hotel they had chosen because it was popular with German officers. Aaron lost no time engaging them in conversation at the bar over glasses of schnapps. Delighted to meet this well-dressed man who spoke such excellent German, they didn't hold back. Before the evening was over, he knew that their commander, General von Kressenstein, was also staying there with his staff and that 50,000 German soldiers were stationed in Palestine. 'We'll soon whip the lazy Turks into shape,' they boasted.

While Aaron was chatting with the officers, Shoshana sat demurely in the spacious lounge with a notebook on her lap as though writing a diary, but she was listening intently to the conversations around her and jotting down interesting snippets she overheard. By the end of the evening, she knew where the Germans were barracked, how many of them there were, and where they expected the next battle to be fought. They even knew how many British troops were stationed in the south of the country.

Their meeting with the engineer next morning exceeded their expectations when he handed them a map of the city clearly marked with all the Turkish fortifications.

Pleased with the results of their trip, they lurched along the road leading north towards home. Shoshana took her almanac from her bulky travelling bag and turned to the page that listed the phases of the moon and turned to Aaron.

'According to this, the next moonless nights will be on Tuesday and Wednesday this week, so we have to get all our intelligence together ready to hand it over to the captain of the British ship.'

Only a few more days and her hope would become reality.

CHAPTER SIXTEEN

The Atlit Shore, 1916

Nathan hoisted the rucksack on his back, flattened himself against the gate of the research station, looked around to make sure there was no one nearby, and step by cautious step began making his way towards the shore. It was 11 p.m., and although he knew the area like the back of his hand, it took a while for his eyes to become accustomed to the dark. His outstretched hands scraped against the knobbly trunks of the Washingtonia palms he had planted at a time when his botanical career was at its zenith and his scientific future seemed assured. But that part of his life was now on hold, and as he crept forward, he reflected that he was sacrificing his passion for botany for something he had never imagined: espionage.

Now that he was able to discern shapes and shadows, he quickened his pace, but when he came to the highway, he heard voices and stopped, hardly daring to breathe. A Turkish patrol! He heard one soldier utter a lascivious belly laugh and then another, probably in response to a bawdy joke. There was an acrid, sweetish odour, and he saw cigarette smoke wisping in the clear night air. When the soldiers' voices died away, he began to cross the road with small, hesitant steps. But despite his caution, his shoe dislodged some pebbles that skittered on the ground, shattering the silence.

'Did you hear that? There's someone out there!' a soldier shouted. 'Stop or I'll shoot!'

He heard the click of a retracted trigger and froze, his heart pounding hard enough to burst through his ribs. He couldn't be caught with the incriminating documents in his rucksack. Terrifying minutes went by until he heard one of the soldiers say, 'You're imagining things. Probably a fox or a jackal.'

As soon as all was quiet again, Nathan let out his breath and waited for the trembling to stop. Then, adjusting the straps on his rucksack he headed towards the wadi. This was a longer and more tortuous route but he was less likely to run into Turkish patrols down here.

They had all been delighted when they saw the naval ship's signal that afternoon. Conditions were ideal for the rendezvous: a moonless night and calm seas. The ship would have no trouble anchoring below Atlit, and its messenger would be able to row ashore easily to collect the oilskin pouch containing the intelligence they had gathered.

Down steep limestone outcrops, Nathan descended into the valley, and soon the sound of lapping waves told him he was close to the water. Almost there. Passing clumps of thorn bushes, he reached the sandy bank on the water's edge, sank down, let out a long sigh, took a flask from the rucksack and gulped some water. Above him loomed the ruins of the Crusader castle; before him the water was as still as a millpond, and all around was darkness and silence. The tough part was over. All he had to do now was wait for the ship to appear.

*

Inside the research station, tension rose as the clock ticked slowly towards midnight. Shoshana sat down, stood up, and paced around the room. Like Eli, who was also restless, she found it difficult to be at the mercy of events outside her control. Every few minutes she went to the window and looked at the dark waters below. The ship was due to arrive some time after twelve. Not much longer to wait.

She glanced at Eli, who was uncharacteristically quiet while she was so keyed up she couldn't stop talking. 'The ship should appear fairly soon,' she said to reassure herself.

During the afternoon she had heard the blasts of the ship's horn and seen the thick smoke. At last! She had immediately flown upstairs to hang the white sheet from the window to let the captain know it was safe to return that night.

She glanced at Eli again. He was standing by the window with his back to her and didn't respond, and it struck her that he hadn't said much in the two days since her return from Afula.

She stood close behind him and encircled his waist with her arms, breathing in the masculine scent that always aroused her. 'I know you've got something on your mind and it's not just the ship. Maybe I'm too direct, but I don't like mysteries. They put me on edge,' she said. 'Whatever it is, I'd rather know.'

He turned around to face her and lightning flashed from his dark eyes. 'How can you not know? You've just spent how many – three or four days? – travelling all around the countryside with Aaron, staying with him in hotels and boarding houses. How do you think that looks, especially with your reputation? What will people say?'

She was taken aback. 'You've never worried about what people thought before. Isn't that what you call bourgeois? You've always said you liked the fact that I wasn't conventional.'

He was looking straight at her now.

'I meant I liked that you didn't wear a corset.'

Their laughter defused the tension, but she felt she had to explain herself.

'Anyway, you were there when Aaron suggested the trip. You didn't say anything then. You know we weren't on a pleasure trip.

We were meeting our contacts and gathering intelligence. Don't tell me you're jealous of Aaron, the friend you trust with your life?'

Before he could reply she clasped her hands behind his neck, pulled him towards her, and kissed him so passionately that the words died in his throat and his body came alive.

At that moment, she glanced past him and noticed something in the distance. She tore away and pressed her face against the windowpane. Was it really there or had she imagined it? No, there it was, looming in the distance.

'This is it, it's here!' she cried. In the blackness of the night she detected a darker shape in the darkness. It had to be their ship.

Now they had to sit and wait for Nathan to come back. She paced around again, impatient to hear about the rendezvous with the ship. Had the rowboat reached him yet? Had he handed over the pouch? How delighted Woolley would be when he received their intelligence and read its contents, and how vindicated he would feel to know that his plan had yielded such valuable information about Turkish troop movements and defences. And what a slap in the face it would be for that arrogant Major Stewart.

More relaxed now, she unpinned her hair, which flowed over her shoulders in auburn waves, and took Eli's hand in both of hers. 'It will take Nathan at least an hour to get back. Can you think of anything we can do to fill in the time?'

He was already unbuttoning her blouse.

'I can't bear to think of you with anyone else,' he whispered. Before he could say anything else, she slipped her hands under his shirt and felt the inviting warmth of his skin. Holding her gaze, he propelled her towards the couch.

*

Some time later, they both sat up with a start. Someone was tapping on the front door. Shoshana struggled to open her eyes as she looked at the clock. Half past four! Relaxed after making love, they must have dropped off to sleep. 'It must be Nathan!' she cried.

They were adjusting their crumpled clothes as they ran downstairs to let him in.

As soon as the door opened, they were both talking at once and asking questions but a moment later they fell silent. He didn't look like the bearer of good news.

'I waited for three hours for the ship to come back, but it didn't,' he sighed. Unfastening his rucksack that still contained the oilskin pouch, he slumped onto a chair.

Shoshana stared at him in dismay. 'I don't understand. I'm sure I saw it from the window just before twelve. And it was here this afternoon and gave the signal and I hung the white sheet from the window straightaway to let them know it was safe to return.'

'I know. I saw it this afternoon too. I was sure it was our ship. It couldn't have been anything else. But for some reason it didn't come back. Whatever you saw this evening must have been something else.'

'Do you think Lieutenant Woolley made a mistake about the meeting place?' Eli asked. 'Maybe he told the captain to anchor somewhere else on the coast?'

She shook her head. 'Definitely not. He said "under the Crusader castle at Atlit". Nobody could mistake that. Anyway that's exactly where the ship anchored this afternoon, so it had to be the right ship.'

They sat in despondent silence until she said, 'The trouble is, we don't have any way of finding out what happened. Perhaps the captain made a mistake after all.'

'But he anchored at the arranged spot this afternoon and gave the right signals and we responded,' Eli argued.

'We just have to be patient,' Shoshana said with a certitude she didn't feel. 'The British want our intelligence, so we'll just go on gathering it and keep vigil for the ship on the next moonless night.'

Neither of the men commented, and she doubted if they took much comfort from her words. She tried to sound optimistic but a heavy weight spread over her chest. What if the ship never came?

It didn't help that her father rushed out of his bedroom early the next morning with an expectant look on his wrinkled face. '*Nu?* Tell me. How did it go? What did Nathan say about the handover?'

After explaining what had happened, she was about to make some positive comment when he surprised her by saying, 'Don't worry. This was only your first chance to meet the ship. You can't expect a complicated plan like this to work the first time. You'll see, next time you'll make contact.'

*

The stress of waiting for the next moonless night sapped Shoshana's energy, and although new information continued to arrive, she found it an effort to resume the task of coordinating the spy operations.

She was looking out of the window of the research station when she saw Tova's carriage pull up. Tova's bubbly nature was exactly what she needed to dispel her anxiety, and she went outside to greet her friend.

'I told everyone at home I was coming to Zichron Yaakov to see my dearest friend. That's you!' Tova exclaimed, beaming as she linked arms with Shoshana. Tova's vitality was infectious.

'I've got good news!' she whispered as they went inside. 'The woman who works for the local pasha told me that a Turkish general came to see him yesterday and told him where the Turkish garrisons were stationed all. Along. The. Entire. Length. Of the Hejaz railway.' She paused between each word to let their significance sink in and looked expectantly at Shoshana.

'Did she remember any details?'

In reply, Tova took out a bulky piece of knitting from her travelling bag. Her eyes sparkled when she saw Shoshana's puzzled expression.

'Did you think I was going to start knitting?' she laughed. Unrolling the unfinished woollen shawl suspended from thick needles, she took out a slip of paper pinned onto the wrong side and handed it to Shoshana, unable to conceal her delight at her own ingenuity.

'Wasn't that a brainwave? I was wondering how to bring it here without arousing suspicion when I hit on this idea. Good thing I did because a self-important Turkish official stopped me on the way and demanded to check my bag. When I showed him my knitting, I asked if he'd like me to make him one as well!' He just laughed and said he didn't think he'd look good in a shawl, but a scarf would keep him warm on his night patrols.'

Carefully she unfolded the slip of paper. 'This is a list of all the places the Turk mentioned.'

Shoshana opened the drawer where she stored their intelligence and placed the paper inside a large metal box.

'That's wonderful, Tova,' she said. 'Please thank your friend and ask her to keep listening.'

Tova was looking around and, anticipating her question, Shoshana said, 'Nathan's out in the field today, probably filling up more notebooks with his observations.'

'He's so clever,' Tova said. 'When will he be back?'

'Not till tomorrow.'

'Not till tomorrow?' Tova didn't bother to conceal her disappointment. 'So I won't see him.'

'Not today. Can I make you some tea?' Shoshana asked, although she knew that tea was no antidote for the pain of unrequited love. 'I've made some almond *rugelech*.'

Tova had a sweet tooth, but this time she couldn't be tempted by biscuits. Shaking her head, she replaced the knitting in her travelling bag.

'I'd better get back,' she mumbled. 'Maybe I'll have more luck next time I come.'

Shoshana stood outside the gate, watching until Tova's carriage became a dark speck on the road lined with Washingtonia palms. Her heart ached for her friend and she wished that Nathan reciprocated Tova's affection instead of chasing married women in other countries.

She was leaning on the gate, deep in thought, when a stranger on horseback rode up and dismounted. 'You must be Mrs Shoshana. I'm Ephraim Shulman and I've brought you a letter from my brother in Afula.'

His face was red and he was mopping the perspiration that ran down his face with a large handkerchief. After leading him inside, she brought him a glass of water and waited while he gulped it down.

He wiped his mouth and sat back. 'Gavriel has always been very cautious, so I couldn't believe it when he told me he was gathering information for you,' he said. 'He's so keen to help that he even got me involved.'

Shoshana smiled. So Dr Shulman had decided to join their network, as she had known he would. 'Welcome to our conspiracy,' she said.

A slow grin spread across his broad face. 'Wait till I tell you what I did. As you probably know, my brother is a great talker. Well, a few days ago when a troop train pulled in to Afula, he climbed into the officers' compartment and got talking to them, and while they were telling him all about their woes, and their attention was on him, he got me to run along the platform to count the number of carriages and see how much ammunition and weaponry they carried. I never thought I'd be a spy! And as you can see, he's turned me into his messenger as well!'

It seemed that, like his brother, Ephraim was also a great talker, although unlike him, he looked like a man used to physical work. Taking a few sheets of notepaper he'd concealed inside a thick newspaper, he said, 'When you see how much information my brother has managed to find out in a short time, you'll be amazed. And this is just the beginning, so you'll be seeing a lot of me from now on!'

After Ephraim left, she sat down to read Dr Shulman's long letter and her admiration for his ingenuity grew with every page.

Being a physician, I have plenty of opportunities to talk to the army officers while I examine them, and they don't hold back. They have been an important source of information about conditions in the army, their orders, and their weapons and supplies. I've also found other ways of gaining intelligence. For instance, I asked Turkish authorities for a daily train timetable. I explained that as I'm expected to get up at all hours of the night to examine soldiers and officers, I need to know when they're arriving.

The quality and quantity of Dr Shulman's intelligence exceeded all her hopes. He listed the names of the Turkish divisions from Constantinople, with the number of soldiers in each one. When he examined German pilots, he encouraged them to describe the structure of their planes, which he included in his letter.

She was surprised to read that he had met top military men, and from Djemal Pasha, General von Falkenhayn and Enver Pasha, he had found out what reinforcements the Turks and Germans were sending to Palestine. His ingenuity and dedication knew no bounds. He even went out and measured the gauge of the railway lines so that when the British needed to carry troops and supplies through the desert, they would know which trains would match the tracks.

Her optimism grew as she turned the pages. Now she couldn't wait for the next moonless night so that they could pass on all this information. Information that would help the British win the war.

*

One week later, having seen the ship's signal that afternoon, Eli and Aaron left the station an hour before midnight with the oilskin pouch and made their way to the water's edge to wait for the ship.

'Have you thought what you'll do when the war ends?' Eli asked his friend. They were stretched out on the sandy bank smoking cigarettes as they listened to the soothing sound of waves slapping against the shore.

Aaron shrugged. 'Wars never end. They just cause other wars.'

Eli nodded. 'Sad but true.'

'I don't really know what I'll do,' Aaron went on. 'I don't fancy going back to my village. Maybe I'll stay in Zichron Yaakov.'

Eli was glad that the darkness hid the sharp glance he shot his friend.

'What about you? What will you do?' Aaron asked.

Eli inhaled and blew a few smoke rings towards the sky. 'When I think about my life after this, all I see is a blank. Nothingness. I can't explain it. Perhaps war fills up the empty spaces in my soul and after living on the razor's edge as we are now, I can't imagine leading an ordinary life.'

'I think you'll become a famous writer and we'll all be characters in your book.'

'I like the sound of that, but for some reason I just can't envisage a future.'

They finished smoking in silence. Tamping out his cigarette, Eli said, 'If anything happens to me, promise to look after Shoshana.'

At this, so many conflicting emotions collided in Aaron's mind that at first he couldn't collect his thoughts. Then he said lightly, 'Don't be absurd. Nothing will happen to you.' To change the subject, he asked, 'Do you believe in God?'

Eli pointed to a tiny crab scuttling in front of them. 'That crab is aware of us and fears us, but it has no concept of what we are. We are too huge and terrifying to comprehend. I could reach out and squash it, or I could decide to let it live. So to a crab, I'm probably God. And who knows what unimaginable force hovers above us, ready to strike us down?'

Aaron shook his head. 'So that's your answer? The notion of God is relative to size?'

Eli shrugged. 'There's no point asking questions to which there are no answers.' In a lighter mood, he added, 'Someone once said there are no atheists during a battle or an earthquake.'

Before Eli could reply, a small ship appeared on the horizon, and they sprang up for a closer view, but although it passed in front of them, it didn't stop. They continued to wait in the hope that it would return, or that another one would pass, but hour after long hour went by, and still there was no ship.

*

At dawn they returned to the station where Shoshana and Nathan were waiting. One glance at their faces told her everything.

'It's simple,' Nathan said bitterly. 'No doubt about it. Woolley has changed his mind. Either he decided we couldn't be trusted, or the British don't care about Palestine.'

Shoshana shook her head. 'That's impossible. I know he was sincere. He wouldn't have let us down. And we saw the boat give the signal this afternoon. There must be another explanation.'

Aaron took off his glasses and sank into a chair. 'Let's say you're right, but on two afternoons now we've seen what we think is the signal and we've waited for his ship in vain. So why hasn't it come?'

'Anything could have happened. For all we know, the Turks might have captured the ship, or some mechanical problem has held it up. The signals we thought we saw in the afternoon may not have been from our ship at all.'

She knew she was clutching at straws but she had to keep their hopes up. She had to appear strong.

Eli was studying her. 'It's not your fault, Shoshi,' he said gently. 'Your arrangement with Woolley should have worked, so something unexpected must have come up. The trouble is, we can't contact him, so we'll just have to go on collecting information in the hope that the ship will come. But for how much longer?'

That afternoon she saddled Zahra and galloped up and down the hills and wadis, past the thorn bushes, oaks and tamarisk trees, and across the dunes, but she hardly saw the landscape. If the ship didn't come soon, most of the information they had gathered would be obsolete. It would all be wasted.

CHAPTER SEVENTEEN

Zichron Yaakov, Berlin and Copenhagen, 1916

It was already autumn, but the longed-for breeze that finally cooled the scorching days of summer didn't bring Shoshana any comfort. The war was already in its third year. On the battlefields of Europe, Germany was inflicting catastrophic losses on the British, while in the Middle East, Germany's allies the Turks were gaining ground. Two more moonless nights had passed without any sign of the ship – no horn blasts or black smoke in the afternoon, no appearance in the darkness of the night. Even if she didn't see the ship in the afternoon, Shoshana always put the sheet out and kept watch through those nights, just in case. They were long nights of fruitless vigils and blighted hopes. Could she have been mistaken about Woolley's sincerity after all? Meanwhile, intelligence from Dr Shulman and their other contacts continued coming in and as she added each valuable piece of information to the metal box, her frustration mounted. Were they risking their lives for nothing?

Rereading some of the documents they had amassed, she was struck by the wealth of information they contained. Every one of them would benefit the British war effort. Locking the lid and sliding the box into its hiding place at the back of the specimen drawers, she wondered what they could possibly do. Continuing to wait for a ship that might never arrive risked wasting precious time. The only alternative was to contact the British again, but there was no way of reaching Egypt now that Nathan was no longer in a position to secure a travel permit for her.

*

The same thoughts churned in Nathan's mind as he continued his reconnaissance of the northern Galilee. He was mourning the loss of the region's forests when he came to a village where he recognised an unusual flowering plant, *ricinus communis*, commonly known as the castor bean plant. As he continued exploring the region, he noticed it in other villages as well. He was puzzled. This plant was potentially toxic, and there was only one reason farmers would cultivate it: it was capable of producing lubricating oil, which was in very short supply due to the Anglo-French blockade.

With this in mind, he stopped to chat to some fellahin, who confirmed his theory. They complained that they only received a minuscule amount of olive oil for their bread and unless they used that to lubricate their wheelbarrows, they had to haul the loads themselves. It got Nathan thinking. If there wasn't even enough lubricating oil for wheelbarrows, how did the Turks manage to lubricate their big machinery?

He found the answer that afternoon when he stopped at a railway workshop and saw engines being dismantled and carried piece by piece on carts pulled by oxen. So the shortage of lubricating oil in the country was even worse than he had imagined. He dismounted and sat against the gnarled trunk of an oak tree, deep in thought. When he rose, he had the answer to their problem.

*

Inside the research station, the mood was glum as Shoshana, Eli and Aaron discussed the situation, but at the sound of hooves their heads swivelled towards the window. Nathan had dismounted and was hurrying towards the door with the bright-eyed expression of someone bearing good news.

It took him a few moments to get his breath back. Panting as he flopped onto a stool he said, 'I've figured it out. It all hinges on sesame oil.'

Shoshana's stool suddenly felt so hard that she had to shift her weight. How could sesame oil possibly solve their problem?

'Sesame oil? How?' Eli asked.

'Wait and I'll explain. We've all agreed that we have to make contact with the British, right? And we're agreed that it's pointless relying on their people in Cairo. The only place where British officials have the power to make important decisions is in England. So we have to make contact with the authorities in London.' He was speaking slowly, pausing and looking at each one of them in turn to make sure they understood.

Shoshana sighed. Nathan's scientific acumen was legendary but he had an irritating way of imparting information like a teacher trying to explain things to slow-witted children.

'So I have to go to London to convince the authorities there that we're serious, that we've collected information that will help them defeat the Turks,' he concluded.

If he had just announced that he was about to travel to the moon, they couldn't have been more astonished.

'There's just one small problem with that.' Eli's words tumbled out in a torrent. 'In case you've forgotten, we're at war with Britain. The Turks will never give you permission to go there and even if they do, as a Turkish citizen, the English will throw you into jail as an enemy spy the minute you land.'

Aaron was nodding. He started to say he agreed with Eli but Nathan interrupted. 'You didn't let me finish. It will definitely be difficult and complicated, but I'm ahead of you. And that's where sesame oil comes in.'

'Sesame oil?' Aaron burst in. 'You're going to get to London on account of sesame oil?'

He glanced at Eli for support but Eli was listening attentively. If Nathan had an idea, it was worth hearing.

'I know it sounds crazy but just listen. The Turks are desperately short of lubricating oil. Before the war, I did some research on sesame oil and I know its potential. If I can convince Djemal Pasha that with more research I can produce a heavier type of sesame oil that could be used as a lubricant, I think he'll jump at it.'

'That's smart,' Eli said.

'But it still doesn't get you to London,' Aaron pointed out.

'If I tell him that I need to confer with fellow scientists in Berlin, he'll probably give me a travel pass for Germany. That shouldn't be a problem as Turkey and Germany are allies.'

There was silence as they absorbed his audacious plan, then they all started talking at once.

'You've got *chutzpah* approaching Djemal Pasha after resigning from the locust eradication project,' Aaron said. 'You're taking an enormous risk.'

Nathan shrugged. 'It's a chance I have to take. It might work because they're desperate for lubricating oil.'

Eli was gazing at Nathan with admiration. 'I think your plan is brilliant. Anyway, was anything important ever achieved without a risk?'

Shoshana was frowning. 'But what happens after Berlin?'

'Obviously I can't ask the Turks for a *wassika* to London but once I'm in Berlin, I'll find a way to get to England, maybe through Denmark, which is neutral. I'll contact the British consul there. When I explain why I need to travel to London, I think he'll arrange it.'

Eli looked thoughtful. 'This is going to be a very long journey,' he said slowly. 'First you have to get from Afula to Damascus, then from Damascus you'll have to take the Baghdad–Berlin railway to Constantinople, and then on to Berlin. That could take much longer than usual because the trains run very slowly these days. And you don't know how long it will take to get from there to Copenhagen, whether the British consul will give you a travel pass for London, or how long you'll spend there trying to contact someone. It might take weeks.'

'What's your point?' Nathan's voice had a testy edge.

'My point is, what are we supposed to do here while you're traipsing all over Europe? You won't be able to contact us once you leave Berlin, or possibly Copenhagen if you get a permit to travel there, so we won't have a clue where you are or what's going on. Are we just going to sit here waiting and wondering when you'll be back? And what's going to happen to all our intelligence in the meantime?'

'Have you got a better plan?' Nathan retorted. 'Anyway, what will happen to our intelligence if I don't go? The way I see it, this is our only hope.'

The late afternoon light was fading and the air in the room had grown chilly. Shoshana shivered. Drawing her rose-patterned shawl closer around her shoulders she said, 'Nathan is right. We don't have any alternative. He has to try and get to London, however long it takes.'

After Eli and Aaron left, she said to Nathan, 'I know someone who will miss you when you're gone.'

'Who?'

When she didn't answer, he said, 'From that little smile of yours I suppose you mean Tova. You're wasting your time with your matchmaking. I've never been interested in country girls who never stop talking. I only like strong women.' His gaze softened as he looked at her. 'Like you,' he added.

'And that woman in Berlin. I've noticed letters in pink envelopes with German stamps addressed to you,' she said. 'You still don't realise that she's playing games to keep you on the hook. She'll never leave her husband.'

'I don't think you're in a position to lecture me about relationships.'

'Touché. I just hope your plan works because everything depends on it.'

*

Two days later, Nathan climbed into a horse-drawn carriage bound for Afula to catch the train to Damascus. As he travelled northwards, he filled his notebook with detailed observations about the villages and fields he passed, lamenting their impoverished condition and depleted crops.

When he entered Djemal Pasha's headquarters, he steeled himself for the onslaught and hoped it would merely be verbal. He flinched when one of the most feared men in the Ottoman Empire sprang from his armchair and glowered.

'How dare you show your face in here after abandoning your post?' he yelled, his eyes bulging. 'I made you commander-in-chief of the locust eradication program and how did you reward me? You had the effrontery to resign before the job was completed. I should have you strung up by the toes and flogged until there's no skin left on your body.'

Nathan tried to keep his voice steady. 'As I told Your Excellency at the time, your soldiers and labourers were lazy and didn't follow my instructions, so I had no hope of succeeding. But I've come to offer you something you need. A plan to boost your supply of lubricating oil.'

At the mention of lubricating oil, Djemal Pasha sat down again but he was still glaring.

'Lubricating oil? How do you intend to do that?'

'I've done some research on sesame oil, and I believe that if we can produce a heavier type, it would be suitable as a lubricant.'

'So do it! What are you waiting for?'

'I can't do it alone. I need to confer with my colleagues in Berlin.'

Half an hour later, Nathan left Djemal Pasha's headquarters with a *wassika* for Germany and an authority to travel by rail to Berlin tucked into his wallet.

*

As Eli had predicted, the Baghdad to Berlin train took much longer to reach its destination than usual, with frequent protracted stops along the way. Nathan was uncomfortable in the shabby compartment, complemented by a dirty toilet in the corridor, but he used the time to plan what he would say to his German colleagues.

This was his second visit to Berlin and he was surprised to find such a light-hearted atmosphere in the city. It was as if the residents were either untouched by the war or determined to ignore it in their pursuit of pleasure. When he ordered a beer in his hotel in the Mitte district, the barman behind the highly polished timber counter complained that the cancellation of the Olympic Games the previous year on account of the war had resulted in a huge financial loss to hotels, which had expected an influx of visitors. That was the only reference to the war Nathan heard during his entire stay. Close to his hotel, he noticed a proliferation of tawdry nightclubs and risqué cabarets, where the war was far from anyone's thoughts.

During the day, he made contact with his academic colleagues and found that many prominent German botanists concurred with his idea about sesame oil and gave it their written support. Armed with their endorsements, he started knocking on the doors of German officials to convince them of the importance of his research and to explain that in order to produce heavier sesame oil and help the war effort, he would need to consult with experts in Denmark.

He wasn't a patient man, and although he tried to control his temper, he grew increasingly irritated after each interview. Why couldn't these obtuse people understand that he was offering them something they needed?

Shoshana had been right in assuming that his enthusiasm to visit Berlin was partly due to his eagerness to see Rachel again. Excited by the prospect of touching her delectable body again, he tried to contact her as soon as he arrived, but each time he dialled the number she had given him, the maid asked him to wait, put down the telephone, and came back after a whispered conversation to say that her mistress wasn't home. Mortified, he realised that, as usual, Shoshana was right.

To distract himself from his disappointment over Rachel, he began a flirtation with a German fräulein he met at the bar one night. Liesl Blucher, a singer at a nearby cabaret, didn't need much persuasion to accept his offer of dinner and champagne in his room. The two evenings they spent together revived his confidence in his seductive powers but she bored him and he was relieved when, on the third day, the German immigration department issued him with an authority to travel to Denmark.

*

As soon as he arrived in Copenhagen and booked into a small inn situated among a row of pastel-painted shops and restaurants facing the marina, Nathan headed straight for the British embassy. He was in high spirits. London was getting closer. It took two frustrating days spent explaining to the staff why he needed to see the ambassador, before he was finally granted a meeting.

Sir Edward Finchley-Smythe had a fine head of closely cropped silver hair that accentuated his florid complexion. He wore gold-rimmed glasses and an air of pained *noblesse oblige*. As Nathan explained his mission, the ambassador studied him with an expression that indicated he didn't believe a word he said.

'Are you trying to tell me that in some godforsaken village in Palestine, a small group of Jews believe that spying on the Turks will help us win the war?'

Nathan suppressed the urge to argue. 'When my sister met Lieutenant Woolley in Port Said earlier this year, he promised to send a ship to pick up our intelligence and deliver it to British Naval Headquarters.'

As he proceeded to explain the arrangements Woolley had made and the signals he had suggested, Sir Edward didn't conceal his scorn. 'I see. White sheets, hooting steamships and black smoke on moonless nights.' He paused for effect. 'Let me guess. Did that ship ever arrive?'

'No. For some reason our line of communication was broken, and that's why I must get to England to organise a reliable way for us to deliver the information we've collected.'

Nathan was struggling to speak slowly and pleasantly but found it difficult to keep his temper in check. All over the world he was feted and honoured in academic circles, yet this pompous diplomat treated him like a supplicant even though he was offering his country a gift of incalculable value.

Finchley-Smythe took off his glasses, sat back in his armchair, and surveyed the man in front of him.

Speaking in a dry voice as if each word was an effort, he said, 'Do you really expect our chaps in Whitehall to communicate with your lot? Do you realise there's a war on, Mr Adelberg?'

'The name is Adelstein. I'm perfectly aware that there's a war on. But perhaps you're not aware that it's being waged in Palestine as well as in Europe, and that's why we've been collecting intelligence for you, because like you we want to defeat the Turks.'

Confronted by this upstart from the other end of the world, Finchley-Smythe made a dismissive gesture with his manicured hand and reached for the buzzer on his desk. 'If you'll excuse me I'm very busy. My secretary will show you out.'

Nathan could no longer control himself. 'I won't excuse you, and neither will your government when it discovers that you have rejected an offer that could mean the difference between victory and defeat. You're sitting here in comfort in this neutral corner of the world, while most of Europe and parts of the Middle East are embroiled in battles where tens of thousands of young men are dying. And most of them are British.'

Clearly taken aback, the ambassador leaned back in his chair, as if trying to put more distance between himself and his unwelcome visitor, his hand poised above the buzzer. Then he hesitated.

'What is it that you'd like me to do, Mr Adelstern?'

This time Nathan didn't correct him. 'I'd like you to give me a travel pass for England.'

'And how do you propose to get there?'

'By ship. I know that ships bound for the United States stop in the Scottish port of Kirkwall. That's where I'll disembark and make my way to London.'

'So you have it all worked out.' There was no admiration in his tone.

'Not quite. If the Turks find out that I've arrived in Great Britain, they will figure out that I'm spying for you, and that will have catastrophic consequences not only for me but for my family and all the people in our spy ring. Obviously that will also mean that we won't be able to continue collecting intelligence for you.'

'Your self-assurance is formidable,' the ambassador said. It didn't sound like a compliment.

'I'm a scientist destined for an academic career, but the war has pushed me in a different direction.'

Finchley-Smythe looked at him for a long time but whether his gaze denoted incredulity, admiration or disdain, Nathan couldn't tell.

Taking an official-looking sheet of paper from his drawer, he started writing and paused every so often to stare at Nathan. When he finished, he inserted the letter into an envelope and sealed it.

Handing it to Nathan, he said, 'Give this to the immigration people at Kirkwall. It should ensure that you won't have a problem.' Rising from his chair, he extended his hand. 'Good luck, Mr Adelstern.'

That evening, Nathan sent a brief cable to Shoshana: *My German colleagues agree with my idea about sesame oil.*

*

Shoshana rushed to the research station as soon as she received Nathan's cable. Three weeks had passed, and every day, as she and Eli filed new information, they wondered where Nathan was, whether he had any chance of getting to London, and whether their intelligence would be outdated before he returned.

But Shoshana didn't doubt that he'd succeed. Nathan had never failed to accomplish anything he had set out to do. Now, waving the cable triumphantly she said, 'I told you he'd get there. He's probably in London by now convincing the authorities to agree to our plan.'

CHAPTER EIGHTEEN

The Negev, 1916

As the carriage jolted its way along a road that wound southward towards Beersheba, Shoshana sat forward, mesmerised by the granite peaks, rock-strewn plateaus and craggy pinnacles, and the rugged wadis whose moisture had been sucked dry by thousands of years of relentless heat. In the shifting light, the mountains on the horizon changed colour as she watched, now blue and mauve, now violet and deep purple. In the distance, as far as she could see, sand dunes curved towards infinity. The landscape surprised her with its savage beauty. Leah's letters, which were always fairly brief, had nevertheless mentioned that Aunt Hannah's settlement was situated on the edge of a desert, but she hadn't described its grandeur. In fact, she had given few details about her new life, and with every turn in the road, Shoshana grew more intrigued at the thought of her gregarious, village-raised sister living in this remote, sparsely inhabited region.

She knew that her father missed his younger daughter, especially now that his son was also away, and that he felt anxious about her welfare. 'Leah has never been away from home before, we should see how she is, why don't you go and visit her?' he kept urging. Shoshana had insisted that there was no need for concern. After all, Leah was staying with Aunt Hannah, who had written to let them know that her niece was settling in well, but he had dismissed that assurance with a disparaging gesture. 'You have to take anything Hannah says with a grain of salt. It's time you went to see for yourself.'

As she sat in the carriage watching the ever-changing colours of the surrounding hills, Shoshana acknowledged that while she also missed Leah, her absence made life less complicated.

She missed Nathan far more. Ever since he'd left, life had become a succession of frustrating daily discussions at the research station where she, Eli and Aaron mulled over the same questions: had Nathan reached London? Had he managed to convince anyone there to take their spy ring seriously? Would he return before the information they continued to gather became obsolete? Shoshana feared that her vision might fizzle out in the corridors of Whitehall.

The sun was blazing and the golden sands shimmered in the haze. Shoshana tilted her wide-brimmed hat to shield her eyes from the glare. In this landscape it was no wonder that tired eyes, fixed on an ever-distant horizon, often conjured a mirage of a verdant palm-filled oasis. She glanced at her wristwatch. In her letter to Aunt Hannah, she had estimated that it would be about twelve by the time she arrived, and it was close to that now.

She felt unsettled. How would Leah react? Would she refuse to talk to her? Would there be recriminations and accusations? Her own feelings were a jumble of apprehension and hope. Relief that her sister wasn't exposed to the danger their spying activities posed, guilt that Eli's love for her had caused Leah to leave home, and longing for the closeness they'd lost. Perhaps she and Leah could never be close again, but Abba was right. It was time to try and heal the rift.

As they neared the farm, the landscape transformed into an agricultural Eden where yellow and green fields of wheat and barley stretched ahead of them. Seven women dressed in loose cotton trousers, kerchiefs tied around their heads, were bent over the soil with their hoes. At the sound of carriage wheels grinding along the gravel road, they looked up, straightened their backs, waved, and returned to their work.

Past a bold sign hand-painted in crimson that welcomed visitors to the Women's Cooperative Farm, Nasser drove through the large gate into the grounds. The carriage stopped at a jumble of low structures that consisted of a main building, what appeared to be accommodation blocks, barns and sheds, surrounded by eucalyptus trees whose grey-green foliage seemed bleached by the sun. Through the partly open wooden doors of the sheds Shoshana saw rakes, hoes, scythes, wheelbarrows and ploughs.

She had alighted and started towards the main building when a thin woman with iron grey hair frizzing around her wrinkled face rushed towards her and enveloped her in a powerful hug that felt like a collision with a bolt of lightning.

'Shoshana! I couldn't believe it when I got your letter saying you were coming! And now you're really here! Let me look at you.'

She stood back and scrutinised her niece with an appraising look. 'You're still a fashion plate, but you've lost weight since I saw you last. When was that? The last time I came to Zichron Yaakov, your dear mother was still with us so I suppose it must have been at least five years ago. And now after all this time you're here. You've made your old aunt very happy!'

She said all this hardly stopping for breath and linked her arm through Shoshana's as they walked in step into the building. Shoshana had almost forgotten how much she loved her aunt's impulsive and affectionate nature, which was such a contrast with her father's reserved character. Hannah always said he thought too much, while he said his sister thought too little.

From what Shoshana remembered, they never saw eye to eye on anything. Their arguments came to a head when Hannah and her socialist husband Yosef joined a kibbutz many years before.

'People aren't sausages, they don't all come out identical from mincing machines, they want to be in charge of their own lives, earn their own money and spend it however they like,' he had scoffed. 'We're not all equal, and your ideal of communal life ignores human nature. You'll see, sooner or later it will collapse.' But as usual, Hannah had ignored his predictions.

'Leah will be so happy to see you. In spite of everything.' It was clear Hannah knew why Leah had left home. 'Don't worry,' she added. 'You'll see, everything will be fine. The bond between sisters is stronger than anything that divides you. Even a lover. Men come and go but sisters are forever.'

After inviting Nasser to come inside for lunch, and reassuring him that he was welcome in their commune, she led Shoshana into a large refectory sparsely furnished with wooden benches on either side of a long trestle table. 'Sit down a minute. I'll tell her you're here. She's helping in the poultry farm today.'

The thought of her dainty sister working with chickens was so incongruous that Shoshana laughed aloud. For a moment, the knot that had formed in her belly at the prospect of coming face to face with her dissolved, but a moment later the churning returned.

She heard swift footsteps on the unpolished timber floorboards and turned to see Leah walking towards her, carrying a wide wicker basket full of eggs smeared with dirt and feathers. She wore a shapeless dark dress covered with a big apron, and her fair hair was tied back from her face with a headscarf that accentuated her finely moulded features.

They confronted each other and stood very still as if suddenly nailed to the floor, and their eyes locked. Leah put the basket on the sideboard and at the same moment, without uttering a word or making a conscious decision, they rushed forward and flung their arms around each other.

'I'm so glad you've come, Shoshi,' Leah said. 'It's good to see you. I've hardly slept since we received your letter. There's so much I want to show you.' She sounded like a child at boarding school who has finally received a longed-for visitor.

'You look very happy,' Shoshana said.

Leah nodded. 'For the first time in my life, I feel I fit in. At home I never did, as you probably know. I wasn't beautiful like you or brainy like Nathan, but here people appreciate me and value what I do.'

Shoshana studied her sister. Leah had lost her petulant expression. Her eyes were shining, and she emanated the radiance of a convert to a religious sect.

'Do you remember the evening we went to hear Olga Mankiewicz speak?' Leah was saying. 'I wasn't even interested in anything she said, so who would have thought that one day I'd be so happy living in one of those collectives she talked about?'

Shoshana could recall every detail of that evening, from Leah's impatience to see Eli, to her furtive glances in his direction throughout the lecture. She also remembered her own chagrin at discovering that she and her sister were in love with the same man. Had Leah forgotten the powerful emotional undertow of that evening and the rivalry it revealed?

As if in answer to her unspoken question, Leah said, 'My life in Zichron Yaakov now seems very distant. Sometimes I think that by coming here I've taken a holiday from myself.'

Just as Shoshana was about to ask what had prompted that insight, Aunt Hannah came out of the kitchen and joined them. 'I'm sure you girls have a lot of catching up to do,' she said, smiling at them benevolently.

Women were coming in and out of the kitchen carrying piles of thick plates that clattered as they set them down on the long table beside jugs of water and platters heaped with dates and figs. Inside the kitchen, others were chopping tomatoes, onions and eggplants, and pulverising sesame seeds and chickpeas. A red-faced figure in a white chef's cap bent over the wood-fired oven, wiping beads of perspiration from her brow as she checked to see if the flat bread was ready.

Shoshana turned to her aunt. 'How long have you been here?'

'I moved here two years ago, after Yosef passed away. I wasn't happy in the kibbutz he and I had joined, although I would never have admitted it to your father. I liked the idea of everyone being equal, working together and sharing the profits, but after a while I saw that the equality only applied to men. Women were never equal. We were relegated to what they regarded as women's work. Children, cleaning and cooking. Here we do everything from ploughing with oxen to mending farm machinery. I've never looked back. But that's enough about me,' she said. 'A couple of years ago your father wrote to tell me that you married a prosperous merchant and moved to Constantinople but later he said you'd left your husband. He was furious. What happened?'

'Abraham was kind and considerate,' she said, 'but I couldn't stand living in Constantinople. Women there are controlled and cooped up behind latticed windows. I missed my family, my freedom, and my life in Zichron Yaakov.'

She was aware of a flicker in Leah's eyes, and she paused for an instant, afraid that she had just opened a Pandora's box of resentments, but the moment passed and she continued. 'I was so miserable I left.' She darted a surreptitious glance at her sister, who was looking down at her work-reddened hands.

Her aunt broke into enthusiastic applause. 'Good for you, Shoshana! I can imagine how much courage that took. But there's nothing as miserable as life with the wrong man. It's hard enough to be happy with the right one!'

She turned to Leah. 'Why don't you show your sister around, while I go and tell the cook we have visitors for lunch.'

Taking her arm, Leah led her across the yard. They were walking past a barn filled to the roof with bales of hay and Shoshana had stopped to inhale their dry sweet scent when Leah turned to her.

'I heard that Nathan's gone away. Where did he go?'

Shoshana was taken aback. How did she find out?

'He had to go to a scientific conference.'

She hoped that the finality of her tone would forestall further questions, but Leah didn't look convinced.

'What conference? Whereabouts?' She spoke in an accusing tone that Shoshana recognised implied she was being excluded from a secret her siblings shared.

'About botanical research, I suppose. In Berlin.' At least that part was true.

But Leah still wasn't satisfied. 'How come he got permission to travel to Germany in wartime?'

'Don't forget Germany is our ally. Come to think of it, he was talking about improving the quality of sesame oil.' It was a relief not to have to lie about everything. She longed to tell Leah the truth but she was determined to keep it secret. The only way to protect her sister was to keep her ignorant of what they were doing.

Before Leah could continue her questioning, she asked, 'How did you know Nathan was away?'

'Tova mentioned it.'

Shoshana tried to conceal her dismay. Tova! The girl was a chatterbox but surely she realised the importance of keeping all their activities secret.

'When did you see her?'

'About two weeks ago she was visiting a cousin here. She told me she hadn't seen Nathan for weeks. You know how smitten she is. I asked Abba about him in my last letter but he hasn't replied.' She looked curiously at her sister. 'Why do you want to know when she was here?'

Shoshana shrugged. 'I didn't know she had a cousin staying here so I was surprised, that's all.'

Changing the subject, she asked Leah about her life on the farm. 'Do you always work in the chicken coop or do you rotate jobs?'

'We rotate, but I like the chickens best. Planting and weeding are back-breaking but it feels good to work in the fields. I hate helping in the kitchen. It's too much like home!'

They laughed and the tension dissipated. As they continued walking in the grounds they came to the barn and through the open door she saw two young women in baggy trousers standing beside a large butter churn, puffing as they beat the milk with a long wooden pole.

'This is my sister Shoshana,' Leah said, and introduced her to Noa and Esther. They looked her up and down, their eyes lingering on her long skirt and the polka dot blouse with the Peter Pan collar. Shoshana and Leah walked on, but when Shoshana turned around a few moments later, the two women were still standing there, staring at her.

Leah resumed her questioning. 'Shoshi, tell me what's going on at home. I can't put my finger on it but it feels as if everyone is hiding something.'

Did we carry our childhood emotions inside us throughout our entire lives? Shoshana wondered, and wished she didn't have to perpetuate Leah's anxiety by dismissing it. 'There's nothing mysterious going on and we're not hiding anything. Abba probably didn't reply to your question because he's busy with the harvest at this time of year.'

But Leah's eyes held a challenge. 'You're trying to fob me off. I know you've been away too. Where did you go?'

Shoshana's heart was pounding. She had to think fast to defuse this potentially dangerous situation.

'I had to go to Constantinople to finalise my separation from Abraham, that's all.'

Before Leah could comment, Aunt Hannah appeared and called them into the dining hall. Lunch was a simple meal of hummus, tahini, roasted eggplant and olives on flat bread.

Conversation flowed easily as some of the women asked about Shoshana's life. Noa wanted to know whether she made her own clothes while Esther suggested she should design smarter trousers and dresses for them, which made them all laugh. Some women asked for news of the progress of the war, while others complained about the relentless work in the fields or told amusing anecdotes about the donkeys.

After lunch, Leah took Shoshana to her tiny room. It was furnished with a narrow bed, a small round mirror above a wooden table, and one chair.

'Very different from your room at home,' Shoshana commented as she sat beside her sister on the edge of the bed, which didn't give under their weight.

It felt good to sit side by side in a bedroom again, just as they used to do so long ago when they were girls and confided in each other about their parents, their friends and their problems. Shoshana sighed. Those times were gone and would never come again.

Leah shrugged. 'It's basic but it's adequate. I think we've spent too much time dwelling on comfort and possessions and not enough on things that really matter.'

Once again Shoshana was lost for words. They sat in silence until Leah cleared her throat and fiddled with the hem of her dress.

'How is Eli?' she asked.

Shoshana stiffened. What was coming next?

'He's in charge of the research station while Nathan's away. That keeps him very busy so I don't see as much of him these days.'

She offered it as an explanation, almost an excuse, but as soon as she said it, she realised it was true. Preoccupied with gathering and sorting all their information, and worried about the future of their spy ring, in recent weeks she hadn't visited Eli as often as she used to.

As usual when she thought about him, she felt a visceral longing to be near him, to see herself reflected in the dark depths of his eyes, and to feel the solace of his warm skin.

Leah seemed to be considering her comment. For several minutes they sat in an awkward silence and Shoshana sensed Eli's magnetic power drawing them apart. It had been a mistake to come, she thought. Leah will never forget him or forgive me.

Just then Leah leaned towards her, put her arms around her neck, and rested her head on her shoulder. 'I don't feel angry with him anymore. I think about him with affection but not longing.'

Shoshana's relief was replaced by scepticism a moment later. Was Leah sincere or was she fooling herself? They sat in silence until Leah said, 'It's wonderful to see you again, Shoshi. I love it here but I miss you. There's so much to tell you and so many places to show you. Do you have to go back this afternoon?'

Shoshana's eyes misted over and she kissed Leah's cheek. She surprised herself by saying, 'I'd love to stay longer. I can ask Nasser to come back for me the day after tomorrow.'

Leah jumped up. 'That's fantastic! Let's go and tell Aunt Hannah so she can arrange for you to sleep in the visitors' room.'

As they walked back towards the main hall hand in hand, Leah said, 'Something strange happened last week. An Australian soldier turned up here on horseback wearing a funny lopsided hat with long feathers. Jack Simpson. Said he was an Anzac and part of the Light Horse Brigade that had fought at Gallipoli, but don't ask me what Anzac means. I have no idea what a Light Horse Brigade is either.'

'What was he doing here?'

'Patrolling the Negev, apparently. It was his day off, and he got sick of seeing nothing but sand, palms and soldiers so he decided to explore further afield. He wasn't supposed to do that but he said he was a larrikin, which I think means a rebel. It was the eucalypts that made him stop here. He called them gum trees and said they made him homesick. You should have seen the way he pulled off a twig, closed his eyes and breathed in the scent of the leaves as if he was inhaling perfume!'

'Sounds as if this Jack made quite an impression on you.'

'He was different. The women here liked him too, even though they couldn't understand everything he said. Before he galloped away he called out *See you later!* and I thought he meant he was coming back that afternoon!'

Shoshana laughed. She had dreaded the prospect of confronting her sister and she was relieved that their conversation was free of tension.

*

The next two days passed with a speed that astonished Shoshana, and her heart felt heavy at the thought of parting with her sister. As she greeted Nasser, who had returned with the carriage to take her home, Esther called out, 'Next time you come, bring simple clothes instead of all this finery so we can put you to work in the fields!'

Aunt Hannah gave her a hug. 'Don't be a stranger, come back soon.'

When it was time to say goodbye to Leah, Shoshana's throat constricted and she couldn't speak. Suddenly everything blurred, and she held Leah close before climbing into the carriage. For the first time in several years, she felt she had lost a rival and regained a sister.

The day was drawing to a close and the late afternoon sun had begun to drop lower in the sky, burnishing the fields with a warm light. As the carriage drove through the gates, Shoshana turned for one last look at Leah, who was standing beside Aunt Hannah. Seeing them together, Shoshana felt as if a rucksack filled with rocks had suddenly fallen from her shoulders, and her heart skipped with a new lightness. Whatever happened, her sister was safe.

The shadows were lengthening. They sharpened the contours of the slopes and leached the colour from the fields. Far in the distance stretched the desert sand, and as she recalled Leah's story about Australians patrolling the area, she felt a surge of hope. Perhaps the British were planning an assault on the Turks in Palestine after all. If only she could let Nathan know. If only she knew how much longer he'd be away. And if he'd been successful in London.

CHAPTER NINETEEN

London, 1917

The voyage from Copenhagen to the northern tip of Scotland passed pleasantly for Nathan, who spent most of the time with Vibeke Rasmussen, a Danish journalist he met on board. He had been sitting in a deckchair, reading a Conan Doyle novel when an alluring young woman who had already caught his eye stopped in front of him and said in a husky voice, 'I love mysteries too. And Conan Doyle is my favourite author.'

From that moment, they spent all their time together. The attraction was mutual. He enjoyed the company of women, especially when they were tall, slim and interesting like Vibeke, who travelled the world reporting the news, while her interest was aroused by this mysterious botanist who was apparently on his way to a conference in Britain. Their days were spent wrapped in blankets on deckchairs, feeling the sea breeze on their faces and salt on their lips as they shared their dreams, and their nights naked under blankets in his cabin. To add to her other attributes, Vibeke was uninhibited and adventurous in bed, arousing him with her erotic imagination. He knew that finally he had found a woman who would never bore him, in bed or out of it, but he also knew that his mission precluded a future for them.

Her soft lips pressing on his woke him early one morning and he reached out for her but when he glanced through the porthole he was startled to see that they were approaching the coast of Scotland where his journey was due to end. With a sigh, he rose, dressed hurriedly, removed his neatly folded clothes from the drawers, and placed them into his leather valise.

'I'm going up on deck,' he said.

She sat up, unable to conceal her chagrin. 'What's the rush? We still have at least half an hour before we dock.'

But he was already at the door, and reluctantly she dressed and followed him. They stood arm in arm on deck as they watched the ship approach the busy port.

As soon as it docked, an announcement over the loudspeaker asked Nathan Adelstein to come to the lounge.

Vibeke looked at him questioningly and when he didn't comment, she supposed that his host at the conference had come to escort him off the ship. But when they entered the lounge, two British soldiers in military uniform confronted him. In a booming voice, one of them said, 'In the name of His Majesty King George V, we are arresting you as an enemy alien. You must come with us.'

Shocked at this unexpected finale to their romantic interlude, Vibeke was astonished that Nathan didn't offer any argument or resistance. 'This is outrageous,' she shouted. 'I thought Britain was a civilised country. As soon as I get to New York, I'm going to write an article about this so the whole world will see how Britain treats innocent visitors.'

'I'd be grateful if you do,' Nathan called out as they hustled him off the ship. He meant it. An international news story describing his arrest in Britain was exactly what he needed to dupe the Turkish authorities and conceal the real reason for his visit to Britain.

Although he regretted being unable to explain it to Vibeke, the whole episode at the dock was a charade organised by Finchley-Smythe in Copenhagen to make him look like a Turkish spy.

Away from public scrutiny, he handed his military escort the envelope from Finchley-Smythe. The senior police officer, clearly astonished by its contents, glanced from the letter to Nathan and back again, shaking his head in disbelief. 'It seems our orders are to deliver you to Scotland Yard,' he said.

They boarded a train bound for London. While his escorts grumbled about food shortages, curfews and horrifying losses in the trenches of the Somme, Nathan looked up occasionally from his Conan Doyle novel and marvelled at British railways. They were clean, punctual and comfortable, a contrast to the dirty, cramped carriages of the Berlin–Baghdad railway on which he had travelled from Damascus. He took it as a good sign. Surely a nation that produced such exemplary trains was superior to the enemy in other ways as well.

It was a dark and foggy night when the train pulled in at Kings Cross station, and he was amused to hear his escorts describe the thick greenish fog as a pea-souper. When he wiped his face with his white handkerchief, it was streaked with soot. On the streets, he noticed a surprisingly large military presence, and read signs warning people of the danger of bombs falling from zeppelins.

As it was too late to meet his contact at Scotland Yard, his escorts dropped him off at a seedy hotel close to the station. After an uncomfortable night in a lumpy bed followed by an unsatisfactory breakfast of weak milky tea and soggy toast and marmalade, he caught a hansom cab to Whitehall Place. A lifelong fan of Conan Doyle's hero Sherlock Holmes, whom he regarded as the epitome of an English gentleman, he couldn't wait to see the famous police headquarters that featured in the novels.

The handsome three-storey building on the Embankment didn't disappoint. Past a small canteen where two motherly women in dowdy skirts, black lace-up shoes and hats like pudding basins jammed low over their foreheads, were serving tea and sandwiches, he was ushered into the office of Sir Rupert Woodbridge, who, according to the sign on his door, was head of the Criminal Investigation Division.

Nathan was intrigued. Criminal Investigation. Did they think he held the key to some mystery?

As it happened, they did. When he entered, Sir Rupert looked up from the papers in his hand. 'This dispatch from our ambassador in Copenhagen suggests I might want to meet you, Mr Adelstein,' he said, and gestured to Nathan to sit down.

'You are a mystery and a conundrum.' Sir Rupert leaned back in his chair. 'I take it you are a Jewish resident of Palestine, but you are also closely connected with one of the most feared men in the Ottoman Empire, Djemal Pasha, who is our sworn enemy. You've travelled across the world, crossing hostile borders under the noses of Turkish and German authorities. And on top of that, you are apparently part of a spy ring that gathers intelligence about Turkish movements to help us win the war. Mr Adelstein, if I were to write a spy novel I would base my protagonist on you, but I doubt if anyone would find it plausible.'

Nathan smiled. 'Whenever I think about my life, I have exactly the same impression.'

Sir Rupert studied him across the desk with a gaze that indicated genuine interest, and Nathan sensed he may have finally met an official who could help him achieve his goal.

Sir Rupert was scanning the dispatch again. 'How did your extraordinary relationship with Djemal Pasha come about?'

'I'm a botanist and an agronomist, and I run a research institute which is funded by American scientists. That's why he recruited me to try and eradicate the locust plague.' He controlled the impulse to mention his international fame, aware that the understated English did not take kindly to self-promotion.

Under his clipped moustache, Sir Rupert's lips were twitching. 'So you have fought plagues as well, like your forebears in Egypt that the Bible tells us about. Is there no limit to your accomplishments? Next you'll be telling me that in your spare time you're a high-wire acrobat.'

Nathan uttered a short laugh. 'As a matter of fact, I've needed the skills of an acrobat to jump the hoops of indifference that we've encountered in our attempts to convince British authorities that we are risking our lives to help you defeat the Turks.'

He stopped. Sir Rupert's raised eyebrows alerted him to the fact that he was speaking louder, faster and more forcefully than the situation warranted.

'I apologise for my blunt words, but you cannot imagine how frustrating it is to offer our help only to be met with mistrust and disbelief.'

'If you are so highly regarded by one of the most powerful men in the Ottoman Empire, why are you going to such lengths to help us defeat them?'

Nathan took a deep breath. 'The Turks are our enemies as well as yours. They have deported and dispossessed Jews in several towns and we believe this is only the beginning. They have cut down our forests to make railway sleepers and requisitioned our crops and supplies to feed their troops. They've crippled our farms by taking our draught animals, tools and farm machinery. As a result, food has become scarce and people are impoverished and hungry. We've seen how they drove out and killed the Armenians, and we are convinced that unless you defeat them and take control of Palestine, we'll be next.'

Sir Rupert steepled his fingers and sat forward in his chair. 'Exactly what information are you offering us?'

'Information you lack. Your government has no idea how weak Turkish defences are. There are no permanent coastal defences between Haifa and Beirut. Not a single gun from Gaza to Beirut. The coast is poorly patrolled, the guards are very slack, and there is no telephone service along the entire coast. We also have detailed information about the equipment and morale of their troops.'

As he spoke, Sir Rupert looked up from the notes he was making, and nodded.

'How do you know all this?' he asked.

'Some of the information comes from members of our group, and some from my own observations. While travelling around the countryside during my scientific studies and later as locust exterminator, I took note of Turkish military deficiencies all over the country. Our group can supply you with information about Turkish troop movements, rail schedules and so on.'

'Your group. Who are they?'

'They are young Jews, mostly from farming families. All committed to helping Britain win the war at enormous risk to themselves, should they be caught. I'm sure you are aware of the way Turks deal with traitors. My sister risked her life several months ago when she travelled to Egypt to make contact with the British. In Port Said she met Lieutenant Woolley, who promised to send a British boat to collect our intelligence, but that boat has never arrived, and that's why I've come to England, to organise a workable method of delivering our intelligence to your authorities.'

Sir Rupert was frowning. 'Woolley? Not Leonard Woolley from Naval Intelligence?'

Nathan nodded. 'For several months we kept watch for the ship he promised to send while our information was becoming obsolete. Finally we gave up waiting. We figured that Lieutenant Woolley must have changed his mind.'

'You have maligned him. Woolley would never have gone back on a promise. The poor fellow was on board a ship that was mined by the Turks three months ago. Luckily he survived but since then he has been their prisoner at Kastamonu.'

So that was why the arrangement with Woolley had broken down.

'Your sister must be a remarkable woman, to have undertaken a journey like that and convinced Woolley to send a ship. Courage and commitment obviously run in your family.'

After a pause, Nathan said, 'Sir Rupert, you asked me before what useful information we can provide, and I'd like to give you an example. Your army transports water to the desert all the way from Egypt, which is extremely slow and is probably the reason why you haven't taken the offensive against the Turks.'

Sir Rupert looked askance. 'But what's the alternative?'

'You should drill for it in the desert, about three hundred feet down.'

If Nathan had suggested drilling for water in the centre of London, Sir Rupert couldn't have looked more astonished. 'Drill for water in the desert? What on earth makes you think that?'

'I've studied the rock formations. Also the Bible. Solomon described flourishing plants and lush gardens, so there must have been plenty of water. For years I've explored the entire area on horseback and there must be aquifers beneath the sand. Accounts by the historian Josephus also support that theory. I could show your engineers where to drill and I assure you they'd find so much water that they'd no longer need to bring it from Egypt. And that could shift the course of the war in your favour.'

In the silence that followed, Sir Rupert studied the young man in front of him with an incisive gaze. 'You have a point. Water supply would certainly ensure greater mobility against the Turks and speed up the offensive. It would also enable us to steal a march on the French, who are jockeying for a commanding position in the north in anticipation of an Ottoman defeat. There's already talk of a secret treaty to carve up the region between us and them.'

He paused. 'But you must understand my situation. Here you are, clearly an exceptional man with an encyclopaedic knowledge of the terrain and a rare understanding of strategy, offering to provide us with valuable intelligence out of the goodness of your heart, unlike our Arab spies who demand hefty remuneration for scant intelligence.'

Nathan was about to reply when Sir Rupert continued. 'I'm cynical enough to realise that a price must always be paid, though not necessarily in gold. So I can't help wondering if the price of your offer will be an expectation that we will support your efforts to establish a Jewish homeland in Palestine. Isn't that what Mr Weizmann is pushing for in London?'

Nathan had heard that Chaim Weizmann, a fervent Zionist from Manchester, had invented acetone, which had produced the explosives that helped Britain's war effort. Again he tried to reply, but Sir Rupert held up his hand.

'I'd like to acquaint you with another vexing scenario. Lawrence, our man in Cairo's Arab Bureau, is apparently embarking on some kind of crusade to unite the Arab tribes. He also has an agenda. In exchange for their support against the Turks, he wants the Arabs to be given their own nation in northern Palestine and Syria. So do you see our problem? If Britain and France have already agreed to carve up that region between themselves, how are all these conflicting ambitions to be reconciled?'

'Excuse my bluntness, but I am not a diplomat,' Nathan said. 'From what I can see, your fight with the Ottomans isn't going well, and we are offering you intelligence that could turn the tide. The terms of peace can be negotiated later, but if I'm not mistaken, your priority right now is to ensure victory.'

Encouraged by Sir Rupert's silence, he added, 'I understand your dilemma. You don't know if you can trust me, but I have sacrificed everything I've achieved in my academic and scientific life to concentrate on this mission and it coincides with yours. Your victory.'

'Are you a Zionist, Mr Adelstein?'

It was a loaded question, and Nathan took his time while he considered his reply. He knew that Zionism was regarded with suspicion, mistrust and even antipathy by some in the British government, even though some members of parliament seemed to approve of the idea, probably because of Weizmann's contribution to the war effort.

'I believe in its ideals, that in the face of recurrent anti-Semitism we should have refuge in our national homeland, land we have continually inhabited for three thousand years. But I don't believe this should exclude the Arabs who live there now. I envisage an inclusive country where Jews and Arabs have equal rights.'

A young woman with large owlish glasses and light brown hair pulled back into a tight bun stood at the half-opened door. 'Sir Rupert, the commissioner has arrived,' she said.

Realising that the meeting was over, Nathan made a final plea. 'At this very moment my colleagues in Palestine are risking their lives to obtain information for Britain. I hope that you will convey the urgency of our plight and the importance of our offer to those who have the power to decide whether to accept it.'

'I assure you I will do what I can. Please give my secretary your address in London so we can contact you.'

*

After leaving Scotland Yard, Nathan walked with a jaunty step along the Embankment. It was a cold autumn morning and a soft mist rose from the river where barges, tankers and craft of all sizes sailed on the grey water that had flowed through this city for thousands of years. He was confident that Sir Rupert would recommend his offer to his superiors.

But as days passed, optimism turned to disappointment. His hopes rose each time he received a message that an appointment had been made for him to meet a major or lieutenant-general at the War Office, and each time he spent a frustrating hour pleading his cause and explaining their offer to yet another official. They kept him waiting for hours in draughty corridors before asking the same questions. The military authorities he met were unfailingly affable and polite, apart from one who pointed out tersely that Britain's priority in prosecuting the war was Europe, not the Middle East. But they continued to bounce him from office to office without making a decision. To avoid losing his temper he had to keep reminding himself of the importance of his mission. Newspaper accounts of catastrophic British losses during the Somme and Verdun campaigns exacerbated his anger with the British authorities. Although the war was going so badly for them, they still ignored his offer to help defeat the Turks.

At night he seethed at the disappointments and frustrations of the day. He missed Vibeke's warm body and her stimulating conversation. Would they ever meet again? And would she really write that article? Perhaps when all this was over, he would contact her. She might even travel to Palestine to write about a group of spies who had helped Britain defeat the Turks. Lost in this fantasy, he would finally fall asleep.

To fill in the long grey days, he walked from one side of London to the other, hoping that brisk exercise would dissipate his anger. He walked past Hyde Park to Buckingham Palace, and as he gazed at that sprawling grey edifice he wondered what King George would say if he knew that his government had a chance to avail itself of help to defeat the enemy yet refused to take it. He walked from Marble Arch to Piccadilly Circus and sat on a bench in Trafalgar Square watching pigeons defecating on Nelson's head.

Near the Guildhall, troops were parading at the Lord Mayor's Show. 'Cor, look at their khaki uniforms,' he overheard a woman comment to her husband, who replied, 'They're our Dominion troops, bound for the front I shouldn't wonder.' Looking at the young conscripts, Nathan wondered if they were heading for the Middle East, and if so where the assault would take place. That fuelled his fury at the incompetence of the authorities who had failed to see what an advantage their intelligence would be in such a campaign.

After two months of waiting, it was with a sense of hopelessness bordering on despair that he stood outside the baroque Edwardian building that housed the War Office and steeled himself for yet another round of questioning that would lead nowhere. As he waited outside Major Tomlinson's office, he drummed his fingers on his briefcase. No doubt this would be yet another official who would look at him as an oddity who had just stepped out of the Arabian Nights and expected to be taken seriously. As he was ushered inside, he took a deep breath and was about to express his indignation when Major Tomlinson said, 'Well, Mr Adelstein, you'll be relieved to hear your waiting is over. We have arranged to send you to Egypt next week. In Port Said you will meet Major Simpson who will arrange a reliable system for picking up your intelligence.'

While Nathan was trying to absorb this unexpected news, the major added, 'I have long believed that we Christians must atone for all the suffering we have inflicted on the Jews, and that you should have your own state in what is now Palestine.'

Nathan was overwhelmed. Finally his efforts were to be rewarded by officials who were not only willing to accept his offer, but appreciated its value. It seemed too good to be true, but he had no reason to doubt the major's sincerity. Nothing stood between them and the realisation of their mission. If only he could share his triumph with Shoshana and Eli, but he knew it wouldn't be long before he'd be able to tell them in person.

CHAPTER TWENTY

Port Said, 1917

As soon as Nathan arrived in Port Said, he made straight for Major Simpson, whose air of cool formality he found disconcerting. He supposed it was typical British reserve.

'So good of you to come,' the major began. He didn't smile and spoke with great deliberation. 'Major Tomlinson has sent a glowing account of your offer, recommending we put Lieutenant Woolley's plan into action as soon as possible. As a result, I have instructed Captain Edwards, the skipper of MS *Victoria*, to sail to Atlit to pick up the intelligence from your people later this week.'

Although Nathan knew he should resist sounding overenthusiastic, he couldn't control his elation. 'You can't imagine what a relief it is to know that we can finally start passing information on to your authorities. It will be an even bigger relief for my colleagues, who must be feeling very anxious as they haven't heard from me in such a long time and have no idea where I am, or whether I've succeeded in contacting you. I can't wait to see them again and tell them the news myself.'

Major Simpson was frowning. 'I don't think you quite understand. You will not be on board the *Victoria*. The people at the Arab Bureau have informed me that you must stay in Cairo.'

Nathan thought he had misheard. 'Stay in Cairo? But I have to go to Atlit and talk to my group.'

'I'm afraid that won't be possible. It's too risky for you to return to Palestine.'

The major's tone had the finality of a military officer accustomed to giving orders that were never questioned, but Nathan couldn't control his indignation.

'I don't think *you* understand, major. I've been away from home for over three months because it's taken all that time to contact your superiors in London to get them to accept an offer that will help your war effort. In all that time, my group have continued risking their lives collecting information, not knowing where I was, whether I'd been successful or when I would be back. And now you're telling me that I won't be able to set foot in Atlit to see them or give them the news in person. Do you really expect them to hand over such valuable intelligence to a complete stranger?'

Major Simpson surveyed Nathan for a time and his eyes hardened. 'Perhaps you fail to place a high enough value on your strategic importance to us, or to understand the perils of travelling to an area controlled by the Turks.'

Nathan couldn't suppress a sarcastic laugh. So after ignoring and dismissing his offer for so long, they suddenly decided he was indispensable.

'The danger is something I am well aware of, having spent a great deal of time exploring the region to gather information that will help you.' His voice rose. 'The people in my spy network are risking their lives every single day right now gathering intelligence in the hope that the British will deign to accept it. I have spent months knocking on doors to convince your authorities that we are genuine. And now that I've succeeded, it's intolerable that I can't see my colleagues and pick up their intelligence.'

Major Simpson surveyed him with an expression that indicated shock at such insubordination, and Nathan knew he had crossed the line between urbane discussion and impolite argument, but he no longer cared. Instead of being appreciative, these people were treating him like a lackey, forcing conditions on him even as they acknowledged his value.

They stared at each other without speaking. Eventually the major broke the silence. In a more conciliatory tone he said, 'I do understand your concern. I will inform Captain Edwards that on this occasion you will sail with him to Atlit and go ashore very briefly to make contact with your people, but you will go back on board for the return voyage. After this, you will have to make further arrangements with Sir Hugh Gardiner-Hall in Cairo.'

It was unsatisfactory, but Nathan realised he had no choice but to accept. At least he would be able to see Shoshana and tell her the latest developments so that they could continue their work with renewed confidence.

He knew he should thank Major Simpson, but the words stuck in his throat. As the horse-drawn carriage trundled over the roads taking him to his hotel, he went over the interview and felt increasingly frustrated at his powerlessness. Inside his hotel room, he unpacked his valise and stared at the grey waters of the Suez Canal. He tried to shake off his malaise and comfort himself with the knowledge that in a few days he would see Shoshana and Eli again.

The following day he met Captain Edwards at the wharf and realised that no matter how bad things were, they could always get worse. The captain was a short, nuggetty navy man whose gruff, contemptuous manner made it clear that he mistrusted Nathan and resented having to take part in what he regarded as a waste of time and effort on behalf of a group of people for whom he had no sympathy. Pointing at Nathan, he said to a crewman, 'You wouldn't believe it, his lot reckon they're going to help us win the bloody war!'

The day before they sailed for Atlit on the small fishing trawler, Nathan bought provisions to distribute among the residents of Zichron Yaakov. But when he arrived at the wharf with bags of flour, sugar, condensed milk, cocoa and coffee, Captain Edwards, arms akimbo, barred his way and refused to let him bring them on board.

'I have to bring them. People there are in desperate need of food. They are starving,' Nathan protested.

Captain Edwards shrugged. 'That's not my problem. My orders are to get there and pick up some so-called intelligence, not to deliver food,' he said.

Pleading, arguing, accusing and appealing to his better nature had no effect and Nathan was forced to leave the precious supplies behind. He tried to calm himself with the thought that he would soon step on the shore of Atlit and see Shoshana and Eli, but he fumed at Captain Edwards' insolence.

*

The first part of the voyage proceeded smoothly and as soon as the silhouette of the ruined castle appeared in the distance that afternoon and the research station came into view, the trawler gave the agreed signal and Nathan was thrilled to see the white sheet hanging from the upstairs window. Only a few more hours and he'd see them again. Focussed on his political quest, he had almost forgotten how much he missed wandering among the hills of Mount Hermon, listening to the soughing of the trees, and breathing in the scent of the wildflowers.

Time passed slowly until darkness fell and the trawler turned back towards Atlit. Although the sea had been calm all afternoon, Nathan felt a strong breeze on his face. The wind picked up and foam-tipped waves slapped against the trawler with increased power. By the time the station came into view again, the boat was rocking so much that he had to grip the rail to stop himself falling. He scanned the balcony with binoculars and to his delight, he saw someone standing there watching the boat. Was it Shoshana? Or Eli? He was unable to make out who it was but their steadfastness touched him. After all this time, they were still keeping vigil.

The wind blew stronger and the sea grew rougher and tossed the small trawler from side to side so violently that the sea towered above the gunwales with a roaring sound. On shore, the wind was thrashing the trees whose branches swished and swayed. Nathan looked anxiously at Captain Edwards just as they heard a clap of thunder and saw lightning zigzag against the black sky.

'There's no way I'm lowering the boat in this storm,' the skipper announced and turned the ship away from the coast back to the open sea.

The station receded and Nathan's heart sank. 'What happens now?' he asked. 'Your orders were to land at Atlit and pick up documents.'

'I don't need you to tell me what my orders are,' Captain Edwards snapped. 'That lightning is like a torch. Makes us an easy target for a Turkish patrol. Besides, even you must be able to see that it's impossible for a rowboat to make it ashore. It would capsize.'

Nathan knew he was right. 'If the wind subsides, shall we try again?'

Without replying, the skipper stomped away.

Half an hour later, a miracle happened. The storm was over, the wind dropped, and Nathan was overjoyed to see the boat turning around and sailing towards Atlit once more. The captain gave the order to lower the rowboat, but when Nathan prepared to step into it, Captain Edwards shouted, 'You're staying on board. I have to get you back to Cairo in one piece. This tide could change in a second. Our boatman Abdul will pick up your so-called intelligence.'

Nathan's mouth tightened into a straight line. He had trouble speaking in a civil tone. 'They don't know Abdul so they won't give him the documents.'

But Captain Edwards was facing him in a challenging stance, and he realised there was no alternative. 'I'll give him my compass to show my sister. She'll recognise it and know she can trust him,' Nathan said, and took it out of his pocket.

Captain Edwards nodded. It was the first time he had shown approval of anything Nathan had said. As Abdul placed the compass in a waterproof bag, Nathan was seething. The skipper had cheated him of his chance to go ashore, but at least when Abdul showed her his compass, Shoshana would know he had returned from London, and had been successful.

No sooner had Abdul started rowing than the wind started whipping the waves until the sea resembled a boiling cauldron and the small rowboat seemed to be swallowed up by the waves. Nathan watched anxiously until it became a speck in the distance and disappeared altogether. He paced around the deck, unable to keep still. Surely by now the boatman would have reached the shore. How long would it take him to row back?

Then he looked down and saw the boat struggling in the waves nearby and heard the boatman's weak cry for help.

'I thought I was going to drown out there,' Abdul gasped as the crew pulled him on board.

'But you got to the shore and picked up the satchel?' Nathan asked.

The boatman was shivering and his teeth were chattering. 'Not a chance. I got close but I couldn't land. The tide kept sucking me back. It was like trying to row in quicksand.'

The captain gave Nathan a disgusted look, swore about the waste of time and effort, and without another word turned the trawler around towards Cairo. Nathan took one last heartbroken look at the shore. Until the next moonless night brought the trawler back to attempt another landing, Shoshana and Eli would not know that he was in Cairo, or that everything was ready to put their plan into action. Had they given up hoping to deliver their intelligence? How long would they continue to gather it? As he focussed his binoculars on the station, he saw a lone figure standing there. He thought it was Eli.

CHAPTER TWENTY-ONE

Atlit, 1917

The atmosphere inside the research station crackled with tension. Eli looked at Shoshana. 'Every month when the moon is dark we keep watch for a ship blowing smoke in the afternoon, and I keep hoping it's the spy ship come to pick up our intelligence. But this is now the third time we have seen a ship appear to give the signal, and we've hung out the sheet, and gone down to the beach in the middle of the night, but no one has arrived.' His face was set. 'It's time to stop hoping for a miracle. We have to do something. It's been over three months now and we haven't had a word from Nathan since he left Denmark. We can't just sit around waiting for him to come back.'

'He's right,' Aaron said quickly. Too quickly, Shoshana thought.

'For all we know Nathan could be in prison or in an English hospital,' he continued.

Beside him, Benyamin hadn't taken part in the discussion. Unlike his companions, he was slow to give his opinion until he had heard all points of view. So when Aaron turned to him for support, instead of replying he glanced at Shoshana and waited to hear what she said.

'I hate this uncertainty as much as you all do,' she said slowly, 'but what can we do except wait?'

Aaron and Eli exchanged complicit glances and in that instant she knew they had already formed a plan.

'We don't know how long it will take for Nathan to get back and we can't contact him,' Benyamin said in his measured way. 'If you recall, it took over a month before he even left Denmark, so who knows how long it will take him to find someone in London who'll listen to him. That's if they haven't already arrested him as an enemy alien.'

He was about to go on but Eli broke in, impatient with his summing up. 'We've already seen how slow the English are at making decisions. And what do we do in the meantime? What do we tell our people? That they should keep risking their lives gathering information that might be obsolete by the time Nathan gets back? Or should we put a stop to everything we've worked for, and disband?'

The same unsettling thoughts had kept Shoshana awake for the past few nights. She sighed. 'So what do you suggest?'

Eli moved towards her but she held herself back, resisting the urge to lean into him and feel his strength.

'As a matter of fact, I've figured out what to do,' he said and again that look passed between him and Aaron, whose eyes hadn't left her face since the discussion began.

Her body tensed as she waited.

'We have to get to Cairo to see what happened to the arrangement you made with Woolley, and to renew our contact with Naval Intelligence,' Eli began.

She frowned. Where was he going with this? They had no way of reaching Egypt. Surely they weren't planning to stow aboard one of the French ships that sailed along the Mediterranean?

'Getting there by ship is impossible on account of the blockade,' Aaron said. 'But there is another way. Eli and I can ride across the Sinai.'

She glanced at Eli but to her dismay he was nodding.

'You can't mean it,' she said. 'Tell me you're joking.'

But he wasn't. She saw that at once from the defiant set of his mouth and the obsidian hardness of his gaze.

At first she was too shocked to speak. Then she said, 'Do you really think that Aaron with his blond hair and blue eyes and that celluloid collar and cravat will fool the Bedouins into thinking he's an Arab?' Her voice rose in frustration. 'I can't believe you're really considering doing this. The Bedouins are tribesmen. They only trust their own clan and kill strangers who trespass on their land. And how do you expect to cross the desert? The minute you stop to drink from their well or rest in an oasis, they'll attack you.'

'We've figured it all out. We both ride camels as well as any Bedouin, and we both speak Arabic,' Aaron said.

Eli broke in, 'The Bedouin chief who tutored me when I was at school has recommended a guide who will fit us out with a traditional thawb robe and a keffiyeh that we'll fasten with an agal rope, so we'll look like Bedouins.'

She was shaking her head. 'This is crazy. Can't you see how reckless and dangerous it is?'

Eli put his arms around her and as he looked deep into her eyes, she felt the steady beating of his heart against hers and couldn't distinguish its rhythm from her own. She looked away.

'Shoshi, what we're doing here every day is far more dangerous. We face a terrible death if the Turks catch us. But unless we get to Cairo and pass on our information to the British, we're all risking our lives for nothing.'

She gripped his hand, digging her nails into his palm. 'There must be another way.'

Benyamin, who had spent many long nights on the beach at Atlit listening to the endless lapping of the waves on the shore as he watched in vain for their ship, looked sympathetically at Shoshana. 'It is dangerous, but Eli and Aaron are right. We have to get to Cairo somehow to find out what's going on,' he said in his considered way. 'Maybe that officer you made the arrangement with changed his mind, or his superiors did. Perhaps the British aren't interested in Palestine. We have to know. But if they're still interested, we need to start passing on information before it becomes obsolete. And I can't think of any other way.'

Eli was nodding. 'And that's why we have to leave tomorrow.'

Shoshana caught her breath. Tomorrow! So this hadn't been a genuine discussion but an announcement, and a justification for action they had already agreed to before last night's failed rendezvous.

Although she was fuming, she said nothing. Here at the station she was outvoted, but that evening, in the privacy of Eli's home and the intimacy of their bed, she would convince him to abandon this reckless plan.

For the rest of the day, she organised their intelligence and attended to the business matters involved in running the station. As usual, she read, collated and filed the secret reports that came in from their members and locked them in the metal tin, and then took care of funding and provisioning the station. Thanks to the high yield of their crops, she was able to distribute much-needed barley and wheat to the impoverished farming families in the area.

But that day she couldn't concentrate. The thought of Eli setting off across the Sinai made her hands shake so much that she had trouble holding her pen. She kept staring out of the window but all she saw was a scene concocted by her worried mind, a scene of two figures wrapped in Arab garb riding across the desert. It was as if a light from some distant galaxy on the outer edge of space had reached her and beamed its menacing message. Unable to continue working, she returned home earlier than usual.

One thought kept hammering in her head. She had to stop him. But while she was rehearsing what to say to dissuade Eli from leaving, she realised she couldn't offer any alternative. Waiting for Nathan was no longer an option, that she knew. Unless they made contact with the British soon, they would endanger themselves for nothing, and her mission to defeat the Turks and liberate the Jews would end as a heap of broken dreams. Reluctantly she confronted the limits of her vision.

That evening when they were alone, she would reason with him, talk him out of this foolhardy plan, and they would find another solution. Her heart pounded with new hope and she rushed to get ready. She brushed her long auburn hair and left it loose and wore the blue skirt and the white blouse with the revealing décolletage that always made his eyes gleam.

Breathless with excitement she was almost out the door when her eyes fell on a porcelain bowl full of fresh dates on the table. They were soft and luscious and on impulse she scooped up two handfuls, wrapped them in a linen cloth, and stuffed them into the pocket of her skirt before rushing to the stable to saddle her mare.

A few heads turned as she rode along the main street of the village, and she noticed a coolness in the greetings she received. Did they suspect her of conducting a clandestine activity that excluded them, or was it just a manifestation of their usual envy? She had expected that to wane when she supplemented their food, but it now occurred to her that perhaps her generosity had only increased their resentment. Perhaps accepting charity didn't engender gratitude.

These possibilities ran through her mind as she rode towards Eli's village but the scenery calmed her unsettled mind. Late afternoon was her favourite time of day. A light breeze eased the exhausting daytime heat, and the setting sun softened the contours of the hills and lacquered the tree trunks and the vines with a golden paintbrush. As she rode over the slopes of Mount Carmel, she tried to focus on the beauty of the landscape and the relaxing rhythm of the mare's cantering gait, but her thoughts continued to slide back into a spongy morass that threatened to suck her down. While she had to try to dissuade Eli from leaving, she already knew she would fail.

She had planned to present her arguments in a quiet, convincing way but as soon as she entered his house, she flung herself into his arms and blurted out, 'Eli, please don't do this. Please. We'll figure out another way but not this.'

He pulled away gently and as he looked at her, the tenderness in his gaze brought tears to her eyes.

He stroked her hair. 'Sit down and I'll put your mind at ease so you can stop worrying.'

She shook her head. How could he not understand that her heart was about to shatter into a million terrified fragments?

'You'll never convince me,' she said. 'I'm so frightened for you, so terrified, I can't think of anything else.'

Sitting side by side on the settee in his living room, he took her cold hands in both of his. He looked into her eyes with an expression that took away her powers of reason.

'You don't need to be terrified. You're my brave warrior princess. Before you know it I'll be back with good news and you'll see that you were worrying for nothing.'

She shook her head. 'I can't shift this blackness from my mind whenever I think of you riding across the Sinai. Don't you realise how dangerous it is, especially now that it's a war zone?'

He didn't reply immediately and the silence implied that he might be considering her words. That he might agree. She held her breath.

He spoke very slowly as if weighing each word before he uttered it. 'Shoshana, the time has come to stop thinking about our own safety. Our cause is much greater than you and me. The only thing that matters is the future of our country and our people. If we risk nothing, we'll gain nothing and we'll lose everything we've fought for. Our only hope is for me to go. You do see that, don't you?'

She swallowed and he tightened his grip on her hands, which he had now warmed with his own. 'My darling, I understand how you feel, but remember that we are two halves of the same soul. Our love will last forever and our souls can never die. Whatever happens we will be together for eternity. Nothing can separate us in this world or the next.'

There was so much she wanted to say but she could not find the words to express the ache in her heart and the depth of her despair.

Instead of returning home that night as she usually did, she stayed with him until morning. As soon as the first light of dawn speared through the curtain, she opened her eyes. She was still cradled in his arms. If only time could stand still so they wouldn't have to move, and the future would never happen. She must have wept in her sleep because her face was wet, and when she raised her hand to wipe the tears streaming down her cheeks, she looked up and saw him gazing at her. Before she could wipe her eyes, he kissed her tears away.

It was time to rise. She was pulling on her skirt when she felt the bulge in the pockets and remembered the dates. She placed them in his hands. 'Take them with you and when you're riding your camel in the Sinai, remember that you're carrying part of me.'

He folded his arms around her and they clung together in the doorway. She felt she was drowning in his eyes, but she was determined to be strong. She would leave him with a smile, not a sob.

'I'll take care of everything at the station until you get back,' she managed to say. Then with trembling fingers she saddled Zahra, mounted, and galloped away. She knew he was still standing there, watching her, and she forced herself to smile as she turned her head for one last lingering look.

CHAPTER TWENTY-TWO

The Sinai, 1917

Eli took one look at Aaron and burst out laughing at the sight of his fashion-conscious friend attired like a Bedouin. 'Your keffiyeh is a bit crooked but apart from that, you look quite convincing,' he said. Eyes sparkling with mischief, he slapped Aaron on the back, excited as a boy heading off on an adventure.

And that's how he felt. At last the frustrating months of waiting were over. The prospect of riding a camel across the Sinai all the way to Egypt to make contact with the British would be an exotic feat straight from the books about intrepid explorers whose exploits he had always admired. How astonished Nathan would be to see them. And Shoshana! He couldn't wait to see her face when he returned triumphant. 'I told you there was nothing to worry about,' he would tease her.

His reverie was interrupted when their guide poked his head into the tent. Faisal was a tall thin man with a turn in his left eye that made it hard to know where he was looking.

'The camels are ready,' he said.

Eli found his gaze disconcerting, unsure whether Faisal was addressing him or Aaron. Faisal had been recommended by Abu ben Abadi, the patriarch of the local Bedouin tribe who had taught Eli to speak Arabic as a boy. He had visited the chief's mud and straw hut to ask his advice about their forthcoming journey. Over warm rounds of flat bread sprinkled with sesame seeds and glasses of cold buttermilk served by his wife, they had sat on rush mats spread on the clay floor and discussed plans for the trip.

Like most Bedouins, the chief resented the Turks and was willing to help Eli and Aaron reach the British.

'You will need a guide,' he had said. 'Faisal is the nephew of my kinsman Abdullah and he knows the desert like the back of his hand. He will provide your clothes and the camels, and he'll guide you across the Sinai as far as Rafah. There you will find the British. May Allah protect you and bless your journey.'

*

Late in the afternoon two days later, everything was ready for their departure.

'We will rest by day and ride by night,' Faisal had announced. 'This will be cooler and also safer.'

Eli had ridden camels since childhood, but he hesitated for a moment before mounting his, bemused that no one he knew would recognise him dressed in a keffiyeh and a robe that flapped around his ankles.

Faisal had finished saddling the camels and stood back watching him. 'I have heard of an Englishman who dresses like a Bedouin and rides at the head of an Arab army that attacks Turkish trains along the Hejaz railway. They trust him like a brother because after they have defeated the Turks, he has promised to give them a homeland in northern Palestine.'

Eli shrugged. 'Then they will be disappointed because it is not his to give.'

Faisal turned away, and Eli wondered if he was offended by his comment. He glanced at Aaron, who was clinging to the reins with white knuckles as his camel unfurled its long legs, dropped on its forelegs and folded in its back legs with a rocking motion, snorting and belching. 'This is like riding a four-storey building,' he muttered.

Eli considered the fading light and looked at Faisal. 'Is it really dangerous to ride by day?'

'Brigands. Armed with rifles and hundreds of cartridges in their belts. If you give a man a gun he is impatient to use it. Sometimes they shoot first and ask questions afterwards.'

As they rode in silence across dunes that undulated like waves of sand towards the horizon, it struck Eli that their route was the reverse of the one taken by the ancient Israelites who had trudged from Egypt to the Promised Land.

The analogy amused Aaron. 'So is Faisal our Moses who will ensure that the sea of sand will open to let us pass?'

Mesmerised by the rhythmic gait of the camel and the hypnotic vistas of the landscape, Eli experienced a rare sense of peace. In his everyday life, his mercurial mind was always planning and analysing, and his body was never still, but now he was forced to slow his pace and allow his mind to adjust to the camel's gait. All around him the sand dunes stretched towards infinity and in that savage indifference of sand and sky, he understood why desert dwellers felt close to God.

Once the blood-red semicircle of the dying sun sank behind the dunes, dark shadows formed patterns on the sand. Night fell quickly in the desert and soon blackness was all around them, bringing with it the blessed coolness that made them shiver.

Eli, familiar only with the desert area close to Zichron Yaakov, was astonished at the variety of landscapes they encountered as they resumed their journey late the next afternoon. The graceful curves of dunes gave way to arid lunar plateaux where lizards darted between clumps of cactus and thistles. Sometimes he looked up to see the horizon blocked by a ridge of purplish mountains whose jagged peaks were silhouetted against the sky as the sun set.

They descended into rugged wadis whose sides had been eroded to form steep canyons where the camels trod carefully on large flat rocks that seemed to exhale the hot breath they had absorbed during the day.

'This is like riding inside an oven,' Aaron mumbled, wiping his forehead as he tilted his head back to drink from his pannikin. Occasionally they heard a flapping of wings high above them and saw the predatory beaks of falcons.

Sure-footed as they were, the camels stumbled as they made their way across the sharp edges of twisting lava troughs, but picked up their pace when they descended to a valley floor whose white sand glittered with quartz. There they stopped to nibble tufts of white-tipped stubble grasses that they chewed until green liquid oozed from their huge lips.

While they rested by day tormented by the savage heat, at night the brilliance of the stars brought tears to Eli's eyes. How beautiful the world was. Humbled by his own insignificance in the face of such grandeur, he wanted to write it all down, to compose a poem that would convey his wonder at the beauty of the desert from its dazzling sunsets to the heart-aching splendour of its dawns, the cosmic miracle that lit up the world every morning.

Throughout the second night they made their way across the desert, grateful for the dawn that signalled they could finally rest. Tapping the camels' necks with the long cane Faisal had provided to make them kneel, they dismounted with a groan and collapsed onto the soft blankets Faisal spread on the ground, too exhausted to eat the burghul and flat bread he prepared for them. Soon they fell into a deep dreamless sleep. When they awoke, it was late afternoon. Time to head off again.

*

Eli woke up to see the sky ablaze in vivid scarlet, flame and tangerine. It was as if he saw the world for the first time. Suddenly it became clear to him that he had spent his entire life struggling against time and yet time was composed of a series of exquisite moments that stretched for eternity. Determined to share this vision with Shoshana before it evaporated into the throbbing air, he reached into his rucksack for paper and pencil, and began to write.

My dearest darling, I feel as if I have just been reborn and under-stood for the first time the unique gift of being alive in this glorious world. I used to think that I could seize the moment and conquer time, but I realise now that I want to savour each moment and gaze at the world with gratitude. Until we are together again, I will hold the silent splendour of the desert in my heart where I hold you. I sense you are with me now, and your heart is beating with mine, for how could it be otherwise when we are two halves of a single soul. My darling girl, I send you a thousand burning kisses, and press them all over your body.

He folded the letter and as he tucked it into a pocket of his robe, his hand came across the small bundle of dates Shoshana had given him, and he smiled. This must be an omen. He took one out and as he chewed its moist sweetness, he knew beyond any doubt that she was there beside him.

He listened for the usual sounds of Faisal preparing their meal or saddling the camels but all was silent. He turned to look at Aaron, who was still asleep. He pulled himself to his feet, stretched, and stood up. That's when he saw that there were only two camels tethered to the thorn bush where there had been three. With a sense of foreboding he looked around. There was no sign of Faisal or his camel.

He shook Aaron awake.

'Faisal has gone,' he whispered.

Aaron rubbed his eyes and yawned. 'Gone where?'

'No idea. He was gone when I woke up.'

'There's probably a simple explanation,' Aaron said. 'Maybe he went to a nearby encampment for provisions and didn't want to wake us. He's sure to be back soon. Anyway, Rafah can't be very far off now.'

But as minutes went by, Eli became more anxious. Without a guide they didn't have much hope of reaching Rafah. And why had Faisal disappeared without a word?

'For all we know, he has a secret sweetheart in one of those Bedouin camps and he stole away to see her.' Aaron was joking but Eli could tell he was concerned.

'We have to make a decision. We're very exposed here by ourselves. How long should we wait for him?'

'Let's wait a while. Anyway, what choice do we have?' Aaron glanced at his watch. 'It's already six o'clock and we should be on our way. If he hasn't turned up by ten, we'll have to get going. We'll use our compasses and head south. Rafah can't be very far from here.'

An unsettling feeling that they were being watched made Eli turn around and his blood froze. Above them, on top of the ridge, seven Bedouin tribesmen on camels looked down on them and nothing about their appearance, from their black garb to the rifles slung over their shoulders, looked welcoming.

Eli leaned towards Aaron. 'That bastard!' he hissed. 'That's why he vanished. He betrayed us!' Turning to the Bedouins he called out with a confidence he didn't feel, '*Salaam alaikum.* We come in peace.'

But there was no customary response and at a signal from their leader, the Bedouins advanced towards them.

The saliva caught in Eli's throat and he couldn't swallow.

'We're with Faisal, Chief Abu ben Abadia's kinsman,' Aaron shouted.

But at the mention of Faisal, they sniggered and repeated the name in mocking voices and that's when Eli knew for certain that Faisal had betrayed them.

Eli scanned their faces and was chilled by the menace in their eyes. Their rifles were pointing at him. 'We are just passing through,' he said, trying to keep his voice steady. 'Tell us what you want. Maybe we can help.'

'Offer them something. My watch or your compass. Anything,' Aaron whispered.

Eli heard something explode inside his head. The sound was deafening and he was about to ask Aaron what it was when to his surprise he collapsed on the ground and saw blood pooling from his chest. Aaron was moving towards him and he gasped, 'Aaron, get away! Go! Save yourself!'

Then he heard another explosion. He opened his eyes and smiled. Shoshana was lying beside him holding him and he felt the beating of her heart. 'Shoshi,' he whispered. 'I knew you'd come.'

CHAPTER TWENTY-THREE

Cairo, 1917

Nathan whistled as he cycled along the paths of the Ghezireh Palace Gardens, past its fountains, grottoes, miniature lakes and ornamental pavilions. For the first time since arriving in Cairo, he felt light-hearted. Finally everything was falling into place.

After the aborted attempt to land at Atlit, he had taken Major Simpson's advice and left Port Said to meet Sir Hugh Gardiner-Hall, the head of British Military Intelligence in Cairo. As usual, what should have been straightforward was complicated by ineptitude. Instead of directing him to Sir Hugh, they shunted him from one indifferent official to another, none of whom knew anything about him. Nathan's temper threatened to explode. He realised he was dealing with an inefficient organisation that consisted of rival groups, each jealously guarding its own little patch; none of them shared information with the others, whom they often tried to undermine.

All this took several infuriating days, but when he was finally led to Sir Hugh's secretary, everything changed. In a voice as crisp as her tailored suit, she said, 'Please come this way. Sir Hugh asked me to show you in at once,' and added, 'He's spitting chips that you've been kept waiting all this time. Heads will roll.'

Hugh Gardiner-Hall sprang from his chair as soon as Nathan came in and pumped his hand so vigorously that it tingled.

'I regret that you've been given the run-around,' he said. 'They should have informed me of your arrival in Cairo but unfortunately this is typical of our bureaucratic organisation where one hand doesn't know what the other is doing. I've been looking forward to meeting you ever since I received the dispatch from England about you,' he said. 'The chaps in London are usually niggardly with their praise, but they lauded you to the skies.'

Picking up a newsletter lying on his desk, he handed it to Nathan.

It was a bulletin the Arab Bureau circulated among its members, and it not only referred to him by name and praised his encyclopaedic knowledge but quoted extensively from the memorandum that he had presented to Sir Rupert in London.

'As you can see, we value your remarkable grasp of the situation on the ground in Palestine and consider ourselves extremely fortunate to be able to avail ourselves of your help,' Hugh Gardiner-Hall said.

Nathan had already been deceived by British officials whose smooth words often served to conceal their true intentions, but this bulletin proved that they trusted him at last. He felt an immediate rapport with this man, but after the humiliation, procrastination and frustration he'd suffered over the past months trying to convince the British to accept their offer, he felt flat. The triumph had been too long in coming.

He looked up from the newsletter. 'Who wrote this?'

'Lawrence in the Arab Bureau. He is convinced that an army comprised of Bedouin Arabs will help us defeat the Turks. He has already led them into battle along the Hejaz railway with considerable success.'

'Lawrence,' Nathan repeated. 'I think that's the man my sister met at Atlit before the war. She met him again in Cairo several months ago and took his advice to see Lieutenant Woolley, who arranged for the transfer of our intelligence. We've been waiting in vain for the ship he promised to send. That's why I've made this journey, so we can set up a reliable way of passing information on to you. Major Simpson did organise a vessel to reach Atlit last week but the seas were too rough to get the rowboat ashore. The ship needs to come regularly so if the weather prevents a landing on one night, we can be confident it will try again the next moonless night.'

Gardiner-Hall was nodding. 'That's exactly what we propose to do. Believe me, I understand how frustrating these delays have been for you. But your waiting is over. The War Office has decided to open a new front in the Middle East and it regards your group as a valuable asset in that campaign. I'm aware that the attempt last week failed due to bad weather, but we will continue to proceed with the arrangement your sister made with Lieutenant Woolley as soon as possible. I heard about your disappointment in not seeing your people, and the next time the ship sails, you will be able to go ashore, but I have to insist that you come straight back here on the return voyage. We can't risk you being captured like Woolley. We will give you an office here at the Savoy Hotel so you can be on hand to advise us.'

'There's something I don't understand,' Nathan said slowly. 'After Lieutenant Woolley was captured, why didn't his office proceed with his plan?'

Sir Hugh made a vague motion with his large freckled hand. 'Because no one knew anything about it. Perhaps he hadn't time to tell anyone about it.'

Nathan remembered Shoshana saying how Woolley's superior had been antagonistic towards her and the plan. That officer certainly knew the details and could have carried them out, but perhaps with Woolley out of the way, he had been happy to bury it.

Now as he cycled out of the palace gardens, still whistling, he couldn't wait to get to Atlit and tell Shoshana and Eli the good news. He tried not to dwell on his bitter disappointment that he wouldn't be able to spend much time with them. The fact that this decision was made on account of his value to the British was a consolation.

Glancing up at the ornate palace building from the street, he saw a row of injured men sitting on the sunlit balcony. Some had white slings on their arms, others had bandages on their heads, and standing behind them were nurses in long white uniforms with red crosses on their caps. He stopped two young nurses walking along the road and pointed. 'Who are those men?'

'Our patients,' one of them replied. 'Many of them are Australians and New Zealanders. After Gallipoli, they had so many casualties that Mena House couldn't cope and they turned this palace into the Australian Hospital. They're waiting up there now to see a convoy of horse-drawn wagons of the 20th Australian Supply Corps coming along the road. If you wait a while, you'll see it.'

At the mention of Gallipoli, Nathan tensed up. It was a stark reminder of British ineptitude and poor intelligence-gathering.

Although he would have liked to see the convoy, he decided to hurry back to his office at the Savoy Hotel, where he was due to brief several members of Military Intelligence about Turkish coastal defences, and to make arrangements for the next voyage to Atlit.

Half an hour later he was sitting at his desk, looking out onto the busy square where horse-drawn carriages were pulling up outside the portico, disgorging visitors and their luggage. Another group coming to see the pyramids. Judging by the voices that floated up to his office, they were Americans. That took him back to his visit to the United States and his meetings with the scientists who had lionised him after his discovery of the original wild wheat.

He sighed. How long ago that seemed. If he had accepted their offer of a professorship in California, he would be pursuing a successful career in academia instead of the precarious existence he was leading now. He had chosen a risky mission of global significance over one that guaranteed personal success but he didn't regret it. In conquering his ego and deviating from the easier path, he reflected that he had finally become the man he had always wished to be.

Lost in thought, he didn't hear the first knock on his door or the second. It wasn't until he heard a sharp rap and a brusque voice calling his name that he sat up with a start and hurried to the door.

Standing there was Captain Edwards, whose abrupt manner had so infuriated him the previous week.

True to form, the captain didn't waste any time on social niceties. 'Where the devil have you been, Adelstein? I've been looking for you all afternoon.'

Before Nathan could reply, he said, 'You're to go to the hospital in Port Said straightaway. They've found one of your people in the Sinai.'

That made no sense. 'It must be a mistake. I don't know anyone in the Sinai. Why do they think it's someone I know? Do you know who it is?'

Edwards shrugged. 'How would I know? The message came from the hospital and they said it was for you.'

There was no point questioning him any further – he was either unable or unwilling to give him any information and, from his past dealings with the man, Nathan suspected the latter.

*

As the train steamed along the track towards Port Said, past fellahin ploughing their fields with oxen in scenes unchanged for centuries, Nathan tried to work out who the mysterious patient could possibly be. It must be either a misunderstanding or a mistranslation. The message was probably intended for someone else.

But as soon as he introduced himself to the businesslike matron inside the hospital, she made it clear that he was the man she was expecting. 'Ah, Mr Adelstein, we've been waiting for you,' she said briskly. Puzzled, he followed her rapid footsteps down long grey corridors, convinced that he would soon reveal her error.

When they came to the end of the corridor, she stopped and gave him a stern look. 'Please don't stay long. After what happened, he is very weak and needs to rest.'

Inside the large ward, men lay in iron beds arranged along the walls. A creaky ceiling fan barely moved the torpid air. A quick scan of the men's faces proved him right. Of course he didn't know anyone here. And then his eyes rested on the man at the far end of the ward. His head and torso were swathed in bandages and his white face contorted with pain, but Nathan recognised those pale blue eyes.

He was looking at Aaron Sokolov.

They stared at each other, Nathan with incredulity, Aaron with relief.

'Thank God you've come,' he rasped through cracked lips. 'I thought I was going to die here without seeing a familiar face.'

A young nurse in a long white apron brought Nathan a wicker chair that took up the entire space between Aaron's bed and the next one, and Nathan sank into it. Of all the things that had happened in the past three months, this was the most baffling.

'What happened to you?' he asked. 'How come you're here? They said something about the Sinai. Is that true? What on earth were you doing there?'

Instead of replying to the barrage, Aaron stared at him and shook with harsh sobs that resounded throughout the ward. Seeing his friend in this state was not only mystifying but alarming. It was incomprehensible.

Aaron's sobs brought the young nurse running back into the ward. 'Are you all right, Mr Sokolov? Do you need anything?'

Aaron shook his head and, with a warning glance at Nathan, she left the ward.

Nathan waited until Aaron's shoulders stopped heaving before repeating his question.

Aaron's voice was so faint that he had to lean closer to hear him. 'We were trying to get to Egypt.'

'What do you mean, we? Who was with you?'

Aaron groaned, closed his eyes, and didn't speak for several minutes while Nathan sighed and tapped his foot on the linoleum floor. 'Speak up. Who?'

In a sepulchral voice, Aaron whispered, 'Eli.'

Despite the heat, Nathan felt a shiver run down his spine. 'Eli? Where is he?' He looked around. 'Is he in here as well?'

In the silence that followed, he wanted to grab hold of Aaron and shake him; he couldn't stand the suspense of not knowing what he already suspected.

'Nathan, Eli is dead.' Aaron groaned and closed his eyes again.

Impatience triumphed over empathy and Nathan hissed, 'For God's sake, man, pull yourself together and tell me what happened out there.'

With a sigh, Aaron struggled to sit up and open his eyes, but before he could get a word out, Nathan asked, 'Why were you trying to get to Egypt?'

One by one, Aaron listed the reasons for their decision: they hadn't heard from Nathan, the ship hadn't come, they were desperate in case their information was wasted. Exhausted by his long speech, he sank back in the bed.

Nathan shook his head. He had a vision of Aaron in his stylish suit and large cravat riding a camel through the Sinai and expecting not to be caught.

'I can't believe you and Eli thought such a crazy plan would work. Did Shoshana know about this?'

Aaron nodded. 'She fought against it, but in the end she realised it was the only solution. We did everything to ensure it would work. We were so well disguised that the Turkish patrols we passed ignored us. And we had a Bedouin guide we thought we could trust, but that's where we made a mistake. On the third day, when we were ready to set off again, he disappeared. The bastard left us there as prey for the jackals he colluded with.'

'Did you know why he deserted you like that?'

'We never saw him again. We'd heard that thieves roamed the desert in search of booty, so I suppose he betrayed us in return for some reward.'

'Then what did you do?'

'Eli thought we shouldn't wait any longer because we were very vulnerable out there by ourselves, and we should ride towards Rafah while it was still dark. We had compasses and reckoned that it couldn't be very far away. That's where the British were.' He stopped and uttered a sound that was almost a chuckle. 'Funny the things you remember. Faisal had left without preparing our meal and Eli was eating the dates Shoshana had given him for the journey. He offered me some but I was too nervous to eat. I couldn't wait to get away. Just as we were about to mount our camels, we looked up and saw a group of Bedouins watching us from the top of the ridge. They were all in black, looking sinister and armed to the teeth. After that everything happened so fast, it's all a blur.'

He shuddered and closed his eyes again.

Without realising it, Nathan was leaning so far forward that he was only centimetres from Aaron's face. 'Go on. You have to tell me exactly what happened.'

'I remember hearing Eli saying *Salaam alaikum*. I think he was trying to explain that we'd come in peace but suddenly they swooped down and started shooting, not just warning shots. I thought that was the end. I yelled at them to stop, that we were friends and meant them no harm but the words froze in my mouth because from the corner of my eye I saw Eli crumple up and fall and blood was pouring from his chest. I rushed over to try and help him up, but he told me to get away as fast as I could. *Save yourself*, he whispered and then he closed his eyes. Nathan, those were the last words he said to me.'

He was sobbing loudly again, and Nathan looked at him with obvious distaste. 'Are you telling me that Eli was wounded, and you just left him there and rode off?'

Aaron looked at him reproachfully. 'I did not abandon him. A moment later I heard more shots. I didn't realise I'd been shot myself. I wanted to reach Eli but I couldn't breathe or move. I thought I was dead.'

'So how come you ended up here and he didn't?' The accusation in Nathan's voice was unmistakeable as he recalled the longing expression on Aaron's face whenever he looked at Shoshana. Had Aaron left Eli alone in the desert to remove his rival?

The look in Aaron's eyes made him ashamed of his suspicion. 'The Bedouins were among us, probably searching for loot, when more shots rang out. I thought they were shooting at us again but the shots came from Australian soldiers who appeared out of nowhere and dispersed the Bedouins. At that point I think I blacked out. All I know is that these Australians saved my life. They brought me here.'

'Why didn't they bring Eli?'

Aaron looked away from his accusing glance and tears glistened in his eyes. 'One of them came to visit me and said Eli was dead by the time they arrived. They were part of a British patrol in Rafah and had galloped towards us when they heard the shots. I asked them to go back and look for Eli's body but they didn't find it.'

There was a tense silence. 'I still can't believe it, Nathan. Our Eli dead. It doesn't seem possible. I wish I had died instead.'

'Still, it was convenient all the same,' Nathan blurted and immediately regretted the comment.

But Aaron had closed his eyes again, so perhaps he hadn't heard.

The young nurse was back. In a disapproving voice she said, 'You should go now. Mr Sokolov needs to rest.'

'I'll come back to see you before I leave Cairo,' Nathan mumbled and hurried from the ward. He couldn't bear to look at Aaron another minute.

*

As he travelled back to Cairo, he kept repeating the words *Eli dead* in his mind but they didn't make any sense. They were merely words with no meaning. That dauntless spirit couldn't have vanished from the earth forever. He could still see Eli's burning gaze and hear the voice that always inspired them to action. He had to be alive. Aaron must have misunderstood. Eli had probably been taken to some other hospital. Perhaps he was one of the soldiers he'd seen on the balcony of Ghezireh Palace.

That possibility sustained him all the way back to Cairo, but as soon as he staggered out of the carriage at the Savoy Hotel, he had to lean against the wall to steady himself as the realisation sank in. Eli was dead, his life wasted, and he lay alone in some part of the godforsaken desert without a grave or even a stone to mark the place where he had died. He would never know that their mission to help Britain defeat the Turks was finally about to bear fruit.

His mind raced. He would be in Atlit in a few weeks, but instead of sharing the triumph of the boat finally arriving, he would be bringing tragedy. How would their co-conspirators react when he told them that one of their leaders was dead? Would they be too demoralised to continue the work? Should he even tell them?

He buried his face his hands. How was he going to tell Shoshana?

CHAPTER TWENTY-FOUR

Zichron Yaakov, 1917

Shoshana woke with a start. Something had pinned her to the bed with a pressure that threatened to suffocate her, squeezing the air from her lungs, the blood from her heart. Her breath came in choking spasms. Trembling, she forced herself to open her eyes. She tried to shift the weight crushing her body but her hands felt only the soft blanket that covered her. She sat up and looked around. Had the ceiling collapsed? But nothing in the room had changed.

Yet nothing was the same and never would be because at that moment she knew beyond any doubt that Eli was dead. She didn't need anyone to tell her. Every cell of her body knew it, every drop of her blood, every vein and every nerve.

Perhaps she was dead too. Was it possible to survive when your heart had been ripped out? She lay down again, then curled up, feeling as if she had shrunk to a dry shell. How could she go on living without him, without seeing his smile or feeling his touch? How would she find the strength to get up in the morning and get through each day when life had become empty and everything in it pointless and futile?

Eli dead? She turned that unthinkable idea over in her mind and rejected it. What had he said that last morning? That their love would last forever. That they shared two halves of one soul. But where was his soul now? How was she to go on living in a world grown dark, its dazzling light extinguished? His energy had always seemed boundless. How could that vanish from the earth?

She went over every passionate word of their last meeting and remembered how she had longed to capture every tender touch, every loving glance, to gather it and hold it tightly and never let go so she wouldn't forget a single moment. She hadn't wanted that night to end and now it would have to last a lifetime.

She didn't know how long she stayed motionless, numb and bewildered, arguing with herself that it couldn't be true, even though she was convinced it was. How could she continue breathing when Eli did not? Did he know he was about to die? She had read somewhere that people always knew. Her mother had known. That's why she had extracted that promise, knowing Shoshana couldn't refuse her dying mother's wish. Deathbed promises were unfair, forcing the living to comply with the desires of the dead. Keeping that promise had almost ruined her life and yet, strangely enough, it had also helped her to discover her destiny. Can we ever foresee the consequences of our decisions?

Her thoughts turned to her mother's death. How had she grieved for her? She remembered keeping busy to dull the ache. Perhaps she had never allowed herself to mourn wholeheartedly, as Leah and her father had, for fear the grief would tear her apart. She had buried it beneath a mountain of household chores.

She remembered how, the day Batya died, they had held a mirror against her mouth and nose, and when no breath moistened its surface, they knew she was dead and gently closed her eyes. Telling their friends and neighbours about her death had intensified the pain she had tried so hard to avoid. They had buried her in the pretty tree-filled cemetery a few hundred metres from their home and carried out the rituals that were supposed to comfort the bereaved but only served to intensify their sense of loss.

But she couldn't close Eli's eyes or follow any rituals because she didn't know where he lay. Had he and Aaron been murdered by a Turkish patrol somewhere in that godforsaken desert? Her grief turned to anger. Why hadn't he listened to her warnings? Was he lying on the ground or was he entombed beneath it? No, not that. She couldn't bear the thought of his warm body lying beneath the suffocating soil.

Was it possible that she was the only person in the world who knew the truth? She sat up again, suddenly enlivened by the thought that if no one else knew, then he wasn't really dead. He would stay alive as long as she kept it a secret from everyone, as long as she didn't say it aloud.

She was startled by a knock on the door. 'Shoshi, are you all right?' It was her father. 'It's almost midday. Is something wrong?'

'My head aches, that's all. I don't feel well,' she mumbled, relieved to find an excuse. 'I think I'll stay in bed.'

'Can I bring you some tea?' he asked. 'You sound hoarse. Do you have a temperature? You might be coming down with a cold. Do you need some aspirin?'

'Don't fuss, Abba. I just need to sleep,' she said.

He must have been undecided what to do but after several moments, she heard his footsteps receding.

She wouldn't tell him. He didn't suspect anything and there was no way for him to find out. But what about their spy network? Should she tell them? Quickly she dismissed that thought. She could never bring herself to tell them. Besides, the knowledge that one of their leaders had died might demoralise them and jeopardise their work.

That must never happen. The work to which they had dedicated themselves and risked their lives, the work Eli had died for, that must not be undermined by fear or grief. Or even death. For one crazy moment it crossed her mind that she should talk to Eli about it and ask his advice as she usually did. He would know the right thing to do and make a joke about it, and they would laugh together. Then the fantasy faded away and she almost laughed at the tragic absurdity of the thought.

If she did tell the others, she reasoned with herself, they would immediately ask for details. How did she know, how did he die, where was he? And what could she answer? The truth was that she knew it in every fibre of her being because they shared one soul. Someone once told her that when one twin dies, the other is immediately aware of their death, no matter how far away they are at the time, and she had always suspected it was true. Now she knew it was true for lovers, too.

She didn't know how long she stayed in her room, dimly aware of footsteps coming and going outside and her father's concerned voice asking how she was feeling as he left a jug of water and bowl of fruit on a tray outside her door. It was only when she heard him say he was about to call the doctor that she staggered from her bed and assured him that she was feeling better. She knew she would break down under the doctor's sympathetic questioning and blurt out her grief. She couldn't risk that. If one person knew, everyone would know.

She glanced out of the window and shielded her eyes, affronted that the sun was shining and the sky was cobalt blue, that the day could be perfect even as the earth spun off its axis and hurtled into space.

Forcing herself to get dressed, her trembling fingers stumbled over buttons as though they had lost the power to carry out any action. Brushing her long thick hair defeated her, and she pulled it into an untidy knot. She sank onto the bed and stared at her hands, wondering if she had the strength to go to the research station and pretend everything was normal. Luckily none of the group would be there, only Dov the caretaker and a couple of Arab labourers.

As she sat there, the clouds that had obscured her mind blew away, and the importance of continuing their mission became clear. She and her small group were waging war against the Ottoman Empire, pitting themselves against its might. No matter what happened to any of them, they had to keep going. Empowered by that thought, she felt stronger. From now on she was in sole charge of their network and she would guide it. Eli had said, *This work is bigger than you and me,* and he was right. She had to steel herself and dedicate herself to it with even more determination than before so that he hadn't died in vain. She had nothing to lose.

The obstacles were merely challenges she would overcome. With Nathan still away, and their fruitless vigils on moonless nights, she knew that the group had become disheartened. A week before she had overheard Benyamin saying to Eli's cousin Berish that Nathan had obviously not succeeded in contacting the British authorities, otherwise why hadn't the ship arrived? They had been devoted and patient, but how long before they lost hope?

She must appear more confident than ever to bolster their belief in Nathan and keep up the conviction that on the next moonless night the ship would surely come.

Her father had already had his lunch and left for the vineyard when she emerged from her room and set out for the research station. Instead of riding Zahra to Atlit as she usually did, she decided to walk. She needed a long walk to plan what she would say next time the group convened.

The air was fresh and pine-scented and as she walked along the avenue of Washingtonia palms, she sensed Eli walking beside her, holding her hand in his. It felt strong and warm, and as always, its grip made her blood race. Then she looked down at her hands. They were empty and always would be. She leaned against the trunk of a palm tree, slid down to the ground and for the first time she wept.

When she entered the station, she was shocked to see four colleagues sitting around the long table. She had forgotten that she had asked them to meet that day to discuss their progress. As she looked around the room, she realised that Aaron wasn't there. She hadn't given him a thought. He and Eli had set out together, so where was he?

She took a deep breath. There was no time to think. She had to get hold of herself and focus so they wouldn't suspect anything. They stopped talking as soon as she came in, and from the way they looked at her, she sensed that she had been the subject of their conversation. They looked subdued and even Benyamin, who had recently managed to obtain information about the Turkish military build-up and the increase in the number of patrols, spoke in a flat voice that lacked his usual enthusiasm.

While he spoke, Shoshana's eyes strayed to the empty chair where Eli usually sat and suddenly the room blurred. Wiping her eyes quickly, she said she had a cold. As soon as Benyamin finished giving his report, Tova glanced around the table as if seeking approval to speak up on their behalf.

'Shoshana, we can't go on like this,' she said. 'We haven't had a word from Nathan in over three months, and we haven't had a word from Eli and Aaron. Surely they can't still be crossing the desert. We're wondering what's the point of all this information-gathering when it's being wasted. It feels as if we're risking our lives for nothing.'

Shoshana nodded. 'I understand how you feel. You've all been doing a magnificent job and of course you need to know what's going on.' She swallowed and cleared her throat. 'I have wonderful news. Eli and Aaron are in Egypt. They crossed the Sinai and are meeting with the British authorities in Cairo to arrange passing on our intelligence.'

They were all talking at once, rejoicing at her news and asking for details. 'That's fantastic. Thank God they're safe,' Tova said.

Benyamin was quieter than the others. 'When did you find out?'

'In a coded letter that arrived yesterday. It sounds as if they have received great encouragement from the British. That's all I know at the moment.'

Her eyes rested on Tova and she remembered that the girl had unwittingly revealed to Leah the fact that Nathan was away. 'But you mustn't say a word about this to anyone. We'll just carry on as usual, but you'll see, it won't be long before a ship arrives to collect our intelligence.'

'And what about Nathan?' Tova wanted to know.

'He has met with Eli and Aaron,' Shoshana said. She forced herself to smile. 'All the authorities are making a big fuss over him. I think they've finally realised how remarkable he is. But we always knew he would succeed, didn't we? As we all know, Nathan never fails.'

She marvelled at the conviction in her voice. She had never suspected she could lie so easily, but the importance of their cause justified the falsehood. They had to continue the work that had become her life's mission. She had concealed Eli's death to ensure that it would continue. But a small voice in her head asked whether that was the real reason, or whether she had done it to protect herself from speaking words she was desperate to deny. What would happen when they discovered her lie?

She couldn't allow herself to dwell on that. Had she crossed the fine line between intuition and delusion? But perhaps it wasn't a delusion after all, because as long as she maintained the fiction, as long as she didn't say the words aloud, Eli was still alive.

*

That evening, she walked to the small cemetery in Zichron Yaakov where her mother was buried and sat on the soft loam surrounded by the cedar and eucalyptus trees that shaded Batya's grave. Here, in the only place where she was obliged to be honest, she allowed herself to admit that Eli had died. Here she didn't have to hide her tears. In the stillness and silence all around her, she heard his voice assuring her that their love would last until the end of time.

Everything depended on her now, she realised as her fingers traced her mother's name on the cold stone. She had brought people into this dangerous enterprise, and no matter what happened, she couldn't let them down. She had to be true to her vision and find the strength to continue the work she had begun. The survival of the Jewish communities in Palestine depended on it. As she rose and walked slowly away from the cemetery, she realised she had just made her mother another promise.

CHAPTER TWENTY-FIVE

Atlit, 1917

'There won't be a moon tonight so we'll watch out for a signal from the British spy ship this afternoon.'

Shoshana's tone indicated her conviction that the ship would arrive and made contradiction unthinkable. 'We'll hang the white sheet from the window even if we haven't seen the signal in the afternoon, and Benyamin and I will go down to the shore to watch for the ship. Tova will watch with Berish from the upstairs window of the station.'

Tova continued staring fixedly at the notes in front of her while Berish and Benyamin glanced at each other and quickly looked away again. Their scepticism was unmistakeable, but Shoshana pressed on with instructions.

Two weeks had passed since their last meeting, and she marvelled that she had managed to collate their intelligence, direct their activities, and run the research station as though nothing had changed. She hardly slept, and the leaden feeling in her chest hadn't lifted, but by some miracle she was still breathing. Why hadn't she broken down, why hadn't her tears dried up and her hair turned white with sorrow? It felt as though she had turned to steel. She had never imagined she had so much strength, but she was convinced that Eli's energy had flowed into her body. Nothing mattered now apart from their mission.

She didn't allow herself to speculate how she would buoy their spirits if their hopes were dashed once again. What if Nathan hadn't contacted the British authorities? Or if the British had changed their minds? She brushed her fears aside. She had faith in Nathan. The ship would come. It had to.

The day dragged on as she paced up and down, unable to concentrate on any task. Late in the afternoon, she was at the window, lost in a reverie about Eli, when she stared at something dark on the horizon. Was it a figment of her imagination again? But it was emitting dark smoke and sounding its horn and her heart thumped against her ribs as she shouted to Benyamin and Tova, 'It's here! Our ship is here at last!' Her prayers had finally been answered. She flew upstairs and hung the white sheet out of the window and watched as the vessel turned around. She knew it would wait out of sight until midnight and then return, just as Woolley had arranged.

This time everything must run smoothly, and Shoshana rushed to prepare. She took the metal box from its hiding place in the cupboard and placed the thick packet containing their intelligence into an oilskin pouch, ready to be delivered.

Glancing out the window, she saw a carriage pull up outside. Two men alighted from it, and she recognised them as botanists from Tel-Aviv who had come once before to study the station's methods of propagating richer yields of wheat and barley. Usually she welcomed opportunities to share their agricultural success with other scientists, but this was the wrong time.

Flustered, she apologised that she had to leave unexpectedly and asked them to come back another time. As soon as they left, she gave Dov the caretaker the rest of the day off. Nothing must endanger their first successful connection.

Close to midnight, she asked Berish and Benyamin to go down to the beach to meet the ship. If the tide was rough, the rower might need two men to help bring the boat ashore. She and Tova would keep watch from the station.

*

On board the MS *Victoria* that afternoon, Nathan could hardly control his excitement as the British boat he had boarded in the harbour of Port Said approached the coast of Palestine and he had his first glimpse of his homeland in many months. Through his binoculars he identified the coasts of Jaffa and Caesarea, and finally the silhouette of the ruined Crusader castle at Atlit came into view. He pointed it out to Zvi Bernstein, who was also on board. Zvi, who lived in a neighbouring village, was a stocky man in his early forties with the broad shoulders of a man used to physical labour. He had been a muleteer with the Zion Mule Corps attached to the British army in Gallipoli and had distinguished himself by being one of the first members of this Jewish supply group to throw himself into the fighting, even though they had not been provided with weapons. When Nathan had run into him in Cairo, he remembered hearing about Zvi's extraordinary courage and swimming prowess and had asked the captain to include him on the voyage in case someone had to swim ashore. This time Abdul had been unable to join them, and although Captain Wilson, the skipper of the *Victoria* on this voyage, had engaged another Arab boatman, Nathan had insisted on bringing Zvi as well.

Now the trawler was belching black smoke and Captain Wilson ordered the horn to sound the signal. Nathan trained his binoculars on the research station and after a few minutes let out a triumphant cry when he saw the white cloth hanging from the upstairs window.

'They're keeping vigil,' he said to the skipper, his voice hoarse with emotion. 'The coast is clear for tonight's delivery.'

Captain Wilson nodded. He was a man of few words, a welcome contrast to the pugnacious Captain Edwards, whose attitude had been a constant source of exasperation. As arranged, he turned the boat around to wait out of sight several miles from the coast.

*

At midnight, when the sky was dark, Captain Wilson turned the *Victoria* back and moored her about a mile away from the coast of Atlit.

'We have plenty of time for the delivery,' he said. 'It won't be getting light until dawn.'

They lowered the rowboat carefully into the water and the skipper, Nathan, Zvi and the young Arab climbed down the rope ladder to step into it. It rocked under their weight and Nathan gripped the waterproof oilskin package with letters and money he had brought. As they drew closer to the shore, he could hardly keep still. It wouldn't be long before he would see Shoshana again. There was so much he wanted to tell her, so much had happened since he'd left home. Berlin, Copenhagen, London, Cairo. He had been tossed about on a rollercoaster of emotions, frustrations and triumphs in the past few months. He had been forbidden to go ashore in Palestine, but if she was waiting on the beach, he would talk to her there. Then he sighed. He would have to tell her about Eli.

He was figuring out how to break the news, when he noticed that the boatman was having trouble keeping the boat steady. The wind had whipped up the waves, which were rising dangerously above the gunwales and tossing the small boat from side to side.

The skipper was saying something but the wind blew away his words. He leaned towards Nathan and spoke into his ear. 'The surf is too wild. This is as close as we can get to the beach. The men will have to swim ashore from here.'

The Arab scanned the water and shuddered. 'Look at the tide. It's too dangerous.'

The skipper shrugged. 'In that case I'm afraid we'll have to return to the ship.'

Nathan looked at him in dismay. Surely not, now that they were so close?

Then he heard Zvi say, 'I'll swim ashore.'

As Nathan surveyed the churning water he felt apprehensive, but there was no choice. Hurriedly he explained what Zvi should do when he reached the shore. If no one was waiting for him on the beach, he was to make his way to the station alone and say he had a message for Shoshana.

Zvi nodded as he stripped off his clothes and strapped a large leather satchel onto his bare back. It contained his clothes, Nathan's oilskin packet of letters, a wad of cash, a torch, and a bottle of whisky that Captain Wilson slipped inside at the last moment.

'I don't need that,' Zvi protested. 'It's going to weigh me down and anyway I don't drink whisky.'

'You'll be glad of it later,' the skipper said.

Just as Zvi was about to dive in, Nathan realised that as no one at the station knew him, they wouldn't deliver the precious documents. His hands shook as he tore his medallion off his neck. 'Give this to my sister,' he said. 'She'll recognise it and know that I sent you.'

A moment later they heard a splash and saw Zvi cutting through the wild waves with strong strokes. Watching anxiously from the boat with his binoculars, Nathan found the tension unbearable. Every few moments it looked as though Zvi had been swallowed up by the turbulent water, and he held his breath until Zvi's head reappeared above the foam-crested waves.

*

Watching from the beach, Benyamin and Berish saw a stranger emerge from the water and collapse on the sand. As they ran towards him, they saw him toss a large package off his back, remove a bottle and take a long swig from it. He had just hauled himself to his feet and was pulling on a sweater when they reached him.

'Who are you?' Benyamin demanded. 'What are you doing here?'

Still shivering and gasping, Zvi couldn't get a word out and his legs buckled under him. 'Shoshana,' he stammered. 'Shoshana.'

'Why do you want her?'

'Nathan. Have to see Shoshana.' Suddenly he remembered the medallion but as he pulled it out of his pocket, it fell from his trembling fingers, and he switched on his torch.

Berish lunged at him. 'Turn that off!' he hissed. 'Do you want the Turks to see us?'

Zvi scrabbled around in the dark until he felt the metal chain and handed it to Berish. 'From Nathan. Said give it to Shoshana.'

'We'll take you to her,' Benyamin said. They started walking but Zvi's muscles were cramping. Benyamin picked up the oilskin satchel while Berish hoisted Zvi to his feet and supporting him on both sides they half dragged him towards the station.

An hour later, Shoshana and Tova heard knocking on the door and saw their colleagues holding up a bedraggled stranger who seemed about to faint.

'He's from the ship. Says his name is Zvi and Nathan sent him,' Berish said, holding out the medallion.

Shoshana's fingers closed around it and she knew that Nathan's mission had succeeded.

She stared at the man whose teeth were chattering. 'You swam all the way from the boat in that wild surf?'

All he could do was nod.

While Tova ran upstairs for a blanket to wrap around him, Shoshana made him tea. She had a thousand questions but knew she would have to wait until he had recovered from his ordeal.

He took the oilskin package from his leather satchel. 'From Nathan.'

She opened it and saw three thick letters. With trembling fingers she tore open one of them and scanned it for news of Eli. Filled with Nathan's small writing, it contained pages of instructions about distributing the cash among their villagers. She put it aside and started reading the second letter which described his experiences in Berlin and Copenhagen and his frustrating encounters in London in minute detail. The third listed the information that the British authorities had asked them to provide about Turkish coastal defences. *They have said I am too valuable to them to go ashore in Palestine,* he wrote. So the British had finally recognised the importance of their offer.

But not a word about Eli. Was it possible that Nathan didn't know? For a comforting instant, she allowed herself to indulge the fantasy that she had been mistaken all along and Eli was alive after all. But she knew that was a forlorn dream. If Eli had survived crossing the desert, he would have reached Cairo long ago, and Nathan would have met him. Nathan was keeping it from her.

After draining two cups of scalding tea, Zvi recovered sufficiently to talk about the voyage and his struggle in the wild surf, but when they asked him about Eli and Aaron, it was clear that he didn't know anything. Shoshana controlled her urge to ask for more details. Having assured her colleagues that Eli and Aaron were in Cairo, she was reluctant to ask too many questions that might expose her lies.

She took the bulging packet containing the intelligence they had gathered from the metal box, wrapped it in the oilskin pouch, and handed it to Zvi, whose hands were still pale and crinkled from their long immersion in water. He seemed to be considering something. 'It's very heavy,' he said.

Making the first delivery of their intelligence was such an occasion that she felt they should mark it with some ceremony. Taking a flask of wine from the kitchen she poured each of them a glass to toast it. Then turning to Zvi, she said, 'We're very grateful to you for braving this dangerous surf to reach us. Thanks to you, we'll make our first delivery, which I hope will be the first of many that will help to defeat the Turks.'

She could see that he longed to stay and ease his fatigued body in that warm room, but it was already past three in the morning and by the time he got back to the beach it would soon be getting light. With a sigh he rose and left the station, accompanied by Berish and Benyamin. Shoshana watched until they disappeared in the darkness, elated and despondent at the same time. If only she could share this news with Eli. How thrilled he'd be to know that they had just made the connection for which he had lost his life.

*

When the three men reached the shore, they looked at each other in alarm. The waves were even wilder than before, and rollers towered above the beach before crashing onto the sand with a frightening roar. Zvi shivered as he stripped off his clothes and stuffed them into the leather satchel with the oilskin pouch. He glanced uneasily from the satchel to the surf as if considering what to do. Then he shook his head and removed the oilskin pouch from the satchel and handed it to Benyamin.

'I don't know if I can make it back to the ship in that surf, but there's no way I'll make it with that weight on my back.'

They stared at him. 'What do you mean?' Benyamin said. 'This is the last stage. You can't leave these documents behind. All you have to do is swim back to the ship. Come on, man, you've already done it once tonight.'

'But not in this surf. If the current rips the satchel off me, as it probably will, your documents will be lost. It's safer to leave them here. Perhaps the skipper will come back tomorrow night.'

And with that he plunged into the roiling water and they watched as he battled waves that threatened to drown him.

The two men walked back to the station in silence, heads down, shoulders hunched, dreading having to break the news to Shoshana.

*

As soon as she saw their dejected faces and the oilskin pouch, the colour drained from her face and she sank into a chair.

'We tried to persuade him to take it but he refused.' Berish almost spat the words out.

The bitter disappointment of that moment almost defeated her, but somehow she found the strength to stand up and look straight into their eyes. In a confident voice she said, 'We can't control the tide. This is just a temporary setback. The main thing is that our connection has been established and everything is in place for our delivery when the ship returns.'

CHAPTER TWENTY-SIX

Zichron Yaakov, 1917

Shoshana turned the pages of the almanac and marked out the next moonless night. Another two weeks to wait. Ever since the aborted mission, time had dragged and she spent most of the day at the research station, trying to pass the long hours cataloguing plants. With a sigh she pushed away the latest slides and glanced out the window. To her surprise, she saw Dan, Miriam's youngest brother, and his friend Noah dart out of sight behind the building.

Apart from occasional visits by botanists, no one came to the research station, and as she watched the boys' stealthy approach, surprise turned to suspicion. The boys ran a few metres, hid behind the trunk of a Washingtonia palm, looked around as if to ensure no one had seen them, and dashed towards the next tree.

What were they doing here? She ran down the timber stairs two at a time, pressed herself against the doorway, waited until they reappeared, and stepped outside to confront them.

'What are you looking for?' she asked.

Startled, Dan backed away and looked down at his feet. 'Nothing,' he mumbled. 'Just came up here to have a look.'

'Nothing wrong with that, is there?' Noah's voice held a challenge. 'We were wondering what you do up here.'

Shoshana looked from one to the other. 'Well, since you're interested, come in and I'll show you. Maybe you'd like to work here. I could do with some help collecting plants and identifying them.'

She saw them exchange an awkward glance, trying to back out of the situation they'd stumbled into.

'It's all right, Miss Shoshana,' Dan said, pointing to the bicycles leaning against one of the palms. 'We're on our way to the Crusader castle anyway.'

But she wasn't going to let them off the hook. She didn't know what had prompted their secretive visit but whatever it was, she felt she had to impress on them that the work they did here was botanical.

She led them into the laboratory and pointed to the glass slides containing plant specimens, and the wooden boxes containing thick folders of catalogued plants.

'Botany is fascinating,' she said. 'It's the basis of life on our planet. Here, have a look through the microscope.'

They were fidgeting and she took her time pointing out the individual properties of various plants, enjoying their discomfiture.

'Next time you want to come here, all you have to do is ask me,' she said. 'You don't have to sneak in.'

They feigned interest in the collection and after apologising for the intrusion, turned to leave. At the bottom of the stairs, Dan turned around. 'It's just that your brother is the botanist and with him being away, we were wondering what you did here.'

It might have been an innocent comment, but she doubted it.

*

Late that afternoon Shoshana was thinking about Dan's comment as she watered the bushes in their courtyard at home when she saw

Miriam cross the street and come towards her with a purposeful step and tense expression. As they rarely spent time together these days, she wondered what Miriam had on her mind. Ever since her return from Turkey, they had grown more distant, and Shoshana knew she was to blame. Whenever Miriam had suggested going for a walk or attending a performance at the community hall, she had made excuses. It wasn't just that she was overwhelmed organising the spy ring and the need to keep it secret. Whenever she saw Miriam she felt awkward, and wondered whether her father had told her about the thoughtless request she had made in Constantinople.

But there was another reason, too. Increasingly over the past year she had noted Miriam's resentful comments about Nathan and realised that her friend was hurt by Nathan's lack of interest. Perhaps Miriam felt that Shoshana could have done more to foster their relationship. 'You're his sister,' she said once. 'Can't you put in a good word for me?'

Shoshana had confided this suspicion to Eli, who had thrown his arms around her and said, 'I love the way you feel responsible for other people's problems.' Although Nathan had never given Miriam any encouragement, Shoshana suspected her friend still hoped that one day she and Nathan might become engaged, as their mothers expected. But it was a vain hope. She felt sorry for Miriam whenever she asked when Nathan was coming home, and dreaded having to explain his protracted absence.

Apart from that, keeping secrets made it impossible to share confidences, and there was too much going on in her life to conduct a genuine friendship. Miriam's inquisitive nature would turn any conversation into a potential minefield and she would have to watch every word she uttered. But it occurred to her now that Miriam's unexpected appearance this afternoon offered a good opportunity to raise the subject of the boys' mysterious visit and find out whether she knew anything about it.

Miriam's expression lightened when Shoshana invited her inside and for a while it felt like old times. She poured two glasses of tea from the samovar and placed them on the table beside a plate of raisin biscuits she had baked.

Miriam looked around the room. 'It's such a long time since I've been here,' she said pointedly. 'We used to be so close. I don't understand what happened.'

Shoshana didn't recall closeness. They had always been friendly but not friends. She remembered Miriam's envious eyes scrutinising her new clothes and her constant questions about Nathan's activities.

'That's life, I suppose,' Shoshana said vaguely. 'People grow apart.'

She asked Miriam about her brothers and soon found the opening she was seeking. 'I hadn't seen Dan for a long time but to my surprise he came up to the research station today. Did you know he was coming?'

Miriam cleared her throat and shifted her weight on the brocade couch. After a pause she said, 'As a matter of fact, I did.' She was fiddling with a loose thread on her blouse. 'Shoshana, there's something I want to talk to you about.'

Shoshana gripped the glass in her hands to keep them steady and waited.

'Everyone is wondering what's going on,' Miriam began in her blunt way.

Shoshana's heart was hammering but she managed to sound calm. 'Going on? What do you mean? And who is everybody?'

'Don't pretend. Nathan has been away for – what is it – three or four months now? Where is he? What's he doing?'

Shoshana shrugged. 'I'm sure I've told you. He's attending various scientific conferences and advising academic groups about increasing grain yield. I don't need to remind you that with the war still raging, and the scarcity of wheat and barley all over Palestine, that's now more important than ever.'

Miriam's expression didn't change. 'So where is he?'

'I don't know. Maybe he's still in Germany. The last letter I had from him was from Berlin.'

Miriam's dark eyes were boring into her face. 'I spoke to the postmistress yesterday and she told me you haven't had a letter from Germany for a long time.'

Shoshana decided to stop explaining and go on the attack. 'Is it me you're spying on, or Nathan?'

'Not spying, just trying to figure out what's happening since you haven't said anything.'

'And why is that your business?'

Miriam reached out and placed her hand on Shoshana's arm, her head tilted to the side in a gesture of conciliation. 'Don't be angry, Shoshi. But it is my business – our business. As you said, there's a war on, the Turks are making bigger demands on our grain and raising our taxes and lately everyone's been nervous in case your activities put us all in danger.'

Shoshana's voice was cold. 'So tell me, how does that have anything to do with me or with Nathan being away? We're all in the same boat as far as Turkish oppression is concerned.'

Miriam's eyes roamed around the room and rested on Shoshana's face. 'It's not just about Nathan,' she said after a pause. 'Your sister Leah has disappeared too.'

'I'm sure I told you that Leah has gone to live in a small settlement with our aunt Hannah. Nothing mysterious about that.'

'And now I hear that your lover, the one who was going to marry Leah, has disappeared. Where is he? No one has seen him either.'

At the mention of Eli, Shoshana swallowed and bit the inside of her lip. That was a subject she hadn't expected Miriam to raise.

'It looks as if my family has kept the entire village busy concocting gossip and innuendo. I don't know who the everyone is that you've mentioned, but you can tell them that Eli has gone home to help his family down south. I'm sure they'll all be disappointed to know that there's a simple explanation for all the so-called disappearances. No one has been kidnapped or murdered.'

She hoped that her flippant comment might cause Miriam to desist, but she was mistaken. 'It's not just your family, Shoshi,' she persisted. 'People have commented on the things going on at that research station of yours.'

Shoshana forced a laugh. 'What next? That the plants have started a revolution and are threatening to burn down the building?'

But Miriam wasn't laughing. 'You can make fun of me but I've heard that people not connected with your plants have been coming and going there.'

'And is that why you sent Dan to spy on us there?'

Miriam flushed. 'I didn't send him. He probably overheard people talking and wanted to see for himself.'

'Well, he solved the big mystery. He saw me cataloguing plants.'

In the awkward silence that followed, Shoshana poured more tea to break the tension and give herself time to redirect the conversation. But arguing back and forth and deflecting accusations wasn't the way to get out of what was a very serious situation. She had to take control of the discussion.

She moved closer to Miriam. 'Listen,' she said. 'We have redoubled our efforts at the station to improve the quality and quantity of our yield so we can provide more grain to the locals who are desperate. You know we already distribute sacks of barley and wheat to villagers in our area, and we are teaching farmers to use our methods to increase their crops. That's why people have been visiting the station. I thought that would have been obvious.'

Encouraged by Miriam's silence, she pressed on. 'Because we've succeeded so well, we've been able to sell much of our yield and everyone in Zichron Yaakov has benefited from that. As you know, I've been distributing cash to some of the farmers who've been ruined by Turkish confiscations and taxes and have had trouble putting food on the table.'

Miriam nibbled a biscuit. 'I know. Everyone appreciates what you've done.'

Shoshana doubted that but she was relieved that Miriam was backing down. Pushing her advantage, she said, 'You know, we're all victims of the Turks here, every single one of us. They would love nothing better than seeing us divided among ourselves, but if we don't pull together, they've won.'

Miriam nodded. 'You're absolutely right, Shoshi. It wasn't easy to raise all this but I'm glad we've been able to talk about it instead of sweeping it under the carpet.'

At the door, she turned back towards Shoshana. 'There's a concert at the community hall next Sunday, a violinist from Tel-Aviv. Would you like to come?'

This time instead of making her usual excuse, Shoshana agreed to go with her. But as she watched Miriam walk away, her spirits flagged. The enemy within could be more dangerous than the oppressors.

CHAPTER TWENTY-SEVEN

Atlit, 1917

Once again it was a moonless night as the MS *Victoria* approached the coast of Atlit. Nathan gripped the rail as he surveyed the water. Although there wasn't a breath of wind and the waves rolled gently towards the shore, he drew no comfort from what he saw. He knew only too well that this tide was too unpredictable to be trusted.

Aaron limped towards him, straining to make out the blurred coastline in the distance. Despite his bullet wounds, he had surprised everyone by recovering much sooner than expected. The only outward signs of his injuries were deep scars on his left cheek and a limp, the result of a bullet wound in his left calf. After he was discharged from hospital, Nathan had brought him to Cairo. Reluctantly, because Aaron's story about the attack in the desert still rankled. He had asked repeatedly for details about his rescue and although the answers never varied, he kept rechecking them like a policeman questioning a suspect. He couldn't leave it alone. He didn't want to accept Aaron's explanation. He didn't want to accept the fact that Aaron had survived while Eli was dead.

He would have been happy never to see Aaron again, but the situation at Zichron Yaakov had forced him to overcome his hostility. With Eli gone and unable to return home himself, the spy ring was seriously depleted. Shoshana would need a second in command, and despite his resentment at Aaron's survival, he knew that the man had the qualities needed to step into the role. He was passionately dedicated to their cause, and although inclined to be reckless, his courage was beyond question.

How Shoshana had managed to direct the spy ring and continue gathering information in Eli's absence he couldn't imagine. As they hadn't been able to deliver their intelligence, he didn't know how much they had or how valuable it was, but now that the British authorities had given him a specific list of the information they needed, it was essential to intensify their efforts. That was why he had urged Hugh Gardiner-Hall to permit Aaron to sail on the *Victoria* with him to Atlit, saying, 'We'll need him to help speed up their intelligence-gathering.'

Standing with him at the boat's rail, Aaron said, 'A perfect night.'

Perhaps it was too perfect, Nathan's subversive mind whispered. It felt as if every nerve in his body was stretched to snapping point. Perhaps at the last moment the wind would whip up the waves, the tide would roar, and once again foil their plans. He recalled Zvi Bernstein's heroic swim a month ago, the way the sea had tossed him about like a piece of cork and almost drowned him. He had managed to make it back and they'd pulled him up on board half-dead, but he'd had to leave the oilskin pouch with the documents behind, and as the wind had shown no sign of abating the following night, they'd had to abandon the attempt and the mission had been a failure.

Aaron was pointing excitedly at the stark silhouette of the Crusader castle on the hilltop. 'I never thought I'd see that again. Never thought I'd get back home.'

Lost in thought, Nathan didn't respond and he felt Aaron's eyes boring into him, waiting for some acknowledgement. When none was forthcoming, Aaron spoke.

'Nathan, I'll be going ashore when we get to Atlit, and I know you're returning to Cairo, so I don't know when we'll meet again, and I want to clear the air between us while I can. I know you resent the fact that I survived. You've made no secret of that. You wish I'd been the one who died and there were times when I did too. You've questioned me over and over about what happened in the desert, and believe me, I've gone over and over it all thousands of times myself to see if I could have done something to save Eli, but there's nothing either of us can do about it.'

Still Nathan didn't respond. He was staring moodily at the water, and in the motion of the waves he saw Eli's face.

'Eli was irreplaceable,' Aaron continued. 'We all know that. But when I get back to Zichron Yaakov, I'll do whatever I can to support Shoshana so we can get rid of the bloody Turks, especially now that we know the British are considering an attack from the desert.' Then he added, 'It seems to me that we should put aside personal feelings and recriminations and redouble our efforts to work together. You should ask yourself if Eli would have wanted his death to create a rift between us.'

Nathan didn't like being lectured but he couldn't deny that Aaron was right. Especially about the urgent need for action now that the desert campaign was a possibility. One of the many rumours circulating around British Military Headquarters in Cairo was that a general called Allenby had been impressed by Nathan's idea of drilling for water in the desert and believed it was the key to launching a campaign to attack Palestine. From Aaron's account of the British patrol at Rafah, it was obvious there was already a military presence in the area. Nathan's heart was racing. This was what he had been hoping for. If they could provide the British with vital information about Turkish defences in the area, that campaign might become reality and the liberation of Palestine would be within reach.

Suddenly he saw how crazily improbable it was, that their little group might be instrumental in defeating the Turks. He recalled something he had once read in a botany textbook. *If you lack belief in your power to achieve something,* the author wrote, *if you think you are too small and your goal is too great, just consider the acorn.*

'What are you smiling at?' Aaron asked

'I'm thinking about acorns,' Nathan replied.

Puzzled, Aaron shrugged and turned to go inside. Nathan watched him limp away, marvelling that his wounds had healed so well, leaving relatively minor disabilities. If only Eli had been able to survive his injuries. Perhaps if someone had rescued him sooner, he would have. He tried to dismiss this resentful speculation as Captain Wilson appeared beside him.

'The tide looks good, so the rowboat should be able to land on the beach this time,' he said. He rested his gaze on Nathan. 'I know it will be frustrating for you but we can only stay long enough to drop off your friend and pick up their intelligence. These are enemy waters and the sooner we get away the better.'

Nathan nodded.

Fifteen minutes later, Captain Wilson moored the trawler a short distance from the coast, lowered the rowboat, and watched from the deck as Abdul, followed by Nathan and Aaron, climbed into it. As the boat neared the shore, Nathan squinted. Although it was dark, he thought he could make out two figures on the beach. Was one of them Shoshana? How would she react if she saw Aaron but not Eli? He was impatient to see her after all these months, but dreaded having to tell her about Eli. He wondered what she had made of his absence. He had avoided mentioning Eli in the letters Zvi had delivered, but now they would be face to face, he would have to tell her the truth.

Sitting beside him in the boat, Aaron shivered, and Nathan realised that his homecoming would be painful, especially when he had to describe Eli's death to Shoshana.

He leaned forward. 'Listen, Aaron. Don't tell anyone what happened to Eli. It will arouse curiosity among the villagers and lead to awkward questions. You know that according to our laws death can't be confirmed without a body, so the fact that they haven't found his body is actually an advantage.'

Aaron stared at him for a moment, shocked at his words. Then he said, 'So what do I tell our group when they ask where he is?'

'Just say that he's been sent to England to train as a combat pilot. Knowing how intrepid Eli is, they'll believe it.'

Almost immediately he realised he'd said *is* instead of *was*, but he was imagining Eli sitting in an aeroplane, a white silk scarf wound about his neck.

The boat was heading straight for the beach when he saw a tall, erect figure standing against the thorny broom bushes. Shoshana! How brave she was. No woman on earth had her courage.

With a powerful surge, the tide launched the boat onto the beach and even before he jumped onto the sand, Shoshana was in his arms and she was sobbing and when he looked into her eyes he could tell that she knew. She clung to him and they stood on the beach without speaking.

She pulled away and he stared at her in astonishment. 'How did you know?' he asked gently.

She shook her head, unable to give a coherent answer. After a pause she said, 'How do you know the sun has stopped shining?'

Her reply left him speechless. For the first time he grasped the depth of their connection and the enormity of her loss, the fragility of life and the finality of death.

After a long pause he asked, 'Have you told anyone? What about Leah and Abba? Do they know?'

'I haven't told anyone.'

He let out the breath he didn't realise he'd been holding. 'That's good. Better if they don't know.'

While they were speaking, she became aware of Aaron's presence. Her eyes widened, as if seeing an apparition. Time was running out and before she had a chance to speak, Nathan handed her a thick envelope. 'This contains cash for you and the farmers. And a long letter in which I've included a list of the intelligence the British need. I've explained everything because I knew I wouldn't have time to tell you.'

She was still staring at Aaron and it took her several minutes to collect herself. Then she looked down at the large oilskin pouch in her hands as if suddenly remembering why she was there and handed it to Nathan.

'Thank God we can deliver it at last. Now they'll have proof that we are genuine and that we have the resources to provide them with intelligence that might swing the war in their favour.'

He looked at his sister. Obsessed with his own problems and frustrations, he hadn't given much thought to the danger she was in. From the age of six she had been his eager assistant, helping him categorise plants and place them in envelopes. He had taught her a code so that they could write notes to each other that no one else could decipher. As an adult she had become his trusted confidante and his respected critic. She was his anchor. And suddenly he saw how vulnerable she was.

'Shoshi, you have to be extremely careful from now on. Don't take any chances. The Turks are suffering losses and wounded beasts are the most dangerous.'

She nodded. 'I'm far stronger than you realise. As a matter of fact, I've realised that I have to reorganise the way we collect information. I've heard that some of the villagers have become suspicious so I've decided that it isn't safe for our group to meet at the research station anymore.'

'What happened? How did you find out?'

She described Miriam's visit in a few words. 'Don't worry, I've dealt with all the gossip and reassured her that there was nothing suspicious going on.'

He couldn't conceal his alarm. 'You can't assume that's the end of it. From now on you have to be more wary. Miriam mightn't be able to stop the rumours and you know how dangerous they can be. We can't give them an opportunity to jeopardise our mission.'

He was speaking in the older brother tone she remembered well and her tone revealed her resentment. 'You don't need to worry. I know what I'm doing.'

He glanced at Aaron, who hadn't taken his eyes off Shoshana from the moment they had set foot on shore, and turned back to her. 'How will you collect intelligence from our members if they don't come to Atlit?'

She was looking at Aaron too. 'I'll have to take the carriage and visit them one by one. Obviously I can't travel alone without arousing suspicion, so now that Aaron is back, we'll go together.'

Nathan opened his mouth to object but closed it again. He felt uneasy at the thought of her travelling all over the country with Aaron, but he was based in Cairo and Shoshana was in charge now. He had to defer to her decisions.

It was time to return to the boat. He placed his hands on her shoulders and looked into her eyes. 'Promise me one thing, Shoshi. If things get dangerous here, you'll take the ship to Cairo.'

Touched by his concern, she squeezed his arm. 'You don't need to worry about me.'

As Abdul pushed the rowboat off the sand, Nathan jumped into it. The only sound he heard was the splashing of the oars taking him away from her. It was too dark to see anything on shore, but he knew she was watching as the boat disappeared in the dark. She was strong, stronger than he had imagined. But was she strong enough?

CHAPTER TWENTY-EIGHT

Cairo, 1917

Several days after arriving back in Cairo, Nathan was in his office at the Savoy Hotel reading the latest bulletin from the Arab Bureau when he was summoned to see Hugh Gardiner-Hall. He set off at once. Like a keen student eager to find out whether he had been awarded a prize, he couldn't wait to hear how the intelligence he had delivered had been received.

Sitting at his large marble-topped desk, Gardiner-Hall puffed on his pipe. 'We have just held a meeting to discuss the information you've brought us, and I would like to convey our gratitude,' he said.

It was a disappointing response, he felt, not commensurate with the value of the information the group had provided, or the cost at which it had been obtained. Although he knew better than to expect effusive praise from the British – their attitude of grudging tolerance had long exasperated him – he had hoped for more enthusiasm.

As if reading his mind, Hugh Gardiner-Hall added, 'You and your espionage group should be extremely proud of yourselves. You've provided us with more valuable information than any of our other informants and I should like to tell you that everyone is most impressed. If you keep this up, you will contribute greatly to our success in the field.'

It was on the tip of Nathan's tongue to add that unlike the other spies who demanded rivers of gold for intelligence of dubious value, his conspirators were providing crucial information free of charge, but he thought better of it and simply nodded. He smiled to himself as he left Sir Hugh's office. Perhaps English understatement was rubbing off on him at last.

He was still smiling as he made his way along the corridor towards his office when he saw a short man swaggering towards him wearing a crumpled jacket and trousers that stopped above his ankles as though the tailor had run out of material.

'I don't believe we've met,' the man said. 'I'm Lawrence. Friends call me Ned. Others call me a pompous upstart.'

So this was the man he had heard mentioned in Military Intelligence circles with admiration but also derision, the man Shoshana had met in Cairo. Nathan extended his hand. 'Nathan Adelstein.'

Lawrence studied him with renewed interest. 'So you're the brother of the beautiful Shoshana, and the author of the splendid article I quoted in our bulletin recently. Congratulations and welcome to our wasp nest of duplicity, ineptitude and mistrust.'

Nathan was taken aback by the sarcasm but he felt an immediate affinity with this abrasive, eccentric man who, like him, had trouble reining in his opinions and didn't fit into this world of false modesty, entitlement and condescension.

'I say, I've had enough of this stuffy place,' Lawrence was saying. 'Feel like joining me at Groppi's?'

Half an hour later, the two men were seated at a round table inside the fashionable café. Lawrence looked up from his fluted glass of iced coffee. 'Do tell me about your sister. What is she doing these days in that village of yours in the shadow of the Crusader castle?'

Nathan hesitated. Lawrence had introduced Shoshana to Woolley, but how much did he really know about the spy ring? And how much should he tell him?

But Lawrence didn't wait for his reply. 'Your sister is an unusual young woman. Clever and courageous. I've only met her twice but I'd be surprised if she was leading a life of backwater mediocrity.'

Nathan nodded. Shoshana's personality was a safer topic than her occupation. 'She was remarkable even as a child. By the time she was six she already knew the botanical names of most plants.'

Lawrence looked thoughtful. 'She was proud of you, too. Said you were a world-famous botanist. What made you give it up in favour of the murky world of politics?'

Another question that Nathan preferred to avoid. He took his time stirring sugar into his porcelain cup of black coffee to delay giving a reply. Despite Lawrence's flippant tone, he sensed an underlying agenda that put him on guard. When he looked up, he saw Lawrence studying him intently.

He decided to counter Lawrence's question with one of his own. 'I might ask you the same thing. You used to study Crusader castles and map coastlines. What brought you to the Arab Bureau?'

'Touché!' Lawrence cried. 'Now let's stop playing games. I know you've just supplied HQ with intelligence about Turkish defences in the area.' He sat forward and narrowed his eyes. 'So you're spying on the Turks. I applaud you. You want them defeated. So do I. But what's your goal?'

'We're desperate to secure British victory so we can expel our Ottoman overlords before they expel us.'

Lawrence gave a lopsided smile that accentuated his long face. 'Aren't you afraid of substituting one overlord for another? Do you realise you're about to open the door to a power-hungry nation convinced of its God-given duty to civilise the savages of this world?'

The bitterness of his remark took Nathan by surprise. 'Is that how you regard your country?'

'I feel about my country the way family members feel about each other, with loyalty, love and also mistrust. It's politics I hate. That's why I'm curious why you gave up an honourable profession for politics, which is anything but honourable.'

'It's not politics I'm interested in. It's survival,' Nathan said.

Lawrence shrugged. 'Then you haven't yet realised that everything is political. But you will.'

He sounded disillusioned and Nathan found it difficult to reconcile his cynical comment with his image of Lawrence as an intrepid warrior riding a camel at the head of Bedouin troops. He was a baffling mixture of supercilious self-assurance, humble self-deprecation, energy and restlessness, but even this brief encounter was enough to indicate why he was the object of ridicule among his fellow-officers, who were probably unable to appreciate his quicksilver mind and subversive ideas.

They had finished their drinks and the waiter, formally attired in a dinner jacket and bow tie, hurried to their table to ask whether they'd like anything else. He spoke to Lawrence in a confidential tone that indicated he was talking to a habitué. Several minutes later he returned with another iced coffee for Lawrence and a silver pot of black coffee for Nathan.

While mulling over Lawrence's comments, Nathan remembered Sir Hugh had told him that Lawrence had recently returned from leading a series of raids on the Hejaz railway: 'To our astonishment, his undisciplined army succeeded in attacking the train and tying down Turkish troops. Of course the Arabs immediately swooped on the train and looted everything they could lay their hands on, but they regard that as their just reward and Lawrence has to go along with it.'

Visualising the small man before him attired in flowing silk robes and riding a camel at the head of a Bedouin army, spurring them on to victory then standing back while they looted the spoils, demanded a huge leap of imagination.

'What about the Arabs whose cause you espouse?' he asked. 'Aren't they also playing politics?'

A rapt expression played on Lawrence's face, softening its bony contours. 'They are fighting a just cause for their independence. It's the Western powers that are playing politics with the Arabs' dreams. I have lived in Faisal's tent, eaten his food, and we have shared our thoughts like brothers.'

It was clear Lawrence had idealised the Bedouins and saw them as heroes fighting an epic battle for freedom, with him at the helm of their noble cause. Nathan understood why a man of such brilliance and vision, misunderstood and ridiculed by his peers, might long to prove his detractors wrong by becoming the champion of a downtrodden people.

'What did you mean when you said the Western powers were playing politics?' Nathan asked.

Lawrence's eyes flashed with anger. 'Britain has lured the Arabs to fight the Turks, promising them a homeland in the north of Palestine, but behind their backs, England and France have already decided to carve up the whole region between them. They wanted to keep it secret but I had to let Faisal know about their duplicity.'

Nathan had heard rumours about this secret agreement, but this was the first time it had been mentioned as a fait accompli.

'You can't trust Britain,' Lawrence continued. 'That's why I warned you. When you change horses midstream you can't always tell how the new horse compares with the old one. The promises they give aren't worth the paper they're written on. There's even some talk in the English Parliament about recognising the right of the Jews to their traditional homeland.'

He sounded scathing but Nathan couldn't conceal his excitement. It was the first time he'd heard that British politicians had discussed the possibility of recognising a Jewish homeland in Palestine.

'Do you know how that came about? Who was involved?'

Lawrence shrugged. 'Who can understand the arcane machinations of politicians? I've heard Lord Balfour mentioned in connection with it but I wouldn't be surprised if the idea originated from Britain's hope of winning over the Jews to support the war financially. It certainly wouldn't be for any idealistic motives.'

Nathan was silent as he surveyed the man in front of him. Lawrence was formidable. Who else would have had the vision and the strength to convince Bedouin tribes to unite and accept him as their leader and commander in battle, and then to convince Britain that Arab troops would be invaluable allies in their fight against the Turks?

At the same time, he struggled to reconcile his admiration for the man with antagonism for his aspirations. They were both on the same side – both determined to overthrow the Turks – but their ultimate goals were irreconcilable. While he was risking everything to establish a Jewish homeland where Jews and Arabs could live together with equal rights, Lawrence was risking his life in battle to deliver Palestine solely to the Arabs. To safeguard a secure future, they had to be reconciled.

He spoke slowly. 'You believe that the Western powers will double-cross the Arabs, yet you continue to lead them in battle. Why? What do you hope to gain? From what you've said, even if you win a battle or two, you'll probably lose your war to establish an Arab state.'

'I've started this and I'll see it through to the end. I intend to push on towards Damascus in the hope of reaching it before the British do. That's crucial, because if we do, then no matter what they've arranged in their secret treaty with the French, they'll have no choice but to install Emir Faisal as ruler of that region.'

Nathan considered this for several minutes. 'Then how do you envisage the future of Palestine?' he asked.

Lawrence shrugged and spread his hands. 'That's something only the future will reveal. The Arabs have a great deal to learn from the Jews. Their stability and loyalty as well as their agricultural skills.

Perhaps they will live in peace. But I suspect not. Before that happens, we must remember that we're dealing with politicians who can't be trusted. They will probably try to sell the same horse twice.'

It struck Nathan that Lawrence was an exceptional young man who was puffed up with his own self-importance, having found fame long before he had reached the maturity to handle it. He was dangerous as all young zealots were who valued ideals above all else.

They had finished their coffees and were now strolling through the bustling souk, past men with huge bellies and exuberant moustaches reclining on armchairs and puffing on hookah pipes. Women scurried among the stalls choosing spices, shawls and sandals. Suddenly Lawrence stopped walking and turned to Nathan.

'Whatever happens in the war from now on, you should be aware that your sister is in great danger.'

Before Nathan could reply, Lawrence was swallowed up by the crowd. He continued walking towards his office in the Savoy with Lawrence's warning echoing in his head.

CHAPTER TWENTY-NINE

Zichron Yaakov, 1917

Shoshana sat at the kitchen table staring straight ahead but seeing nothing. The determination that had buoyed her until now had abandoned her and she felt cast adrift and alone. Had she been fooling herself, imagining a strength she didn't have? She fixed her gaze on the wall to blot out all thoughts and feelings. That state of suspended animation dulled the pain gnawing at her bones, a visceral pain that twisted everything inside her, worse than any physical pain she had ever suffered. But she could only maintain that frozen state for several minutes before the pain came bursting back, like blood when a bandage is ripped from an open wound.

She sighed. All this effort to stem the pain sapped her energy, and she would need strength to confront Aaron, who was due to visit her that morning – a meeting she wished she could put off forever. What could she say to the man who lived while Eli did not? How could she conceal her disappointment that the wrong man had survived? She longed to know all the details of Eli's death but at the same time she dreaded hearing them. How could she control her fury and resentment and continue working with him?

The work, she reminded herself. That mattered more than ever now. Not her feelings. She mustn't allow anything to distract her from that.

With that resolve, she felt her strength flowing back. She knew it was vital to overcome her resentment. She and Aaron had to work together for Eli's sake. Lost in thought, she was startled when she heard the squeak of the gate and footsteps on the flagstone path. Someone with an uneven gait was approaching the front door. A moment later, she heard a knock and Aaron's voice, quiet and hesitant.

'Shoshana?'

She swivelled around and saw him limping towards her. Despite everything that had happened, Aaron hadn't lost his sense of style and her resentful eyes took in the bow tie and the celluloid collar that now accentuated the deep scar on his left cheek. Her gaze travelled down to his left leg, which was stiff. She hadn't noticed the limp while walking back from the beach with him three days before. She had been aware that he had trouble keeping up with her but she had assumed it was a temporary weakness or that he was tired. Perhaps she had been too upset to pay much attention to his disability.

He followed her glance and shrugged. 'A souvenir from the Bedouin bandits.'

It was no longer possible to avoid the conversation she had been dreading.

He spoke slowly, describing every moment, every word of that fatal day, and she listened as though in a trance, because it sounded unreal. It was just a story, her numb mind kept telling her. Just a story. He finished speaking and they sat in painful silence. She couldn't speak. Her tongue seemed stuck to the roof of her mouth.

'I've just remembered something,' Aaron said after a long pause. 'The dates. He said you gave them to him just before he left. He was still eating them when we were ambushed, so he would have been thinking of you.'

She realised he was trying to comfort her but she couldn't bring herself to respond. When she looked up she noticed that behind his glasses, his eyes were bright with tears.

She roused herself. 'Tell me again. Who shot him? Where was he shot? Did he say anything before he lost consciousness? When did you realise he was dead?' Her voice rose with every question. It was as though she had heard nothing and demanded to hear the details once again.

He went over the incident again as patiently and in as much detail as he could. After he'd finished, he took off his glasses, and took a long time polishing them with his handkerchief.

'I know how terrible this is for you, Shoshana.'

'Know how terrible it is for me? Know how terrible it is for me?' she was suddenly screaming. 'Have you ever had your heart ripped from your chest with a grappling hook? Did a wolf's claws ever tear through your flesh? Don't tell me you know how it feels.'

Shocked by her own outburst, she buried her face in her hands. He watched her with concern, longing to comfort her but fearing to provoke another overwrought response if he tried.

After a long pause, she raised her head and in his eyes she saw concern and a desire to comfort her. With an effort she reminded herself that this wasn't only her loss, that he had gone through a traumatic experience himself. He'd been ambushed, witnessed the murder of his closest friend, whom he'd been powerless to save because he'd been wounded himself. He must have thought he would die as well.

'You would have died too if those Australian soldiers hadn't turned up when they did. Just as well they got there in time to disperse those tribesmen and save you.' She hoped she sounded sincere.

Suddenly a new thought struck her. 'Can you remember where exactly this happened? If you can find the place, we'll be able to bring his body back here and bury him.'

Aaron swallowed. 'The Australians visited me in hospital and said they went back to that spot but when they got there, they saw that it had been levelled and there was no sign of his body. And when Nathan told the British in Cairo what had happened, they also sent people to look for him, but they couldn't find him either.'

'How is that possible?'

Aaron shrugged. 'Nobody knows. Someone suggested that perhaps the Bedouins buried him because they were afraid that if his body was found, they'd be charged with murder.'

'So we can't even bury him. We can never visit his grave.'

Aaron was silent. Empty words of consolation would only intensify her grief. Then he thought of something to raise her spirits.

'Just before the bastards descended on us, I saw Eli taking some paper from his rucksack and writing furiously. Maybe he was writing a letter to you.'

She almost stopped breathing. 'Do you know where he put that letter? Maybe it's still out there in the desert.' It felt as if all hope hinged on finding Eli's last words.

'I think he put it in his rucksack, but that's missing too.'

Had he really written to her? What was in his letter? She would never know, and that torment reopened the wound.

She rose and paced around the room, her arms folded tightly around her, as if afraid she would fall apart.

Finally, exhausted, she sat down again. 'We can't tell anyone that Eli is dead,' she said. 'Not even Leah. It's for her own protection. I know Eli will agree.'

He didn't comment on her use of the present tense.

'What about Eli's family? Shouldn't they be told?'

She shook her head. 'Definitely not. If they find out, his cousins, who are in our network, will probably be too disheartened to keep working with us and everything will fall apart. Can you imagine how distraught Berish would be? We must maintain the fiction that he is in England, training to be a combat pilot, as long as we can.'

Aaron studied her for a moment. It crossed his mind that this deception fulfilled another need – it prevented her from facing the truth.

He leaned towards her. 'Shoshana,' he began, 'you know I'd do anything for you. You just have to say the word.' He saw the warning look on her face, and added, 'Eli once said that if anything happened to him, he wanted me to look after you.'

She raised her eyebrows, and he realised she didn't believe him. 'Really? I don't need anyone to look after me. But I do need a deputy in our espionage work because I can't do it all by myself. Just remember there's nothing personal between you and me, and there never will be.'

He looked away and in the awkward silence that followed, she realised she had spoken more sharply than she had intended.

'We can't meet at the research station anymore, so when we need to discuss anything, we'll do it here,' she said. 'The neighbours will still gossip but at least they'll just gossip about your visits.'

'Speaking of gossip, I should tell you that a friend of mine who is part of that security group I belonged to told me they've warned their members to watch us, as we are endangering the safety of the whole community. They suspect we're making contact with British vessels.' He paused. 'You know those vigilantes have had it in for me ever since they expelled me. The last thing I want is to put the spy ring at risk, so if you decide I should drop out, I'll understand.'

She looked straight into his eyes. 'I appreciate your offer, but you're my deputy and I certainly don't want you to quit now that we have the British on side and everything is organised to pass on our intelligence. We're all at risk, especially as time goes on, but we just have to keep going and do all we can to avoid scrutiny.'

Her tone became more decisive. 'In a few days we'll set out to visit our people and collect their intelligence, but first I need time to go through the letter Nathan gave me listing the information the British have asked for so I can decide who we should see and in what order. Can you come back tomorrow afternoon so we can plan our route?'

As she spoke, she was aware that her voice sounded strong and resolute. No longer cast adrift, she was a leader again.

CHAPTER THIRTY

The Negev, 1917

Leah looked up from the eggs she was collecting in the barn and gazed at the fields that stretched towards the horizon. Tender ears of barley had already pierced the soil and, moved by the sight of the earth's perennial renewal, she recalled Nathan's passion for plants, which she now shared.

But where was Nathan? According to Shoshana, he was attending scientific conferences somewhere, but he must have been away for over six months by now and she hadn't heard from him in all that time. As for their father, he occasionally added a few lines to Shoshana's letters, but he never mentioned Nathan. It aroused her suspicion that something was going on in Zichron Yaakov, something they were keeping from her.

She was walking towards the main building when she heard a clatter of hooves and looked around. Beaming down at her from his saddle was Jack Simpson, sweat beading on his forehead.

When she invited him inside for a drink, he shook his head. 'I can't stay, but I heard something I wanted to tell you,' he blurted out.

She listened with growing astonishment as he talked. 'Some of my mates were out patrolling the southern part of the desert a few weeks ago when they came across two fellows who'd been attacked by a band of Bedouins. At first they thought they were Bedouins as well, because they were wearing those long robes and head cloths, but then it turned out they were your people.'

'My people?'

'Jews.'

'How come they were disguised as Bedouins?'

Jack shrugged. 'Dunno. Spies maybe. One of them had been shot but the patrol turned up in the nick of time and took him to the hospital in Port Said. I heard he recovered and by the time he got out, all he had was a scar on his face and a bad limp.'

'And the other one?'

'Poor devil was dead when they got there.'

'Do you know who they were?'

Jack shook his head. 'Wish I could tell you.'

She wanted to know more but he was looking at his wristwatch. 'Struth, it's getting late. I'd better get going or I'll be in trouble.'

It was an intriguing story, but once Jack had galloped away, Leah's mind returned to the vexed problem of Nathan's absence. There was no point writing yet another letter to Shoshana asking about him, but it struck her that if they were face to face, her sister might find it difficult to persist with her evasive replies.

*

It was late in the afternoon two days later when Shoshana heard Leah's carriage pull up outside the house in Zichron Yaakov, followed by her father's surprised greeting as he opened the door.

'Leah!'

'Abba, it's so good to see you!'

As Shoshana ran down the hall, she saw her father disengage from Leah's embrace and ask, 'Is everything all right? Has something happened to Hannah?' He turned and called out, 'Shoshana! Did you know Leah was coming home?'

Shoshana came forward and hugged her sister.

'Nothing's wrong, Abba,' Leah said lightly. 'I missed you and wanted to see you.'

Shoshana wasn't fooled by her words.

'Come in, come in,' her father was saying. 'Put down your bag and relax. Come sit and tell us about your life in that settlement. Shoshana, bring Leah a glass of tea and something to eat. She must be starving after her long journey.'

Shoshana brought refreshments and listened as Leah answered her father's questions. Why had she come? Why now?

'That's good, that's good,' their father was saying. 'I'm glad you're happy there, though I did have my doubts. Hannah isn't the easiest person to get on with, and I've never understood the point of working hard and owning nothing.'

Leah entertained them with stories about the farm as they ate the simple meal Shoshana had prepared. When evening fell, Moshe rose and stretched. 'My old bones are tired. I know it's still early but I'm up every day at five so I'm going to bed. I'm sure you two have plenty to talk about.'

The moment they heard his bedroom door close, Shoshana said, 'Tell me why you've really come, Leah.'

'First tell me why you're so shocked to see me. And don't try to deny it. I saw it in your eyes the moment you looked at me.'

'You took me by surprise, that's all.'

'You can call it what you like but I know you and I know shock when I see it.'

Shoshana studied her sister and realised that she would have to think fast to allay her suspicions. Of all the secrets she needed to conceal from her, the least dangerous was Nathan's absence.

'To be honest with you, I've been worried about Nathan,' she began, but Leah interrupted.

'I've noticed that when people begin by saying *to be honest*, they're usually about to conceal something.'

Shoshana was taken aback by her bluntness. Leah had certainly matured during her stay at that settlement. No longer willing simply to defer to her big sister's judgement, she was challenging her.

'Nathan is the reason why I came,' Leah was saying. 'I feel there's something you're not telling me. What does he write?'

Shoshana shook her head. 'That's just it. He hasn't written.'

'I don't get it. If he was in Berlin six months ago as you said, there's no reason why his letters wouldn't have been delivered. Do you think something happened to him?'

Shoshana sighed. In trying to solve one problem, she had created another. 'There's no reason to think that. There's probably some simple explanation.'

Leah narrowed her eyes. 'Unless he's not in Berlin at all. But where could he be? There must be some way of finding out.'

'I've been trying to contact some people he knows in Berlin and as soon as I have some news, I'll let you know.'

Leah drained a glass of water but pushed away the flat bread and fig jam that Shoshana had placed in front of her. It was hard to tell if she accepted the explanation. She looked tired.

'I'm going to bed,' she said. She was almost at the door when she suddenly turned around.

'I heard about two Jews who were disguised as Bedouins and attacked in the Sinai. Do you know anything about it?'

Alarmed, Shoshana stopped clearing the table and stood very still. If she told Leah the truth, her next question would be *What was Eli doing in the Sinai disguised as a Bedouin?* and she couldn't reveal that without exposing the spy ring and that was something she was determined to keep from her sister.

She decided to play for time. 'Who told you?'

'That Australian soldier I told you about. I can tell you do know about it. What have you heard?'

Shoshana was about to reply when they heard the front door open and a man's voice calling out, 'Shoshana?'

It was Aaron. He was limping and had a deep scar on his cheek.

CHAPTER THIRTY-ONE

Zichron Yaakov, 1917

Leah stared as he hobbled towards the couch.

'What happened to you?'

He hesitated and glanced at Shoshana who flashed him a warning look before fixing her gaze on something on the floor.

'An accident,' he said.

'What kind of accident?'

He cleared his throat and looked at Shoshana again. 'A riding accident.'

His brief replies piqued Leah's curiosity. She had only met Aaron a few times but from what she remembered, he enjoyed talking about himself. Why was he being so cagey and why did he keep looking at her sister?

'Where was that?'

He waved a dismissive hand in the air. 'Out in the desert.'

In the desert. She looked at him again. 'It was you, wasn't it?' she said slowly. 'You were attacked by Bedouins out there. That's how you were injured.'

He didn't deny it. Shoshana bit her lip. It was clear Leah wouldn't be fobbed off.

'Who was the other man? The one who died? Who were you with, Aaron?'

Shoshana turned away but not fast enough to conceal her stricken expression.

'It wasn't Eli, was it? Tell me it wasn't Eli,' Leah cried out. She grabbed her sister's arm. 'You have to tell me the truth.'

But there was no need for Shoshana to confirm it. The tears in her eyes said it all.

Leah slumped into a chair and Shoshana could see the emotions flowing across her sister's face one after the other – shock, disbelief, confusion, grief, her eyes pleading that this not be true. Then she covered her face and wept.

The three of them sat in silence for long moments before questions began to tumble wildly from Leah's mouth. Why had Eli been in the desert with Aaron? What were they doing there and where were they going? And why hadn't Shoshana and Aaron come straight out and told her?

In a resigned tone, Shoshana said curtly, 'They were trying to get to Egypt.'

But she should have known better than to hope that Leah would leave it at that.

'What on earth for?'

Shoshana finally realised that she would have to reveal the secret she had been guarding for so long. For the next hour, Leah listened transfixed as her sister told her about the spy ring. Why she had decided to form it, how essential it was to convince the British that they had valuable intelligence, and the problems they'd had trying to find a way of delivering it. She finished by explaining why Eli and Aaron had set off across the desert.

As she talked, no one moved. For a long time Leah continued looking at her hands, avoiding their eyes. Then she looked straight at Shoshana.

'So it was your fault. You and your grandiose scheme killed Eli.'

Shoshana was shocked. She had expected horror or outrage, or an outpouring of grief, but not an accusation. Struggling to speak calmly, she said, 'Eli was as keen to defeat the Turks as I was. He couldn't wait to start collecting intelligence for the British. Do you really think he would have been involved if he didn't believe in our cause? Don't you remember him saying that he despised people who just sat back and did nothing?'

Leah turned her fury on Aaron. 'You were supposed to be his friend. Why didn't you talk him out of it?'

'I agreed with him. It was the only thing we could do to try and reach Egypt. Don't forget that I took the same risks.'

He was hurt by her accusation but more upset on Shoshana's behalf. 'I know this has come as a terrible shock to you but you're not being fair. Shoshana tried to talk him out of riding across the Sinai but you know how he was. Nothing could stop him. He was afraid that all our efforts would be wasted unless we got to Egypt, met the British authorities and started passing on the information we'd gathered. He convinced me. He didn't doubt we'd make it across the Sinai and he couldn't wait to go. He saw it as an exciting adventure.'

'You probably thought it was a great adventure too.'

There was no mistaking her implication, but Aaron didn't react and Leah sat in silence, considering what he'd told her. Eventually she turned to Shoshana.

'So you've been lying to me for over a year. I kept saying you were keeping things from me and asking you what was going on but you kept dismissing my questions and denying everything. When were you going to tell me?'

'I'm sorry I lied to you, Leah, but I was trying to protect you. What we are doing is extremely dangerous and I wanted to keep you safe.'

Although she didn't expect gratitude, Shoshana did hope for some understanding, but Leah's response was cold and resentful.

'You've always treated me like a child. What makes you think I need protecting? Did you ever think of asking what I wanted? Maybe I would have wanted to be part of what you're doing but you've always been the big sister, the one in charge. You always knew everything, and you always got your way.'

Shoshana reached out to take her hand. 'Please don't be angry. I thought it was better not to let you in on our spy activities for your sake. I couldn't bear to expose you to such danger.'

'It's all about your feelings, isn't it? What you thought best, what you couldn't bear. Well, now the genie has escaped from the bottle and you can't push it back in. In spite of all your efforts, I know everything now and you can't exclude me any longer.'

Shoshana looked helplessly at Aaron, who shrugged. For a moment she was at a loss. Incurring her sister's anger for trying to protect her was something she hadn't envisaged. It was unfair, but she would have to deal with it. Whether Leah liked it or not, she was in charge and she was prepared to pay the price of leadership. Now that the British authorities were waiting for their intelligence, they would have to redouble their efforts, and she couldn't allow herself to be distracted by her sister's hurt feelings.

'Leah, I understand your grievances, although you must admit you've harboured some of them since childhood. I can't help being older and feeling protective, and perhaps you can't help resenting it. But you're right about one thing. You won't like me saying this but I am in charge and as the leader of this spy ring, I'm the one who has to make decisions, and I can't allow you to be involved.'

Leah was taken aback, as if she had thought her complaint would result in a softening of her sister's attitude. 'You say you're trying to keep me safe, but if the worst comes to the worst and the

Turks find out what you're doing, don't you think they'll come for me as well?'

'As you're living far away, there'll be nothing to connect you with what we're doing.' Shoshana looked deep into her sister's eyes. 'Someone in our family has to survive, and I want it to be you.'

Leah opened her mouth to argue but closed it again as the significance of Shoshana's words sank in.

'Is it really so dangerous?' she whispered.

Shoshana nodded.

Leah's anger was replaced by concern. 'It seems to me that what you're doing is insane. It's already cost Eli his life. Why are you risking yours?'

'Some causes are bigger than ourselves.' It was as though Eli was speaking through her. 'If we don't fight for our freedom, we'll be at the mercy of the Turks forever.'

Seeing her sister's worried face, Shoshana brightened her tone and tried to smile. 'We're talking about the worst-case scenario, which will probably never happen. I've been very vigilant to make sure they don't find out what we're doing, and I've trained our members to be very discreet.'

Leah glanced at Aaron. 'So you're one of the spies. Who are the others?'

Shoshana shook her head. 'I can't tell you that. The less you know the better.'

Leah let out a long-suffering sigh. Then she remembered what had originally prompted her visit home.

'What about Nathan? Is he part of this? Where is he? Surely you can tell me that at least.'

Shoshana nodded. 'He is part of it.'

'So he isn't attending scientific conferences after all. But what about his scientific work, the research he was doing?'

Shoshana explained that Nathan had decided to put his botanical research on hold and devote himself to their cause instead. He was based in Cairo, where he was highly regarded by the British authorities, and thanks to him they finally had a reliable method of transmitting intelligence.

'But no one must suspect where he is or what he is doing so please don't breathe a word about any of this to anyone, not even Aunt Hannah.'

Leah pulled a face. 'I'm not stupid.'

'I'm not implying you are, but it's very easy to reveal something that seems harmless during a pleasant conversation.' She reminded Leah of Tova's inadvertent comment about Nathan's absence several months before. 'That's why I didn't want to tell you about this. I didn't want to burden you with secrets.'

Leah looked straight at her sister. 'You probably didn't trust me, but that doesn't surprise me. I'm going to bed now and I'll go back to the settlement in the morning, but you don't have to worry, I won't breathe a word about any of this to a soul.'

Shoshana sighed. She had hoped they would part on good terms but if Leah's resentment was the price she had to pay to keep her safe, she accepted it.

Leah was still looking at her. Then she said, 'Shoshi, I do understand what you're doing, but I'm worried for you. Be very careful.'

CHAPTER THIRTY-TWO

The Galilee, 1917

As the large wheels of the horse-drawn carriage jolted and lurched over the rocks and potholes in the road heading southwards several days later, Shoshana ran through the members of their spy ring in her mind. There were thirty-four of them now, spread all over Palestine, and as she thought about each one, she was proud that she had enlisted a whole cross-section of the community: doctors, farmers, businessmen, porters and guards, women as well as men, including one of Nasser's relatives. Each one was committed to their secret mission and brave enough to carry it out. She was humbled by their dedication and loyalty to their cause. But as the carriage turned inland onto the narrower road towards Afula, she was assailed by doubts about her own strength and the enormity of the task she had imposed on others. Had she allowed hubris to spur her on? Was she attempting to become more than she was? She expected so much of others but was she strong enough to live up to their trust and fulfil her own dream?

She sensed Aaron's yearning gaze and reflected on the potential problem of their situation. To strangers, they would appear to be a couple travelling on vacation, but to people who recognised her, she was an immoral woman, behaving in a scandalous manner. She knew the villagers disapproved of her behaviour, but there was nothing she could do about it. She couldn't travel around the countryside alone. Aaron's feelings for her complicated the situation. But far more dangerous than gossip about her morality were the rumours about her activities. If what Miriam had reported was true, those suspicions had to be quashed before they endangered them all.

If only Eli were here, he'd know what to do. If only. She sighed, tightened her lips and stiffened her back. Missing him was a visceral ache that nothing could assuage. She felt like tearing her hairs out one by one or slashing her skin to distract from her emotional pain, but she couldn't wallow in despair. She had to strengthen herself with his spirit. With an effort she turned her attention to the landscape. They were approaching Afula, which was surrounded by the verdant Jezreel Valley. The treetops flared with light and their foliage glistened in the morning sun as though brushed with silvery paint. She gazed at the huge round leaves of the almond trees, the spreading branches of the oaks, and the dwarfish trunks and canopies of the acacias. Nathan had once described them as wide skirts billowing above stumpy legs. She longed for the day when they'd be together again.

She mused that some of these oaks had probably stood when Solomon's temple was razed to the ground. How ancient this land was. Today Afula was an important railway junction, but thousands of years ago, back when Moses had led his people across the desert, it had been a Canaanite settlement. She strained her eyes to make out the smudgy peak in the distance – Mount Tabor, which loomed over the plain that the Old Testament called Megiddo. Armageddon.

She felt Aaron's eyes lingering on her again and thought back to the first time they had travelled together to visit their contacts. Back then, their communication with the British had been uncertain, but now that reliable contact had been established, and the military authorities had given Nathan a list of specific information they needed, collecting intelligence had become a matter of urgency.

The scope, variety and details required were daunting. How could they comply with a request to provide details about 125-millimetre guns? She was more confident of finding the location of Turkish ammunition, food and fodder stores as well as troop movements and the condition of coastal defences. And about extensions to roads, bridges and railway lines. But as for discovering the weight of railway traffic passing over the entire region, from Afula to Beersheba and from Dera'a to Medina? Surely that would be impossible. One aspect of Nathan's letter had irritated her with its implied criticism that her reports included too many 'emotional' comments. He wanted only facts and full stops, not feelings and exclamation marks. Writing her reports was the closest she came to talking to him, and she enjoyed expressing excitement or disappointment, but she supposed that all he needed were objective facts to pass on to his superiors.

He had added a request of his own, one that obviously hadn't come from the British authorities: to observe and report on the economic conditions of people in the Jewish communities, their morale, and the state of their fields and crops. To meet all these requests, they would have to redouble their efforts, which meant that collecting information would place their members in even greater danger.

All this was going through her mind as they arrived in Afula to see Dr Shulman, the first contact on her list. Dr Shulman's unique position as physician to the Turkish army had provided the British with information that had astonished them. According to Nathan, his British contacts had marvelled at the vast amount of valuable information the doctor had gathered, and at the high-profile Turkish military officers who had talked to him so freely and provided so many details.

Ever since the doctor had joined their spy ring, his genial brother Ephraim had been delivering intelligence to the research station at Atlit on horseback, and it was always a pleasure to see his beaming face, but his visits would now have to end to allay the suspicions of the villagers.

When Shoshana and Aaron entered the clinic, the waiting room was empty. It was eight months since she had last seen Dr Shulman. As he came out of his consulting room and recognised them, he looked around to make sure that no one had seen them enter. She noticed that he had lost weight, his cheeks had become more lined, and his eyes had acquired a watchful expression. She hoped that spying on the Turks wasn't taking a toll on him.

Dr Shulman looked around again before ushering them into his consulting room and quickly closed the door. He seemed puzzled to see them. 'Is there a problem? My brother was planning to bring you the latest information next week.'

He spoke faster than usual and glanced repeatedly towards the door. Shoshana explained why she had come to Afula in person instead of waiting for Ephraim. Choosing her words carefully so as not to alarm him, she said, 'Some people in the area have been wondering why so many strangers have been coming to see us at the research station, so from now on we'll collect the intelligence ourselves.'

She looked at him intently. 'Are you all right, Dr Shulman? You seem tense.'

He hesitated before replying and she could see that he was unsure how to answer. 'Nothing to worry about,' he began. Then he added, 'Even though I'm very cautious when I talk to the officers, and never ask questions that would arouse suspicion, I have the impression that some of them are wondering why I'm so interested in their activities.'

'Is that a hunch or have any of them said anything?'

'I suppose you'd call it a hunch, but in years of medical practice I've learned to read facial expressions and interpret tones of voice that often reveal far more than words.'

Before she could comment on this, he went on, 'I'm not suggesting I'm in danger or that I want to stop what I'm doing. It's just an impression and I wanted you to be aware of it. For your sake as well.'

She was relieved that he was willing to continue, but she felt uneasy. If he was exposed and arrested, the entire network would be at risk and they would all have to go to ground. But if he decided to stop, they would lose his valuable intelligence. She was responsible for his safety as well as for supplying intelligence to defeat the Turks. Was it possible to reconcile both?

While she was considering this, he reached into the lowest drawer in his desk, unlocked it, pulled out a thick folder and handed it to her, saying in his understated way, 'I think you'll find this interesting.'

Before secreting the folder in a concealed compartment of her large travel bag, she scanned its contents with growing admiration. It seemed that, using his proficiency in German, he had talked to high-ranking German officers and then interpreted for the Turks. In the process, he had noted detailed information about their aircraft. Their latest aeroplanes were apparently armed with an innovative machine gun that could be turned to fire in all directions. His notes about the condition of the Turkish soldiers who had recently arrived from Lebanon were particularly revealing. He thought they looked malnourished and noticed that many were barefoot, an indication of inadequate rations and supplies.

Flicking through the pages, she came to the location of soldiers stationed along the front. It appeared that much of the army was close to Aleppo, while some divisions were in Beersheba. Then she read something that made her widen her eyes and she reread it.

According to many of the Turkish officers, the forthcoming battle would probably be fought in Gaza. Her hands trembled. This information had to be delivered to the British as fast as possible.

She closed the folder and looked up. 'I can't thank you enough for what you're doing. The intelligence you've gathered will help the British plan their strategy and bring victory closer. We'll be back in two weeks' time, but until then, please be very vigilant.'

Back in the carriage, she looked troubled. Turning to Aaron, who had remained silent during the meeting, she asked, 'What do you think about what he said about the officers becoming curious? Do you think they suspect him?'

He looked at her and quickly looked away. 'If they did, they wouldn't give him so much information. They probably just regard him as a friendly physician who is interested in them.'

She knew that his brusque manner covered up feelings he tried to suppress. Although he didn't refer to it, the tension between them was palpable. Perhaps it had been a mistake to bring him on this journey. She turned her thoughts back to Dr Shulman. She was inclined to trust his judgement more than Aaron's, but she said no more about it as they continued their journey.

Feeling the need for some relief after the intensity of their meeting with the doctor, she suggested stopping for lunch at a café near the station that catered for Turkish soldiers. They were the only customers and the moustachioed chef, who also served as the waiter, came out of the tiny kitchen with a broad smile, wiping his hands on his stained apron. 'Today we have borek, gozleme, dolma and kofta,' he said. He stared at Shoshana with unconcealed admiration but addressed Aaron. 'I haven't seen you here before, *effendi*. Where do you come from?'

Aaron made a vague gesture towards the coast.

'And you are going where?'

'Visiting relatives.' Shoshana's tone discouraged further questioning, and with a laugh the chef said, 'You are lucky the train is late as usual, or we'd have nothing left.'

When they had finished their spinach gozleme, fried eggplant and lamb kofta, the chef brought them tiny cups of thick black coffee and squares of rose-flavoured sweets. After complimenting him on his delicious food, they left to continue their journey. As the carriage moved off, Shoshana looked back and saw the chef standing on the doorstep, watching them.

'Just shows how careful we have to be,' she said. 'Even the café owners are on the lookout for strangers, and we certainly don't look like typical travellers. He might even now be contacting the local pasha about us.'

They urged Nasser to take back roads as they hurried south to visit Eli's cousin Berish at Rishon-le-Zion. It was a meeting she dreaded and, as she had anticipated, his first question was about Eli. 'Where on earth is he? I haven't seen him or heard from him for ages.'

Studiously avoiding Aaron's clenched jaw, she said as nonchalantly as she could manage, 'He's in London on a secret mission but don't breathe a word to anyone.'

Berish threw his head back and laughed. 'That doesn't surprise me. Trust Eli to get involved in something like that.'

He stopped talking, and rested an unfriendly gaze on Aaron. 'So has he taken Eli's place now?'

Startled by his words, she thought he was referring to their relationship, but realised in time that he meant in their organisation. Either way, the comment was provocative. The last thing they needed was internal jealousy. She hurried to defuse his resentment.

'I can't travel all over Palestine alone. With his experience as a security guard, Aaron was the best person to accompany me.'

Too late she realised that mentioning Aaron's former position with the local militia had been a mistake, given the animosity with which they regarded him, but Berish shrugged and changed the subject. He was eager to impart the information he had gained from Turkish officers who visited his winery. While he had plied them with wine, they talked about their military activities and complained about the slow progress of the defence trenches being dug around Gaza, and the posts being erected for gun batteries. They said that mountain guns had already been sent to the Gaza front where a battle was imminent. They had even revealed the gauge of the guns to be used.

The three of them were sitting under a vine-covered pergola, and as Berish poured them glasses of cabernet from his vineyard, Shoshana couldn't resist swirling the crimson liquid around in her glass and breathing in its full-bodied aroma as her father had taught her to do.

'So does it compare with your father's cabernet?' Berish wanted to know. After chatting about the problems of growing grapes in their arid climate, he returned to the information he'd gathered. One of the Turks was aide-de-camp to a German general, and had not hesitated to share his boss's opinions.

'According to General Kress von Kressenstein, who apparently doesn't think much of Turkish soldiers, they are deserting in droves, which is seriously reducing the numbers in their battalions,' Berish said. 'That says a lot about their morale.'

For the first time since they had set out on their journey, Shoshana's spirits rose. His words confirmed what Dr Shulman had reported. Turkish soldiers were demoralised, inadequately equipped and diseased, and their army was much weaker than they had imagined. It also reinforced her suspicion that the British had vastly overestimated Turkish strength.

Before they left, Berish handed them a letter for Eli. 'I've told him off for not writing to me,' he said.

Shoshana promised to send it on.

As they left the vineyard, she felt troubled. 'Did you notice that Berish avoided looking at you? For some reason he seems to resent you.'

Aaron shrugged. 'He's got a bee in his bonnet about something. Maybe he's jealous that I get to travel with you.'

She dismissed that idea but remained troubled – their spy ring needed cohesion.

Their next stop was the village of Eliahu to see Tova. As Shoshana expected, her first question was about Nathan. Where was he? When was he coming home? Shoshana had no qualms about lying. 'He's still giving lectures at botany conferences,' she said. Seeing Tova's crestfallen expression, she was tempted to add that in his last letter he had asked about her, but thought better of it. No point raising her friend's hopes.

Tova didn't spend much time lamenting Nathan's absence. She was bursting with news. Her contact, the woman who cleaned the German general's villa, had overheard submarine officers talking. Eavesdropping on their conversations while serving coffee and cake, she had learned that there were six German submarines in the Mediterranean. One of the officers mentioned that there were thirty sailors on his boat and that mostly they only searched for large ships to attack. He said their torpedoes were too valuable to waste on small ones, as each weapon cost 30,000 marks. Thanks to her retentive memory, the housekeeper remembered exactly where the ammunition for the submarines was stored. When the officer proudly held up a photograph of his submarine, she noticed that on the back it gave its number as 63 and its length as fifteen metres.

Their last visit that day was to Benyamin, who had discovered the location of a Turkish oil-producing factory.

'That would be a good target for British aircraft,' Shoshana commented.

Benyamin had other news as well. A Turkish army officer he had befriended during his high school years in Tel-Aviv had told him about a German radio station near Damascus. He said it linked Damascus with the Middle East and its coded messages were used to transmit military orders. He even divulged the code. 'The British will be thrilled with that information,' he said.

As the carriage returned to Zichron Yaakov, they passed a group of men deeply engaged in conversation on the corner of Ha-Nadiv

Street. They turned at the rumble of carriage wheels and exchanged disapproving glances when they saw her sitting beside Aaron. She recognised one of them as the chairman of the local Jewish community, a man determined not to upset the Turkish authorities. She dreaded to think what would happen if the rumours about their espionage reached him. She forced herself to smile.

As soon as she stepped inside the house, her father greeted her with a barrage of questions, but before giving him an account of the journey, she pulled out her almanac to check the date of the next moonless night. Two more weeks and the spy ship would arrive. She couldn't wait to pass on the intelligence they had just gathered.

CHAPTER THIRTY-THREE

Atlit, 1917

Two weeks later, Shoshana took up her position by the upstairs window of the research station. For the hundredth time that day she picked up her binoculars and scanned the horizon. And finally there it was, the signal she had been waiting for, three horn blasts from a small vessel emitting thick black smoke. Almost throwing the binoculars on the table in excitement, she ran upstairs, hung out the white sheet, ran back to the window and clamped the binoculars back to her eyes, watching the ship continue on its way. She knew it would return later that night.

At midnight, Shoshana, Aaron and Benyamin crept towards the highway in the dark. Although by now they had made this journey several times and were familiar with the rock-strewn terrain and its cliffs and treacherous slopes, they were aware of the risk of being detected and stood very still, pressing themselves against bushes and boulders whenever they heard the voices of Turkish soldiers who patrolled the highway.

After crossing the highway, they heard a strange noise from a nearby field. A branch snapped nearby, and a moment later a huge shape hurtled towards them. They hid behind a large boulder, almost afraid to breathe. To their relief, it was a cow that had escaped from its barn. They were about to move on when Shoshana motioned them to keep still. A loud Arabic voice broke the silence. It was the cowherd chasing his cow.

After he had disappeared, they hurried towards the shore, desperate not to keep the ship waiting. Every minute mattered. They paused on the clifftop, listening to the roar of the surf. In the darkness they could make out the little boat rowing towards the shore and heard the occasional splash of oars in the water. They were about to make their way down to the beach to meet it when the crack of gunshots and the sound of male voices made them freeze. Soldiers on patrol! Almost before she heard the sound of bullets being fired terrifyingly close, she felt the air shimmer around her. Before she had time to react, Aaron grabbed her arm and pulled her down onto the ground. Had the soldiers heard rustling in the bushes? Or had they seen the boat and, suspecting a secret rendezvous, were they now lying in wait for them? But after the initial salvo, there was no more firing and the voices receded. Shoshana breathed out again. They scrambled to their feet and made their way down the rugged cliff, grabbing hold of bushes and slipping on loose rocks until they reached the beach just as the rowboat was being dragged onto the sand.

In hurried whispers, Shoshana handed the skipper the oilskin pouch containing their reports. He glared at her. 'I said I didn't want to take provisions on board. You'd better get a move on and unload this stuff before we all get shot.'

In silence they began unloading sacks of grain, barley and tea as well as the bags of gold coins intended for the ruined farmers of

Palestine and the destitute Jews who had been expelled from Jaffa
and Tel-Aviv and desperately needed help.

Just as they were unloading the provisions, they heard the
unmistakeable sound of camels approaching along the sand, their
bells tinkling in the night air. 'This is madness,' the skipper fumed.
He ordered the boatman to start rowing back towards the boat
while they threw the boxes, cases and sacks back into the boat in
a panic.

'Quick, in the water!' Shoshana whispered, and fully dressed,
they all waded into the sea until they were submerged up to their
necks. Shivering with cold and fear, afraid of making a sound, they
watched from the water as what seemed an endless line of camels
trudged past.

As soon as Shoshana gave the signal they emerged from the sea,
water dripping from their drenched clothes. She gave a sign to the
boat, wondering if the truculent captain would agree to return, and
what she would do if he didn't. The boat turned towards the beach
again, and the skipper cursed profusely while they began unloading
it once more with feverish haste.

Loaded up with sacks and boxes, they made their slow way back
to the station, across the wadis and sand dunes. It was close to four
o'clock when they returned, exhausted and freezing. After secreting
the gold, concealing the letters, and stacking the provisions in the
cellar, Shoshana made them tea. Her hands gripped the warmth
of the glass and she gave an involuntary shudder. It felt as if someone was walking over her grave, but she dismissed that depressing
thought and said in a bright tone, 'We made it!'

*

Two days later in Cairo, Nathan was fuming. He had been called
in to the office of Sir Hugh Gardiner-Hall, which was filled with
aromatic smoke from his pipe. Facing Sir Hugh, Captain Edwards
was sitting on the edge of his chair, drumming his fingers on his
knees.

'I said from the beginning that this plan of Woolley's would never work,' he burst out.

Ignoring the man, Nathan looked questioningly at his superior. 'Why was he back on the *Victoria* and not Captain Wilson?'

Aware of the antipathy between the two men, Hugh Gardiner-Hall shot Nathan an apologetic look. 'Captain Wilson has been transferred.'

He rested his pipe in the ashtray and turned to the skipper. 'Perhaps you'd like to explain to Mr Adelstein what happened during your voyage to Atlit.'

'First it was the bloody camels. We unloaded the stuff, and then we had to load it up again and row back to the ship, and when the caravan had passed, we had to go back and do it all over again. It's a preposterous misuse of navy resources. I always said we shouldn't be carrying provisions for civilians ...'

Nathan tightened his lips and shifted in his chair. This wasn't the first time Edwards had opposed bringing the desperately needed food and money for the refugees who had lost everything.

'And what happened after that?' Sir Hugh asked.

'On our way back a bloody German U-boat pursued us! I had to wheel backwards and forwards and make several detours to throw it off our scent.' He glared at Nathan. 'We could have been torpedoed for risking our lives to take sacks of grain to some so-called spies.'

Sir Hugh was puffing on his pipe again. 'Those so-called spies, as you call them, provide us with valuable information.'

'Valuable information!' Captain Edwards scoffed. 'We've got other spies on the coast. His people are amateurs. It could be done far more efficiently by other people.'

Nathan could no longer stay silent. He felt as if some unseen power was about to eject him from his chair and he had to grip the sides to remain seated. 'Those "other people" you mention are in it for the money and the information they provide at exorbitant fees is useless. My sister and her group are endangering their lives because our only motive is for you to defeat the Turks.'

Captain Edwards' eyes had a sly glint. 'If you're doing all this from the goodness of your hearts, where's all this gold coming from?'

'Certainly not from the British government!' Nathan retorted. 'It's from Jewish organisations in America and England who want to help the refugees and feed our people who are starving.'

Hugh Gardiner-Hall intervened. 'Apart from the value we place on the information we obtain from the group in Atlit, we regard Mr Adelstein as an invaluable advisor. There is nothing he doesn't know about the topography, geography and geology of Palestine. He even knows the right treatment for malaria.'

'Then you're lucky to have such an oracle at your disposal,' Captain Edwards sneered. 'So I suppose being torpedoed in the process of delivering his provisions is regarded as a small price to pay for his services.'

He rose abruptly, scraping his chair on the floor, and with a curt 'Goodbye,' stormed out of the office.

Nathan flashed an angry look at his superior. 'I'm sick and tired of those derogatory comments. Whenever I encounter such ignorance and ingratitude, I wonder why we are risking our lives to help you. It makes me feel like throwing it all up and walking away.'

Sir Hugh sucked on his pipe for several moments before replying. 'Edwards is old-school navy. Competent but stubborn and somewhat bigoted. I'm sure you are aware that his views don't represent the opinions of those who count inside Military Intelligence. Please sit down. I'll have my secretary bring us tea. There's something I'd like to ask you.'

Although Nathan was still agitated, he felt mollified. He could never resist the surge of pride at being praised by an Englishman in authority.

'We've been wondering whether we could organise a supply service for the cavalry between Beersheba and Hebron.'

Nathan hesitated before replying. Were they planning another campaign? The second battle of Gaza had been a disaster like the first. No wonder, he thought. It was Gallipoli all over again. After the first debacle he had urged General Murray to avoid a frontal attack from the south and suggested an outflanking attack to the east instead, but Murray had ignored his advice and lost the battle. And now the second battle of Gaza had also failed. It was typical of British incompetence and arrogance. Murray had forged ahead without studying the terrain and had overestimated Turkish strength on the coast. Were they about to embark on a third battle that would repeat the blunders of the first two?

As if reading his thoughts, Sir Hugh rested his pipe and leaned forward. 'We've replaced General Murray with General Allenby. We have every confidence in him. Now, tell me what you think about the supply road to Beersheba.'

'From the military information in my sister's latest reports, I think the main offensive should be at Beersheba, not Gaza.'

Sir Hugh nodded. 'That's very interesting and I shall pass it on to Allenby. Now there's something else I should like to discuss. That business with the submarine. If German subs are cruising those waters, that makes it increasingly dangerous, not only for our ship and crew but also for your people and our entire arrangement.'

He sat back, puffed his pipe, and paused for a few moments to give Nathan time to consider his words. Then replacing the pipe on the ashtray, he continued. 'From what Captain Edwards has said, there seem to have been numerous problems with delivering your intelligence. I know that wild seas have made landing impossible at times. And now, on top of that, we have submarines in the area, Turkish soldiers shooting at the spy group, and passing caravans of camels. It seems to me that we must look for some other way of transmitting information between us and Atlit.'

Nathan nodded. The same thing had occurred to him while Captain Edwards was talking. Sending the ship on moonless nights was fraught with uncertainty and danger from the start. And now submarines. And Sir Hugh didn't even know about the suspicious neighbours that Shoshana had mentioned during their brief meeting on the beach at Atlit. They did need to find some alternative method of delivering their intelligence. But what?

He returned to his office feeling increasingly agitated as he turned the problem over in his mind. Then he thought about the recent military disasters. They were risking their lives to secure victory for an incompetent nation whose generals and policy-makers ignored his advice.

He sprang up and paced around the room. While he was focussed on military strategy, Shoshana was exposed to increasing danger, probably more than she realised. He had to get her away from Zichron Yaakov while there was still time. Taking a sheet of paper from his drawer he hurriedly scrawled a letter. He wanted to send it straightaway but knew it wouldn't be delivered until the spy ship arrived at Atlit on the next moonless night.

CHAPTER THIRTY-FOUR

Cairo, 1917

The fact that delivery of his letter to Shoshana depended on so many variables beyond his control preoccupied Nathan after his meeting with Sir Hugh. Over time, he had reluctantly resigned himself to the inevitable frustration of the long delays in transferring intelligence, but now he felt an increasing sense of urgency to warn Shoshana of impending danger. He had to find a faster way of communicating with Atlit.

He began investigating other options with the fervour he had always devoted to his scientific pursuits. It didn't take long to hit on the obvious answer. The telegraph! Invented about sixty years before, it was generally regarded as a swift and reliable way of transmitting information. Delighted with his solution, he almost ran to Sir Hugh's office to suggest it, but instead of sharing his enthusiasm, Sir Hugh poured cold water over him. It was beyond dispute that this method was swift and efficient, he conceded, but the messages were too easily intercepted to be used for espionage.

Crestfallen but undaunted, Nathan continued searching. Looking into other possibilities, he thought of using some kind of wireless technology and was overjoyed when he heard there was an Englishman in Cairo who was regarded as an expert in this field.

Did this man hold the key to swift and safe transmission of information between Cairo and Atlit? Nathan couldn't wait to meet him. Behind the city's main palm-lined boulevard, he wandered into a rabbit warren of crooked alleys, and from the tapping, hammering and sawing all around him, he realised he was in an area of tradesmen and artisans. As he walked towards Richard Hawkes's workplace, he had to jump out of the way as bicycles carrying planks of timber and donkey-driven carts loaded with sacks of cement barrelled along the narrow street.

Richard Hawkes was a tall man with a bony face and large ears set unusually high on his head. He pumped Nathan's hand energetically as he ushered him inside. Instead of the well-equipped laboratory Nathan had expected to see, he was led into a shed-like workshop at the back of a house, its shelves overflowing with cables, its benches covered in coils of wire; piles of papers and journals obscured the tabletop. Struggling to find something for his visitor to sit on, Hawkes pulled out a rickety stool, apologising profusely. Few people were aware of the new technology, and fewer still crossed his threshold to discuss it, he explained, so he was delighted to meet a like-minded person interested in his research.

With that introduction, there was no need to waste time on small talk, and Nathan launched straight into the subject that preoccupied him. 'I wonder if we could lay a telephone cable from a spot on the coast a distance out to sea, lay a second one from further out at sea to a point about twenty metres from the first, and then connect those two cables by some kind of wireless transmission.'

Hawkes listened eagerly and his eyes didn't leave Nathan's face. He had spent the last few years investigating the possibilities of wireless technology and his eyes lit up as he listened to a man he recognised as a kindred spirit who shared his inquiring mind.

'That's a very interesting idea,' he said slowly when Nathan finished. 'Two separate cables coming from distant places connected by wireless under the sea. I've never heard of that being done, but it might be possible.'

As he escorted Nathan to the front gate, he promised to investigate this possibility straightaway. Nathan left his workshop with a light step, but as weeks passed, his frequent inquiries met with excuses and prevarications. Finally it became frustratingly clear that he had wasted valuable time waiting for something that Hawkes was incapable of producing.

He was mulling over his disappointment one morning when Sir Hugh knocked on his office door. 'You'll be relieved to hear that we've sorted out our communication problem,' he said, pulling up a chair and placing a thick manila folder on Nathan's desk. Without waiting for a response, he said, 'Carrier pigeons.'

Nathan's initial reaction was incredulity. Surely he wasn't serious?

Sir Hugh was watching him with an expectant smile, clearly waiting for some enthusiasm, but all Nathan could summon was a frown. 'Carrier pigeons?'

'It's not as bizarre as you might think.' Sir Hugh sat forward, placed his elbows on the desk and rested his chin on his folded hands. 'Pigeons have a long history of carrying secret information. We know from hieroglyphics that the ancient Egyptians used them. Back in the fifth century BC, Cyrus the Great organised a network of pigeon messengers in Persia, and Genghis Khan established a postal service using them to carry messages across Asia. During the first Olympic Games in 776 BC, every single athlete brought a homing pigeon from his village so that in case of victory, the bird would carry the triumphant news home. In 58 BC Julius Caesar informed the Roman senate of his victories in Gaul by pigeon post. And in 1815, Napoleon Bonaparte used pigeons to carry news of his defeat at Waterloo.'

He has come well prepared to persuade me, Nathan thought. In all his extensive reading of Palestinian history he could only recall one incident involving carrier pigeons, and that had ended badly. During the First Crusade, about a thousand years ago, when the Crusaders were encamped in Caesarea, a carrier pigeon sent by the Turkish governor of Acre was killed by a hawk and fell into the hands of one of the Crusader bishops, who noticed something tied to its leg. It was a message urging the Muslims to rebel against the foreign invaders. The fact that this failed pigeon post had taken place uncomfortably close to Atlit had lodged in his memory. It did not seem auspicious.

'The examples you mentioned all happened a long time ago,' he said. 'But surely no one uses pigeons these days?'

Sir Hugh smiled. 'In 1849 the Reuters news service used carrier pigeons to relay advance notice of stock market prices. You can imagine how top secret that information was. And in 1896, New Zealand introduced an airmail service using pigeons. They called it the Pigeongram. And, to put your doubts at rest, just three years ago, when this war started, we established a Pigeon Corps on the Western Front, which apparently has been extremely successful. They've placed lofts along the English coast so pigeons could be dispatched in case of invasion. I recently heard an extraordinary story about one of our pigeons. Although he was wounded during his flight, the brave little fellow didn't stop until he reached his destination, even though he was shot through the chest, blind in one eye and had one leg almost falling off. Thanks to him, the lives of hundreds of soldiers were saved!'

He sat back, pleased that he'd provided incontrovertible proof of the value of a feathered delivery service. But Nathan wasn't convinced.

'The distance between Cairo and Atlit is far greater than any locations on the Western Front. How can we expect pigeons to fly all that way and back?'

Sir Hugh pushed the folder across the desk towards Nathan. 'This contains information about carrier pigeons from the Directorate of

Army Signals, which manages the service. I believe you'll find the answers to all your questions in there. Read it and let me know what you think.'

After Sir Hugh left, Nathan stared at the folder for some time before opening it. Ornithology was a science he knew nothing about, but it seemed to him that, compared with the telegraph, using birds was a retrograde step. Despite what Sir Hugh had said, the idea of using carrier pigeons to transmit secret information on which his sister's life depended unsettled him.

Opening the folder, he flicked through a thick wad of papers that described in off-putting detail the selection, training and use of carrier pigeons. With a sigh he sat back and began to read.

Although he had always considered pigeons to be the least interesting members of the bird family, unremarkable in plumage and vocalisation, he soon discovered he had underestimated them. There was nothing ordinary about these birds. Far from being the rank and file of the avian world, they were elite troops that had become indispensable to humans for thousands of years.

Fascinating as that was, it didn't clarify how the birds found their way home. This was explained in other articles. Apparently they had a surprising ability to navigate using the earth's magnetic field, a skill that enabled them to find their way home over large distances and complex and changing landscapes.

Nathan paused to consider this remarkable skill. Then another question struck him. They must have been trained to fly home, but how? The answer lay several pages away. Food was the incentive. It was kept only in the loft that was the pigeons' home so that they would return there to be fed.

Another issue puzzled Nathan as he read on. How could the pigeons be trained to fly from Atlit to Cairo and back again? Apparently they could. The trainers created a route between the two locations by taking the pigeon from its home base to the second location where he would be provided with food. After feeding there, the bird would return to its home base until eventually it learned to fly between the two locations. On the day the owner wanted the pigeon to deliver a message, he would remove food from the home base and release the hungry bird which would then fly to its second location and deliver the message.

So that's how it worked. Nathan sat back and went over the entire process in his mind to familiarise himself with it. Then he rose and knocked on Sir Hugh's door.

'I've read those articles. Fascinating stuff. I think I understand how it's done. But I'm wondering if anyone has done a study to assess their success rate in this region.'

'The Directorate claims 97 per cent success on the Western Front. That's rather encouraging, wouldn't you say?'

It bothered Nathan that no studies had been made closer to home, but he supposed the difference in locations wouldn't affect their success if the pigeons were trained by the same people.

'One more question. How will these birds be delivered to Atlit?'

'By our spy boat. For the time being we will continue our arrangement, but if the pigeon mail lives up to our expectations, it will eventually supersede the sea route.'

Nathan returned to his office, musing that the day had begun with hopes of modern wireless transmission and ended with the pigeon mail of the ancient Egyptians. He took out his fountain pen and began writing a letter to Shoshana to explain the surprising delivery the next spy ship would bring.

CHAPTER THIRTY-FIVE

Atlit, 1917

As the rowboat approached the shore, Shoshana listened for the splash of its oars among the roar of the surf. Flattened against the thorny broom bushes behind the beach, she watched two men wade ashore, leaning against the weight of the boat they were pulling onto the sand. She motioned to Aaron and Benyamin, who were waiting nearby, and together they crept towards the boatmen. After exchanging whispered greetings, and handing over the precious intelligence, they began unloading the boat, tossing the cartons, boxes and sacks from one pair of hands to the other with a graceful economy of movement that was almost balletic in its precision. Not a moment to lose.

When all the provisions had been unloaded, one of the boatmen leaned into the boat. He pulled out a large oddly shaped object covered by a thick cloth and handed it to Shoshana.

'I was told to deliver this to you in person,' he said. 'The skipper said to tell you it's from your brother.'

Puzzled, she raised a corner of the cloth, but it was too dark to see inside. There was no time to stop and investigate, and bent under the weight of their provisions, they started trudging back to the research station. The rhythmic sound of the oars receded as soon as they left the beach behind and started climbing the steep slope that led to the wadi. Curiosity spurred Shoshana to hasten her step. What had Nathan sent her?

Even before she had time to light a candle inside the station to examine the contents, she became aware of fluttering sounds and soft cooing. Her heart sank. Surely Nathan hadn't sent birds? She pulled off the cloth and her worst fears were confirmed. She was staring at ten pigeons.

Attached to the cage was an envelope addressed to her in Nathan's florid handwriting. Slumped on the couch, she began to read his long letter, which explained in stultifying detail why they had decided to use carrier pigeons. She was so agitated that her eyes leapt from one paragraph to the next before her brain had time to absorb their meaning, and with a groan she went back to the beginning. With each sentence her indignation grew. She didn't like pigeons and had no confidence in them as messengers of vital intelligence. Besides, she already had her hands full running the research station and organising the spy ring without embarking on an activity she knew nothing about. What was Nathan thinking?

You are stronger and braver than anyone I know, Nathan wrote. *Your courage is a flame that illuminates everything and inspires everyone around you.* She put down the letter and exhaled in exasperation. It was all very well for him, safely ensconced in his office in Cairo, to dump this on her and try to sweeten it with flowery words. She knew her strength and courage weren't in question. She was ready to face any danger, but she had a bad feeling about this.

Aaron hadn't taken his eyes off her while she read Nathan's letter and as soon as she placed it on the table, he broke his silence. 'You look upset. What does Nathan say?'

'He expects me to use carrier pigeons! Read this!' and with an abrupt movement she thrust her brother's letter into his hands.

He read it slowly, nodding from time to time. When he had finished, he said, 'I can see his point. The pigeons will deliver our intelligence faster and more reliably than the spy ship and we won't have to wait for moonless nights and calm seas. Remember how heartbroken you were each time the ship didn't come or the rowboat couldn't reach the shore? This will solve our problem. It's exactly what we need.'

Although his argument was logical, it didn't shift the heaviness that pressed on her heart, but she decided to say no more about it.

'I'm exhausted. I'm going home to bed. I'll leave the birds some water and tomorrow I'll go through all the instructions.'

He responded to the anxiety in her tone. 'Don't worry, I'll help you with the birds,' he said and placed a comforting hand on her shoulder. She shot him a warning glance and recoiled as if stung by a wasp.

He looked hurt. 'You've changed,' he said. 'You've become harder. It feels as if you don't trust me.'

Shocked, she tried to gather her thoughts. Since Eli's death, she had become more focussed on their work than ever, and perhaps that was why he saw her as hard and distant. His feelings for her posed a problem she had to deal with. His contribution to the spy ring was invaluable and she didn't want to alienate him, but she couldn't risk encouraging him either. Was it possible to sustain a friendship with a man whose desire was written in his eyes whenever he looked at her? Navigating her way through this relationship was like steering a boat between rapids and shallows.

'Of course I trust you. We're partners in this work. I don't know what we would do without you,' she said after a long pause. 'I know I've become very single-minded, but this is the only thing that matters to me right now. Eli gave his life for it, and I have to continue the mission he died for. Perhaps you mistook my friendship for something it can never be.'

He gazed at her as she spoke, and she realised that although they shared a common goal, on a personal level they were at cross-purposes and always would be. For her, the spy work was everything, but for him, she was everything and his loyalty was to her above all else.

'Don't worry, I didn't mistake your feelings, but I will always do whatever I can to help you,' he said.

She thanked him and left the room without another word, conscious of his eyes on her back.

*

Next morning she returned to the research station and, like a child glaring at homework and wishing it would disappear, she forced herself to pick up the instructions Nathan had enclosed with his letter. The first step was to erect some kind of loft where she was supposed to leave water and birdseed every day so that the pigeons would regard it as their home. The loft was to have a landing board and a one-way trapdoor through which the pigeons would return. This had to be kept closed to prevent them from flying away and she was only to open it when she wanted to release them to deliver a message.

Dov the caretaker, an elderly man whose greatest enjoyment in life was tinkering with tools to fix things, was delighted when Shoshana asked him to build a loft for the pigeons with a landing board and a trapdoor. He had no idea why she had suddenly decided to keep pigeons, but he knew better than to ask. For some time now he had been aware of strange goings-on at the station and he heard rumours in the town, which he always ignored. In any case, keeping pigeons wasn't unusual. His brother had kept them for many years, and used to bore the family with stories about their amazing sense of direction. He had said that he was in good company – a Turkish pasha in the region kept pigeons as well.

It didn't take Dov long to measure out the timber, saw the planks, and nail together a timber loft with shelves inside just like the one his brother had. Proudly he led Shoshana to view the finished product. As soon as she transferred the birds from their cage, they started pecking the grain inside, and as she looked at their iridescent neck feathers and red and white feet, she decided they weren't as plain as she had initially thought.

But despite Nathan's assurances about the inbuilt compass and navigational sense that enabled them to compare where they were with where they aimed to be, and his assertion that they were able to fly ten to fifteen hours at a time between two locations, she doubted their ability to fly to El Arish, where they had been trained, and then back to her in Atlit.

Inside the cage, she found a small package with tiny aluminium cylinders not much larger than her thimble. When she was ready to send a message, she would insert one inside the cylinder using a code. Nathan suggested using the code they had invented as children. She hadn't forgotten it and smiled, thinking back to the time they wrote messages that no one else could decipher, and recalled how frustrated Leah had always been at being excluded from their secret game. She felt a pang of guilt. It had always been her and Nathan. Little did she imagine as they played their game so long ago that one day this code would have an important role in a game on which their lives depended.

Nathan suggested a trial run as soon as the birds had grown accustomed to their new home. Using fine paper that was almost transparent, she penned a message in tiny letters. It was a long time since she had used their code and she checked repeatedly to ensure she hadn't made a mistake. Each letter she wrote was shifted four letters to the left of the one she wanted, so if she wanted to write 'n' she had to write 'j'. The word she wrote – *Greetings* – was a nonsensical jumble of letters that no one could possibly make sense of.

She inserted her message inside a cylinder that she attached to the foot of one of the pigeons and released it. After hesitating for a moment, it flew off. Shading her eyes, she followed its flight until it disappeared. Part of her hoped it wouldn't reach its destination. If the initial attempt failed, they might abandon the idea and the weight she couldn't explain would lift from her heart. Throughout the day she glanced anxiously at the sky every few minutes, hoping she would see it and hoping she wouldn't.

But next day she heard a flutter of feathers and ran towards the loft in time to see the pigeon pushing its way through the trapdoor. Nathan had inserted a message of his own inside the cylinder and when she decoded it, she read *Eureka*. So the bird had found its way to Egypt and back to Atlit! Perhaps she had been wrong about the pigeons after all.

Her second attempt at using pigeon post proved less successful. Several days later, she sent two pigeons to El Arish, each bearing intelligence she had collected about Turkish troops massing around the Gaza-Beersheba area. The sun blazed relentlessly in a cloudless sky that morning and, bathed in perspiration, she went down to the sea to cool off, confident that the pigeons would soon deliver her messages. She was luxuriating in the water, swimming in the dark blue waves, wondering whether the pigeons had reached Nathan, when to her dismay she saw one of them pecking grass nearby. Alarmed, she ran out of the water and shooed it on its way. It flew off, but for the rest of the day she was anxious, wondering whether it had reached its destination.

The following day Nathan's reply arrived with both pigeons. *Great news*, he wrote. *Send more.*

Over the next two months, she sent pigeons with information she gathered. Nathan's continued demands for detailed information ensured that the intensity of their work never slackened. Her fingers shook as she attached the capsules with their coded messages, and she paced nervously until the pigeons returned. Much of the newly gathered information concerned the continuing build-up of Turkish forces near Beersheba and described where they dug their trenches, where they placed their artillery, where they stored their ammunition, and what kinds of guns were being transported to the front.

Then she obtained vital information she knew might change the course of the war in Britain's favour. It described Turkey's advanced aeroplanes at a time when no British aircraft had been sent to Palestine. Despite the safe delivery of her messages, she couldn't relax until the birds returned, and on this occasion she was so overwhelmed by a sense of dread that she released two pigeons at the same time to increase their chance of success. At least if one lost its way, the other might deliver the message.

Churned up, she couldn't wait for the spy ship's next visit. She was relieved that for the time being the arrangement with the ship was due to continue, so that they weren't solely dependent on the pigeons. At least when she handed her intelligence to the boat-man she knew it would be delivered in Egypt. And the ship could continue to deliver much-needed supplies. The uncertainty about the pigeons was too wearing. For the next two days she scanned the sky. At last she heard the flutter of wings, and the sound of the hinged trapdoor being pushed open. But only one of the pigeons had returned.

CHAPTER THIRTY-SIX

Caesarea, 1917

Osman Bey sat on the balcony of his palatial home overlooking the ruined Roman amphitheatre of Caesarea and contemplated the fate of empires. Scattered below him were pillars, statues, and the broken stones of a hippodrome, all that remained of the ancient Romans who had thought their power would never end. Caesarea, he reminded himself, had been so named by Herod in honour of the emperor in Rome. Smoothing down the loose white shirt that had bunched up around his large belly, Osman smiled. He was the representative of the great Ottoman Empire that had superseded that of Rome.

Sipping grape juice from an enamelled goblet, he listened to the cooing of his pigeons, a sound that always soothed him. He had reached an enviable stage of life: all his goals had been fulfilled and he was free to enjoy the fruits of his labour. Of his shrewdness, too. He was aware that being a vocal supporter of Djemal Pasha had been instrumental in his recent promotion to chief of police in this Mediterranean port.

Although he didn't always see eye to eye with Djemal, he had placed ambition ahead of ideals, knowing that to advance in life, one needed to be pragmatic rather than judgmental. Just the same, he couldn't understand why Djemal had allowed himself to be hoodwinked by that Jewish botanist who, despite his promise, had failed to eradicate the locusts, offering the feeble excuse that his labourers were lazy. Osman's policy was that if someone has betrayed your trust once, they would do it again, but for some reason Djemal was so bewitched by this Jew that he had trusted him to produce oil from the sesame plant and had given him a pass to travel to Germany. Not only had the man failed to achieve what he'd promised, he had never returned. Vanished without a trace. There was an article in the American press that he had been captured by the British as an enemy spy, but Osman had his doubts. He would have found out where he was and hunted him down. The man had a family, didn't he? A few well-aimed blows with a whip would soon have revealed his whereabouts. The fellow had made a fool of Djemal, something Osman would never have countenanced and could not comprehend, especially now that Djemal was one of the most powerful men in the Ottoman Empire.

Life had been good to him, he mused as he cast his gaze past the ruins to the port and the sparkling dark blue sea beyond it. He lacked for nothing, and his recent promotion ensured the wealth he needed to support his luxurious lifestyle. Like most affluent people, Osman Pasha did not consider himself wealthy or extravagant, but he hadn't been able to resist the lure of exacting additional taxes, confiscating farm machinery and commandeering grain in this backward part of the Ottoman Empire. He had to keep his wives happy and for some reason all the women in his life were so infatuated with gold and precious stones they couldn't have enough.

He turned his thoughts to the subjects in his fiefdom. Thankfully the Armenians were no longer a threat. The new Turkish rulers had made sure of that. As to the Arabs, they wouldn't fill his coffers. Certainly not the backward fellahin who ploughed their plots of land and lived from hand to mouth. No wonder some of them had sold their land to the European Jews. They posed no threat to their Turkish overlords. The Bedouins, however, were a different breed. Wily, tribal, duplicitous and vengeful, their greed had no limits. They exacted bags of gold from the British in return for information that was useless while at the same time purporting to spy for the Turks.

He knew that they had fallen for the propaganda of the messianic Englishman they called El Aurens and believed that with him at the head of their so-called army, they would unite to defeat the Turks and lay claim to the whole of Palestine. Every age produced its own messiah, he reflected, like Jesus and the Mahdi, but they were all betrayed in the end. Perhaps the mesmerising quality of deserts with their shimmering dunes and ever-shifting horizons had seduced this Englishman into thinking himself the saviour of the Bedouins. It was true that they had won some victories attacking the Hejaz railway, but a close friend stationed in Dera'a had confided that they had captured the Englishman and humiliated him in a way he would never forget. The Ottoman Empire would never be at the mercy of such adventurers.

The Jews were another matter. He felt a grudging admiration for them, the way they had bought swampy, malaria-ridden land and turned it into fertile orchards and vineyards, and he intended to profit from that. That's where the money lay. Here too he opposed Djemal's policy. These people needed to be handled with a firm hand. Expelling them as Djemal had done had been counterproductive. What was the point of getting rid of successful people who could be taxed and replacing them with peasants who lived in penury? The answer was to impose harsher taxes on those who could pay.

This group did pose a danger to the empire, however, and he had heard murmurs of rebellion after the deportations from Tel-Aviv and

Jaffa. Just the previous week he'd heard that some British politicians were talking about creating a Jewish homeland in Palestine, but that assumed they would win the war, which, judging by their recent defeats in Gaza, was highly unlikely. His spies informed him that the Bedouins had already staked their claim on Damascus, based on their Englishman's promise of an Arab homeland, but he knew that in the event of a Turkish defeat, the French would grab that region before the Arabs did. With Allah's help, they would defeat the foreign infidels. In the meantime, he would send two of his officers to investigate the state of the orchards and vineyards in the Galilee region and demand higher taxes.

Warmed by the sun, he closed his eyes and was drifting off to sleep when the fluttering of wings reminded him that it was time to feed the pigeons. Reluctantly he rose, walked to the other side of the balcony, plunged his hand into the bag of grain and poured it into the feeding bowl. As the birds flew towards him, he regarded them with an indulgent smile.

'Here you are, my beauties,' he called. 'Dinner's ready.'

There was something very touching about the relationship between man and bird, he thought, a fine balance between dependence and freedom that he controlled. He had started keeping pigeons ever since his arrival in Caesarea several months before, but already they knew his voice and their feed times.

As he watched the birds crowding and jostling around the bowl, he noticed one he hadn't seen before. A stranger had joined his flock for a free meal. Where had it come from? Coming closer, he noticed a small metal capsule attached to its leg. A carrier pigeon that had obviously lost its way. Who had sent it and what message was it meant to deliver?

He clapped his hands for a servant, who materialised immediately as if he had been waiting to be summoned. 'Yes, *effendi*?'

Osman told him to fetch a pair of scissors.

The man returned several moments later and Osman, who hadn't taken his eyes off the strange pigeon, reached out, grabbed hold of

the bird, and cut off the capsule. Prising it open, he found a fine slip
of paper with words that he couldn't understand. They weren't in
Arabic, Turkic or Hebrew script. He studied the Roman letters and
concluded that they were some kind of code. His eyes narrowed.
Who was sending coded messages and who were they intended for?
He would send it to Constantinople where they would have experts
in deciphering codes, but one thing he didn't need an expert to tell
him was that there was a spy ring operating in this area. It had to
be run by Jews. He wouldn't rest until he found out who they were.

*

Shoshana wasn't worried when only one pigeon returned from
Egypt. She had learned from experience that pigeons often strayed
and she assumed that the other one had got lost or been injured
along the way. The important thing was that one of them had
delivered the vital intelligence that the Turks were using advanced
aircraft.

Two days later, she looked out of the window of the research
station and to her dismay saw Daniel Skovron, one of the members
of the spy ring in the Caesarea region, galloping along the road
towards the station. Flushed and out of breath, he dismounted and
tied up his horse. Before he could knock on the door, she opened it
and hastily ushered him inside, glancing around to make sure that
no one had seen him before closing the door.

Her eyes flashed with anger as she confronted him. 'Why did
you come? I told you that Aaron and I would come and collect
intelligence from now on. You're risking our lives coming here.'

He was still panting after his long ride and she brought him a
glass of water, tapping her foot while she waited for his explanation.

'I wouldn't have come if it wasn't urgent. I heard from my contact
in Caesarea that the Chief of Police has found a pigeon with a message
tied to its foot. He can't decipher it and he's sent it to Constantinople,
but he's convinced it was sent by a Jewish spy ring somewhere in the
area and he's determined to find out who's behind it.'

Shoshana's face went white. Her worst fears about the pigeons had been realised. Of all the mishaps that could have befallen them, the worst was for a pigeon to fall into the hands of a Turkish official. And of all Turkish officials, it was Osman Pasha, who was notorious for his oppression of the Jewish communities.

'You did the right thing coming to warn me, but hurry back before anyone notices your absence.'

She had to act fast. What if someone found the rest of the pigeons and traced them to her? She cursed the day Nathan had brought the birds, but her mind was clear and she didn't panic. As she ran to find Dov, she knew exactly what she had to do.

Dov was humming as he hammered nails into the stable door and didn't hear her until she repeated, 'Listen, Dov, we have to kill the pigeons.'

He stared and his jaw dropped. 'But Miss Shoshana ...'

'I haven't got time to explain. We have to do it now.'

Looking at his horrified expression, she said, 'Believe me, I wish we didn't have to do it but there's no choice. If you can't bring your-self to do it, I'll do it myself.'

He was still staring at her. 'I'm sorry, I can't do it.'

There was no time for discussions. She swallowed hard. 'I under-stand. I'll do it. Will you dig a trench in the barley field so we can bury them?'

His shoulders slumped as he walked towards the field, looking back several times as if hoping she'd change her mind.

She walked slowly towards the loft then paused. Aaron was in Afula, collecting intelligence from Dr Shulman. He'd probably be back late that afternoon. Perhaps she could wait ... but she couldn't risk waiting. Osman's men might be scouring the area right now. Somehow she had to find the strength within herself to kill the birds, no matter how repugnant it was.

She put her hand through the trapdoor, grabbed hold of a pigeon, stroked its soft feathers and squeezed her eyes shut as she closed her hands around its neck. As if they sensed the danger, the other pigeons started squawking and flew to the most distant part of the loft. Fighting nausea, she continued, knowing she had to finish the horrible job before anyone heard them. She left one pigeon so she could let Nathan know what had happened.

The documents! She couldn't risk them being found. Bunching her skirt to enable her to run faster, she hurried inside the station, grabbed the metal box with the latest intelligence, and ran outside to bury it in the trench Dov had dug.

Tears poured down her cheeks as she laid the limp little bodies inside the trench, and shuddered at the enormity of what she had done. Then she filled in the grave with shovelfuls of soil.

'You're stronger than most men, Miss Shoshana,' Dov said as she replaced the shovel in the barn, and she sensed disapproval as well as admiration in his tone. But there was no time to analyse his words or her own emotions.

'We have to dismantle the loft and destroy all evidence of it,' she said. 'If anyone asks you, you never saw any pigeons here and you don't know anything about them.'

She had managed to hold herself together until that moment but suddenly the smell of dead pigeons overwhelmed her and she rushed around the side of the barn and retched until she tasted bile.

CHAPTER THIRTY-SEVEN

The Sinai, 1917

Wiping the sweat off his face as the desert sun blazed on his head, Nathan sank into the shade of a palm tree, took out his flask of water and gazed at the dunes rolling towards the horizon. The edge of the Sinai was the closest he had come to the land he loved for over a year, and he felt the heart-racing joy of an animal that has picked up the scent of home.

He had been sent here by General Edmund Allenby to show Anzac engineers where to find sources of water along the route they were eventually to take on their way to Palestine. His reverie was interrupted by a sudden burst of ribald laughter. The Australians were talking about a commanding officer one of them described as 'a bloody mongrel'. Nathan chuckled at their colourful expressions. This was his first encounter with Australians, who fascinated him with their high spirits and their ability to make fun of everything. They were irreverent and independent, and their refusal to respect authority almost amounted to insubordination. He liked the way they called everyone 'mate'. They were a refreshing contrast to the stuffy English officers he had encountered in London and Cairo.

Nathan was in his element. Here he felt he could breathe freely. Apart from spending time with people he liked, he was thrilled to be out in the field again. He was a country boy at heart and loved being under vast skies, in wide open spaces. To outsiders this would appear to be a monotonous landscape of endless sands and scrubby plants, but he saw millennia of wondrous ecological development. Wind, sun and water had eroded rocks and transformed the topography, and shrubs and grasses endured despite the forces of nature.

It was a relief to be away from the claustrophobia of his Cairo office where the soundtrack of daily life was the whirring of ceiling fans and restrained English voices. He had aspired to be recognised and accepted by the British authorities, but the price he paid was being continually on his guard, watching every word in an effort to curb the natural spontaneity and outspokenness that shocked them.

Looking back over the past few weeks, he felt vindicated. Finally they appreciated the invaluable contribution the spy ring could make, especially after the last intelligence Shoshana had sent about Turkish plans to launch an offensive at Gaza. This had led to his meeting with Sir Edmund Allenby, who had recently replaced General Murray as commander of the Sinai campaign.

Nathan recalled that meeting with a satisfaction bordering on incredulity. Allenby's reputation as a legendary martinet preceded him and Nathan's associates in Cairo had told him about the general's volcanic temper – one story even claimed he had yelled at a dead soldier to obey orders. Maybe that one was apocryphal, but just the same, it put Nathan on his guard: this wasn't going to be a relaxing encounter.

When he arrived at their meeting, he found General Allenby the image of a highly decorated general. Tall, erect, with a neatly trimmed moustache and an intimidating presence, he surveyed

Nathan with a piercing gaze and demanded to know why he advocated drilling for water in the desert. Nathan had steeled himself for ridicule and dismissive comments, so he was delighted to have the general's undivided attention as he explained his reasons. Allenby had listened intently, followed his explanation, and then asked for details, impressing Nathan with his incisive mind.

In the course of their conversation, Nathan became so relaxed that after they had discussed the issue of water sources, he gave the general his opinion about Turkish troops. 'They are not as well equipped or as well motivated as our men, but it would be a mistake to underestimate them,' he said. Allenby had responded with a restrained 'I see,' and it was only in retrospect that Nathan realised how presumptuous he had been, offering military advice to a general. And how gracious Allenby had been to receive it.

Before wrapping up their meeting, General Allenby returned to the subject of water. 'If, as you have intimated, you can help our engineers source an adequate water supply in the desert, we will be forever in your debt because it will make our victory possible, Mr Adelstein.' Then he added, 'I believe we are already greatly indebted to your sister and the spy ring she has organised for intelligence that will dramatically alter the thrust of our campaign. When, as I expect, we have defeated the Turks, I will go on to fulfil my greatest dream. I will enter the holy city of Jerusalem and liberate it.'

Nathan was elated. Finally everything was coming together and he would play a role in British victory.

And that was why he was now sitting in the shade of a palm tree in the Sinai desert. While he waited to talk to the Anzac engineers about drilling for water, he gazed at the desert sands and thought about Eli. Where did his body lie? He wished he could tell his friend about the meeting with Allenby. Some evenings when he looked up and saw something flash across the night sky, he thought that Eli had been a human meteor, illuminating their lives for an instant and disappearing into the void, leaving a blazing trail behind.

He heard the nasal twang of Australian voices and wondered how they would react to his revolutionary plan.

'You might be surprised to hear that I'm quite familiar with the water sources in this area because I explored it before the war,' he began. He went on to describe how he had followed the Biblical descriptions of the ancient route of wells, waterholes and springs mentioned in the Book of Joshua, a route that had been followed by the early Israelites and by Bronze Age traders as well.

He paused to assess their reaction. Someone muttered something about a bloody Bible lesson but the others listened intently and he continued. 'I realise that these sources alone won't be enough to provide water for all the men, let alone the camels and horses that the campaign will involve, or the mules that will be needed to pull the covered wagons of wounded soldiers to medical tents after the battle, so I'd like to explain what I have in mind.'

They leaned forward as he traced a map on the sand with a fallen palm frond. Pointing to several places on his diagram, he explained that they would draw water from the plain with spring drills and filters and prepare sufficient lengths of pipe that would provide Jerusalem with water after it had been liberated.

At the mention of Jerusalem, an excited murmur rose from the group. Encouraged by their interest and fired by his own enthusiasm, the ideas poured from his mouth. They would have to build a filtering plant large enough to purify 600,000 gallons of water a day on the Sweet Water Canal that already supplied Port Said with fresh water. To store the purified water, they would have to construct a reservoir. A long pipeline would carry the water from the reservoir to El Arish. To bring the water to the battlefield, they would need to construct a broad-gauge railway. A convoy of trucks would eventually carry the water from the pipeline to the railway, and finally camels loaded with metal tanks would transport the water from there to the battlefield.

As he finished explaining his visionary plan, he looked around, expecting a barrage of questions, but they looked back at him in thoughtful silence. Some were frowning, others raised their eyebrows or turned to their colleagues while they considered his proposal. He realised how revolutionary his ideas were. Perhaps he had talked too fast and they hadn't followed his explanation. But suddenly they were all talking at once, and their comments and questions showed that they had understood his plan but needed more details about the logistics involved in carrying it out.

After addressing their concerns and admitting that he didn't know exactly how long it would take or how much it would cost to implement his plan, Nathan reassured them that General Allenby himself had sent him to brief them on it. 'He regards this as the key to his victory,' he added.

After several more days in the desert discussing various aspects of his proposal, Nathan returned to Cairo, confident the Australians would put his plan into action. Although he regretted leaving the open spaces of the desert he loved, he had achieved something close to his heart. He had long been convinced that water played a crucial role in international conflicts and believed it might also ultimately hold the key to peace.

As soon as he walked into his office at the Savoy Hotel he saw the dispatch on his desk. As he opened it, he felt something contract in his chest. It was a message Shoshana had sent by carrier pigeon that had been forwarded to him from El Arish. He read it several times and felt a chill rise from the base of his skull. Everything stopped and he turned to stone, unable to think or move. His sister had worded her desperate message with an attempt at humour. *My lost pigeon has visited Osman Bey in Caesarea. I wonder what they talked about.*

His initial apprehension about the pigeons had been prophetic. Why had he allowed himself to be persuaded to use them? He again recalled the story of the carrier pigeon during the First Crusade that had been intercepted by the Catholic bishop, not far from Caesarea where Shoshana's pigeon was caught.

But it was too late for recriminations. He felt ashamed that he had been so absorbed in his own plans he hadn't given his sister a single thought. For as long as he could remember, he had felt closer to Shoshana than anyone else in the world, but while he had been pursuing his selfish ambitions, basking in the recognition he received from General Allenby and the admiration of the Australian engineers, she was in Zichron Yaakov facing catastrophe.

He picked up the dispatch again and tried to think calmly. Osman Bey wouldn't understand what was written in the capsule attached to the pigeon's leg, but he would know it was in code. Even before he had it deciphered, the Roman letters would have told him that the sender was probably Jewish and that a spy ring was operating nearby. How long before his inquiries led him to Zichron Yaakov? And once there ... Nathan shuddered. The consequences were unthinkable. There was only one solution.

He checked his almanac. The MS *Victoria* was due to sail for Atlit in a week's time, but the Turks would be watching the coast more closely from now on, searching for signs of espionage. He hoped the British would continue to send the spy ships now Shoshana would no longer be able to send the carrier pigeons. His mind was racing and his hands were shaking. When the ship docked at Atlit the following week, it would deliver his letter to Shoshana. She must sail to Cairo on its return voyage.

He began writing the letter but stopped after a few words and propped his head in his hands. What if she didn't agree? He knew how stubborn his sister was. No, not stubborn. Idealistic. Selfless. Brave. Over the past year, he had invited her to come and visit him in Cairo several times but each time she had refused. She couldn't leave the work to others. Perhaps she hadn't trusted anyone else to shoulder the burden or felt guilty leaving them. But this time he wasn't suggesting a holiday. This time she would have to remain in Cairo, he would make sure of it. He picked up his pen again. There was no choice. This could be her last chance to leave.

CHAPTER THIRTY-EIGHT

Atlit and The Negev, 1917

Shoshana was in a frenzy of activity but her mind was calm. The chaos in her head had subsided and the world had become very quiet. She knew exactly what she had to do and the order in which to do it. Her first task was to safeguard Nathan's precious botanical collection and his scientific papers. When the Turks came to search the station, as she was certain they would, they would find nothing, and in their fury they would probably destroy everything, smash the glass specimen plates into splinters, rip up the research papers, set fire to his treasured books.

She opened the filing cabinets one by one and contemplated their contents. She was looking at the results of years of meticulous documentation of the geology, botany and water sources of Palestine, folders bulging with research notes and analysis. She paused, overcome with admiration at the breadth of her brother's knowledge and his ever-expanding scientific curiosity. All this must be preserved for posterity and it was her duty to do so.

Next she inspected the drawers full of plant specimens pressed onto glass plates. She had been allowed to label the envelopes herself from the age of six, and remembered recording the strange words in her best writing to avoid making a mistake and incurring her brother's anger. For an instant she was overwhelmed by a sense of helplessness. There was so much of it. How could she save it all? Should she bury everything in the trench together with the metal box that contained their intelligence documents and reports? But if she did, would the dampness of the soil damage them?

Then she remembered the wall recess and the momentary panic passed. When the station had been erected, the builder had concealed recesses behind the double walls, probably at Nathan's suggestion, whether due to instinct or prescience, she didn't know. But as soon as she pressed the button that slid open the false wall and saw the extent of the space behind it, she breathed out. Stacking Nathan's specimen plates into neat piles, she arranged them inside the recess. That still left room for his files. Running back and forth for the next few hours, she filled the space with the papers that had gained him international renown.

Exhausted, she sank onto a chair. If Nathan had carried on his scientific research instead of abandoning it to take part in her mission, he would certainly have continued making contributions to science. Did he ever regret his sacrifice? Despite their closeness, she had never asked him, and now she wondered why. It wasn't that she lacked empathy. Since childhood, she had been Nathan's adoring shadow, and it seemed now that there had never been enough time to talk about personal matters. When they met again she promised herself she would pose the questions she had never asked.

She cast a regretful gaze at his bookshelves. There wasn't sufficient space in the concealed recess for all the books, so she selected the rarest tomes, the ones she knew meant most to him, and stacked them inside the remaining space. In the far corner of the recess, her hand brushed against something hard and metallic. Curious, she closed her fingers around it and rolled it towards her. She was looking at a small ivory-handled pistol. It was the one Nathan had brought her from America before the war. She used to take it whenever she rode alone in the hills and valleys of Mount Carmel, more to put her mother's mind at rest than for any thought of her own danger, never believing she would need to use it. When she moved to Constantinople with her new husband she had left it at home, and Nathan must have placed it inside the recess for safekeeping.

She turned it over and felt its heft. After all these years, it still rested comfortably in her hand, reminding her of those long rides she had taken when the only thing on her mind was the wild beauty of the landscape and the breeze ruffling her hair. After a moment's hesitation, she put the pistol inside the pocket of her skirt. She would take it home.

Night had fallen and there was a chill in the air. She had run out of the tea that the spy ship had delivered during its last visit, and for the past two weeks had drunk hot water with lemon instead. As she closed her hands around the glass to warm them, she was grateful that there was no shortage of lemons and oranges in her father's orchard.

Thinking about her father unsettled her. Although he still worked in the orchards and vineyards and protested that he was stronger and more energetic than men half his age, he looked frail, and she worried about him. Ever since Osman Bey had found their pigeon, she had tried to persuade him to leave Zichron Yaakov, at least until the danger passed, but as she had expected, he had refused.

'Move where?' he had retorted. 'Don't talk nonsense. My place is right here in my home.' Then he had placed his arm around her shoulders, and added in a more conciliatory tone, 'My place is with you. No matter what happens.'

That's when she realised that he was fully aware of the situation they were in and was not afraid to face it.

Her thoughts turned to Leah and she was churned up again. In her last letter, her sister said she intended to come home for the High Holy Days.

A shiver had run down Shoshana's spine when she read that. Rosh Hashana, their New Year celebration, was only two weeks away. On no account should Leah come. She had to be stopped. Shoshana's impulse was to write back at once but she couldn't risk committing a warning to paper. She had to visit Leah as soon as possible.

*

September rain was falling more heavily than usual when she set out for the women's settlement the following day. The horse stumbled on the rutted road that had turned to mud, and Nasser cursed as he tried to manoeuvre the carriage around the potholes and the slush. 'This is not a good day for travelling such a long distance, Miss Shoshana,' Nasser grumbled as he jumped down to lead the horse out of the boggy ground and brushed away the rain that dripped off the brim of his battered hat. Shoshana sat in the centre of the wooden seat, hugging the hood of her coat close to her head to keep dry, but gusts of wind drove the rain into her face. As she gazed at the misty landscape, she wondered how to present the situation to her sister in a way that would convince Leah to stay away from Zichron Yaakov without alarming her.

Suddenly the sky brightened, the sun dazzled her eyes through the grey clouds, and through the rain Shoshana saw a perfect rainbow arcing across the sky. *Rainbows are God's smile, his signal that he loves the world*, her mother used to say. She had believed that as a child, and even after Nathan had explained rainbows were a scientific phenomenon caused by the refraction of light, she continued to regard them as magical. Even now, burdened with responsibilities and apprehensive about the future, she couldn't resist seeing this one as an omen of hope.

By the time they turned off onto the rutted track leading to the settlement, the sky had darkened again, and the rainbow had vanished as if it had never existed. There was no one working in the barley field, and there was no activity in the courtyard when Nasser brought the carriage to a halt outside the main building.

Shoshana walked inside and followed the sound of voices until she came to the kitchen where a group of women were slicing tomatoes, carrots, cucumbers and onions for their midday meal. They looked up when they saw her, and Esther, whom she recognised from her last visit, pointed to the far corner where Leah was stirring hummus paste and spooning cottage cheese into large serving bowls. Shoshana stood watching her, waiting for her to turn around, but Esther's voice boomed through the kitchen.

'Leah! Look who's here!'

Leah put down the ladle, wiped her hands on her large apron, rushed towards her sister and threw her arms around her.

'Shoshi! What a surprise! But how come you're here? Didn't you get my letter? I wrote I was coming home soon.'

Aunt Hannah, who had been bent over the wood stove, took out three wheel-sized rounds of bread from the oven, placed them on the oak table to cool, and turned when she heard Leah's voice. She hurried to greet her niece but from the way she was frowning, Shoshana saw that she suspected something was wrong.

In an urgent tone she said, 'Is everything all right at home? Is it my brother?'

Shoshana hugged her aunt. 'Don't worry. He's fine.' She was about to add that he sends his love but decided against it. That would really make Hannah suspicious.

It was hard to make herself heard above the clattering, banging and chattering in the kitchen. She glanced at Leah. 'Let's go to your room so we can talk.'

Inside Leah's monastic bedroom, she sat beside her sister on the narrow bed while Leah chattered about life on the farm. After she had made several perfunctory replies, Leah stopped talking.

'Shoshi, you haven't been listening to anything I've said. Why did you come here? There's something wrong, isn't there?'

Shoshana hesitated before replying. 'I came to tell you not to come to Zichron Yaakov. It isn't safe.'

'Not come home for Rosh Hashana? Why? What's happened?'

Speaking slowly, Shoshana told her about the pigeon that had been found by Osman Bey. 'So things are a bit uncertain at the moment and we don't know what will happen but ...'

Leah interrupted her. 'I still want to come.'

'Listen, Leah. You have to trust me. It's far too dangerous for you to come home right now. And in case they start making inquiries, you shouldn't have any contact with me.'

Leah tightened her lips. 'But you're still there and so is Abba. I've been looking forward so much to coming home for Rosh Hashana.'

'So was I, but the situation has changed. I can't risk you being caught by the Turks. Please try to understand. We'll celebrate Rosh Hashana together next year.'

Leah said nothing. Suddenly Shoshana blurted out something she had no intention of saying. 'Leah, I have no idea what will happen but I promised our mother that I'd look after you so I have to keep you safe.'

Leah's face was pale and she was silent. Then she said, 'Does Nathan know about this Osman Bey? Maybe he can do something?'

'There's nothing anyone can do. Maybe he won't even come and I'm anticipating things that will never happen, but I have to be prepared in case they do. In the meantime, please don't write to me and don't come home. As soon as things settle down, I'll get in touch.'

Leah put her arms around her sister and they clung to each other in silence. When Shoshana rose, her eyes were full of tears. 'I should go. Can you apologise to Aunt Hannah for me and tell her I had to hurry home?'

'She'll wonder why you came all this way for such a short time.'

'Tell her I wanted to discuss a personal problem and had to get back early because of the weather.'

Leah looked dubious. 'She wouldn't believe it. You saw the way she looked at you when you arrived. She's too smart to be fobbed off with such a story.'

'It doesn't matter if she believes it or not. The important thing is that she doesn't know anything. You wanted to be part of the conspiracy. So now you know how hard it is to keep secrets.'

As she climbed into the carriage, she breathed out. No matter what happened, Leah would be safe.

As the carriage lurched north towards Zichron Yaakov, the rain eased to a drizzle. From time to time the clouds parted to allow sunlight to shine through, but although she scanned the sky hoping to see another rainbow, the clouds darkened and hung low above the earth.

CHAPTER THIRTY-NINE

Atlit, 1917

Aaron stomped into the research station, flung himself onto the nearest chair and started cursing. Shoshana, who had been sorting the last of the provisions from the most recent ship delivery, looked up in surprise at his dishevelled appearance. Usually he looked impeccable, but now the top button of his celluloid collar was undone, his shirt sleeves were unevenly rolled up, and fury blazed in his eyes.

'That blasted idiot Berish. You'll never believe what the fool has done.'

'What happened? What did he do?'

Shoshana forced herself to stay calm. After all, Aaron was a hot-head and he and Berish had never got on, so it wasn't impossible that they'd had an argument when Aaron had arrived to collect the latest intelligence. She shouldn't have sent him on his own, but she had been overwhelmed by all the things she had to do in case the

Turkish police came to search the premises, as they were bound to do as soon as they'd decoded the message attached to the pigeon's leg.

As she waited for him to explain, she surveyed the meagre supplies stacked inside the cupboard. All the tea and coffee were gone, but a couple of sacks of grain and barley remained, as well as a small bag of gold coins. Time was running out. If she didn't distribute it all before the police arrived, the Turks would grab the lot. That would be a terrible loss but discovery of the coins would seal her fate. As soon as the Turks saw the image of George V, they would know the coins came from Britain.

She had already begun to sort out the cash and provisions she wanted to distribute to the Village Committee. As she removed the bag of coins from the metal box secreted at the back of the cupboard, she thought about the people whose lives it would ease. It would help them pay their ever-increasing taxes and buy food for themselves and their animals. Life these days was reduced to bare essentials. Thinking about the risk she and her companions had taken lugging the heavy sacks from the ship past Turkish patrols, she couldn't quell a bitter sense of injustice. She had played a vital role in supporting the community, and she had done it because it was in her power to do so, to help the people she had grown up with. She hadn't done it to earn their gratitude, but from the rumours she overheard and the suspicious glances cast her way, it was clear she wasn't trusted, and she resented their malice, despite the eagerness with which they accepted the provisions and money she distributed.

All this ran through her mind as she waited for Aaron to catch his breath and explain himself.

His jaw was clenched and his scar looked more livid than ever. When he did begin to speak, the words that poured out were so incoherent she had to ask him to stop and start from the beginning. With an effort he spoke more slowly and her curiosity turned to alarm. It seemed that as soon as he'd walked into the vineyard,

Berish had challenged him in an aggressive tone to explain the whereabouts of his missing cousin.

'Where is Eli? First they told me he was in Egypt, then they changed the story and said he was training to be a pilot in Britain. So which is it? And wherever he is, why hasn't he written? I only joined your spy ring because he was involved. I'm sure you're hiding something and I won't rest until I find out what it is.'

Shoshana understood why he was so angry. She had insisted on keeping Eli's fate a secret to prevent the group from panicking, but now hearing Berish's accusations, she wondered if her plan had misfired.

'It sounded as if he blamed me for Eli's disappearance,' Aaron continued. 'It's just as well he doesn't know what really happened. Can you imagine what he'd do if he found out that I'd been with Eli when he was shot, and I was the one who got away?'

He stared at his hands and sighed. 'When he got that off his chest, he had another complaint. He said he'd heard a rumour that the farmers around here suspected we were involved in some illegal activity that put them all in danger. He blamed me for that too. Said I was reckless and untrustworthy, that even my former colleagues in the militia didn't trust me.'

Aaron hesitated for a moment before continuing. 'He even criticised you. Said if you took off your rose-coloured glasses, you'd get rid of me before it was too late.'

Shoshana wondered if Berish had noticed the way Aaron gazed at her and whether he suspected a personal relationship between them.

'I shouldn't have sent you there alone, knowing how he feels about you. But let's move on. Did he have any intelligence for us?'

Aaron made a scornful sound. 'Intelligence? Wait till you hear this. You know that his main informant is the Turkish officer who is the aide-de-camp of the German general? Well, that Turk has now deserted from the army.'

Shoshana frowned. 'Why is that a problem?'

Aaron's voice rose again. 'Because that bloody fool Berish is hiding him!'

Now she understood his fury. A Jewish member of a secret spy ring protecting a deserter from the Turkish army was not just the height of recklessness. It was potentially fatal for Berish – for all of them. How could he have exposed them to such danger?

It was too late for recriminations. They had to act fast. 'We have to get that deserter away from there as soon as possible.'

Aaron nodded. 'If the army finds him they'll hang him. And Berish, too, but not before they get information out of him. The deserter was wondering if we could put him on the spy ship next time it visits Atlit so he can get to Egypt.'

Shoshana was speechless. How did the deserter know about the ship? Surely Berish hadn't been careless enough to tell him? But it looked as if he had.

'What did you tell him?'

'I told him I'd have to discuss it with you.'

'Do you know where Berish is hiding him?'

'In a shed in a remote corner of his vineyard. He says he'll be safe there for the time being.'

'I doubt it. The Turks will scour every farm and vineyard until they find him. He's a high-ranking officer and they'll make an example of him. Our only hope is that it might take them a couple of days. That's our only chance of extricating him from Berish's vineyard and finding a safer place to hide him until the ship's next visit.'

After Aaron had left, she paced around, too restless to finish sorting the remaining provisions. One thought pounded in her head. *That's all we need right now, a Turkish informer who has deserted from the army and is hiding in the home of a Jewish spy, just as the Turks are probably about to swoop down on us any day.*

Sleep didn't come easily that night, and as usual when she couldn't sleep, her bed felt cold and empty and she yearned for Eli's warmth. Grief wasn't just a wolf with sharp claws, it was a cancer that invaded every part of the body, lodging its tentacles inside the pathways of the brain, the joints of the bones, even the follicles of hair. It never forgot what was lost and could never be regained. Grief was the price of love.

She must have drifted off to sleep because she dreamed she was running across wadis and sand dunes, searching for Eli, calling his name. Finally exhausted, she sank down in despair. He had gone and she would never see him again. Suddenly she heard his voice. So he wasn't dead after all, he was only hiding! Overcome with joy she reached out to touch him and woke up hugging her pillow, tears streaming down her cheeks.

*

The messenger arrived at her home early the next morning with a curt letter summoning her to the Village Committee that afternoon. Shoshana had already figured out where to shelter the Turkish officer. Dr Shulman's brother lived in a modest brick house on the outskirts of Afula. He had once told her that its basement was accessible only by a hidden trapdoor. As no one would think of looking for him there, it would be the ideal place to hide the deserter until they could get him out of Palestine. The problem was to find a way of transporting him from Berish's vineyard to Afula. She was considering the possibilities when the letter arrived.

She had no doubt what the committee wanted to talk to her about, and she was still contemplating her response as she walked along Ha-Meyasdim Street after lunch. A light breeze ruffled the leaves of the oak trees and almost blew off her wide-brimmed straw hat. Occasionally it flurried the hem of the navy taffeta skirt she had copied from a French fashion magazine before the war. The design was tricky and she recalled asking her mother's advice how to make the concealed pleat. She sighed. The memory of her mother was a wound that never healed. She calculated it must have been seven years ago, a carefree time when dressmaking had given her so much pleasure. It felt as if a hundred years had passed since then.

The street was unusually quiet, and no children played hopscotch or chasings in the street. A cat looked up and resumed licking its paw. She heard a door open and saw Miriam coming out. It had been several weeks since their last meeting and Shoshana looked at her friend, eager to see a friendly face. Just then Miriam's mother appeared behind her, locked accusing eyes with Shoshana, and grabbed Miriam's arm and pulled her inside, quickly closing the door.

The Village Committee met in the Town Hall built by Baron de Rothschild. At the time of its construction, it had appeared pretentiously ornate and excessively large for a town that was little more than a settlement, but since then the founder's vision had been validated, and Zichron Yaakov had grown into its communal centre like a child that eventually fits into an older sibling's clothes.

As she pushed open the heavy oak door carved with floral emblems, she had a vivid memory of her last visit to the Town Hall. That was before the war, when she and Leah had attended the lecture given by Olga Mankiewicz. That evening her sister's mind had been more on Eli than on revolution. Witnessing the intensity of Leah's love, she had realised that her sister was her rival.

Five members of the committee were seated at the conference table upstairs and they turned unsmiling faces towards her when she entered. She was immediately struck by their attire. They were farmers, millers and vignerons, but on this occasion they had dressed formally in suits with stiff-collared shirts. The committee's president, Lev Bernstein, whom she had called Uncle Lev when she was small, was frowning, which deepened the lines running down his cheeks. Next to him sat Mendel Bukowski, who used to give her sweets whenever he saw her, but now regarded her with a disapproving expression.

She was shocked to see Miriam's father, Joseph Steinman, sitting there. He had never referred to the embarrassing request she had made in Constantinople, but she knew she had shocked him, and didn't expect him to support any activity she was involved in.

He nodded briefly in her direction when she came in but quickly looked away and didn't meet her eyes again. So that explained why Miriam's mother had pulled her daughter inside to avoid her. The other two men were citrus farmers she knew only by sight.

Lev Bernstein spoke first. 'We've summoned you here because you are violating the rules of our community and endangering our safety. You and your family have lived among us ever since this town came into existence. In fact, like me, your father was one of the pioneers. I don't know what he thinks of your illegal activities because he refuses to discuss you with us, but you are endangering the entire village, if not the entire Jewish community of Palestine. I won't comment on your association with a man who was expelled from a local militia for insubordination, except to say that it shows a serious lack of judgement on your part. We have asked you to come here today to inform you that we are unanimous in our demand that you stop your espionage, which is likely to bring the wrath of the Turks on all our heads.'

'I have the feeling you are threatening me,' she said quietly.

'It's you who are threatening our existence. As you well know, life here is already precarious and you are poking the tiger. We insist that you put a stop to this now.'

She took a deep breath before replying. 'I'm trying to liberate us all from our Turkish overlords but it seems to me that you prefer serfdom to freedom. You'd rather cringe in corners like scared mice at the mercy of the Turks than support the people who are fighting for you.'

The men started shaking their heads, all trying to speak at once. It was Miriam's father whose voice rose above the others. 'We are much older than you and less impetuous, Shoshana. We want to enjoy what little we have rather than be slaughtered and driven out.'

She could see that he was trying to be reasonable, but Lev Bernstein, who had been drumming his fingers on the table, broke in. 'You are not in a position to criticise us or our desire for safety. As in generations past, we will ride out this storm while hotheads like you only bring disaster. You and your associates have besmirched your brother's research station by using it for criminal purposes and we insist that you stop this dangerous business that puts not only our own community but all the Jewish communities at risk. You want to be a spy and risk your life, be a spy. But carry on your dangerous work somewhere else. You are not going to do it in our community. And if despite our warning you persist in it and the authorities come after you, don't expect any support from us. I hope we have made ourselves clear.'

While he was speaking, she looked around the room. Instead of being among the friendly neighbours she had known all her life, she felt she was facing a medieval court of fanatical judges like the ones who had sent Joan of Arc to the stake.

'Very clear,' she replied. Without another word, she left the council chamber.

For the first time, her faith in her mission faltered. Too shaken to walk home, she leaned against the doorway of the Town Hall as disturbing thoughts flooded her mind. Why was she risking her life and the lives of her group on behalf of people who would probably betray her? Did she have the right to force her beliefs on them against their will? What if they were right and her actions resulted in massacres and more expulsions? What if, despite her efforts, the British lost the war?

Unable to answer these questions, she gathered herself and began walking home, but her footsteps led her to the little cemetery. Sitting on the soft loam in front of her mother's grave, she heard herself say, 'Ima, what should I do?' The wind had picked up and the birches and oaks soughed above her head, as if whispering secrets that only they could hear, and she smiled to herself. That's what Nathan would have said. Thinking of her brother, she realised how much she needed him, and how alone and vulnerable she felt.

It was almost Rosh Hashana, the time of year when she missed her mother the most. They used to go to synagogue together and return for a celebratory dinner beginning with apples and honey and ending with honey cake that filled your mouth with sweetness, a symbolic start to the Jewish New Year. Rosh Hashana marked the beginning of the High Holy Days that heralded a period of deep reflection. The answer would come to her then.

CHAPTER FORTY

Zichron Yaakov, 1917

Head held high, Shoshana stepped out of the house accompanied by her father, and arm in arm they walked along Ha-Meyasdim Street. It was named in recognition of the founders of the town, and Moshe Adelstein could never resist smiling when he read the street sign. After all, he was one of the pioneers it celebrated. Overhead, dark clouds threatened to turn the drizzle that fell from the sky into heavy rain, and light filtered grudgingly between the palm fronds, the pines, and the bare branches of the mulberry trees lining the street. Every few minutes, Shoshana's buttoned shoe tripped on the uneven paving and she lifted the hem of her long skirt that trailed on the wet ground. Her father gripped the edge of his prayer shawl to stop it from slipping. In his other hand he carried his burgundy velvet prayer bag containing his prayer book.

'It's the only thing I have that belonged to my father,' he said as they walked along. 'I still remember walking beside him to *shule* in the old country while the Romanian thugs jeered at us.'

Just then his hand flew to his black homburg to stop it from blowing away. September was an unreliable month. Sometimes it prolonged the bright days of summer but on that first morning of Rosh Hashana, the sky hung low over the town and sharp gusts of wind presaged an early winter.

The street was full of worshippers heading for the Ohel Yaakov synagogue, the men in suits, the women decked out in floral dresses that created a splash of colour on this dull day. As they drew level with their neighbours, Moshe raised his hat and inclined his head in greeting as though this was a normal Rosh Hashana morning. He nudged Shoshana to acknowledge them but she looked straight ahead at an invisible spot in the distance.

'I'm not going to pretend,' she murmured. 'They hate us.'

'That's exactly why you should act as if everything is normal. You know, when my father and I walked to synagogue in Romania, we never let them see we were afraid. We ignored their threats.'

'But they won just the same,' she said, recalling her grandfather's horrific death and the pogrom that had forced her parents to migrate to Palestine.

Moshe shook his head. 'That's where you're mistaken. They lost. Thanks to them, we've built a new life in our ancient homeland.'

She decided not to point out that once again they were at the mercy of despotic rulers and hostile neighbours. It was painful to compare the attitude of their neighbours to that of the anti-Semitic townsfolk of Romania. She hadn't given her father a full account of what had transpired at her meeting with the Village Committee, but from his shrewd expression and the way he had kept shaking his head when she talked about it, she knew he had filled in the blanks.

Just then they drew level with Miriam, who was walking with her parents. Shoshana and Miriam stopped and looked at each other, uncertain how to react as they weighed up the bonds of old friendship against the recent conflict. Miriam broke the impasse. Reaching out, she kissed Shoshana's cheek and wished her *Gut yontov*, happy holiday. Shoshana returned the greeting with a surge of gratitude. Miriam's mother, who had been standing nearby in obvious discomfort, muttered a perfunctory greeting without meeting Shoshana's eyes; her father had continued walking, ostensibly to catch up with a friend, but Shoshana knew it was to avoid acknowledging her.

At the intersection of Ha-Nadiv Street they came to the synagogue. Small groups had gathered outside to chat with their neighbours. The women complimented each other on their outfits and boasted about their children while their husbands lamented the economic situation that threatened imminent ruin. Although the harvest had been good that year, the wine prices had collapsed while everything else had become prohibitively expensive.

As Shoshana and her father approached, people stopped talking, nudged each other and looked uncomfortable, like children caught with their hands in a jar of forbidden sweets.

'*Gut yontov!*' Moshe's voice boomed, breaking the silence. Embarrassed, people returned the traditional greeting and hurried inside, the men downstairs and the women to the wraparound gallery upstairs.

Before entering the synagogue, Moshe turned to Shoshana. 'I've lived among these people most of my life. I never imagined they would turn on us like this after all you've done to help them. But I won't give them the satisfaction of seeing that they've upset me, and you shouldn't either.'

Shoshana sat in the front row of the upstairs gallery gazing at the dazzling white marble of the Holy Ark. De Rothschild had spared no expense in decorating the synagogue he had named after his father. Although there were seats on either side of her, she was relieved that no one ventured to sit beside her. She needed time to think without the distraction of accusing eyes and whispered remarks. She hadn't resolved the conflict that had gripped her after her meeting with the Village Committee, and although she had never enjoyed a close relationship with God and didn't set much store in the power of prayer, she welcomed the calming aura of the synagogue and the meditative New Year prayers. Perhaps they would clarify her thoughts.

During past visits to the synagogue on Rosh Hashana, while the devout raised their faces to the Almighty in fervent prayer she had appreciated the tradition of the festival more than the praises sung to the love and compassion of the Almighty whose benevolence she doubted. But as she listened to the soulful melodies, she was moved by the faith that had endured and sustained worshippers for several thousand years.

Usually the prayers and supplications of the service passed in a blur, but on this occasion she paid close attention to the liturgy, as if the solution to her dilemma lay in the ancient words that celebrated the birth of the world. The cantor rose, the velvet curtains across the Holy Ark parted, and the Torah scroll was taken out of its ornate silver case topped by small *rimonim* bells that tinkled as the scroll was passed among the men. The cantor's sonorous tenor voice resounded in the synagogue as he sang about redemption. '*Once we were in bondage, then we became free. We affirm the power of freedom as we celebrate our deliverance from Egypt and all bondage. Redemption will come when we overcome the violence in the world.*'

She sat up very straight, every nerve taut. Deliverance, bondage, violence and redemption. She had never noticed these references to oppression and freedom that might have been referring to their present situation. Deep in thought, she tuned out until the liturgy focussed on the theme of Rosh Hashana, the Day of Judgement, and she listened to the terrifying words repeated from time immemorial: '*Let us proclaim the sacred power of this day, the Day of Judgement. What we have chosen to become, stands in judgement over what we may hope to be.*'

Her body tingled in recognition. *What we have chosen to become.* She knew what she had chosen to become, a spy in the service of her people. But was she brave enough to carry that choice to its conclusion?

The cantor raised the ram's horn to his lips and his cheeks puffed out with the effort of producing the strange discordant sound that heralded the Day of Judgement and linked their congregation all the way back to the time of Moses.

Then began the incantation whose atavistic prophecy made worshippers tremble. '*On Rosh Hashana it is written how many shall pass on and how many shall come to be. Who shall live and who shall die. Who shall see ripe age and who shall not. Who shall perish by fire and who by water ...*'

As he went on to enumerate all the terrible ways people might die, a shiver rippled down Shoshana's spine. Irrational though it was, she felt this incantation was directed straight at her. When would she die? And by what means? How would she be judged?

Then the rabbi said something that startled her with its unexpected insight. '*It is not God who inscribes us in the Book of Life: we inscribe ourselves by our deeds.*'

With an effort she turned her attention back to the service.

'*Each of us is a shattered urn, grass that must wither, a flower that fades, a dream soon forgotten. Only when the vessel of the self shatters can the divine spark shine through.*'

Mesmerised by the poetry of the language, her mind drifted until the next part of the service brought her back with a shock. '*On this day the fate of nations is in the balance, for war or peace, for famine or plenty.*'

Once again, she couldn't escape the conviction that the author of this prophecy was addressing her, urging her to take a stand for what she believed in.

The cantor raised the ram's horn, and filled the synagogue with its harsh jagged sound a second time. '*The sound of the* shofar *proclaims our freedom and raises the banner for the redemption of the oppressed. Reach as high as you dare and follow the path of goodness to prevent the death of the heart.*'

As she listened, the weight of uncertainty dropped from her shoulders and by the time the service was finished, she had resolved

her conflict. There was no longer a question whether she had a right
to save people in spite of themselves. The celebration of the world's
birthday had strengthened her resolve to follow the path her destiny
had mapped out, to continue her fight for freedom from oppression.
No matter what it cost, she would reach the limits of her dreams.

Feeling strong and grounded, she came out of the synagogue and
looked for her father among the throng spilling into the street. He
was among the last to emerge and from his slow gait and downcast
eyes, she knew something was wrong. Without a word, he took her
arm and steered her towards their home. The crowd had thinned
out and when they reached their front gate he looked around, leaned
towards her and whispered, 'They've arrested Berish.'

The blood coursing through Shoshana's veins turned to ice.
Rigid with terror, she stared at her father. Berish arrested!

She stumbled inside the house and sank into an armchair. Panic
threatened to overwhelm her. She had suspected this might happen
but now she struggled to come to terms with the reality. When did
it happen? How? Where did they take him? What would happen
next? Moshe kept shaking his head. He didn't know.

'I overheard Leibel Bialik whispering to David Gross during the
service that someone up north had been caught harbouring a Turkish deserter. That's all he said but I realised it was Berish.'

Shoshana's mouth was dry. She had to think quickly but her
mind was paralysed and she had no idea what she could do to avert
the catastrophe that loomed. Berish had been dangerously reckless.
If only she'd had time to find a safe hiding place for the deserter.
She had no illusions about Turkish efficiency at extracting information from suspects. Would Berish be strong enough to withstand
torture? Everything depended on that.

CHAPTER FORTY-ONE

Zichron Yaakov, 1917

Shoshana was on tenterhooks. She walked back and forth, stared out the window and forgot what she was doing, unable to think about anything but Berish. If only she knew what was happening to him. The scenarios her mind conjured made her shiver but she was afraid of making inquiries for fear of attracting attention. She had never felt so alone or so afraid. If only Nathan was here to support and advise her. She had never needed him so much.

Another issue preoccupied her as she paced around the research station. When would the spy ship arrive? She needed provisions and cash urgently to pay their workers and she was anxious to deliver the latest reports even though there were fewer than usual. Since Berish's arrest the previous week, she and Aaron had used the pretext of the holiday period to call on the members of their spy ring and alert them to the danger. But Meyer Baruch, their contact in Hadera, had important information. An employee of a German businessman who delivered supplies in a horse-drawn wagon to the Turkish army along the Gaza front, Myer had unique access to the Turkish camps and fortifications. He always travelled with bottles of wine to treat the Turkish officers, one of whom had told him that if the British had any hope of breaking through Gaza, they would have to capture Beersheba first. Meyer had reported that conversation and described Turkish machine gun positions, information Shoshana knew would be invaluable for the British.

Although she was distracted, she kept glancing out the window in case the spy ship approached. Wild seas had prevented it from docking on the last moonless night but she hoped it would soon make another attempt. Suddenly her eyes widened. Had her hope conjured up the vision? But it really was the MS *Victoria*, and thick black smoke was pouring from its funnel. So it was coming to Atlit after all. She raced to hang the sheet from the window.

Close to midnight, when the world was plunged in darkness, Shoshana and Aaron crept across the highway and down the wadi with the oilskin pouch. When they reached the beach they sat on the sand and waited for the ship to return. The sea was calm with promise as the ship appeared on the horizon, but a moment later the wind blew up and within minutes the water became a cauldron of churning waves, too treacherous to attempt a landing.

She pushed her windblown hair from her face and clenched her fists as the turbulence showed no sign of subsiding. Surely this couldn't happen again, especially as this might be their last rendez-vous. Apart from collecting urgently needed supplies and delivering Meyer Baruch's intelligence, she was desperate to hand over the letter she had written to Nathan to let him know about the Turkish deserter. Enraged by the prospect of being unable to make con-tact, she seethed at the British authorities. Why were they dragging their feet? If they really valued their intelligence, as they claimed, why hadn't they organised a more reliable form of communication? The pigeons had been a dismal failure and endangered the entire operation. And why didn't they capitalise on all the intelligence she was supplying, and engage the Turks in battle at Beersheba and throw them out of Palestine?

As she listened to the roar of the water, she contemplated the sea, mesmerised by the motion of the waves and the implacable majesty of their power. We are the playthings of the ocean, she thought, and the wind decides our fate. Awed by the grandeur of the sea, she sensed her own insignificance and remembered Nathan saying that we all came from the water.

She felt Aaron's eyes on her and turned to face him and as she did so, she realised that her hair had stopped blowing around. She gripped his arm. Was it her imagination or had the wind begun to subside? Had the waves stopped churning?

He placed his hand over hers and squeezed it. 'It's calming down. The rowboat will come ashore after all,' he whispered.

And as they watched, they saw the boatman's oars slicing strongly through the waves. As they ran forward to pull the boat onto the sand, she saw that in addition to the two boatmen, there was another man on board. Nathan.

She ran towards him and threw her arms around him like a child greeting a long-lost parent. As she clung to him, she allowed herself to feel her vulnerability, the enormity of her situation and the weight of all the responsibility that rested on her shoulders.

'I had no idea you were coming. I can't believe you're really here. So much has happened lately, I hardly know where to start.'

He pulled away, and his expression alarmed her. 'Listen, Shoshi, I shouldn't be here. I disobeyed their orders but I had to talk to you. You have to leave right now. You can't delay. You must come to Cairo.'

Startled by his outburst, she began to argue but he cut her short.

'There were rumours in Cairo that someone in Hadera has been arrested and I put two and two together and realised it was one of ours. I'm right, aren't I? You're in grave danger, Shoshi, and you have to get away from here while there's still time.'

She shook her head. The sense of weakness that had overwhelmed her earlier was replaced by steely resolve. 'I'm not leaving. I can't desert the others.'

'Once you're gone, they won't be in danger,' he insisted. He turned to Aaron, who was unloading burlap sacks of grain and had flung one over his shoulder. 'You could leave too.'

Aaron put the sack down and looked at Shoshana standing erect and resolute as she faced her brother. 'And leave her here alone?'

Nathan made an impatient motion with his hand as if pushing away the words. Turning to Shoshana, he said, 'The war is coming to an end. There's no need for you to expose yourself to more danger. This isn't the time for noble gestures. I don't think you realise that this is a matter of life and death.'

Her reply was quiet but defiant. 'I understand perfectly. The war might be coming to an end but its outcome is still uncertain. I will not run away. I know you want to protect me, but the spy ring is my responsibility and mine alone. I will be the last to leave, not the first. I won't abandon the others. My destiny is here.'

Nathan placed his hands on her shoulders and looked deep into her eyes. She looked straight back, unflinching, and she could see he knew there was nothing he could say in the face of her resolve.

They stood still, gazing at each other in silence. With an awkward movement he leaned forward and gently stroked her cheek. Then he turned and stepped into the rowboat without looking back.

*

Back in his office in the Savoy Hotel, Nathan shifted papers on his desk, moved files back and forth, played with the lid of his fountain pen and stared into space, unable to focus on the work that had piled up during his absence. The irony of his situation didn't escape him. He had achieved what he had longed for, recognition, acceptance and status, and he was now a policy advisor to the inner sanctum. These days his superiors relied so much on his expertise that he frequently took work to his hotel where he worked until the early hours of the morning, collating information, interpreting reports and assessing strategy, on the basis of which he would offer advice.

But after returning from his secret trip to Atlit, it was Shoshana's decision that weighed on his mind far more heavily than drilling for water to supply the army for their imminent battle in Beersheba. Too restless to do any work, he pushed back his chair so hurriedly that it scraped along the timber floor, and as he walked out of the office, he closed the door behind him more forcefully than he had intended. He had to get fresh air and clear his head.

As he approached the entrance he saw a familiar figure strutting towards him. Lawrence, fresh from one of his successful raids, was quaintly attired in a long white robe and keffiyeh as if to ensure that no one forgot who he was. Preoccupied with his thoughts, Nathan would have preferred to walk past but their eyes met and it was too late to avoid him.

'I say, haven't seen you around for a while. Heard you're in Allenby's good books these days.'

He sounded bitter, Nathan thought, and surmised it was on account of the Sykes-Picot agreement, which was now an open secret; a pact that carved Syria and Palestine like a Christmas turkey between Britain and France, despite Britain's promises to the Arabs. But as Lawrence continued to make forays at the head of his Bedouin army, Nathan suspected he hadn't given up hope of placing his Bedouin protégé on the throne of Syria. Although he and Lawrence were working for opposing goals, he admired this eccentric man who, like Shoshana, had such a powerful sense of his own destiny.

He made a vague reply, hoping to move on but Lawrence was still talking.

'I can't stand this pretentious place and its small-minded officials another minute. I'm going to Groppi's for an iced coffee. You look as if you could do with some refreshment yourself. Feel like joining me?'

Nathan surprised himself by agreeing.

As they waited for their coffees in the café Lawrence leaned forward. 'That sister of yours in Atlit. How is she? I hear from our honourable – or rather, dishonourable – superiors that she has supplied them with valuable information at enormous risk to herself now that the Turkish pasha has caught her carrier pigeon.'

Nathan recalled Lawrence's comment about Shoshana the last time they spoke. He had warned that she was in danger, and suddenly, without intending to discuss this painful topic, he told Lawrence about her decision.

'It's like watching someone walking into a burning building and being helpless to stop them,' he concluded.

Lawrence listened intently and nodded, concern on his long face. 'You urged her to leave with you but she refused? That doesn't surprise me. Your sister is worth a hundred men, Adelstein.' He stopped talking and the unfocussed look in his eyes suggested he was contemplating the future rather than the past. After several moments he added in a gloomy tone, 'Unfortunately there's no room for heroines or heroes in this world of ours.'

Nathan wondered if he was thinking about himself. He finished his coffee, counted some piastres out onto the table, thanked Lawrence for his concern, and stood up. It was time to get back to work. Gardiner-Hall was waiting for his assessment of Turkish troops at Beersheba.

On the way back to the office, he quickened his step. It would be good to focus on the task ahead. But back at his desk, he resumed shuffling papers as he tried in vain to dismiss the insistent image of a house engulfed by flames.

CHAPTER FORTY-TWO

Zichron Yaakov, 1917

The sound of hooves thudding along the road made Shoshana look up. She had been counting the last of the coins left in the metal box, wondering how she would manage to run the station and pay all the outstanding expenses with the meagre pile that remained until the next ship arrived. Already most of the money Nathan had given her had been used to pay outstanding wages as well as debts for supplies, and knowing there would not be another ship for several weeks made the blood pound in her ears.

The rider was a welcome distraction and she narrowed her eyes, straining to see who it was. He was still a considerable distance away but she sensed desperation in the set of his jaw, the way he leaned forward in the saddle and dug his spurs into the horse's flanks to maintain a galloping pace. This was clearly a man with an urgent message to deliver and her muscles tensed as she watched him. News that couldn't wait couldn't be good.

Her suspicion intensified as soon as she recognised him. It was Berish's brother Joshua, whom she had met in the vineyard while collecting intelligence. Like all the members of the spy ring, he had been warned not to come to the station, so she sensed something must have happened for him to disobey her order.

As soon as he got to the station, he brought the horse to a halt so suddenly that it reared up and whinnied. He slid off the saddle, tied up the reins with hands that shook, ran to the front door and rapped three times. He was about to rap a fourth time when Shoshana, pale and rigid, opened the door. With a quick glance outside she gestured for him to come in.

She was shocked at the change in him. Instead of the genial laid-back fellow she remembered with ruddy cheeks and a ready smile, his face was chalk-white and his eyes were full of panic.

'It's Berish,' he gasped. 'We need money or they'll finish him off. Cash. We need cash. Three hundred pounds. Today.'

The words shot from his mouth like bullets and her heart was hammering so fast she couldn't get enough air into her lungs.

'I don't have anywhere near that amount,' she said. 'What is it for?'

He grabbed her arm. 'Shoshana, we have to get the money together to save him before it's too late.'

Shaken, she poured him a glass of water. 'What happened? Where is he? Have you seen him?'

Joshua sank into the closest chair, closed his eyes and clasped his head in his hands as if trying to contain the thoughts rioting through his brain. Then he uttered a sigh that seemed to emerge from some deep well of despair.

'They let me see him once,' he began. 'It was that damned deserter. I don't know how the Turkish police found out that Berish was hiding him but someone, probably a disgruntled employee in the vineyard, must have noticed and reported him. There was a fellow who always complained about long hours and low pay.'

Now that he was sitting down, refreshed by the cold water, he sounded calmer and took his time coming to the point but she couldn't sit still. One question was drumming in her head.

'Do you know if he told them anything?'

Joshua looked at her reproachfully but whether it was because she had interrupted his train of thought or because her question revealed a lack of empathy with his brother's plight, she couldn't tell. She realised she would have to let him tell the story in his own time.

'They've taken him to the prison in Damascus. In chains, Shoshana! Berish in chains!' The image was clearly vivid in his mind, and he shuddered and kept shaking his head in sorrowful disbelief. 'We need the money so we can bribe his guards and the police.' He grabbed her arm again. 'You know how things work here. Money is the only thing that can save him.'

He was obviously fixated on the idea of a bribe. 'Go on,' she said. 'Tell me what happened.'

It was a long story and she knitted and unknitted her fingers while he told it. Apparently Berish was initially taken to the prison in Caesarea where he was thrown into a filthy windowless cell that stank and crawled with vermin. When the obese guard gloated that they had already hanged the Turkish deserter, Berish was convinced he'd be next. And he would have been if Osman Bey hadn't intervened.

Apparently Osman Bey had been obsessed with uncovering the spies ever since he found the straying pigeon, and he realised that the message attached to the pigeon's leg held the key to the mystery. Despite his repeated requests to the authorities in Constantinople, however, no one had yet deciphered the code, but from its Roman script he deduced that it must have come from a Jewish espionage group operating in his area. When news reached him that a Jew had hidden a Turkish deserter, he became suspicious. Why had the deserter sought this man's help? Could this be the connection he was searching for? He decided to use the considerable powers of persuasion at his command to find out if the Jew had any connection with the spies.

Joshua stopped talking and sighed again as if in pain. 'For a whole week they interrogated Berish and didn't give him any food, but he managed to remain silent. Didn't tell them anything. Said he didn't know how the deserter came to be hiding in his vineyard. He'd never seen him before, hadn't heard of any spies, didn't know anything about espionage or a code, and didn't believe such a network existed.

'But Osman Bey wasn't convinced by his denials. Seeing they weren't getting anywhere, the crafty bastard thought up another scheme. He told Berish he believed his story and was going to set him free. In fact, as an apology for treating him so harshly, he invited him to his home for a banquet that would be held in his honour.

'You'd think my brother would be too smart to fall for that story, but after being starved and interrogated for a week, he was probably too weak to resist and too excited at the prospect of being released and fed to suspect a trick.' Joshua drained his glass and held it out for Shoshana to refill before he continued.

'The banquet inside Osman Bey's villa was opulent, and from the way Berish described it, I can imagine how hungrily he surveyed all the platters set out on the table and how his mouth watered at the aroma of whole lamb cooked on the spit, iskender kebap skewers, vine leaf dolma, spinach borek, pilav, spiced kofta meat balls, and imam bayildi eggplant stuffed with tomato and covered in yoghurt. And the desserts! Turkish delight, baklava, walnut and honey slices, rosewater sorbets. What he didn't notice while he was eating was that they kept plying him with wine. Glass after glass. Unfortunately that wine loosened his tongue.'

At this point, Joshua paused and Shoshana asked, 'How much did he tell them?'

'He couldn't remember the details but he thought he admitted spying on the Turks.'

She groaned.

'It wasn't his fault, Shoshana. He felt he was among friends. Told me they must have spiked his wine with hashish to induce a state of relaxed euphoria to make him talk. I had the impression that Berish wasn't himself somehow. He sounded vague, as if he was in a fog. I think it was the hashish.'

He paused again, as if to elicit her sympathy but she was appalled that Berish had made such a damning admission.

'What else did he tell them?'

'Obviously not much more because they haven't killed him yet. They've taken him to the jail in Damascus. But it's obvious they'll torture him until he tells them everything he knows.'

He fell silent and stared moodily at the floor before continuing. 'And when he does, they'll hang him.' He sat forward and locked eyes with her. 'Don't you see, that's why it's urgent. We have to pay off the guards and get him out of there as soon as possible.'

Shoshana bit her lip and was silent for several minutes while she considered the situation. As the leader of their spy ring she knew there was only one solution to the annihilation they all faced, only one effective way to prevent Berish from exposing them all, but she knew she couldn't bring herself to say it.

She turned to Joshua with a troubled expression. 'This is a terrible situation for Berish and for all of us. But I don't have three hundred pounds or even a quarter of that. And even if I did, it wouldn't help. It's not a matter of bribing a single prison guard or police officer to release an insignificant prisoner. He is too important and there would be a heavy guard outside his cell. And do you really think the jailers would free the man Osman Bey had captured?'

All the colour drained from Joshua's face. 'So what do you suggest? We have to do something.'

She didn't reply.

'You're not going to do anything, are you?' he shouted. 'You're just going to let him die!'

'Joshua, he signed his own death warrant when he hid that deserter. All we can hope is that he doesn't take us with him.'

He stood up and stomped towards the door. At the last moment he turned to confront her and spoke very deliberately. 'His blood will be on your hands.'

After he left, she buried her head in her hands, unable to shake off his curse. Had she made the right decision? Perhaps she should have tried to buy Berish's freedom in the forlorn hope that the jailers would free him. But she knew there wasn't enough money to induce them to take that risk. They would simply accept the bribe and do nothing. Should she have tried to raise more cash? The philanthropic Jews of Britain were her only source of cash, but by the time the next ship arrived, it would be too late.

Unable to stop tormenting herself, she went over the situation several times, visualising other scenarios and searching for solutions, but each time she came to the same conclusion. There was no other option. Her decision had been pragmatic, but that didn't ease her troubled conscience. Had it also been heartless?

She was still mulling it over when Aaron arrived to discuss the latest intelligence. He sat down beside her and saw the distress in her eyes. 'What happened?'

Relieved to share her dilemma, she told him about Joshua's visit and his curse.

'Don't let that upset you. He's just trying to make you feel guilty. And don't waste any sympathy on Berish. That idiot brought it on himself and now he's put us all in danger. I should have killed him the day he told me about the deserter.'

She studied the man in front of her, intrigued by the contrast between his appearance and his personality. Dressed like an English gentleman, with an academic's round wire-rimmed spectacles over his blue eyes and a pirate's scar on his cheek, he was a man of action who spoke with the recklessness of a revolutionary.

Now he drummed his fingers on the table, deep in thought. Then he said, 'There is something we could do. A group of us could get hold of pistols, disguise ourselves as Turkish policemen, ride to the prison, take the guards by surprise, and free Berish.'

She stared at him. His eyes were shining at the prospect of this daring exploit. It reminded her of that other audacious adventure he had undertaken that had also involved disguise, and she controlled the impulse to point out how that one had ended. It crossed her mind that if Eli was there, he would probably have encouraged his friend and joined him on this escapade that would turn out to be another tragedy.

'I can't believe you're serious. That wouldn't save Berish and it would get you all hanged. I wouldn't consider allowing you to risk your lives in such a reckless exercise.' Then in a softer tone she added, 'I couldn't bear it if you were captured and killed.'

He looked at her questioningly but she didn't say any more and they proceeded to read the latest reports in silence. Every now and then Shoshana looked up from her work and closed her eyes. Joshua's curse was a relentless cymbal reverberating in her head. Suddenly the words in front of her blurred. She was crying for Berish.

CHAPTER FORTY-THREE

Zichron Yaakov, 1917

Two days later, the news that Berish had been hanged in the square outside the jail in Damascus spread swiftly through the community, as bad news usually does. His body had been left dangling from the gibbet as a warning to other spies. In Zichron Yaakov, it reinforced the Village Committee's conviction that Shoshana's activities would lead to their destruction.

Although Shoshana had known that Berish would be executed, hearing it confirmed shocked her. Even though his own actions had caused his death, she felt responsible. He was in this situation because he had shared her vision of the future and agreed to take risks to realise it. The heartbreaking image of his limp body displayed in public haunted her imagination. At the research station she sank onto a chair, unable to form a single coherent thought or plan of action. When she forced herself to rise, her legs seemed filled with lead. Immobilising grief at Berish's fate combined with the dread of a prophecy fulfilled. No matter how often she reminded herself that Berish had brought this on himself, that it hadn't been in her power to prevent it, Joshua's curse resounded in her head.

But this was no time to indulge in recriminations and regrets. She had to focus on the situation that now threatened them all. There was no way of knowing what Berish had told his torturers, but the fact that they had hanged him indicated he had told them all they needed to know. If that included the names of the members of the spy ring, it wouldn't be long before the Turks came to arrest her and the others.

She struggled to clear the paralysing terror from her mind, to think rationally and decide what to do. She was responsible for the members of the spy ring and she had to try and save them. If she had been able to keep their identities secret from each other, no interrogations would have succeeded in eliciting names, but their communal and familial ties had made that impossible. The spy ring was mostly composed of friends, cousins and siblings, but as she ran through her co-conspirators, it struck her that Berish didn't know them all. He couldn't have named Dr Shulman or his brother, or their members in the south whom he had never met.

She had to rescue the ones he would certainly have named, like her father, Aaron, Benyamin, Tova and Joshua while there was still time. But how? She paced around the house as she rejected one plan after another until she came to the only possibility. Evacuation. The spy ship was due to arrive within the next few days and she would send a message for them to gather on the shore ready to sail. Once in Egypt, they would be safe.

Of course that would depend on the tide that night. If the sea was calm, the vessel would anchor off Atlit and launch the rowboat and they would get away. But what if it couldn't? She cursed the arrangement that left them at the mercy of wind and water. But this was her only hope and even though she couldn't be certain that the ship would arrive, she had to send a message for them to come to Atlit just in case. Time was running out. She couldn't risk travelling herself, but she could send Nasser instead. No one would suspect him and if the Turkish police did stop him, he could say he was travelling to see his sick mother in Haifa.

In the meantime, she had to conceal her plans. She had to keep everything going as usual so that the people in the village wouldn't suspect that Berish had been part of her spy ring or that she was planning an evacuation. The recent events in Tyre added to her anxiety. Abdul, the Arab boatman, had boasted about being aboard a British ship and someone had reported him to the Turkish police. Under torture he admitted his connection with a spy vessel and was hanged. Whether he had divulged anything else she didn't know, but in reprisal the Turkish authorities arrested the prominent citizens of Tyre and executed them. News of their fate had already reached Zichron Yaakov and made the Village Committee even more anxious about her activities.

Although Shoshana was on edge and lay awake all night imagining one dreadful scenario after another, she had to appear calm to allay suspicion while she continued making plans. Everything had to appear normal. Anyone who visited Atlit would find the fields ploughed, the horse stamping in the yard and Dov and the labourers busily sawing timber or repairing broken doors. Inside the research station, Shoshana paid bills and wrote letters and tried to control her trembling hands.

As soon as evening fell, she returned home. The long walk refreshed her spirit. The Washingtonia palms that Nathan had planted were lush and tall, and this peaceful interlude in her anxious day was a reminder of the eternal beauty of nature that was impervious to human suffering. The palm fronds shimmered in the breeze and made a cracking sound as they slapped against each other, and the setting sun silvered their razor-sharp edges. But her troubles soon resurfaced. She would have to broach the subject of imminent evacuation with her father, and she tensed at the prospect.

He looked up eagerly from his newspaper when she entered. 'You're late tonight, Shoshi. Everything all right?'

She took a deep breath and told him about her plan to evacuate him along with the others.

'So you plan to put me on a ship like a sack of grain? And you expect me to go? And what about you, are you leaving too?'

She met his gaze. 'Not yet. If we all leave at once it will look suspicious. I'll be the last to go.'

He surveyed her with a stern look. 'Do you think you'll still have the opportunity to leave?'

'That's a chance I have to take.'

'Then it's a chance I'll take too.' He held up his hand to forestall any argument. 'Don't try and talk me out of it. I will stay with you and that's final.'

She looked down so he wouldn't see the tears welling in her eyes.

*

When Aaron came over that evening, he found her in a sombre mood.

'What are we going to do about this?' he asked as she made tea. 'We can't just sit here and wait for them to arrest us.'

She put down her cup and sat forward. 'You have to get away as soon as possible. The spy ship may not arrive in time to evacuate everyone. You know lots of people up north. Surely they'll hide you until this blows over.'

'I doubt it. Don't forget I'm not very popular with the security group that controls the area and they disapprove of our activities. I think they'd be quite happy to hand me over to the Turks.'

He fell silent but his searching eyes never left her face. 'Shoshana, do you really think I'd abandon you?'

'You wouldn't be abandoning me. Go before they arrive. Before they start on you. Imagine how you'd feel if they made you betray me.'

'I'd rather die.'

'You mightn't get the chance.'

He was still looking at her, and she saw him struggling with his emotions. Finally he blurted out, 'This might be my last opportunity to say this. I've been in love with you from the first moment I saw you. Eli was my closest friend, a brother couldn't have been closer, and yet there were times when I daydreamed that he was out of the way and you loved me instead. When he died, I felt I'd been punished for my terrible wish. You have no idea how I ached to touch you when I sat beside you on all the journeys we took together. I will go, but I don't care what happens to me. In a way my life is over. I'm already dead.'

He had never said so much and the honesty of his confession moved her. She was tempted to console him, to say that in time his feelings would change, that he'd probably fall in love again, but she couldn't bring herself to trivialise his feelings with clichés. Instead she put her arm around his shoulders and pressed her lips against his cheek. He took off his glasses and polished them more energetically than usual. A moment later she heard the click of the front door closing and he was gone.

*

The following evening heralded the start of the holiest day in the Jewish calendar. Even unbelievers, sceptics and agnostics observed Yom Kippur, the Day of Atonement, which focussed on repentance and forgiveness: acknowledging sins committed against others and forgiving those who had sinned against them. It demanded that everyone look deep into their hearts to reflect on their behaviour and strive to become the people they yearned to be.

Yom Kippur began at sunset on the preceding evening with the Kol Nidre service, which Shoshana regarded as the most beautiful and most meaningful of all the religious holidays. In accordance with the custom, she wore white, a demure dress with long sleeves and a pin-tucked bodice. She had sewn a similar one for Leah as well, and it was comforting to think that her sister was probably wearing it that evening. White symbolised purity and rebirth, for on this day they were spiritually reborn. It was also a reminder of death, as white was the colour of the burial shroud, so in that sense, the holy day represented a rehearsal for death.

Shoshana and Moshe set out for the synagogue just before sunset. It was a pleasant autumnal day. A light breeze brushed her skin and the street was bathed in golden light that lit up the sky and tinged the clouds a heavenly shade of rose. People walking towards the synagogue stopped and pointed at the sky with delight, as if seeing an omen for better days.

Their neighbours walked past them without a word, not even the slightest pretence of civility. Many of them stepped to the other side of the street and averted their gaze. Moshe gripped her arm and held her closer. 'We are pariahs,' he said.

'I know the theme of this service is forgiveness, but I'm not in a very forgiving mood,' she murmured. 'I know that I've exposed them to danger but all I wanted to do was set them free.'

He squeezed her arm. 'It often takes a long time for people to look outside their own limited interests and comprehend the bigger picture. And sometimes they never do. After all, we are all strangers even to ourselves.'

She looked at her father. He wasn't a philosophical man and his comment surprised her.

The haunting melodies of the Hebrew liturgy moved something deep within her, perhaps an atavistic recollection of millennia of Jewish history. When the cantor raised his powerful tenor voice in a supplication to God, for the first time in many days she felt as though a mantle of peace had landed upon her. *'Avinu malkienu,'* he sang, and the soulful prayer stirred something deep in her soul.

The rabbi returned to the theme of the service. 'What matters when we confront our end is how we have lived. That is why during this festival, we focus on our death and, in a sense, rehearse it, because it is our deeds that determine how we face our inevitable end.'

Once again Shoshana had the feeling that he was speaking to her.

The service ended and, as usual, the worshippers hovered outside the synagogue wishing each other well over the fast and sharing praise and criticism of the cantor's voice, which according to some was not as good as in previous years. But everyone agreed that the rabbi's sermon had been too long.

Shoshana and her father were making their way out of the synagogue when they heard a commotion outside. They heard panicked voices and the sound of people rushing along the street, men shouting and women crying.

Shoshana and Moshe stood still and looked around, wondering what was going on when Miriam's father caught up with them and called out, 'Get home as fast as you can. We heard that Turkish soldiers are heading for Zichron Yaakov.'

She looked at her father. 'Our hours are numbered,' she said quietly. She wondered if Nathan knew.

CHAPTER FORTY-FOUR

Cairo and London, 1917

Nathan tossed from side to side and listened to the whirring of the ceiling fan, which seemed to echo the whirring inside his head. Giving up all hope of sleep, he uttered an irritated grunt, jumped out of bed, pulled on his shirt and trousers, and grabbed his bicycle. Only physical activity would relieve his agitation. It was past midnight and the lobby was empty except for the bored night manager who was leaning back against his chair, staring into space behind the reception desk, his arms clasped behind his head, and the bellboy dozing on a velvet couch with his fez askew.

In the square outside, street lamps illuminated horse-carriage drivers loitering near the park and shadowy figures of long-robed Egyptians pushing barrows of food destined for the city's hotels and restaurants. Cycling away from the square, Nathan followed Cairo's quiet, deserted streets and the noise in his head began to clear. The elation he had felt at the thought of Allenby's impending triumph at Beersheba, the victory of the British and the freedom of Palestine, was dampened by unexpected global events that threatened the outcome he longed for. The golden apple was about to be plucked from his reach.

The problem was Russia. The tsar had been overthrown, the country was in turmoil and there were rumours that the new government might abandon the Allies and make a separate peace with Germany, which would jeopardise victory unless America entered the war.

Closer to home, he was increasingly concerned by the attitude of the head of British intelligence in Cairo. General Clayton made no secret of his strong support for the Arabs and his equally strong dislike of the Jews, whom he held responsible for every misfortune that befell Great Britain. As it happened, Clayton was Lawrence's boss and supported his aim of Arab nationhood. This was increasingly worrying as the Allies proceeded to make arrangements to carve up the Ottoman Empire. While Britain and France had signed a secret treaty that divided the entire area of Palestine between them, Lawrence disputed the French claim to a nation called Syria, which he saw as merely a political construct created to further their ambitions in the area. Nathan knew that Lawrence had ambitions of his own, which included installing his protégé Faisal as ruler in Damascus.

Like Lawrence, Nathan also disputed the creation of a Syrian nation, but for a different reason. Until a map of the entire region could be agreed upon by all parties, there was no possibility of a just political solution or peaceful coexistence between Arabs and Jews. As he continued cycling, he no longer saw the shadows cast by the lampposts in the moonlit streets or heard the occasional stamping of the mules tethered to their carts. He had a vision of the future where access to water would be the basis for delineating borders and creating a just solution for all the people who lived there. With his unique understanding of the geology and water sources in the region, he knew he was the ideal person to draw up such a map.

With that thought in mind, it struck him that there was no point remaining in Cairo. Since their meeting on the beach at Atlit, he knew that he would never be able to change Shoshana's mind about staying in Palestine, despite the increasing danger. She would continue running the spy ring with her usual dedication and efficiency as long as she could, and the spy ship would continue to pick up the intelligence she and the group collected. But his work in Cairo was done. His input was needed in London, where he could influence the important decisions being made. By the time he returned to his room in the hotel, his mind was calm and he fell asleep almost instantly.

When he presented himself in Hugh Gardiner-Hall's office the following day, he outlined his reasons for leaving and asked his superior's permission to travel to London.

Sir Hugh rested his pipe in the ashtray. 'I shall be sorry to see you leave,' he said, and added with a smile, 'After all, everyone says you run General Headquarters.' He paused, as if weighing up how to express what was on his mind, before saying, 'You are a remarkable man, Mr Adelstein. I have always felt you were destined for great things.'

Nathan knew he would never receive a more heartfelt compliment.

*

Shortly before embarking for London, Nathan ran into Lawrence in the Savoy Hotel. Their last meeting had ended with mutual respect, but on this occasion Nathan found Lawrence more pumped up with self-importance than usual. No doubt his recent victory at Aqaba had made him something of a hero among the top brass at General Headquarters.

Without any preamble, Lawrence launched into a diatribe about Bedouin victories, Arab nationhood, the difference between Jews who had lived in Palestine for centuries, who he approved of, and those who had migrated from eastern Europe, whom he despised and called colonists.

Nathan, who resented attempts to trespass on his area of expertise, didn't mince words and, despite his resolve to keep calm, he lost his temper. 'You're lecturing me about the Jewish population of Palestine and the Jewish mentality as if you're an expert on the subject,' he scoffed. 'You haven't spent any time in Galilee, you've done no research on the terrain our people have reclaimed and farmed, you haven't spoken with our people, you can't speak Hebrew, Yiddish or Turkish, yet you're lecturing me on things I've experienced and studied all my life. In short, I'm sorry to say you don't know what you're talking about.'

Lawrence surveyed him with a supercilious stare. 'I mapped that coast eight years ago. That's when I met your sister whose charm you unfortunately lack. As for Palestine's Jews, I don't need to be there to know what the Zionists are planning. My protégé Faisal wants to know what the British have promised them because, as we all know, with their usual duplicity, the British government has very likely sold the same camel twice. But no matter what they've promised, in the end the Jews of Galilee will have to accept their fate. If they don't learn to live with the Arabs, they'll end up with their throats cut.'

Nathan was fuming – he had always envisaged a land where Jews and Arabs were equal – but he decided against continuing a conversation with a bigot whose fame had gone to his head and was incapable of carrying on a civilised discussion. Their altercation reinforced his conviction that he should travel to London. He would talk to Mark Sykes, a member of the British parliament who was sympathetic to Jewish claims in Palestine. He had heard about the memo Sykes had written to the War Cabinet, in which he praised Nathan's advances in agriculture at Atlit and argued that the farming success of the Jewish communities throughout Palestine proved that the region could sustain increased Jewish immigration and make the creation of a Jewish homeland viable.

Nathan thought back to his initial meeting with Sykes during his first visit to London and marvelled at the change in his attitude.

When they had met, Sykes had been overtly anti-Semitic, but since then he had become supportive of Zionism.

It seemed as if the tide of opinion in British government circles was changing. Nathan knew that several factors had contributed to this. One was the lobbying of Chaim Weizmann. Another was the conviction of evangelical Christians that the Second Coming would only take place when all the Jews were living in the Holy Land. Pragmatic politicians suggested that a declaration in support of the Jews in Palestine might counterbalance the commitments made to the French and to the Arabs, and muddy the diplomatic waters in a way that might be to Britain's advantage.

*

As Nathan's ship docked in England, he couldn't help recalling his previous visit when he was shunted from one sceptical official to another. This time he came as a highly valued advisor.

In London, the future was hurtling towards him with dazzling speed. The corridors of the Foreign Office were buzzing with the news that a declaration in favour of establishing a Jewish homeland in Palestine was being discussed by the foreign secretary, Arthur Balfour, with the proviso that the civil and religious rights of non-Jewish communities in Palestine be guaranteed.

Curious to know what had prompted that initiative, he was told that, according to Lloyd George, the declaration was largely due to the influence of Chaim Weizmann. Cynics suggested that it was a public relations exercise to arouse support for the war among the Jews of the United States.

After several days in London, Nathan received an invitation to have lunch with Weizmann. It was a drizzly autumn day when he set out, and his feet kept slipping on fallen leaves. He wasn't looking forward to the meeting. There was only one thing he wanted to talk to Weizmann about, and that was Weizmann's opposition to the spy ring, which he considered reckless. He believed that Zionism should be neutral.

Sitting across from the Zionist leader at an East End restaurant jocularly nicknamed the Kosher Ritz, Nathan studied the slim man with the dark moustache and dark eyes that gleamed with intelligence, and he sensed the dynamic personality and consummate political skill that had propelled this man to the corridors of British power. He knew that his rise to prominence was the result of his scientific work at the University of Manchester, which was all the more extraordinary as he was a Russian immigrant. He had invented a method of developing acetone, which was essential in the production of artillery shells for Britain.

So he and Weizmann shared a scientific background that they had both set aside in favour of politics. But neither that nor their common goal of a Jewish homeland was sufficient to foster friendship or cooperation. Their personalities were at odds. Nathan, bluntly outspoken and impatient, lacked Weizmann's diplomatic skills, while Weizmann had no confidence in Nathan's ability to negotiate.

So the proposal Weizmann made over the beef brisket, potato latkes and pickled cucumbers set before them on the white damask tablecloth caught Nathan by surprise.

They had been discussing the forthcoming Balfour Declaration when Weizmann put down his knife and fork and sat forward. 'I'm in favour of the clause that the rights of the resident non-Jewish population must be guaranteed. I believe that we will be judged in years to come by our relationship with the Arabs. As we build up our state, we mustn't violate their legal or civil rights. I hope we agree about this?'

Nathan nodded. 'I've always thought that.'

Weizmann gave him an approving smile. 'We still have a great deal of work ahead of us but miracles only happen when we work hard to achieve them.'

And then he made his proposal.

'Mark Sykes and the Foreign Office have recommended that you go to the United States as a liaison officer to publicise Balfour's declaration.' Before Nathan had time to ask the obvious question, Weizmann added, 'They said it's on account of the connections you made over there with prominent Americans some years ago.'

Nathan thought it might have had more to do with his expertise and the contribution he had made to the British war effort rather than his contacts, but he swallowed the retort that rose to his lips. 'Will they provide written instructions for the trip?'

Weizmann pulled out a sheet of paper. 'This is a draft suggested by Sykes, who I believe is a friend of yours.'

As Nathan read it, he smiled at Sykes' enthusiasm, so rare in a highly placed British politician. After praising Nathan's unique qualifications for the mission, he suggested that as well as publicising the Balfour Declaration he should cooperate with the representatives of the Arabs and the Armenians.

*

With his instructions safely stowed in his leather briefcase, Nathan boarded the *St Paul* in Liverpool bound for New York, confident that his goal was in sight. The war would soon be over, Britain would defeat Turkey, and Palestine would be free.

Sitting on a deckchair, he remembered the boat trip from Denmark to Scotland and thought about Vibeke. He sighed. He'd probably never see her again. What was it that Shoshana had said about his love life? That the only women he wanted were unavailable? Perhaps she was right. No one understood him as well as she did and it occurred to him that perhaps all his life he had unconsciously searched for a woman like her. He felt a prickle of guilt. Absorbed in his meetings and exultant about his future, he hadn't given much thought to Zichron Yaakov. He would write to Shoshana from New York.

CHAPTER FORTY-FIVE

Zichron Yaakov, 1917

As soon as Shoshana heard that Turkish soldiers were advancing on Zichron Yaakov, the calm resignation she had been feeling was replaced by dread. She had known that time was running out, but now it was too late to tell the members of her spy ring to congregate at Atlit, and she realised that the ship she had pinned her hopes on wouldn't arrive in time. Knowing she would be unable to evacuate them aroused desperation that almost paralysed her.

They had believed in her vision and risked their lives to follow her. They had trusted her with their lives, and now she couldn't save them. Distraught, she ran to those who lived nearby and warned them to run and hide in the barley fields and vineyards. Luckily, those who lived in nearby villages had come to Zichron Yaakov to attend the Yom Kippur service, so she was able to contact them.

She was out of breath and her chest was heaving as she told Tova, Benyamin and Reuben to use side paths and avoid main roads and to hide until the Turks had left. It wasn't only the Turks she feared: she was aware that the townspeople might betray them. And if by any chance they were caught, they should tell the Turks that she was the leader of the spy ring.

Never had they seen their leader in such a state and their concern for her added to their terror. They pleaded with her to flee or at least to hide but she refused. 'I won't run away. I'm the one who brought all this on you and I'm responsible. If they come for me, I'll tell them that.'

She knew her arrest was imminent. She was hurtling towards her destiny.

*

Shoshana was back at home when Ha-Meyasdim Street vibrated with the pounding of galloping horses and the rumbling of military vehicles. From behind her curtained window she peered out at the street and sensed the terror of her neighbours shivering behind their locked doors, waiting for the inevitable raid. At that moment, she understood the animosity of the Village Committee. Although she had acted for their benefit, she had done so against their will. They hadn't consented to her actions and those actions now exposed them all to danger. There was no time to acknowledge her responsibility, but as it was Yom Kippur she hoped they would forgive her, as she forgave them.

She didn't have long to consider her responsibility for what was about to unfold. Someone was yelling outside the house and banging on the door. When she opened it, she was looking at the *kaymakam*, the district governor of Haifa, who was accompanied by three guards with rifles slung over their shoulders. She had heard him described as the Hangman of Haifa.

Shoshana's face was as white as her dress and beneath it her heart was hammering, but she managed to keep her voice steady as she asked what they wanted.

The *kaymakam* was a man of imposing stature with a black handlebar moustache that touched the edges of his jaw, and a large stomach that bulged against his gold-buttoned jacket. His eyes, merciless and obsidian, impaled her.

'We want the Jewish spy Aaron Sokolov.'

'You've come to the wrong place. He's not here.'

'Then you will tell us where he is. Don't try to fool us. We know he's the leader of the spy ring that's been operating here.'

So that was it. Under torture Berish must have told them that Aaron was the ringleader. Had he done it to protect her or to take revenge on the man he blamed for his cousin's disappearance? She would never know.

'I don't know what you're talking about.'

Just then her father appeared behind her. As soon as the *kaymakam* saw him, he raised his hand and motioned to the guards to grab hold of them both.

'Stop wasting my time. You and the old man are coming with us,' he snapped.

Their arms were roughly yanked behind their backs and the soldiers pushed them along the street, prodding them with rifles as raindrops from the trees overhead dripped on their heads. Shoshana looked anxiously at her father, who stumbled a few times on the slippery pavement, but when she asked if he was all right, he whispered, 'Don't worry about me.'

As they passed their neighbours' homes, she noticed curtains moving in the front windows. Had any of them directed the Turks to their house?

They turned into a crooked lane off Ha-Meyasdim Street. The soldiers kicked open the door of a building and pushed them inside. The place was empty and had the musty smell of abandoned houses. Shoshana remembered that the owners had moved to their son's village the previous year when taxes and confiscations had ruined them and they could no longer support themselves.

The only furniture in the room was a long wooden table and two chairs, one of which had a broken leg. The rain had stopped and the weak sunlight of the dying day slanted through the grimy windows onto the dusty floor. Shoshana had no illusions about what awaited her in that room and she was terrified. She knew only too well how the Turks extracted information from their captives. Bracing herself, she took a deep breath and hoped she had the strength to remain silent. Only her silence would ensure the safety of the rest of the group.

The soldiers pushed her onto a chair and wound thick rope around her several times so that her arms were pinned by her sides. Then they grabbed hold of her father, hauled him to his feet, laid him on the table, tied his hands and feet with leather straps, and pulled off his shoes and socks.

Her heart almost stopped. *Falaka*. It was the most common form of torture used by Turkish police, but she hadn't expected them to use it on him. Then she understood. They expected that she would break down and tell them everything when she saw her father being tortured.

Straining against the ropes that bound her, she tried to sit forward. 'Stop!' she shouted. 'Even you couldn't stoop so low to torture an old man! He doesn't know anything!'

The *kaymakan* gave an insidious smile. 'Maybe not, but you do! We'll apply *falaka* to your father until you tell us where that fellow in charge of the spy ring is hiding.'

'You've got it wrong,' she said. 'He isn't the leader. I am.'

The *kaymakan* burst out laughing as if he had just heard a good joke. 'You! You're the leader of the spy ring! Now I've heard everything!' He looked at his companions for confirmation and they laughed too. 'When we find your leader Aaron we'll take him to the prison in Nazareth where he will tell us everything, but in the meantime you'll tell us what you know.'

At this, the terror she felt was replaced by fury at his derision. He couldn't envisage that the person in charge of a spy ring that had been operating under their noses for over a year was a woman.

Turning to the guard who had picked up a thick baton, the *kaymakam* nodded for him to begin. The first blow on Moshe's bare feet made him cry out.

'Tell us where Aaron Sokolov is hiding!' the guard shouted, raising his baton.

The second blow made Moshe scream.

Shoshana winced and closed her eyes. She couldn't look. She was in turmoil. Hearing her father's cries was unbearable. If only she could clamp her hands over her ears to shut out his suffering. But at the same time she didn't want him to give in and reveal the names of the members of their spy ring. Suddenly, to her surprise, he started reciting passages of the Yom Kippur liturgy, yelling the ancient words of prayer at the top of his voice as the baton struck his swollen feet.

She was desperate for them to stop. How much could her father take before he told them everything? 'Stop!' she shouted. 'You can see he's innocent. He doesn't know anything.'

The *kaymakam* hadn't taken his eyes off her throughout her father's ordeal. Whether because he thought she was telling the truth, or because he sensed that torturing the old man wouldn't break her, he signalled to the guard to stop beating him.

'Perhaps not,' he said. 'But we'll soon find out if you do.'

She was relieved when they untied him and she watched anxiously as he staggered and almost fell, unable to stand on his swollen feet.

'Take him away,' the *kaymakam* ordered. One of the soldiers grabbed his arm and propelled him towards the door. 'Don't touch her!' Moshe shouted. 'I know that Turkish law forbids the torture of women.'

The *kaymakam* gave a derisive laugh. As they were dragging him out of the house, he whispered, 'God bless you, my Shoshi.'

Her heart was pounding against her ribs. At least his ordeal was over. Now hers would begin.

The two remaining soldiers released the ropes that bound her to the chair, tied her hands together, nailed a hook high on the wall, raised her arms above her head and looped the rope that bound her hands over the hook. She was fixed to the spot like a butterfly pinned to a sheet of paper, unable to move a centimetre because the slightest movement stretched the tendons in her shoulders to snapping point. Each second felt like an hour and she groaned. How long would she be able to stand this agony?

Her suffering ended when the guard cut her down but her relief was short-lived. He tied her to a wooden post, picked up a whip and stroked it for several minutes, looking at her with a cruel smile. She held her breath and tried to steel herself for the flogging.

The whip whistled in the air above her head and came down on her bare arms, lacerating the flesh. 'You are no better than wild beasts!' she shouted despite the pain. 'Nothing you Turks do can shock me. I saw with my own eyes what you did to the Armenians!'

Her defiance infuriated him and he struck her with redoubled force until her white dress was streaked with blood and her whole body was on fire. She longed for the pain to end but the scourging continued until it felt as though her flesh was in shreds.

Finally the flogging stopped. They untied her and she slid to the floor. They left her there and went into another room. Shivering uncontrollably and whimpering, she tried in vain to find a position where she could lie without excruciating pain. There was no possibility of rest, and she spent the night in agony. At least she had remained silent, but for how much longer?

Suddenly Eli appeared beside her and her heart leapt. So he was with her! But when she opened her eyes she was shocked to see the *kaymakam* standing there.

'If you're really the leader, tell us who your associates are and we'll let you go,' he said.

'I despise you. I'll never tell you anything.'

'We'll see about that,' he said with his reptilian smile.

The guards laid her down on the table and pulled off her shoes. She comforted herself with the thought that her father had withstood the *falaka*, and she would too. But this time the guard wielded his weapon with such ferocity that the blow seemed to explode inside her like a bolt of lightning. The pain was unimaginable, worse than anything they had inflicted so far. It took all the air from her lungs. She opened her mouth but no scream came. She couldn't breathe. It was as if she had been electrocuted. She fainted. They revived her only to continue the torture. She howled with pain but whenever they repeated the question, she said nothing.

*

She spent a second night huddled on the floor shivering violently, unable to find a place to rest her throbbing legs. How long would she be able to hold out? Next day they continued. But *falaka* was only the beginning. When they saw that reducing her feet to a bloody pulp didn't shake her resolve, they assaulted every part of her body in turn using hot irons, pincers and pliers. Maddened with pain, she cursed them but she knew she wouldn't be able to hold out much longer.

Another day passed. Half-conscious, she heard the *kaymakam* say that they would take her to Nazareth for more interrogation that afternoon. She knew they had worse tortures in store for her, tortures she wouldn't be able to withstand. One thought drummed in her head. She had to do something before she betrayed her colleagues.

'You can't take me to Nazareth in this blood-soaked dress. At least let me go home and change my clothes,' she mumbled through her broken teeth and bleeding lips.

They conferred among themselves and agreed.

Escorted by two guards, she stumbled from the house. Every step was like treading on shards of glass but she refused the support of their offered arms. Head held high, she staggered along the empty street towards her home. She sensed that behind their curtained windows, her neighbours were watching in silence.

As soon as she entered her home, she turned to the guards. 'Surely you're not going to come into the bathroom with me? You can see I can hardly move so I won't run away. Wait outside while I change.'

They looked at each other, embarrassed and uncertain, wondering what the *kayamakan* would say, until one of them came to a decision. 'Don't be long,' he said.

On her way to the bathroom, she paused for a moment in the hall, slid open a secret panel behind a bookcase, and took out the pistol she had secreted there several weeks earlier.

Her hands were shaking and as she tried to steady them, she thought of Eli. Ever since his death she had tried to define inconsolable loss. She had compared it to being torn apart by a wolf's sharp claws, but she suddenly saw it simply as love that roamed the earth with nowhere to go. He appeared before her now as he had looked the last time she saw him, smiling at her as he took the dates from her hands.

She placed the cold muzzle in her mouth and pressed the trigger.

EPILOGUE

Leah, 1967

Now that you know our story, you can understand my obsession with memory. As the sole survivor of our family, I've become the custodian of our past, and like that legendary ancient mariner, I buttonhole everyone who passes by our house and tell them what happened here. Just as I'm telling you now.

I'll go back to the terrible day when they told me Shoshana had killed herself. In that initial moment, before the shock of reality sank in, my mind flew to a story we had read in the newspaper long ago. It was about a girl who had committed suicide, and I recalled that unlike me, Shoshana seemed to understand the depth of despair that might impel someone to end their life. Perhaps I'm reading too much into it, but did she already feel the shiver of a presentiment? Did she foresee her own future? No matter how hard I try, I can't even begin to imagine the courage it must have taken her to suffer such agony and then kill herself to avoid betraying her comrades. I often wish I knew what went through her mind as she pressed the trigger, but how can we understand the thoughts of others when we are a mystery to ourselves?

Weeks passed before I could face the fact that my sister had died. How could I still be alive when she was dead? And what was I supposed to do with all the conflicting emotions I'd felt throughout my life? All those unresolved resentments? I told you at the very beginning that I loved and hated her in equal measure. Did I love her more now that she was dead? Did it even matter anymore? Those feelings were irrelevant, they no longer served any purpose, like the skin a serpent sheds as it slithers on its way. But the guilt remained. She was so much nobler than me. Why was I still alive?

I felt as though my mind had been anaesthetised and part of me had been sheared off, leaving a truncated body that had lost its equilibrium. Our bond was much stronger than I had realised, but it took her death to make me understand that.

We buried Shoshana in the little cemetery near our home and she lies next to our parents' grave in the shade of the oak and pine trees whose intertwined boughs whisper the secrets of the dead. At least that's what our brother Nathan once said.

Ah, Nathan. I'll never forget his grief when he returned from America. He sank to the ground beside her grave and sobbed. I knew he was mourning a part of himself. As you know, that's how it had been between them from the very beginning. I didn't cry with him. I was still numb.

Not long after that, Nathan received accolades he could only have dreamed of. After entering Jerusalem, General Allenby acknowledged that his victory at Beersheba had been largely due to Nathan's advice. He also praised Shoshana for the intelligence the spy ring had gathered that had contributed to the British victory. He thanked her for her steadfastness and her sacrifice. And that's when I cried.

It was Jack who told me about the Turkish defeat at Beersheba. He boasted that the British victory was due to the Australian Light

Horse, and insisted on describing the entire campaign, sparing no details about his commander Chauvel, their wild ride, the gallant walers and even the mules that pulled the ambulance carts. But I could only think of one thing: Shoshana hadn't lived to see the British victory she gave her life for.

That was Jack's last visit before his regiment was sent north. There was a race between the British, the French and the Arabs to reach Damascus, but I've never understood politics so the reason behind this international competition escaped me. I heard later that the Australian Light Horse reached Damascus first, and I can imagine how proud Jack would have been to be part of that. After the war ended, he returned to Australia and from time to time his letters arrived in envelopes stamped with the head of King George V. He wrote that he was restless and found it difficult to settle down to normal life. In his last letter he said he'd decided to marry his childhood sweetheart. I never heard from him again.

War connects strangers and then separates them, but I like to think that in a small town somewhere in Australia, Jack is telling his grandchildren about a Jewish woman he met on the other side of the world during the war. Connections are stones flung into deep waters whose ripples reach distant shores.

Whenever I think of Nathan I see him as Icarus who flew too close to the sun. His flight was as spectacular as his fall. After the war ended in 1918, the victorious powers invited him to draw up a map that would decide the borders of Palestine. From what I recall, he based his borders on fair access to water, which he always maintained was the key to peace. He was asked to present his map at the Peace Conference due to be held in Paris the following year. In his last letter he wrote how thrilled he was that his expertise was recognised at the highest levels of world politics. He was convinced his map would ensure that the nations of our region would coexist in peace. I think he felt Shoshana would have approved, and that his contribution to peace and freedom was predicated on her sacrifice.

After the Peace Conference, he intended to spend time exploring and rebuilding his botanical collection. He thought science was the key to the future of Palestine. I think he missed his research and was ready to give up political life with its duplicity and diplomacy, a life for which his personality wasn't suited. But he never reached the Peace Conference.

My hands shook as I read the newspaper report that described what happened in horrifying detail. It was a foggy May morning when he turned up at the Kenley RAF airfield in Surrey for his flight to Paris but discovered that his flight was cancelled due to bad weather. Determined to reach the conference in time, Nathan found the pilot of an Airco DH-4 who was willing to make the flight. I can picture him clutching the leather document case containing his precious maps as he boarded the plane, relieved to be on his way. But shortly after they took off, the pilot was forced to return to the airfield on account of poor visibility. I can imagine Nathan's frustration. He succeeded in pressuring the pilot to try again later that day. This would be his third attempt to reach Paris. That would have been a warning to most people, but Nathan had an iron will that didn't allow him to give up. And being a scientist, he scoffed at premonitions.

As the tiny plane headed over the coast, it was buffeted by strong headwinds. It never reached France. Although ships searched the English Channel, no trace of the plane or the pilot was ever found. No trace of my brother or his document case or maps, either. It was as if they had vanished from the earth. A mystery. There were rumours of sabotage but nothing was ever proved. Nathan made many enemies during his life but I can't believe anyone would have been prepared to blow up a plane to kill him. In any case, no potential murderer could possibly have known that due to bad weather he would make that third attempt to reach Paris.

Nathan's death killed our father. He was a broken man after Shoshana died, but Nathan's death sapped his will to live. He sank into melancholia, stopped eating and drinking, and within a week he had stopped breathing. As I buried him in the little cemetery where our mother and Shoshana lay, I wondered if I was doomed to spend the rest of my life sitting *shiva* for people I loved.

During his political career, Nathan rubbed shoulders with many illustrious people. One of them was Mark Sykes, the co-architect of the infamous Sykes-Picot agreement that divided the Middle East between France and Britain. Curiously, he died the same year as Nathan, during the influenza epidemic that killed millions around the world.

Perhaps the most colourful character Nathan crossed swords with was the man known as Lawrence of Arabia. They were meteors bound on a collision course. Both were mavericks, extraordinary intellects who shared a passion for Palestine, which they attempted to shape in ways that were irreconcilable.

I don't know if you believe in coincidence, but there are times when it makes the hairs on the back of my neck stand up. Like Shoshi, whom he had met and admired, Lawrence was also tortured by the Turks. I know this because I've read his book, *The Seven Pillars of Wisdom*. When I opened it, I couldn't stop staring at the dedication. He had dedicated his book to S.A. He never divulged the identity of the mysterious S.A., but as far as I'm concerned, he didn't need to.

If you believe in coincidence, here's another one. Just two days after Nathan boarded his fateful flight for Paris, Lawrence was flying to Cairo via Rome. When his pilot tried to bring the plane to a stop on the runway, he crashed into a tree and was killed on impact. On that occasion, Lawrence survived, but you can't escape your destiny. Sixteen years later, while riding his motorcycle along English country lanes, he crashed and died.

They say that those the gods love die young. Whether it was on account of an excess of godly love, or the cold finger of fate, all four – Shoshi, Nathan, Eli and Lawrence – died violent deaths long before their allotted span of three score years and ten, but their visions still linger in the desert air.

Shoshi, Nathan and Eli helped Britain to defeat the Turks. But as it turned out, in overthrowing the yoke of the Ottoman Empire, we merely changed masters. I often wonder how they would have reacted to the British Mandate. By imposing a quota on Jews desperate to escape from Europe to save their lives, they were responsible for thousands of deaths. It's ironic that Shoshi had formed the spy ring to prevent the Turks from committing genocide against the Jews of Palestine, but less than four decades later Hitler almost succeeded in annihilating the entire Jewish population of Europe.

After the Holocaust, we fought for our independence, which the United Nations granted us in 1948. But that wasn't the end of our struggle. Since independence, we have had to defend ourselves in two wars, the second of which, called the Six Day War, ended recently and restored Jerusalem to us. It seems we are doomed to keep fighting for our existence and I can't help wondering whether our situation would have been more secure if Nathan had been able to present his maps for our borders at the Paris Peace Conference.

By now you're probably wondering why I've waited so many years to tell our story. The answer might surprise you. It certainly surprised me. Several months ago a group of Bedouins noticed a lone tree growing in the Sinai, a wild date palm. One of them mentioned it to his grandfather, who recalled an incident he'd heard of long ago. According to the story, some tribesmen had come across two men disguised as Arabs and, believing they were spies, had fired at them. One of the strangers got away but his companion was shot dead. Some time later, when they noticed a wild palm tree growing on that very spot, they called the site the Jew's grave.

News of this tree reached Ari Ben-Menashe, an Israeli police officer whose curiosity was piqued. He knew about the mysterious disappearance of Eli Ginsberg and decided to investigate. It was partly curiosity but also a desire to clear the name of his great-uncle, Aaron Sokolov, who had been accused of killing his rival. Aaron, who had always denied the accusation, had been hiding in a friend's barn when he was caught by the Turks, and after days of torture, they hanged his broken body in Damascus. He never revealed the names of the other conspirators and tried to protect Shoshana to the very end. But the question mark about his role in Eli's death still hovered over him.

After we won the Six Day War, Ari was able to travel to the Sinai to investigate the story of the Jew's grave. With the help of a local Bedouin, he began to dig. From the position of the tree roots, they deduced that the date palm had sprouted from dates the men had brought with them. Beneath the tree they found human bones and a knapsack containing a crumpled piece of paper. The writing had grown faint with age but had been conserved by the dry desert air. When the bones were examined at the Institute of Forensic Medicine in Tel-Aviv, they were identified as Eli's. And the paper in his rucksack was a love letter to Shoshana.

You can't imagine the tumult in my head when I stood in front of that wild date palm. On impulse I reached out and wrapped my arms around the trunk. It felt rough and knobbly, embossed for its entire length with deep scars that might have been carved by a loving sculptor's hand. I laid my head against the trunk and didn't want to let go. When I finally tore myself away, the imprint of those scars patterned my face. I hoped they would never fade.

Recovering his remains after all this time should have conferred what people these days call closure, but it stirred up dormant emotions like a sudden gust of wind that swirls among layers of long neglected dust. They gave me Eli's letter but it would have felt like betrayal to read it, and I never did. I placed it on Shoshana's grave and secured it with the stones I leave there after each visit. I hope it brings solace to her soul.

Once Eli's remains had been identified, the conscience of our government was stirred up. After decades of wilful blindness, the politicians finally confronted the fact that they had never acknowledged the role Eli and Shoshana had played to free Palestine from the Turks, despite the hostility of the people they had tried to liberate.

Things move slowly in our country and political gestures of forgiveness are slower still, so it was with a sense of triumph that I travelled to Jerusalem last week to attend Eli's state funeral with military honours on Mount Herzl. Situated in the shadow of the Judean Hills, Israel's national cemetery is a sobering sight with its rows of identical flat graves stretching far into the distance. Most of these are the graves of soldiers who have given their lives for their country as Eli and Shoshana did.

In the name of the Knesset and the government, the politicians asked forgiveness of Eli and his comrades for failing to recognise what they described as 'their great achievement'. I wonder if Shoshana would have forgiven them. I didn't, and I doubt Eli would have.

When I looked around, I saw a group of elderly people sitting together. There was something familiar about them and they must have thought the same about me, because when the service was over they came over to wish me long life as we always say to the bereaved. The first person I recognised was Tova. Her thick black hair had turned white but her eyes were as lively as I remembered. Standing next to her was Benyamin, and I gathered they were married. He was shuffling and his hands shook as he patted my shoulder and talked about Shoshana in a tremulous voice. 'She was an inspiration,' he said. Joshua talked about his brother Berish. 'He was convinced that Aaron had killed Eli. I wish we had known the truth.' Then he added, 'Berish also died for the cause. He deserves a hero's funeral as well.'

I watched them as they dispersed. No one who saw these grey-haired people would have guessed that in their youth they had risked their lives to spy on our Turkish rulers. I think they are all heroes.

As I left Mount Herzl, I couldn't get the image of the wild date palm out of my mind. That tree had sprung from the dates Shoshi had given Eli, a miracle of nature that was a monument to the power of their love, a memorial more enduring than any inscription on a gravestone.

All my life I saw Shoshana and Nathan as comets that blazed across the sky while I was the pallid satellite following in their wake, irrelevant and insignificant. They had their hour of glorious life and they died for it, scattering stardust over several continents. But here's the irony. Their death has finally created my purpose in life. I'm the one who became the guardian of the flame they lit, the custodian of their memory. It's through me that their story lives on and inspires us with a glimpse of the nobility that our little lives are capable of. So when you come to Zichron Yaakov and visit our home, I will tell you about my sister and take you to the little cemetery where she is buried. Perhaps you'll even hear the trees whispering above her grave.

AUTHOR'S NOTE

People often ask me where the ideas for my novels come from and why, out of the thousands of stories I hear each year, one stirs my imagination so powerfully that it develops into a novel.

I can pinpoint the exact moment I heard this one. During a tour of Israel several years ago, Bert and I were passing an area famous for the vineyards that were started by Edmond de Rothschild in the late nineteenth century when our guide pointed to the pretty little town of Zichron Yaakov in the distance. She mentioned that during World War I, some young Jews called Aaronsohn had formed a secret spy ring to defeat their oppressive Turkish rulers. They were desperate to help Britain win the war.

The idea that young people living in an Ottoman backwater had the audacity to try to affect the course of the war by spying on the mighty Ottoman Empire intrigued me, and although at the time I was writing another novel, I never forgot the story of the Aaronsohns.

Several years later, we visited Zichron Yaakov. Inside the Aaronsohn home, which has become a museum dedicated to the memory of the family, I discovered the tragic story of Sarah Aaronsohn. Hanging in the bathroom was the pale blue suit she wore on that terrible last day, and in a display case lay the pistol with which she shot herself rather than betray her comrades.

Later I stood beside her grave in the small cemetery. Someone had placed a red rose on her grave. As I walked away, I knew that I would write a novel based on her life.

I have always found my subjects in the footnotes of history where I have encountered people whose actions have illustrated the unfathomable extremes of human behaviour. But writing a historical novel based on heroic young people who sacrificed their lives in pursuit of freedom posed many challenges.

When I began to research the extraordinary lives of the Aaronsohns in biographies, history books and articles, I was inspired by their story but wondered whether there was room for a novel. I decided there was. Non-fiction presents objective facts, but by fictionalising their story I hoped to provide an emotional and imaginative dimension to their experiences which would breathe life into the historical facts.

But these astonishing facts posed another challenge. It's been said that the difference between fact and fiction is that fiction has to make sense. So while I was excited that so many aspects of this story were incredible, I foresaw a problem: would readers wonder if the incidents in this story could possibly have happened? It seemed paradoxical that my task was to turn incredible facts into believable fiction!

Apart from the extraordinary young activists, I was fascinated by the setting. World War I in the Middle East offers a rich and unfamiliar tableau of exciting action and larger than life characters. One of them is Lawrence of Arabia. While researching this novel, I was fascinated to learn that he had actually visited Atlit and sketched the ruined Crusader castle that dominates this coastline. But did he ever meet Sarah? We know that he met Sarah's brother in Cairo and that during her visit to Cairo, British officers praised her beauty and courage, but the trail ends there, offering a writer of historical fiction the opportunity to explore the potential. To add to the mystery, Lawrence dedicated his remarkable book *The Seven Pillars of Wisdom* to a certain 'S.A.' whose identity he never revealed. Scholars and historians have long debated who the object of his passion might have been, and some believe it was Sarah Aaronsohn. I would like to think so.

Although Lawrence's conversations in the novel are fictional, I have drawn on the thoughts and opinions he expressed in his letters, articles and his book.

Like Lawrence, Leonard Woolley was also a real person and the two knew each other through their pre-war passion for archaeology. During World War I, Woolley worked for British Naval Intelligence in Port Said, and played a vital role in organising the delivery of secret intelligence from the spy group in Zichron Yaakov.

I have based my character Nathan Adelstein on Sarah's brother Aaron Aaronsohn, a world-famous botanist, geologist and ecologist whose ideas were far ahead of his time. He discarded international academic success in favour of political activism that ultimately cost him his life.

Eli, the love of Shoshana's life, is based on Avshalom Feinberg, a charismatic member of the spy ring whose burial place was discovered many years after his death just as I have described.

Sarah did have a younger sister, Rivka, who survived her siblings and ultimately became the guardian of their stories, but in telling the story, I've taken a novelist's liberty to imagine characters, interactions and relationships. However, Sarah and Rivka were both in love with Avshalom Feinberg. Jack Simpson is a fictional character.

At a time when conflicts between Jews and Arabs often make news headlines around the world, I found it enlightening during my research to learn that during the early twentieth century the major powers played a large and duplicitous part in carving up the Middle East between them. Aaron Aaronsohn was on his way to the Paris Peace Conference in 1919 with maps outlining possible borders in the Middle East based on access to water. Like his body, his maps were never found, and we will never know if they would have been the key to future peaceful coexistence.

But politics was far from my mind when I felt compelled to write this novel. I was inspired by the audacity of a young woman who fought an empire and sacrificed herself in her fight for freedom. As I write this, an image flashes across my mind: Sarah galloping across the dunes and wadis under the shadow of a ruined Crusader castle, her long hair streaming behind her.

ACKNOWLEDGEMENTS

Writing is a solitary occupation fraught with anxiety and doubt, and waiting for the publisher's judgement on a completed manuscript is a nail-biting experience, especially when you venture into new territory as I've done with this novel. So I was thrilled when I received Jo Mackay's enthusiastic response to *The Wild Date Palm*. I'm extremely fortunate to have such a warm and insightful publisher. Jo heads a dedicated and hard-working team at HQ Books, which includes the super-efficient Annabel Blay. Working with Josey Bryant is a real joy. Also, a big thank you to Annabel Adair for her painstaking proofreading.

Linda Funnell has edited five of my books, and I am in awe of her meticulous attention to every detail, her understanding and sensitivity. Linda is a dream editor, always open-minded and willing to consider my point of view. Her literary taste is impeccable and her invaluable suggestions have greatly enhanced this novel. Any inconsistencies or errors of style are mine.

I have chosen Ottoman Palestine during World War I as the setting of this novel, and to ensure that I haven't made any historical errors, I asked Australian historian Leslie Stein, who has written three volumes about the history of Israel, to fact-check my manuscript. I am very grateful for his attentive reading and illuminating suggestions.

Kim Swivel was kind enough to read the manuscript and I appreciate her helpful comments.

I'm grateful to Israeli journalist Gil Zohar who has shown much interest in this novel and sent me information and articles about this period.

Ever since I wrote my first book, *Mosaic*, Selwa Anthony has been my literary agent. From that moment, she has been unwavering in her support and encouragement. Her incisive and wise comments have been invaluable. Selwa is always accessible and ready to help me solve any problems I encounter on the long road of creating a novel.

As I mentioned at the beginning, writing is fraught with insecurity, and it never gets easier because every book brings its own challenges. Dasia Gutman always asks the questions that point me in the right direction.

My wonderful family has always been encouraging and interested to know about my work. Justine, Jonathan, Adrianne, Sarah, Maya and Allie, I'm very grateful for your love and support.

The moment I print out a chapter I can't wait for Bert to read it. After considering it, he asks 'So what happens next?' which is exactly what I need to continue writing. Bert, you are generous, unselfish and understanding, and I feel very blessed to share my life with you.

BOOK CLUB QUESTIONS

- *The Wild Date Palm* is based on a true story. Do you think that is an advantage?
- Why did the author call this novel *The Wild Date Palm*?
- What role does the landscape play in the lives of the main characters?
- How does the relationship between Shoshana and Leah change over time?
- Leah remarks that we can't understand others when we are a mystery to ourselves. What do you think about this?
- How does Shoshana keep the promise she made to her dying mother?
- What is the significance of Shoshana's train journey across the Anatolian plateau?
- Does this story relate to world events today?
- How do the main characters reach the limit of their dreams?
- What are the questions at the heart of this novel?

talk about it

Let's talk about books.

Join the conversation:

f @harlequinaustralia

♪ @hqanz

◉ @harlequinaus

harpercollins.com.au/hq

If you love reading and want to know about our
authors and titles, then let's talk about it.